John Evans was born and raised in East London. After working as a carpenter he went back into education and ended up in the financial sector where he still works. He now lives in West London and is currently writing his next book.

GOD'S GIFT

John Evans

Published by Arrow Books in 1997

3 5 7 9 10 8 6 4

First published by Arrow Books in 1997

Arrow Books
Random House UK Ltd
20 Vauxhall Bridge Road, London, SWIV 2SA

Random House Australia (Pty) Limited
20 Alfred Street, Milsons Point, Sydney, New South Wales 2061, Australia

Random House New Zealand Limited
18 Poland Road, Glenfield
Auckland 10, New Zealand

Random House South Africa (Pty) Limited
Endulini, 5a Jubilee Road, Parktown 2193, South Africa

Random House UK Limited Reg. No. 954009

A CIP catalogue record for this book is available from the British Library
Papers used by Random House UK Limited are natural, recyclable products made from wood grown in sustainable forests. The manufacturing processes conform to the environmental regulations of the country of origin

Typeset by Deltatype Ltd,
Birkenhead, Merseyside
Printed and bound in Great Britain by
Mackays of Chatham PLC, Chatham, Kent

ISBN 0 09 922582 4

For my mother,

And in memory of my father
where all stories began and ended.

Pre-Text

The Voice of The Book

Does it begin as a small dot of light, no bigger than a full stop on a page of complete darkness? Is that distant spot your life?

Somewhere in this tiny speck is everything you could ever imagine, so utterly small and dense it is almost infinite. Something is falling towards the light, something from outside of everything. Through a vacuum, silent and empty, it tumbles with the weight of billions of years, the precision brought about by an eternity of planning making a mockery of chaos and complexity. Inside the distant pinprick, far inside, a universe is revealed and within it, perhaps, is your life.

Unseen and unheard, it drops from the sky. It lands exactly where it was always meant to, at the precise moment ordained by itself. This is the touch of God's Gift.

Is this where it begins and ends?

No.

It begins and ends, and begins again, with The Book.

This is the real secret of God's Gift.

The First Knot

God created the world by a Word,
instantaneously, without toil and pains.
The Talmud

Chapter 1

The day it began again, when the knot tightened and things changed, was a Monday. A day so ordinary in itself, it was the perfect clean page of banality upon which The Book could begin to write.

Michael Kavanagh ascended swiftly through the main artery of the Pendulum building, alone in the elevator. It was just before eleven and already that day he had one meeting and a dawn workout behind him. The stainless steel lift doors distorted his image, rendering more like a gargoyle what should have been handsome. Kavanagh turned and looked at himself in the long strip of mirror in the rear corner of the compartment. Back to wearing his dark hair slightly longer now it was streaking with early grey, at any time of day Kavanagh looked like he could have just stepped off a tennis court. Kavanagh knew that two of the younger salespeople who worked for him hummed the theme to the Gillette razor advertisement when they saw him coming, always looking sharp and the best he could in a man's man way. Kavanagh didn't mind. In fact, he quite liked it.

The oversized, soft leather satchel bumped at the side of his leg as the lift stopped, the only indication that the metal cubicle had ever been in motion. The bag contained several files, his laptop, lunch and, pushed into one corner in a plastic pouch, the smallest assemblage of sports kit he had achieved so far. He took a breath, savouring the last moment of soundproofing the lift afforded before it would open onto the main sales floor of Pendulum.

Noise and heat hit him, like stepping off an aeroplane in a foreign country. Half a dozen brands of aftershave and at least five variations of shirt stripe vied for his attention. Immediately, he tuned into three different telephone conversations, able to interpret at the rhythmic level what kind of day his people were having. Five at their desks and three out, he hoped, with clients. Not quite an even split, but good enough for the start of the week.

Everyone was Monday-smart, no time for blues at Pendulum. Male faces were shaved the closest they would be all week following two days of stubble growth. By dress-down Friday, chinos, check shirts and bright floral dresses would adorn the stressed-out and tired bodies as the party atmosphere tried to take hold, but that was still four days away.

Ten years ago, Kavanagh had seen the office at its height, the sweat visible and the flow of faces through the company so rapid it was impossible to keep track. He had witnessed three fist-fights and watched one salesman actually pull a gun on a senior credit analyst, paper flying and desks suddenly clearing as people scrambled under them. In that decade, other finance companies had crashed or burned out, trying to ride the crest of the cycle and extending themselves into too many bad deals, gift-horses that were all mouth and no legs. Pendulum had got through it, got big, got bigger and decided to get smaller again, aiming for quality instead of quantity. Through all the toil, the rhetoric and the outright bullshit, Kavanagh had been there.

Now, it was different. A couple of veterans from the old days, fused with newcomers, comprised his people. The two blended into a different kind of ruthlessness, a more switched-on and caring face grafted onto it. Everyone was still overpaid, still greedy, still more hungry than they needed to be and still overworked. There was still the rush for year end, quarter end, month end, end of the week, end of the day, by lunchtime, by first thing in the morning or by yesterday, but the fire of the game had lost the old ferocity. At thirty-six, Kavanagh felt like a lounge singer in Las Vegas, ploughing through the greatest hits and making money based on some forgotten glory, still addicted to the drug of performance.

Desks were staggered six feet apart to accommodate the eight finance salespeople that worked for Kavanagh. Their sales support were set off at one end of the room in a huddled group of three, secretarial support peppered around the fringes. Kavanagh had fought to keep the credit and legal people on another floor, happy to see the top of the building dedicated to sales, their desks at the centre of the room.

Kavanagh weaved through the office, the activity around him resembling a busy television newsroom. On his walk, he made no eye contact, knowing if he did, someone would want a piece of him right away.

Kate, his secretary, filled the doorway instantly.

'Not now, Kate,' Kavanagh said.

'Paul wants to see you. He said as soon as you got back.'

'When did he start asking for me?' Kavanagh asked.

'About an hour ago, but he only tried once. I told him where you were. Dennis called—'

Kavanagh held up his hand and stopped her, smiling as he did. 'I have to see the boss, remember?'

He gathered up his leather folder and strode out, stopping at a desk on the way. 'Chris, how close are we to the LKG deal?' he asked Chris Carson.

'Closer.'

'Will we fund it tomorrow?'

'I hope so.'

'We fund tomorrow.'

Kavanagh walked away. LKG manufactured wafer silicon chips and needed 200 million pounds to fund development over the next five years. Kavanagh had put a forty-million-pound credit line in place for them three years earlier and when the current deal came up, eyebrows were raised that Chris Carson, twenty-six and the newest addition to the asset finance team at Pendulum, was to be put on it. Kavanagh saw something familiar in Carson and made the call, knowing his boss, Paul Baran, thought it was risky. Kavanagh had piloted the deal through, but it was Carson who would close it finally. Transactions that size closed in so many stages it was hard to tell when the deal was actually done.

It was a short walk round the corner to Paul Baran's office, but the quiet was already noticeable, the carpet an eighth of an inch thicker, the art less corporate, actual brush-strokes visible. Kavanagh knew which part of the floor he preferred.

Paul Baran was chief executive of Pendulum. As the finance arm of the Cameron Trust, Pendulum sat at the rarefied end of a highly diversified chain so complexly constructed it would be impossible to unpick. The combined work of several lifetimes had gone into creating the structure of the Cameron Trust and, as it was, no one individual would have enough time in their life to work it all out. Not even Alexander Cameron himself, if he were alive.

Kavanagh chatted with Baran's PA and was announced over the phone.

'You can go in.'

Baran might have been at Pendulum forever as far as Kavanagh was concerned. For all Pendulum employees, even Kavanagh as sales director, Baran was the only visible face of the Cameron Trust. The responsibility of it wore into his features and created a mix of worry and stature that fascinated Kavanagh. Paul Baran was forty-eight, only twelve years older than him, yet Kavanagh looked so far up to him, the man could have been two hundred years old.

'Morning, Kav,' Baran said, leaning back in his chair.

The office fitted him as well as the handmade suits and the detachable-collar-and-cuff shirts. Bigger than a good-sized living room, it still ought, Kavanagh thought, to seem cramped with so much furniture, but it didn't, and Baran moved around it with the easy confidence of a blind man. The space was divided into three areas and Baran would occupy a particular one according to the nature of business to be done. The low, comfortable leather chairs clustered around a coffee table were the usual venue for cosy chat, shooting the shit as Baran liked to call it. The oval teak table with six swivel chairs was the place where sleeves were rolled up and deals thrashed out. To find Baran in the third area, behind the expanse of his desk, illuminated by the mid-morning sun and framed in the giant floor-to-ceiling window, threw Kavanagh off his mental stride.

'Morning,' Kavanagh said, not hesitating to sit on a high-backed chair which was one of three in front of Baran's desk.

'Kate tells me you were amongst the Arabs this morning. How'd it go?' Baran asked.

'Very well. I'm going to talk to my friend at Citibank and see what she can tell me about creating Islam-friendly financial products. Chris Carson is going to bring LKG in tomorrow,' Kavanagh said.

Baran smiled. 'You knew he would. Watch your back, Kav. They're catching you up.'

'They're not that far behind you,' Kavanagh replied.

There was silence. Ten years ago, when they were both still boys, Kavanagh might have filled the gap with a question, but this was a game he had been playing so long, he knew what to do. Sit tight and wait for the point.

'When would you like to retire, Kav?' Baran asked into the air-conditioned stillness of the office.

Kavanagh sat across the desk from his boss and let the question settle in his mind. It could have been a question constructed to elicit a response that would reveal a seemingly unrelated attitude towards something. Kavanagh waited, letting the query hang in the air between them. He wasn't going to answer this one without more data, and Baran knew it too.

'I'm serious,' Baran continued. 'Don't tell me you've never sat and thought about it. Everything has to stop sometime, Mike.'

Kavanagh looked over Baran's shoulder and took in the familiar pattern of the rooftops, spread out like a contour map. The glass dome of the Opera House in Covent Garden, the chimneys of Battersea Power Station, Centrepoint, all reaching out towards heaven. It was September and the city was still overheating from a Summer that had flourished late. The scene was placid through the tinted glass and Kavanagh wondered what would happen if he tried to open a window and let the noise blast in. There could have been a war going on outside and they wouldn't have known or cared, unless it affected a deal.

'I guess it stops when I decide it isn't fun any more,' Kavanagh said.

'You haven't been enjoying this, Kav, not for two years now. If that were your criterion, you'd retire now.'

'Where is this going, Paul?' Kavanagh asked, ignoring the comment.

'What are your share options worth at the moment, based on the Trust purchasing them?'

'Do you want me to wait a few seconds so it looks like I don't calculate that once a week?'

'Whatever.'

'Well, I have thirty-one thousand ordinary shares in Pendulum and I estimate they'll see me out with around one hundred and fifty thousand, currently.'

'You were the first person off the Cameron Trust-sponsored MBA, Mike. I can still remember your first proper day here, after all those days you spent while you were in your final year at Birmingham and then on through LBS.'

'Why did you ask me about the shares? Are we about to be bought?' Kavanagh asked.

'Not quite. The Trust, as you know, has a business plan for the Cameron empire as a whole. These strategies will outlive all of us, in the long term. In the short term, however, probably when we're too old or rich to care, they are going float off the whole organization, across the board. They may spin it off in sections – finance, leisure and chemicals would be obvious – or they may try to sell the whole thing as one giant diversified monster.'

'Are we about to be bought?' Kavanagh asked again. 'Are we in play, Paul?'

'Kav, if we were, you'd be the first person here, after me,

to know and you'd be hearing it from me. In the short term, up to the end of this century, it's been decided Pendulum should broaden its sweep, push out into a new market for us. To do this, there was talk of acquiring someone, maybe a whole company, possibly just their portfolio, assets and receivables but no people. I thought it was the usual games, trying to buy in tax capacity, reduce funding costs or that fucking securitization all over again. But they're serious.'

'So, we're not going to be bought and we're not going to buy anyone?'

'That's right. The Cameron Trust want Pendulum to find a joint-venture partner.'

'Really?' Kavanagh asked. His mind turned it over, thinking of situations he'd seen where joint ventures had made jobs and destroyed them. Baran had kept this close to his chest and Kavanagh wondered if the conversation was leading out the door as far as he was concerned. The danger with a joint venture was that for every job it created in the new company, there were two people, one from each company, chasing it.

'I know. Cooperation with someone else – it threw me too. Buy or be bought, I thought, but a middle way?' Baran said, raising his eyebrows.

'It'd be more fun to tee up a company and swing in with the Pendulum cheque book open. It worked in Belgium and in France.'

'The Trust want to get something bedded in before the next stage. They have a vision for the way this joint venture will work and they want it up and running before the sell-off. This venture will be seen as crucial to the next few years and it'll put us at the front of the Trust again, a chance to win back some ground.'

'So,' Kavanagh said, 'India, China?'

Paul smiled. 'Oh no, that would be far too obvious for them. That's why they're going for something even more obvious. They want to form a venture with an American company.'

'The Cameron Trust is off to discover America? Very forward. Who are we going with? GE? IBM?' Kavanagh laughed.

'Don't tell me you wouldn't like to try that. There's a finance company called Trellis, based out of Los Angeles, offices in Boston, Seattle, Chicago and Dallas,' Baran said.

'I know the name. What would we be getting for our legal fees?' Kavanagh asked.

'They've done receivables financing on soft products as well as a few clever double-dip structures. Also, they're holding solid residual positions in some extremely big corporate accounts.'

'So we're trying to buy our way into a blue-chip American client base and Trellis get the same from us in the UK and bits of Northern Europe, Southern if we get into gear down there. Has an approach been made?' Kavanagh asked.

'In the stratosphere, yes, an approach has been made. Several members of the Trust have met informally with Jack Burns, who owns Trellis. There have been other companies approaching Trellis recently and I understand an offer fell through less than two months ago. This is the time to capitalize. They've got him switched on. Now, they want to see how we dance.'

'And you want me to put on my tap shoes?'

'Kav, I hate to say this, but not even I could do it as well as you,' Baran said. 'When it comes to the beauty pageant, you're our secret weapon.'

'I don't want to be the one to bring this full-circle, but where, in general, does this leave Pendulum and, specifically, where does it leave me?'

'If you play this one right, Kav, it can leave you wherever you choose. The way it's planned, a cooperation agreement will regulate both Trellis and Pendulum in the short term and each will retain autonomy, but eventually all business will merge into the venture. I think they view it as a gradual thing. "Evolutionary merger" was the phrase used. It's not going to be just a vehicle. They're serious about this, the Trust.'

'Okay, Paul. Given that I've never once seen you ask a question you don't already know the answer to, when would I like to retire?'

Baran paused for a second and the silence thrummed in Kavanagh's ears. 'I've seen preliminary projections on what the joint venture with Trellis is expected to return in the next ten years,' Baran said. 'I've been given authority to offer you three hundred and fifty thousand shares in the venture which the Trust will purchase from you the day the cooperation agreement between Pendulum and Trellis is signed, the vehicle in place. At the float point, the estimated share price is seven hundred and twenty and that's what they'll pay day one. You don't need me to tell you that's a shade over two and a half million pounds.'

Kavanagh's chest was palpitating and he hoped it wasn't showing through his jacket. If this was being fired, two and a half million was some handshake. 'What happens if they float and the share price is nine hundred?' he asked.

Baran snorted. 'You were a fucking Marxist when I met you. If that happens, they've agreed to pay you the difference at the time.'

'And if it floats at six hundred?'

'Nothing. You've taken the money and run by then. Someone up there likes you, Kav. You sit on the beach and worry about skin cancer. When Lucy finishes school, you could put her through university anywhere in the world, take the two of you off somewhere, leave all this shit behind.'

'Why is the Cameron Trust willing to pay me two and half million pounds to set them up a joint venture you could get a few accountants to do? It's America, for Christ's sake, not Italy – they can do this stuff on their own. Why aren't you doing it?'

'I'm a lifer, Mike. People get shorter sentences for murder. In the great scheme of Cameron, what do you think a couple of million looks like? If they get the leverage in the States they're thinking of, you'll be working cheap, trust me.'

'Did you negotiate this deal, Paul? Is this a charitable act?' Kavanagh asked.

'Mike, I remember your and Helen's fifth and tenth wedding anniversaries, holding Lucy when she was a baby. I know that out there they don't think I'm a good people-manager, and maybe they're right, but when Helen died, I saw something switch off in you.'

'I stayed on board here, Paul. I was here for Pendulum.'

'That was what scared me the most, Mike. After what you and Lucy had been through, you just held it in check. It would have been easier for me if you'd gone fucking mad, stood on the ledge and threatened to jump. Tell me you don't want out on these terms.'

Baran was right and it hurt. Kavanagh put the pain somewhere else.

'Tell me some more,' Kavanagh said.

'Naturally, as we get closer, there'll be heavy legal support – our investment bankers, a member or two of the Trust jumping out of the cake – but in the early stages, Kav, it will all be down to you.'

'Not a problem.'

'Trellis is a one-man show. Jack Burns still has his fingers all over it and it'll take some persuading to pry them off, more than just money.'

'I'll have Library dig me out what we have on Trellis,' Kavanagh said.

'I've already got them doing it. This is going to hang a lot of your time, Mike. You'll have to pass any current transactions down to Ray or up to me, if necessary.'

'Sure. When do we get started?'

'That's a small wrinkle.'

'Why?'

'We're talking tight timescales. They want you out there next week.'

Kavanagh exhaled. 'Shit.'

'I know. Until we can get Burns online, we need you to

be out there with him. I know it's short notice, and close to the anniversary,' Baran said.

Kavanagh sighed and wondered if this was going to be worth two and a half million pounds.

Chapter 2

'It's Inoperable'

Nancy Lloyd, on the afternoon it began for her, stood in the 'newborn' section of Gap Kids. She was twenty-eight and, as of the last forty minutes, dying. Nancy had always nurtured the fantasy of being successful before she died, she just never realized how close together fate was going to place the two events.

'Inoperable? You mean it doesn't work?' Nancy had asked.

'No,' was the reply. 'That would be inoperative. If it didn't do anything, I guess that would be benign. This isn't.'

Being told you were going to die was no better in a cool Californian accent, Nancy had discovered, even if the privilege was more expensive than in England.

Was there was a trans-national smell which all Gaps adopted? Nancy was overcome by the familiar odour of the place. It was an identical smell to the shop on Oxford Street in London, and the one she had been to in Hyannis. It created a déjà vu as insidious as the aftershave of the first man she ever slept with.

Carefully she lifted a hanger, as gently as if it were the child itself, and held the material to her face. A milky, biscuit-like essence rose and, even though she knew she was imagining it, Nancy let the scent flow over her, wondering why one sense was heightened above all others on this particular day.

Inoperable. Now I know why I'm blocked, she thought. Who wouldn't be? This wasn't a simple, everyday writer's block. It was the real thing, a tangible foreign object taking up residence.

There was a small dress, no bigger than a face-flannel, black with red flowers on it. What a morbid colour, she thought, something you'd bury a child in. The miniature basketball boots could have been for a toy, intricate reworkings of adult fashions, turning the wearers into mini-people long before they were due to mature. I wouldn't dress my child like that, she thought. If I had one.

Nancy wondered what she was going to tell her agent. It was almost embarrassing. Could she just call her and say, I know we're on the verge of your biggest-ever deal for an unfinished script by a novelist untested as a screenwriter, but I'm afraid I'm dying. Coming to Los Angeles had not merely been about leaving London behind her, but abandoning a whole life. It was not in her plans, however, to come out to the far end of America only to find she would very soon be leaving life itself.

On a practical level, if nothing else, being able to establish an approximate timescale on her demise might just give her a new currency. Surely Los Angeles would be able to pin a value on death, if only a monetary one. Even in nine weeks there, Nancy had learned that much. In her agent's eyes she could already imagine just a flicker of excitement when Nancy revealed the fact of her impending death. Something as mundane as mortality would be no problem for Nancy's agent.

For Nancy, however, it was going to be more difficult. The dying part, she assumed, would be easy. It was the writing, the living, that was difficult. From an early age, she had reached an uneasy peace with her finiteness and saw it unfolding over a number of years. As she discovered her creative gift, she expected at the end of these years to realize a vision of some kind. Nancy hadn't directed a pen towards paper, or tapped her fingers over a keyboard, in eight months, long before the first contact with a doctor.

When the prognosis had been drawled to her less than an

hour earlier, Nancy didn't think, I'm going to die, but, This is it, I'm going to write.

Even on the drive to Gap, she had tentatively felt around parts of her mind to see if anything had been awakened, shocked into life by a bolt of lightning.

Nothing.

Nothing had become a big factor in Nancy's life and she assumed death would bring that very much to the fore. Now at least she'd have the satisfaction of calling Colin in England and being able to deliver the rhetorical line, You wanted to know what the fuck was wrong with me?

Tomorrow, over lunch, her agent would ask how the script was coming and Nancy knew she would make something up to pacify her. From the most devastating treatment imaginable had flowed studio interest in an English author. What had not followed on from the treatment was the script itself, which Nancy saw as very much her end of the bargain. Well, her agent did tell Warner, Sony and Fox that the script would be 'to die for'.

Nancy looked around at the collection of tiny clothes and the biggest conglomeration of the shamelessly fat she had seen since arriving in Los Angeles. It's all here somewhere, she thought, like a dictionary waiting to be made into a book. It's just a simple process of ordering everything. Art as process. Everything's a process.

When the headaches began, she thought, as usual, it was a brain tumour. The same one that had been killing her with every headache since she was twelve.

Surely it was just a brain tumour.

Wrong.

It had turned out to be *the* brain tumour.

When it came down to the range of diseases she believed herself to have at any single time, Nancy cried wolf to herself, always ready for the doctor or a bout of her own rationality to rescue her. When she was told she had a brain tumour, she just nodded her newly sick head. If any organ was going to let her down, it would be her brain. Not content with its size and capacity, it had to try and expand beyond all control, the cells spinning off at wild axes. That's what made me run from England, really, she thought. Once it had become clear something serious was wrong, Nancy had ignored it and hoped she would leave whatever it was languishing in London with her now ex-lover.

In the library-like atmosphere of Gap, so familiar and safe, and she a barren impostor in it, the idea of death seemed absurd, as if she could just shrug it off or ignore it. In the scope of all time, she was on the planet for only a brief moment and when she went, she would be gone for as long as she had never been there. It made her calm and then it made her want to scream and run and run. It gave all her actions meaning at the same time as it stripped them of any.

The shop could have been a fast-food chain, bright ash floors and chrome. Along the white walls were alcoves, clusters of inactivity filled with helpfully pre-dressed headless mannequins. On the stairs to the basement, there were low-level kiddie handrails and a lift for people with strollers. In her arms, Nancy cradled the white baby-grow, supporting it under the rear and at the neck, where a head should have been.

It wasn't like this in Mothercare, she thought. What was it like?

Very special and very nice.

It hadn't been that special or nice, as she recalled it. Either in Mothercare or how she had ended up there in the first place.

He was older than her, quite a bit, and he knew how to get his way. An assured thirty-one-year-old. Could I have done that to a sixteen-year-old if I'd been him? she wondered. Nancy tried to stop using her brain, worried it might advance the tumour, give it nourishment. Perhaps it was a big globule of all the bad thoughts and experiences she'd ever had, the pus of a million rotten moments in her short life. Perhaps it looked like a big brown piece of liver.

‘Is it for you?’ an assistant asked with global Gap friendliness.

‘I don’t think it would fit, do you?’ Nancy said in her best English teacher’s voice, holding it up to herself and giving a gentle smile.

The girl fumbled with the irony and blushed. She was no more than eighteen, her hips the sort that had never passed anything big through them, and Nancy hated her with passion and without reason. Another time, Nancy might have made more of a joke or gone in the other direction and delivered a barbed comment. Instead, she stood there dying, not sure which way to go, and the girl withdrew.

Nancy had not been drunk, just a bit woozy – and that shouldn’t have made a difference anyway, she kept telling herself afterwards – when he helped her into the back of his car and then helped her off with her knickers.

‘What are you doing?’ she asked him.

‘*Something very special and very nice.*’

The knickers made a scratching sound as they came down her legs and it had felt good to be able to close her ankles together so he could work them off her feet. While she was closed up, she felt safe. Once they were off, however, he made it clear he wanted her legs open again. Knickerless and with her knees wide, she suddenly found the small space in the back of the car impossibly tight and she a vulnerable, gaping body in its midst.

I should have worn trousers, she thought. Tight jeans. She had caught a glimpse of three boys skinny-dipping in a river one dappled summer, but this was different. It was heavy and grown-up, a foreboding and ponderous part of him that he wanted to put into her, never mind what she wanted. My mother would be so pleased to be right, she thought, crying out in pain and grappling for the back door handles, which she later realized didn’t work because he had set the childproof locks. The force of his thrusting lifted her behind clear of the seat and banged her head against the window, pushing her neck at an uncomfortable angle. She frantically tried to cling on to any small area of pain she could, using it to focus away from the real agony she felt in the very centre of her.

He growled, sounding angry, his hot breath on the shoulder of her blouse turning to damp. When he reared up and shouted, he used his big hands to pin her shoulders back against the seat. He was staring at her. She closed her eyes tightly, turning her head to one side. Then she felt his hand lock onto her chin, cupping her jaw and forcing her head round to face him. Air escaped her lips in a sputter and when she opened her mouth to cry out properly, she felt his thumb push into her cheek, indenting the flesh where her jaw had opened.

'Look at me,' he grunted.

As she made eye contact with him, her upper body still pinned to the leather of the seat and her lower body shoved back and forth by the dog-like movements of his groin, he seemed to weaken, as if something more powerful had taken hold of him. The movements became impossibly fast and hard in the dry channel between her legs, so much so she thought he would tear her open. Then the actions of his body disintegrated into frantic spasms and it seemed as if, had she wanted to, she could easily have killed him at that moment. Afterwards, for a long time, she found herself wishing she had.

She felt raw and there was warm, gooey liquid running from her. He pulled out and looked down at himself. 'No virgin, then?' he asked, pleased with himself as he put it back in his trousers.

Nancy watched the red brake-lights of the car get smaller in the distance as she stood on the edge of the green, clutching her knickers in her hand, her nose running snotty from tears.

She was gripping the small white baby-grow so hard, she had creased it and she hung it at the back of the row. Her eyes were moist and she felt a twinge of pain in the left side of her head, followed by the feeling her eyes were swelling. In the memory, she knew, her own name never came up.

She was never Nancy, only ever she. And it was the same with him.

It should have stopped then and there. Nancy never saw him again and she thought that was it. It was over. Of course, it wasn't, and she spent three anxious weeks willing her period to arrive, checking her underwear obsessively, a tampon in her purse the whole time. It never came.

In Mothercare, it started as a cheerful event. Nancy was slim and showed quickly, making it hard to hide from her parents for too long. When, after an hour of blunt aching, the first real stab of sharp pain in her lower abdomen brought her upright and to attention, she had been standing near an assistant. A smile broke out over the middle-aged woman's face, as though she were about to witness a birth in the shop; a birth in the style of an American TV movie, where Nancy would name the child after the shop assistant.

A small crowd, three or four people, gathered. One, a woman with a pram containing a sleeping baby in a white wool hat and next to the pram an inquisitive-looking girl clinging to her arm, regarded Nancy with disdain, as though all of this were her own fault. Nancy remembered locking stares with the small girl and seeing the fear in her young eyes, as though she were the only other person in the shop who knew something was going terribly wrong.

Something very special and very nice.

I should have worn trousers.

Even on the yellow-white of the Mothercare linoleum, Nancy was shocked at how red the blood was. It had run in a long dribble down her left leg and the first drop on the plastic surface looked like a spot of paint. Nancy felt queasy, drunk almost, and her legs disappeared from her consciousness as she fell into the assistant and was lowered to the floor. If her mind had been kinder, it might have let her pass out.

On what would be the last occasion for eight years, Nancy allowed a pair of strange hands to work her knickers down. This time, she could not have kept her legs closed even if she had wanted to. Inside, she felt her muscles let go, as though they had been clenching something without her knowledge. It was as if her stomach muscles had sighed and given up some sort of ghost. Down between her legs, it felt nasty and meaty, part of her and yet not part of her, and Nancy was certain she could sense something flapping about as she expelled what he had put in there thirteen weeks earlier.

Again Nancy looked at the little girl, conscious in the periphery of her vision that the onlookers had all taken a step backwards. Nancy watched the girl's eyes, wondering what was going on behind them and if the child had enough knowledge to process what she was seeing. A security guard in uniform appeared behind the pram and Nancy thought he was an ambulanceman, but the look on his face soon dispelled that illusion.

Forcing herself upright, the sharp pain in her lower back now returned to a numb ache, Nancy looked at the patch of floor between her open legs. It looked like a big piece of liver, brown and shining as it lay on the floor surrounded by a garish wash of amniotic fluids.

It moved.

Like a fish out of water, it flipped. She saw it. Nancy glanced up at the child and knew she had seen it too. A quick scan around the other faces and Nancy knew they had seen nothing, all the expressions locked in masks of revulsion as the image burned itself into their memories. It did move, just once in a sharp pulse, but it definitely moved.

As she stood in Gap, even its all-pervasive perfume could not blot out the recollection of the aroma that piece of meat gave off. Now, in remembrance, the smell was coming from deep inside her head and she knew if she held her nose, rather than ward it off, she would trap the fetid stench inside. Instead, Nancy took several deep breaths, purging her head of the scent and the memory in equal measure.

With weak legs and a slight shake to her hands, Nancy charged the black dress, basketball boots and the crumpled white baby-grow she had retrieved from the back of the rack. She would take them back to the rented apartment in West Hollywood and place them with the collection she had been amassing since her arrival.

Outside, she stopped. I should write this down, she thought. Write what? What had she just been thinking about? Nancy turned her head quizzically back to the shop, trying to remember. Something about liver? Was this a symptom of the tumour, the one thing she would never forget, which would always be on her mind?

Into the remnants of the California day she drove, her mind, for the time being, still mercifully blocked to the real truth.

Inoperable.

Chapter 3

Garth Richards might just have killed someone in any case, even if he had never been brought to Book. All it would have required was the right set of circumstances, a context. As Garth sniffed loudly and then swallowed, readying himself for the sixteenth cold call of the morning, he was both unhappy and unknowing. Garth was oblivious to the joy that should have resulted from such ignorance. He was still twenty minutes away from the call that would be the death of him and, in the interim, The Book opened its pages wide and granted Garth a small moment of unknowing respite. It let him remain illiterate, an innocent, for a few minutes longer before it would snap shut and fold its pages over him.

The phone continued to ring at the other end and Garth's insides felt watery, but he tried to stay calm above the chest, taking a quick gulp of coffee and getting ready to make his voice a note lower and his accent a shade better. The phone was answered and his breath caught for a second, as if a small stitch was holding it in. Garth glanced down at the call sheet in front of him, unable to remember the company he had rung or the person he wanted to speak to.

'Molton-Williams,' a female voice said at the same time as his eyes fell onto the name at the top of the page.

'Adrian Hawley, please,' Garth said, trying to sound as if he were a personal friend of Hawley's.

Without speaking again, the woman at the other end transferred him, the ring muffled at first and then becoming loud as a proper connection was made. Part of him wished he had floundered at the receptionist stage. Pendulum had been targeting new business in a wide market, a scatter-gun approach to anyone who bought anything they might be able to finance. The campaign had been aimed at finance directors, but people at board level were well protected from door knockers like Garth Richards and he knew there would be another hurdle before the man himself. The most difficult obstacle of all – the personal secretary, more loyal than a pit bull and harder to get past.

'Adrian Hawley's office,' a female voice said, in an accent so upmarket Garth knew it would be folly to try and match it.

'Can I speak to Adrian Hawley, please?' he asked politely.

'May I ask who's calling?'

'Garth Richards from Pendulum.'

'Will he know what it's regarding?'

'It's about a letter I sent him.'

'May I ask what it was about?'

'I'd prefer to speak to him directly,' Garth said, trying to give the sentence an air of finality.

'Just a moment,' she said.

The depressing, vacant sound of hold forced itself against his ear, not even any pathetic music to laugh at, and Garth wondered what was being said behind the silence. He braced himself for the moment when he would be put through. The line crackled like the needle being put into a record groove and Garth breathed in, ready to go into his pitch, which was laid out in bullet points on the card in front of him, empty diary poised in case he got an appointment.

'I'm afraid he has someone with him at the moment. Can I take your number and get him to call you back?' the woman's voice asked.

'That's okay. I'll try later. When do you think he'll be free?' Garth asked.

'He's in meetings for most of today. Can I take your number?'

'I'll try tomorrow. Thanks,' Garth said, smothering her

next sentence and wanting nothing more at that moment than to put the phone down.

Around him, he was conscious of eyes watching. One or two of the other salesmen were eavesdropping and he could sense their amusement. Failing on a cold call was like asking someone out in front of your friends and being turned down. Garth's face reddened and he looked away, feeling hotter than he would have liked. When Mike Kavanagh found out he had been using one of the meeting rooms to make his calls, he had not been happy, making Garth come back out into the open-plan office, as though it would be good for morale. It was certainly good for the spirits of the other sales staff as it gave them a good laugh at his expense. Of course, Kavanagh had run the most successful cold-call campaign in Pendulum's history, generating sixty-four million in eight months from a standing start.

How much more of this? he thought. Garth had to close off the outstanding letters, forging the call sheets if he had to. Copying names out of company guides, writing to people, phoning them, trying to get an appointment and only getting a brush-off was tolerable for just so long. If he'd been in his early twenties, it might have been fun.

Garth was thirty-nine and, as far as work was concerned, he had seen just about everything. There had been enough companies in his life to take away even the hope of being surprized. He would never be paid what he was worth or given the tools to do what he was good at. There would always be too much work, superiors who should have been inferiors and the medieval impingement the company tried to make upon his personal space, as though he were in tithe rather than waged employment. What he *had* come to expect were the feelings of isolation, resentment and boredom, leading to unhappiness. Garth couldn't think of anyone he knew who was happy at work. If there was that strength of feeling, why didn't it just collapse? Every morning on the Northern Line he wanted to start shouting, 'What the fuck are we all doing this for? Let's just stop, now.' One day he would be at the head of a revolutionary crowd, leading them along the platform and above ground, into a better world. Garth had never thought of himself as a communist or a utopian, but each day at worked increased his sense of what an absurd way it was to organise life.

With his compact body, Garth could have passed for a middleweight boxer, his nose also evidencing the right degree of flatness, even though he had never donned a glove still less thrown an angry punch in his life. Garth would have made a bad boxer since his head was a shade too large, accentuated by business attire where no shirt, however expensive, looked comfortable on him. He had been wearing a suit for nearly twenty years and still carried it with the gawkiness of a fifteen-year-old at a wedding.

He wasn't ugly, he knew that. Garth's smiles always started somewhere deep in the brown of his eyes, which would widen almost imperceptibly, the grin slowly revealing teeth just uneven enough for the recipient to notice and want to straighten them. True, his features were buttery, a sheen of moisture glazing him in a way that suggested patches of sweat gathering in unseen places. Still, Garth knew that if people got to know him, they liked him. It was convincing them to stop and take a second look that was the problem. People looked just the once and registered nothing special. He didn't have the instant, sunny yet patrician likability of someone like Kavanagh.

When Garth had entered the asset finance industry eight years earlier, there were a few people his current age already retiring. Certainly by now most would have leveraged themselves into overpaid jobs, positions they could not afford to leave any more than their employer could bear the cost of firing them. Garth earned less now than two years ago.

There had been a peak. Six or seven years earlier. Garth had scaled it and then no sooner had he reached the apex than the ground moved under him and he toppled. Two years in a row Garth failed to make his numbers and then lost his job. By the time he found the next, there was an ugly nine-month gap on his CV, accounted for by the industry-standard apologia of 'self-employed consultant'. And that wasn't the only consequence. There was also the aching chasm between his old lifestyle and the inability of his current income to fund such high living. That was what happened when you fell off the peak. You hit the ground fast and lived with the results for years.

If Pendulum were a family, its elders men like Baran and Kavanagh, with the new twenty-something kids seemingly born to greatness, Garth felt as though he were the bastard son or, worse, someone who had married into it and was tolerated. It was true that Garth did have a highly tenuous family connection to the Cameron Trust, but he did his utmost to play that down rather than mobilize it as a resource. Garth had only been at Pendulum eight months and had turned down worse jobs in his career. The moment something better came along, he would get out of Pendulum.

The ringing of the ship's bell brought him upright, startling him.

Garth looked up and saw Chris Carson standing by the bell, holding his briefcase out in front of him and smiling beatifically.

'LKG, two hundred million, seventy-five basis points over. Ready to drawdown,' Carson said.

The four other salespeople present clapped and there were some whoops and whistles. Kavanagh was on his feet in his office, staring impassively through the long pane of glass, trying to appear his usual self, both distant and connected, benevolent and cruel, like some mafioso.

It took Garth a moment to realize that he had been frowning and not applauding. Quickly he pushed his face into a smile and tried to clap enthusiastically. The salespeople gathered around Carson, obviously hoping some of the gleam would rub off. Garth knew he would be expected to go over and join in the congratulation session.

'Well done, Chris,' he said, keeping something of a distance. For a moment he was going to shake Carson's hand, possibly even grip his elbow in a manful gesture of mutual recognition, but something stopped him. It was as if touching Carson would be like grabbing a live cable – that an unpleasant force would jerk through his body. Garth tried to ignore the feeling.

'Unless anybody thinks they're likely to bring something bigger than this in by month-end – and if you do, I'll want to know why the fuck it wasn't prospected – I think we have a new king.'

It was Kavanagh, who had sidled up to the fringe of the group and was carrying the brass crown stolen from a banqueting evening the team had been on.

'Long live the king,' Kavanagh said, placing the crown on the loose curls of Chris Carson's goofy head.

Long live the boy king, thought Garth. I could bring in 200 million if I was given a warm lead by 'Kav', who knew everyone at LKG anyway and already had a facility in place. Try some cold calling, Garth thought through his smile and the resumed salvo of clapping.

'We have some drinking to do,' Kavanagh said, looking at his watch. 'The Latchkey in ten minutes?'

There were nods and smiles, the usual happiness a deal engendered buoying everyone up. Everyone except Garth, who nodded and smiled while inside he felt himself oozing despondency, as though his body had sprung a leak.

'Are you coming, Garth?' Chris asked after the team had assembled itself and argued over whose credit card would be put behind the bar of the Latchkey.

'I've got a couple of things to do here. I'll catch you up,' Garth said, the thought of spending two hours singing, playing drinking games and listening to war stories making his insides feel like they'd been through a food blender.

Carson barely registered the response and, in under a second, five men in suits were heading for the door, their new king leading the way and singing the title music from *Reservoir Dogs*.

Garth let out a breath and gazed at the call sheets in front of him. There was a moment of panic as a whole afternoon of trying to leapfrog secretaries crystallized in his mind. Dread flashed past him like the life of a drowning man and he wondered why he didn't just get up and walk out of Pendulum right then, and never come back.

He was doodling idly on the sheet in front of him, making a long swirling figure of eight with his biro, keeping it moving around the arc he'd drawn as the paper gradually gave under the pressure of his pen. The more he trailed the nib across the page, the less conscious he became of his actions and when the phone on his desk rang, Garth reached for it without even looking up.

'Garth Richards,' he said, gripping the pen tight and pressing hard with it.

The Book opened itself.

'It goes on forever, but you can see it,' a man's voice said at the other end of the line.

'Sorry?' Garth asked, as though not hearing him the first time.

'The knotwork goes on forever but you can see it. Infinite patterns visible to the eye. It's seeing forever.'

Garth continued to gaze at his drawing, unable to look up from it. This was what the voice was talking about, the spaghetti-like knot he had inscribed into the paper. His mouth felt dry.

'You could move that pen round and round all day and never stop. Unless you got tired,' the voice said.

'You'd have to stop somewhere. Back where you started,' Garth said, wondering why no one else seemed to be around him at that moment. He could have been sitting in the middle of an aircraft hangar. The words came out of Garth's mouth, but he could tell they didn't belong to him. And yet there was an exhilarating feeling about being used in such a way, a violation that was almost sexual. Garth felt a stirring in his underwear.

'Besides,' Garth continued, 'you can start anywhere you want. It's arbitrary. And it doesn't really go on forever, it's only a line joined up,'

'I agree. If you think of it as a line that only goes in one direction. When did we start doing that? Thinking of things as a line? Don't you find the pattern of infinity comforting?'

The movements of Garth's pen left gold trails, as if a snail had crawled over the knot pattern. When the man spoke again, it felt like the voice was inside Garth's head.

'Have you ever seen the rooms on the ninth floor?' the man asked.

'There aren't any. There's only eight floors. We're at the top,' Garth responded with the quick petulance of a nine-year-old interrupted during a favourite television programme.

'You should go and look. You might find something.'

'What?' Garth asked.

Something very special and very nice.

Did the man say that?

So you trust me then?

Yes.

Take off the rest of your clothes then.

'I think you would be well-advised and well-rewarded to check into it,' the man said.

Garth smiled at the piece of paper and touched the warm breast-pocket of his jacket, trying to feel with his fingers the shapes it concealed.

'Don't you think . . .' Garth looked back down at the page, words failing him.

The phone was dead.

Staring down at the knot he had drawn on the blank page, Garth felt it stretch his eyes as he made the figure blur and then come back into sharp focus. A thin line of dribble trickled from the corner of his mouth, as though he had been asleep, and he noticed how slack his jaw felt. He paused, still looking at the lines on the page, and searched his brain, trying to find the words he had just said and heard during the phone conversation. They weren't there, not in any manner he could define. Instead, he felt as though deep indentations had been made into his brain, like the press of fingers into clay. He could not remember the words, but he knew what to do.

Garth entered the small toilet for the fourth time that day and locked the door behind him. The stall, one of three, had a small gap above and below the door. He put the seat and then the lid down, sat on it and felt the rigid plastic under his behind. With his head lolling to one side as though he were dropping off to sleep, Garth stared listlessly at the door while rummaging about in his pocket.

The outer door of the toilets swung open and Garth heard it with dog-sensitive ears, alert to the minutest changes in air pressure during his most solitary moments.

David Roke from legal. Garth knew him by the footfalls alone. He was approaching the urinals. The sound of a zip. A flow. A clearing of the throat. A breaking of wind. A sigh. The zip. The tap running. The towel dispenser spinning. The door opening. The air still once again.

From his jacket pocket he retrieved a small mirror and looked at himself in it, holding it close to see only his eyes. Carefully he rested the mirror on the edge of his knee while he found the square plastic pouch, the size of a tea bag, in the far corner of the jacket pocket. The polythene was smudged with sweaty fingerprints. Garth emptied some of the white powder onto the surface of the glass.

In the shrill acoustics of the toilets, the razor blade made a clicking noise that echoed around the tiled walls. Garth looked at the powder and wondered if it really did look potent or if it was his imagination. What dreams were locked up in the crystals, waiting to be released in his head, what visions and feelings he knew did not belong to him? Forming the small pile lovingly into lines was like measuring out his prospective happiness. A move to the left or right, making the line fatter or thinner, was like deciding on a few seconds more or less of freedom.

The blank cheque from his book was beginning to wrinkle from use but would serve its purpose a few more times. Garth's spine stretched and he felt the vertebrae separating as he leaned forwards, bringing his head down to his knee. The inhalation always required less force than he expected, making him think he had a knack for it. Garth loved, really deeply loved, the way the dust entered his head, going up his nose and disappearing into a secret passage. It insinuated itself into hidden corners of his skull, unleashing things that would otherwise have remained buried.

All morning the world had been viewed through a badly focused pair of binoculars, making everything blurred and too close at the same time. Now everything was sharp, every edge geometrically defined and able to cut him to pieces. The sense of danger the world suddenly gave off was exhilarating and Garth soared into it. He wasn't sure if he was happy, but he knew he felt different.

Inside him, from a place he could not quite pinpoint, a feeling was stirring. The awareness that despite all the boring stuff around him, the deadening routine that permeated him like cold and damp, something was about to change. It came over him with such a profound certainty yet he had never sensed it at any other moment in his life. It was as though the notion had been planted in him from somewhere outside. Even outside the seductive white powder. As though it had dropped out of the sky.

Something very special and very nice.

The landing for the back stairs, which served as a fire exit, was cold. It was dull and damp, the paint a sickly green and the stairs drab stone, pitted and worn into a dalmatian pattern. Nothing here would burn, he supposed, which was why they were the fire stairs. It was like being backstage, seeing the reality behind the veneer. Was there really a ninth floor? How many people would go outside and count the number of floors and then go inside and reconcile it? The health and safety, the building people, they must know about it.

Working on the eighth floor, the top of the building, Garth had never thought to climb the stairs at the back – he just assumed they led to the roof. He trotted up them quickly, his shoes loud on the stone, and came to a green fire door with a small window and a foreboding steel bar across its middle with the instruction 'Push To Open'. The door was probably alarmed and the last thing he wanted was to set it off. Cautiously he peered through the small pane of glass. It was the roof, a big rectangle of pebbles, like an enormous Zen garden, with metal boxes at intervals, air-conditioning fans spinning lazily within them.

Garth turned around to go back down and saw the other door. It had not been there before, he was certain.

Something very special and very nice.

'Garth.'

The Book called him.

He turned, confused, sure he had heard his name whispered. It had slipped in between a breath, finding a gap in the quickening beat of his heart. Garth listened, waiting to hear it again, but there was nothing. There were stories about people who heard their name called by loved ones who were in trouble. His own voice started to address him, telling him to go back down to his desk and get on with some more calls. What was he doing up here anyway?

Certainty tugged at Garth once again, jerking him along as if he were attached a piece of string.

Opening the door, he half expected a dingy old corridor, full of cobwebs and with the odd mouse scurrying along. But everything about the passage on the other side was bland and neutral, the decor not much different from the rest of the building, apart from the lurid Seventies pattern of the carpet.

The oddest thing about the passageway was that it led only to another single door at its end, ten feet away.

'Garth.'

This time he did not mistake it, had heard it for definite. He felt like an intruder but knew something worthwhile lay hidden at the end of the short walk. It was like the time he had sneaked into his parents' room and gone through Mum and Dad's things.

The door opened unaided, silent and confident as it swung inwards.

Scrunching his eyes closed, Garth shook his head as though trying to rid himself of the vision. This is paranoia and I'm just hallucinating, he told himself. I have to stop snorting. This is paranoia on top of paranoia, anxiety that feeds on itself. What if those things people whispered about the Cameron Trust were true, about Alexander Cameron and what he had done to his family in this very building? Supposing the stories his father so loved to tell were really true? They never found him, he heard his father's voice murmur. They say he's still here, hiding somewhere in the building, watching and waiting.

'Garth.'

Where would the door lead? For the first time since he was a child, Garth felt truly scared. What frightened him most was the sure knowledge that he had to find out. He walked slowly, the sides of the hall feeling close. There were no windows and no lights, yet he could see perfectly.

The room at the end of the hall was a large square, twenty by twenty and empty except for a circular table placed in its centre. On top of the table, also at its centre, was a book.

'Garth.'

It came from the table.

He drew nearer, looking at the dense beam of light that came from above, afraid to get too close. There didn't seem to be a hole in the roof. It was at that moment he realized the light was coming out of the book, not shining onto it. He stopped and tried to walk backwards.

'Garth,' The Book said, more commandingly.

He remained still, sweat now trickling off his face and onto the collar of his white shirt.

There seemed to be two equal forces, his own volition trying to pull him away and some other will attempting to pull him forward. He let his own inner strength match the unseen energy, as if he were stretching a muscle, before yielding, his fear evaporating like a small drop of water thrown into a raging fire.

It was simple, and at that second, in the moment of no

fear and no words, he knew exactly what was going on. It began and ended, and began again, with The Book.

The Book wanted to read him.

Garth approached the table, no longer afraid. The book was no more than ten inches long and seven wide, a little over two inches thick. Looking at the leaves tightly compacted between the covers, he saw they were perfectly flat and white, no damp waves to the paper or dirty smudges marking well-read pages. It seemed clean and new, ready for someone to open and begin writing in like a journal.

Walking round the table, not wanting to touch anything, he squatted and looked at the spine to see if there was a title. There wasn't. He moved his face closer, testing if the volume would smell as new as it looked. The light coming from it warmed his nose like morning sun and made his face form into a broad grin. The material on the cover was closely woven into small divots the size of pinheads.

Then, when Garth stood to look at it from above once more, it no longer appeared new.

The green binding was covered in veins and there were some small dents in it, like craters. The fine weave was replaced by what could have been a dark green wood, almost like green ebony. The pages now looked yellow and the book ancient, as though opening it would raise dust and cause the tearing of paper. It smelled of damp, of earth and of wood. In the tiny part of a second it had taken Garth to stand, the book had aged thousands of years, to a time before books even existed. Now it looked as though every story written might be writhing beneath the jacket, waiting to spill out like disembowelled guts. Its antiquated appearance did not put Garth off. It looked much less antiseptic than it had in its pristine form moments earlier. Something about the earthy well-worn look was seductive, as if indicating secrets worth knowing.

The light was warm on his hands as he reached out, smiling, a feeling of happiness shining through him that he had not felt in a long time, if ever.

Opening the book somewhere near the middle, Garth looked down. The page was blank. Keeping the place with his finger, he looked at the preceding pages, which were also blank. He looked at the ones that came after and they too were the same.

The Book began to read.

It made the drugs seem like nothing more than a placebo. Garth had never felt so certain about where he was at any other moment in his life. Every thought, feeling and word that had ever passed through him or would pass through him was defined in absolute and perfect clarity. He no longer needed other people or other words to define himself or his experience. As The Book pored over him, he became complete in himself. The Book read on, cross-referencing and indexing him, sorting through all the facts of his life and reordering them in the fashion it chose. The Book worked through the text of Garth's life with absolute rigour, finding every contradiction and every small, apparently unimportant moment. When it did, it pushed them to the fore, made them dominant and then crossed them out again, erasing them in a way that meant he still saw them.

It took The Book almost an hour to pull Garth apart, and when it was over, he was fully present to himself for the first time, every thought in his head reverberating with precision and suffused with purpose. The Book had placed him at a very special point in the text and Garth knew it signified something about him. The Book had called him, chosen him.

And read him.

It was such a magnificent and shining gift, it blinded Garth with gratitude, made him so blind, in fact, that he was completely unable to see for several minutes. Supporting himself against the edge of the table, he blinked into a light so bright it became darkness itself and, in doing so, he missed the chance to watch as The Book opened itself wide and displayed the intricate plan it had spent all of time putting into place and of which Garth was only the smallest part.

The Book was as good as the person it read.

The room was quiet and dim again, the balance between light and dark restored once more.

The Book was no longer present and, because of this absence, everywhere at once.

Inside him, all Garth's carefully scrutinized feelings were as tender as if he had undergone surgery, and he tingled as they settled down into their new order. The experience had shaken him and the buzzing sensation in his head was electric, like putting his tongue on a battery.

Garth Richards, for the first time, felt confident and in control.

What was he meant to do with it, this gift?

Something very special and very nice.

The thought trilled in his head. And led into other thoughts, things he would be able to do, choices he could make. He wondered where he should start and it came to him as clearly as if it had been in his head from the moment of his conception. The place to start.

The kid Carson . . .

Garth stepped through the door of the empty room and back into the corridor, which was lit with an orange glow as though from some unseen fire. She was kneeling on the floor, naked and with her back to him. Her behind was on display and the cheeks had deep welts on them from what looked like a wide leather belt. She reached under with her hand and parted the pink flesh, opening herself like the pages of a book.

He managed several heavy blinks over his tingling eyeballs and then saw her perfectly. It was the first reward.

'Garth,' she said.

When the woman spoke, it was with the voice of The Book.

Chapter 4

Kavanagh let the BMW roadster use its own weight to roll down the incline and into the garage under the house. Behind him the electronic door was easing silently shut, and the gentle thrum of the car's engine was barely discernible. He waited, sitting perfectly still for almost a full minute until the motion-sensitive lights inside the garage switched off. The headlights cast pointed shadows across bare brick and Kavanagh sat staring at the wall in front of him. He had parked the low-set car at an angle across the expanse of floor in the two-car garage, its wide tyres hugging the gravelly surface. Perhaps when Lucy turned seventeen he would get her some lessons, and the sort of safe car he would have hated at that age, and then they could share the garage.

Two and a half million in equity. A guaranteed buy-back from the Trust. Good. Time in Los Angeles. Away from Lucy. So near to an anniversary, and then only the third. Bad. He had let telling her slip by for a day, but now he had to tell her.

How many times since Helen's death had he driven the car into the garage and thought about sitting there until fumes filled the space and carried him off to a dizzy, drunken heaven? He didn't have just himself to think about, so the luxury did not exist for him. Kavanagh switched off the engine and opened the door of the car abruptly enough to reactivate the overhead light.

It was almost eight and the smell of cooking filled the house. Kavanagh was no slouch in the kitchen himself, having moved beyond the three basic meals he could make when he was a student, but it was Helen who had the touch and it had passed on to Lucy.

'Hi,' Kavanagh called out into the hall. The lights of the house seemed bright after sitting in the garage for so long.

'Hi,' came Lucy's voice like an echo of his own.

'What are you making?' Kavanagh asked, standing at the kitchen door and inhaling.

Lucy was at the worktop by the window, back to him, and he saw her look up and find his reflection in the glass. Kavanagh could just make out the movements of her lips, her mouth barely open as she appeared to be gnashing silently or muttering something under her breath. It stopped and she spoke aloud.

'A red pasta sauce. I'm doing a big pot so we can freeze some of it. It'll be ready in fifteen minutes. The pasta water's been simmering for the last twenty.'

'I had to stay late and finish up. There was some tidying up on the deal we closed yesterday. Did you go and see Kim?' Kavanagh asked.

'Yes. I haven't been back that long, really,' she replied, the last of the sentence partly blocked by the wooden spoon she was tasting sauce off.

Lucy turned and faced him. She was in there somewhere, Helen, whispering beneath the surface like a subliminal voice. Taller than most girls her age, long-legged and not far off being a woman, Lucy looked at him and Kavanagh felt like he was home. The top half of her face was all Helen. Lucy's eyes were still as profoundly blue as when he had first held her, her nose displaying the same occasional flare of the nostrils Helen's had and her short hair close enough to blonde to lighten in the sun. He wondered if her black garments had grown looser from repeated wear or if she had dropped some weight. Kavanagh knew better than to ask and, as far as he could gauge, she was eating well enough. Small items of silver and gold jewellery garnished her, glinting against the dark clothing and sometimes clinking together if she moved quickly. There were bangles of her own, earrings that had been Helen's and other things Helen had made for her.

'What deal did you close?' Lucy asked.

'Did I tell you about the company that makes the wafer chips?'

'LK something?'

'LKG. I'm impressed. Half the salesforce wouldn't remember that. What did you and Kim talk about today?' Kavanagh was interested as always, but more so now he had something to tell his daughter.

'The usual. It's going okay, Dad, honest.'

Kavanagh still didn't like to leave her alone in the house, afraid lightning could hit twice and take both women away from him. As surely as Helen was embedded somewhere in Lucy, so too was what she had found that afternoon almost three years earlier – the afternoon her mother was killed. Lucy had still to talk about that day, arriving back from school, entering the house, finding Helen. Kavanagh knew what she had found because he had insisted on knowing. Even if Lucy had blocked it out, Kavanagh wanted to know. He wanted to understand what had happened to his wife and what to expect when it did come back to his daughter, the way Kim said it would. Lucy went to see Kim once a week, just for an hour. If she felt the need to go more often, she could, but never had so far. According to Kim, it was vital to put a therapeutic relationship in place with Lucy so it would be there for her when she was ready to talk.

It was frustrating for Kavanagh, like playing a game where he had to make somebody say a particular word, one they might not ordinarily say. What would it take to make the muttering sensible? To insert the necessary pauses and gaps that would allow the guttural noise to shape itself into words? All the time Lucy spent with Kim, as far as Kavanagh understood it, was about trying to bring words to the surface and organize them in a pattern that was meaningful, however painful. Kavanagh knew too well the carnage his daughter had stumbled into that Thursday. 'Don't protect me from anything,' he had told one of the officers. 'If you do that, you might hurt my daughter. I have to know everything.'

'Are we going to sort out a holiday this year?' Kavanagh asked, feeling it was a good entrée into the subject of travel. He was leaning against the frame of the kitchen door, jacket still flung over his shoulder.

'I've only just gone back, but I can take time off school whenever, really. You're the one we have to work around,' she said.

'Instead of me trying to block some time out and then us thinking of somewhere to go to fill it up, why don't we do it the other way? Let's think of somewhere really good to go and then I'll make time,' Kavanagh said.

'Okay,' she said. 'I'll think about it.'

Lucy turned to the stove and Kavanagh gazed at her back for a moment. When would he tell her? What would he say? I've been offered the chance to get out, to get away from this. Both of us. Kavanagh decided to wait until dinner, or afterwards, to sound her out. Something nagged at him, a feeling that he wasn't going to get away that easily, that running off was not an option. He'd never run away from anything in his life. On his left thigh was the deep bite-wound of an angry dog he'd tried to face off when he was twelve.

'I'll go and change,' he said.

The killer had dragged Helen through every room in the house, a trail of blood marking out the route. Up every flight of stairs, each storey of the building. What had the killer been looking for? Whatever it was, he must have thought Helen knew where it was or else she would have been killed first and then the house pillaged. But it hadn't happened that way.

Did the murderer even find what he was looking for? Kavanagh wondered. It was a grim calculation to make, a gruesome algebra in which he continually substituted x's and y's until he came to the same conclusion, over and over: no, the killer hadn't found whatever it was. The house had been turned over, from top to bottom, but Kavanagh knew the search had been fruitless because, then, the killer had ransacked Helen.

A screwdriver, with a four-sided shaft shaped like a diamond, the tip blunt but one edge sharpened, had been pushed into the fleshy part of her belly, just under the navel, and lifted with more force than Kavanagh could imagine. The killer had opened his wife up and rummaged about in her. All through the investigation, it had been so obvious to Kavanagh and yet it was never mentioned. It was simply assumed that what had been done to Helen's body was a defilement, almost ritual in its intensity. It wasn't, not to Kavanagh. The semen, that was defiling. But what had been done to his wife was nothing more than an extension of the search. He hadn't found it in the house, so he looked in Helen.

Kavanagh wanted to think about it like that, in the most brutal and detailed way he could, trying to imagine every second of Helen's suffering and pain, because to sanitize it was to try and stop himself being angry, and he wasn't ready to do that just yet. Kavanagh had told Helen that, the last time he had spoken to her, though a pane of glass after a sheet had been pulled back to reveal her body.

He pulled open the top drawer of the tall chest that faced the foot of the bed, the misshapen wood squeaking on the aged runners. It had been refinished after the murder but Kavanagh knew there was a long indentation near the back corner, a fingernail trail where Helen had grabbed and tried to hold on. The room had been redecorated in the same greenish hue, too feminine for Kavanagh but always her favourite colour. How many layers of paint would it take? he wondered.

Sixteen years earlier, Kavanagh and a pregnant Helen had stood at the foot of the steps that led to the front door of the house, neither of them moving. It was as though each were waiting for a shove between the shoulder-blades from the other, neither wanting to be the first to commit. The building stood detached and looked solitary, as though the houses either side were gradually inching away from it. The front garden had grown over and a sheen of sticky-looking dirt made it impossible to see through the curtainless windows. Looking at the house was a formality. The rent the Trust had agreed to charge on an unused property was virtually token and Kavanagh could not countenance the prospect of still being at his parents' when the baby was born. They would have taken the house whatever happened. Paul Baran had arranged for some money to spend on its redecoration. Kavanagh was a new arrival at the Trust and this was their way of welcoming him and Helen. Of course they were going to move into it.

Kavanagh's first, and lasting, impression of the house was that it could have been an inverted funnel, broad at the base and tapering off to the roof. The underground garage and the cellar formed a wide base on top of which the ground floor spread into more reception rooms than they needed, an oddly shaped dining-room and the kitchen, which was built as an extension and which, even on first sight, he knew was the place they would spend most of their time. The bedrooms were on two levels, separated by a low landing and a passage, reminding Kavanagh of the rooms in a country pub they'd stayed in. At the top of the house, perched on it like a pointed hat, were two attic rooms, one filled with storage boxes and the other the room Helen made jewellery in. It used to be her retreat, set far up and away from the rest of the house and getting the best of the sun through the fanlight window.

On the face of everyone he knew, even now, almost three years afterwards, he would see the question. How the hell can you stay there, after what happened? He could not explain it to anyone else, but to Kavanagh it was perfectly clear. The house had the answer. It was the reason his wife had died. Kavanagh didn't know why, but he was certain something in the walls which surrounded them, the space that was carved up by bricks and mortar, held the truth. That was why to run from it was to run from the truth.

Kavanagh threw his shirt onto his side of the double bed and changed into the same casual attire he had worn over the weekend, pulling the chambray shirt over his head, not bothering to tuck it into his trousers or to do up the top three of its buttons. He took a breath, pushed the drawer shut and went to talk to Lucy.

'I have to go away on business,' he said.

'Okay,' Lucy said.

Dinner was over but they remained at the table in the kitchen, Lucy seeming to sense that Kavanagh had lingered for a reason, that he had something to say.

'I'm going to call your Aunt Karen and see if you can stay with her. We'll work something out,' he said.

'I'll be okay. I can stay here,' she said.

'No,' Kavanagh replied, almost butting across her words. 'Luce, even if you'll be okay, I'll feel better knowing you're with Karen.'

Kavanagh looked at her, watching her jaw working away, almost as if she were chewing something. Spit it out, he thought, and felt guilty for it.

'Where are you going?' she asked.

He paused, trying to make himself seem serious. Before he spoke, he rested his hand on the table, towards her, and looked down at it for a moment. Finding her gaze, he spoke.

'I'm going to Los Angeles, probably next week. I'm not expecting to be there more than a week, ten days at the most. There's something going on at work, Luce.' Kavanagh paused. 'The Trust want to set up a relationship with a company that we'll be merging with in the future. Paul Baran has offered me a lot of money to do it.'

'How much?' she asked.

'A lot. Enough to do whatever we want.'

It had not occurred to him like that, the notion of doing whatever they wanted. Saying it gave him the first glimmer of liberation, a glimpse of something different that suddenly made him realize, in the most banal way, that there was more than Pendulum and the Trust.

'What's a lot, Dad?' Her voice was more inquisitive.

'Enough,' he said, nodding. 'I could retire and so could you.'

'I haven't even started work – how can I retire?' she said, a smile lifting one corner of her mouth.

'Setting this up is going to mean some time away in the States, on and off. I think I can tie it all up in six months, nine tops, and then we're free.'

'God, Dad, we're not exactly prisoners. Look at this house, the car, all the other stuff. You make it sound like we're on the breadline.'

'I know. You're so humbling,' he said and they both smiled. 'Once I've been out to Los Angeles and sounded it out, I thought we could turn one of the trips into a holiday. I could stay on a bit longer. There'd be lots of things we could do.'

'Why don't you think of somewhere to go and I'll make time, Lucy,' she said, mimicking his voice and earlier words.

It was one of the few things that almost made him blush, when she caught him out and made him feel heavy-handed and obvious, though always letting him off with her good humour.

'And you wouldn't like to go to Los Angeles?' he said. 'You'd be the only person in Disneyland dressed in black. You don't mind me going away?'

She shook her head. 'Of course not. I'll go stay with Aunt Karen.'

'It's three years soon,' Kavanagh said.

'In three weeks' time,' Lucy said, her hand lying on his.

In a way that was familiar to them both, they held the silence for a moment, breathing it in and exhaling it as though changing the rhythm of their feelings. The pause was like an adjustment, a way of letting themselves move on, trying to be happy but still thinking about Helen. The moment passed.

'I've got us tickets for *Hamlet*,' he said, pleased to veer away from the previous subject, done with it for the time being.

'When for?'

'Friday. I know it's short notice but it closes soon and

the tickets are hard to get. Why don't you come into the office and we can go eat first?'

'Okay.'

Lucy stood and picked up plates.

'Leave that. I'll do it,' he said.

'Are you sure? You look tired, Dad. Why don't you have an early night?'

'On a Tuesday?' The small of his back ached as though it had been compressed. 'Maybe I will. Go on, leave these,' he said, taking the crockery from her.

Kavanagh lay awake and tried on the idea of two and a half million pounds, getting used to the feel of it. It was like a great soft mattress on which he could stretch out and no part of his body would ever be over an edge. It felt safe and it felt secure. That amount of money opened up possibilities as surely as it closed off uncertainties, a balance that was almost too delicious to contemplate for long.

Around him, the house was familiarly silent and Kavanagh listened to it the way he used to listen to Lucy sleep as a baby, the occasional creak like the restless mutters she used to give, and now gave again. When he had watched over his daughter as she slept, observing the sometimes jerky manner of her rest, he was able to sense precisely when she was about to open her eyes.

Lying in his bed that night, he was troubled by the feeling that the same was true of the house – that it too was about to stir. On the stairs that led down from the attic, the same way it had happened off and on for the three years since her death, Kavanagh heard the squeak of Helen's foot as it pressed on the second step from the top, the way it always did the nights she was up there working on jewellery and he was in bed, drifting towards sleep.

The thought came back to him for the third time since arriving home.

I'm not going to get away that easily.

Chapter 5

Nancy looked at her full-length reflection in the mirror by the bed, smoothing her hands over her stomach, pressing the fabric of the small Armani dress closer to herself, willing it to become a second skin in which she felt comfortable. Whatever the supposed confidence-boosting effect of designer labels, Nancy never felt it. If anything, they made her feel more awkward and jittery, as though she were afraid she might do something to embarrass her clothes.

Staring closely, bringing her head almost to the glass, she thought, What's going on in there? She wondered what the tumour was doing at that moment. Did it sleep or rest in between eating her? Nancy pouted her small mouth. It had the effect of making her nose appear thinner than it was, her slender face a pleasing oval shape with a nicely defined profile. Her heavy eye lids were skilfully shadowed and contrasted against a gap of white skin that was framed by thin and well-tended brows. Her eyes were on the part of the spectrum where green turned to blue and she had a habit of blinking slowly, as though taking a moment for herself in the brief second she could not see. Still with her face near the mirror, she flicked her long black hair off her breastbone, the gentle wave of her last hair appointment in England still giving it a pleasingly tousled look.

Lying down on the bed, sun bright on the white ceiling, Nancy crossed her arms over her chest and kept perfectly still. She stopped her chest moving, letting her diaphragm rise and fall in one steady action to ease the air from her. There she stayed, like a dead person, trying to get her mind around something as big as forever. As a girl, she had played the same game, pretending to be dead. Her mother told her it was a wicked thing to do. 'Who made the world?'

Nancy would ask. 'God,' her mother replied. 'Who made God?' 'Get washed now, Nancy.' Never an answer for it. What was here before the universe? And then before that? And before that? Where was she then? Where would she be?

A long tingle of panic energized her body and Nancy was up, moving around the room in a life-affirming way. The dress rode around her hips and wrinkled across the lap. Nancy fiddled with it, inching the hem down her stockingless legs.

On the waist-high counter in the kitchen, open and ready as though she might walk up to them and start writing, were a pad and pen. Nancy had thought that perhaps even the short-lived novelty of American-sized pads instead of A4 might be a spur for her to write. All over the apartment's seven rooms the same blank tablets were scattered, ready to catch a passing thought. That was in addition to the notebook and pen and the tiny microcassette dictating machine in her bag.

Nancy looked at the page, the only thing marring it a long and pointless doodle that swirled up and down, the lines going back over themselves. She could not remember doing it, most likely because she had been on the telephone at the time. Many times she would put a phone down and find she had been writing her own name and address as she had been reciting them to someone at the other end. Doing it without thinking was at least different from doing it without knowing, she reasoned, wondering if memory loss was to be expected. She looked at the scribble and was struck by how careful its construction seemed, and wondered what precise part of her unconscious she had tapped into mid-conversation with some now forgotten caller. She was about to tear the sheet off and drop it in the bin when she looked at her watch and realized she would be late for lunch. Gathering her purse, the keys to the rented car and some driving-away chocolate to set her on her way, Nancy rushed out of the apartment.

The light was painful in her eyes, so much so that she

scrabbled for her sunglasses as she trotted towards the car. Her apartment was only a short drive along Sunset until she reached the outer fringes of Beverly Hills. She was impressed at having a sense of direction after only a brief time in the city and was also satisfied to learn that the sharp driving skills acquired in London were more than adequate for the supposed nightmare scenario of LA. Nancy saw the sign for the restaurant and pulled in sharply, cutting across two lanes. Taking a ticket from the valet with as practised an air as she could muster, she sensed him run his eyes over her absently and she could tell he was being appraising, negatively appraising. She wished she'd worn a different dress.

Julia Summers, Nancy's agent, was perfectly at home with her labels. Back in London, Nancy's literary agent was the sort of person she wanted to flick a duster over every time she saw him. Not Julia. Each time Nancy had met her, Julia might well have been through a total makeover only moments before. Fresh and bright as sunshine, with a cool breeze thrown in, Julia was soothing. She was already seated, talking quietly on her phone. She seemed to sense Nancy's entrance and looked up, smiling and waving with her free hand. By the time Nancy reached the table, the call was over and she knew Julia would have massaged away the person on the other end without them ever realizing they were being closed off.

'Hi,' Julia said, standing. 'Let me turn this off.' She pressed a button on the phone and put it away.

They sat. The glass to Nancy's right hand was immediately filled with ice water by a waiter who disappeared with the same stealth with which he had appeared. Tables were set far enough apart to allow staring and she spotted a face that was vaguely recognizable, possibly from some barely remembered television show she had devoured as a child. Tablecloths were white, the decor relaxed pastel and, she suspected, the food expensive and anodyne.

'I love that dress,' Julia said. 'I called to say hi yesterday afternoon but you weren't answering.'

'I had the phone off, working,' Nancy said, disappointed at having to begin the lying so soon.

'How's it going?'

'Well. Really well.'

In London, Nancy's literary agent Malcolm had gradually ebbed in the same direction she had herself, realizing Nancy was not likely to produce another novel in the immediate future. When she took him her first effort at a screenplay, Malcolm had been flummoxed by it. Malcolm saw everything in the most vivid way possible, but only as far as the confines of his head. He had no way of seeing her words projected onto a screen. Malcolm was a decent man and he did the decent thing, putting Nancy in touch with the only person he knew connected with Hollywood, and that person had, in turn, led to Julia Summers.

Nancy's first script was about a woman leaving her life behind by going missing, only to find herself so deeply entrenched in the emotional crossfire of her new circumstances that she returns to the old ones. Malcolm had plenty of ideas about how to make it more literary, more of a book, while as soon as Julia read it, she jumped on ways to make it more filmic.

Several transatlantic calls at odd times of the day later and Nancy was looking at how much she had left in her savings account, already knowing both that she would go to Los Angeles and that the money she had would last for the rest of her foreshortened life. This is what it feels like to have enough money for the rest of your life, she thought.

The giddiness and excitement brought about by making such a journey spurred Nancy on and she found herself listening without question or reservation to Julia's suggestions, the bizarre result being that her original script ended up as a six-page treatment about a woman professional thief falling in love with one of the men she robs. The genesis of the character, who came from her original script into the new treatment with her name and most of her characteristics intact, was something which confused Nancy, as though this woman were an uninvited guest. It was when

Nancy felt herself yielding to Julia's suggestion the script be called *Stolen Hearts* that she knew that, like London, integrity was now some way behind her.

Now Julia reached towards Nancy without actually touching her and spoke in a conspiratorial way. 'I gave a copy of your book to my friend yesterday and she called this morning to say she'd finished it already.'

'Thanks,' Nancy said, wondering if she were turning red.

'Do you think Malcolm would be willing to let me market the film rights for your book?' Julia asked.

'I can't imagine how it could work here. It's so English. So London, I suppose,' Nancy said.

The last serious relationship in her life had been with the novel. In a guileful distillation and convergence of her life's many straggling ends, Nancy had taken all the moments, repackaged and sold them wholesale, losing as many friends as she made new ones. She had, she was sure, enjoyed it at the time. The downside of such vitality was that it gave the book all the immediacy and longevity of a magazine. Already, Nancy could open it and hate what she saw, wondering if she were really its author.

'We might get a lot of money for it, some day,' Julia said. 'I can talk to Malcolm, make sure he gets a cut on the deal.'

'Let me talk to him and see what he says,' Nancy replied. 'How are things going with the treatment? Has anyone looked at it seriously yet?'

Nancy had expected Hollywood to be breakfast meetings, the sound of a buzzer indicating the need for silence on set, the snap of a clapperboard and the call for action echoing into a sound stage. It might yet turn out to be like that, but so far she was still on the edges of it, an initial thrust of enthusiasm, mostly Julia's, having propelled her into orbit on the outer rim of the universe. The proposal for her script, the treatment, the last solidification of ideas she had managed, was now being chewed up by machinery, left in the hands of people who had their own agenda, driven by ideas and motives Nancy could only guess at. In England, her book had been different, the publishing industry a dependable, if long, worm that passed things through itself in a straight line. With the novel, it was possible to believe that, at some level, she was the one at the nexus, the person on which it all turned in a no-Nancy, no-book equation. In Hollywood, she was beginning to understand her position as a cog, one of the smallest, that merely drove other parts of the machine, a contraption which could, if pushed, grind on without her or easily find a replacement. It was frustrating, but there was a palliative – money.

'Lee Mitchell at Conical has seen the treatment and wants to meet with you. It'll be a chance for you to pitch the idea at him, let him see how it's developing on from the treatment. Also, it'll give you the chance to hear his thoughts, see where he'd like it to go. Conical might be able to attach a name to the project and that way it has a strong chance of breaking out of development.'

'How will they attach someone?' Nancy asked, ill at ease with a foreign vocabulary.

'Conical will keep its ear to the ground. They might know, say, that Sigourney Weaver is interested in this sort of part at the moment. If they can get a name on board, it opens lots of doors, gets the interest of people who can give the green light for a picture, and there aren't too many of those.'

'One thing I was thinking, about the script, is if she could die at the end. I know it's morbid, but it's interesting,' Nancy said.

'Absolutely not,' was Julia's instant reply. 'At the end of the movie, she gets it together with the guy or else there's no movie. Do you think people are gonna pay seven dollars to see Sigourney Weaver die? Well, maybe that's a bad example, but you see what I mean?'

'Does it always have to be such a pat ending?'

'Nancy, go back to writing books if you want to kill people off. If you want to be in movies, start listening. Hey, kill off someone in your fourth or fifth script, when you call the shots. Right now, we need to get you a deal. Conical are a good outfit and I know Lee Mitchell's seen your book and he asked to see the first script.'

'What does he do at Conical?' Nancy asked.

'He's Head of Development. I've known him for six years. He's a good guy,' Julia said, leaning back and flicking hair that was the deep red colour food companies referred to as nature-identical, while her eyes were bluer than anything that could be created in a laboratory, although Nancy suspected she wore colour contacts.

When Julia spoke, her words insinuated themselves into Nancy, like a whisper, but rhythmic enough to hold her in a way that was almost transfixing. Julia made Nancy believe it was all possible because she was so relaxed with her power. By taking her fifteen per cent of each of her clients, Julia must have contrived to end up with more than most of them, apart from the two biggest, a writer and an actress. It was much more fun talking to her than having to sit and look at a blank page or screen, trying to dirty it with some words, possibly an idea or two.

A waiter appeared and they ordered. The service was brisk and lunchtime-efficient and they filled the short wait with chat, Julia asking her how the apartment was, what was hot in London before Nancy left and expounding her views on the state of Hollywood. They were well into their food when Julia asked a more focused question. Too focused for Nancy's liking.

'When will I be able to see some of the script for *Stolen Hearts*?' Julia asked.

Nancy's fork hesitated in her hand, but she recovered.

'Soon. The structure's all there and I've sketched out most of the scenes for the first act. The ending's already well worked out in my mind. Once I've pulled the second act into shape, I'll give you a look at it.'

'It really is a great treatment. Lee Mitchell was excited by it. I mean that. You're going to be very successful once this takes off.'

Nancy was still not sure how successful she really wanted to be. Many of the major movements in her life, backwards or forwards, had resulted from some sort of outgrowing. The years at university had been more of a confusion than a clarification and she had lost herself in the middle of a field of undirected energy, hurling herself at whoever was nearest. Whether she did it to hurt herself or her family, she wasn't sure, but, after she graduated, Nancy spent four years avoiding any sort of job that might conceivably had led somewhere, moving through an initially painful and ultimately numbing sequence of jobs, flats and boyfriends. The eventual destination, the arrival at a stable job, was ludicrous. There could be no career in advertising copy-writing, surely? The short-lived but repeated bursts of energy a job like that required fitted her perfectly, enabling Nancy to commit, but only in the short term. It was the ideal sort of lustful, serial monogamy, the only problem with it being that, quicker than she expected, both it and she got old.

'When does the guy at Conical want to meet?' Nancy asked.

'Day after tomorrow, ten-thirty at their offices. I can come with you if you'd like.'

'I'll be fine on my own. You'll just need to give me directions.'

'They have an office out at Burbank, I'll write it down for you,' Julia said.

A day and a half, almost two days, gave Nancy time to think of something, a way out. Even if it meant getting on a plane and flying home, wherever that was and whatever it meant. The left side of Nancy's head began to ache like a tooth and she remembered she was going to die, soon. I'm blocked, haven't written a word of the screenplay, and I'm dying, Nancy wanted to say to Julia.

There was something else Nancy wanted to tell her, she was certain, and yet it was as if there were a wall in her mind behind which it hid. Nancy was aware of its presence, could feel it there, but could not form it into a tangible thought. A feeling came over her, not quite anxiety, but something like it. At first, she thought she was going to vomit spontaneously, the way she had during what she now knew were the early stages of the cancer, but it wasn't that sort of feeling, not exactly. It had been so long since she felt it. Nancy reached to her side and pulled the spiral notebook from her bag, Julia watching. She laid it on the table and opened it so that the cover formed a shield from Julia's fascinated eyes. In the grip of a force she knew was practically spent already, Nancy's hand moved over the page with strokes that were as heavy as they were sharp.

Staring down at the page to see what the combination of hand and brain had yielded, she knew the words had been concealed behind the screen in her head. It was a never-ending chain of meanings in which every word or feeling referred to another with no chance of getting to the end and understanding what it all meant. Even as she looked down at what she had so spontaneously written and felt its familiarity, Nancy knew it was only the start of what needed to be brought out of her head and onto the page if the anxiety were ever to stop. Six words was only a small beginning, but it was a start.

Something very special and very nice.

Chapter 6

And The Book whispered on.

Garth stood at the cash machine outside his bank in Covent Garden and reinserted his card for the third time, ignoring the sighs that came from the queue behind him. Again he entered his four digit code and again he pressed the balance request, the same way he always did before taking out his next lump of sixty pounds. Garth made a certain number of trips to the bank each month, withdrawing sixty-pound units with the diligence and respect of a someone going to a well and paying his respects to the water god. He looked at the balance on the screen, holding his hand over its side to cast a shadow in case the sun were distorting it.

Ninety-eight thousand four hundred and ninety-one pounds, no pence.

There should have been about four hundred pounds in the account.

Garth entered the bank, the air inside it arid and smelling like an old carpet. He rarely went into any branch, happy to transact with anonymity. Leaning all his weight against a side-table and with as careful a hand as he could manage, Garth wrote out a cheque for two thousand pounds to cash. Standing in the queue, two people ahead of him and all four cashiers busy, he felt himself getting angry, the voice in his head getting slower and slower, just like the actions of everyone else in the bank.

The hair on the back of the head of the man standing in front of Garth looked blue, shining like a fluorescent tube, and he could smell every strand of it – car fumes, some sweat, shampoo. There was a warm, toasted smell, perhaps what the man had made for breakfast, but it was more like meat cooking, the warmth of the man's brain in his head.

Garth held his breath against the smell and felt heavy liquid roll in his oesophagus. The words of his own mind were so slurred and heavy he could discern every gap between them as though it were an eternal pause. He closed his eyes and waited for the feeling to lift.

Motion returned to its normal speed and he let out a sigh. For the past two days, since the day he'd gone exploring on the roof and . . . what? Whatever, something had changed and Garth had not yet worked out if it was he who was different, the things around him, or a mixture of the two. Smell, touch and taste, as well as sight and sound, were functioning in overdrive, sometimes fast, sometimes slow, together or separately.

And it wasn't just that.

Discreetly, Garth adjusted the front of his trousers, trying to conceal the erection that was now almost permanent. He was sore down there and had to be gentle with himself. While his hand was in his pocket, it lighted on the small piece of Chris Carson he had been carrying around with him since yesterday night. Garth did not want to think about it, but, like a disturbing scene from a film, it lingered in his mind. The struggle, the pleading, the noise and, then, the awful begging sobs that had lasted almost half an hour. Carson had cried for his mother. Garth pulled his hand from his pocket in recoil, as if not touching it would break the circuit of memory. He shuffled to the front of the line, ready to collect his reward.

'Hello Sally,' he said through the glass, grinning at the cashier and using the words to block out the waft that came, even through the thickened pane, just from his glance at her grey badge. The blend of deodorant, heavy perspiration and hot elastic bra strap was fetid but also exciting. 'I'd like to take out some cash.' He let the cheque float into the stainless steel valley.

Sally looked at it. 'Have you got some form of identification?' she asked politely.

'Driving licence and credit card?'

'Fine. I'll have to go and check,' she said, as she picked up his licence, credit card and the cheque.

'Of course,' Garth said, pushing himself against the counter, the strain in his groin rapidly turning into an ache. Gently, he rocked himself from side to side, feeling the tingling and the rigidness, riding it as his breathing speeded up.

'How would you like it?' Sally had returned.

'In your mouth,' came the spontaneous words.

'Sorry?'

She hadn't heard him.

'Twenties, please. Could you hurry, as I'm late?'

Garth kept the walk up as far as the door of the bank and then he was sprinting across the piazza, the elation of the money already gone as he headed for the toilets. He bundled down the stairs, taking them in a mixture of ones, twos and threes, the heady smell of disinfectant and urine, which he'd picked up halfway across the cobblestones, now whistling in his head. He almost slipped on the wet red tiles as he made for the stall, feeling a muscle in the back of his thigh pull from the sudden elongation in a strange direction.

As at work, the stall had a small gap above and below the door. Garth unzipped, unbelted and unbuttoned his trousers. Within seconds they were round his ankles along with his underwear. He lifted the toilet seat and knelt, prayer-fashion, in front of the bowl, his testicles resting on its cold lip. His penis was swollen from his erection and the foreskin puffy and crusty from constant use.

Outside, people came and went. Water and urine ran, toilets flushed and wind was broken. It was the most public of private places but he could not help himself. He scrabbled in his jacket pocket for the bag, wet his finger, put it in and retrieved it, quickly stuffing it up his nose. Two thousand pounds would buy plenty more. As his vision went starry, he sprinkled some of the powder over the shining head of his straining shaft.

The stone floor was hard and cold on his knees, a length

of harsh paper stuck to the back corner of the floor by a yellowy liquid, a drowned turd fraying in the bowl. Garth reached back into his trouser pocket and brought out the memento of Chris Carson, the earlier images which had so appalled him now flashing before him in a violent and erotic slide-show.

Garth gripped and pulled on himself expertly, ejaculating quickly and quietly, closing and then opening his eyes to watch the thin dribble of semen run down the inside of the pan.

'Kill me. Kill me. Kill me,' he gasped quietly with each lash of the orgasm.

Eventually, The Book would.

Chapter 7

Nobody could die in the morning.

Nancy lay in bed thinking about the meeting with Lee Mitchell at Conical, her thoughts quickly leading down a dark road.

Mornings used to be Nancy's favourite. So hopeful. She found she could spend a long time thinking about death at daybreak. It did not seem as frightening. Was that why duels were always fought at sunrise? Her brain was only able to be confident for so long before the effort of being awake all day wore away her good intentions.

Nancy did not understand enough about biology to know what life really was. A friend who worked as a lab assistant told her it had something to do with carbon, bits of electricity and things like that. Nancy thought that explanation could simply be wrong. Perhaps nobody was actually alive, not in the way their conscious minds told them they were. Maybe her brain, each and every brain in the world, was playing a trick, like a déjà vu, creating a false feeling of what it was to be alive. She was not spiritual enough to believe in some ghostly soul occupying the machine, able to float free of it when the time came, like a cartoon character jumping out of the falling hut a nanosecond before it hit the ground. Still, if she were just a machine without the ghost, not really alive, surely she couldn't die.

But she would die. No casual slip of the tongue from inoperable to inoperative would spare her, leave her feeling elated like the time she had managed to miss an injection at school because she was absent. Nancy waited for the rest of the term for the nurse to return, needle in hand, but she never did. Unfortunately, death would be there, however much she hoped it was all going to be some kind of joke.

Would she lie on her death-bed with her heart and lungs stopped and still be able to think for a little while? She hoped her brain would die as soon as her heart stopped, that there would no last moments for dreams, as the final thoughts trickled out. Again, some half-remembered anecdotal chat with a forgotten friend reminded her that the body died in stages, not in one final moment. What would be the last thing she ever thought? Nancy's heart was thudding solidly in her chest, full and lively with blood. What would it be like to lie on the bed and wait for the banging to stop? Would it happen at the same time as her breathing stopped?

Silence.

How long had the symptoms been evident, without her realizing? Was all of this programmed into her genes like a computer virus waiting to activate at a set moment in time? Could a small ache in her knee when she was six have been a clue? Or the way her left eye twitched over a period of three months when she was twenty? The way her right eyelid felt loose if she tapped her right cheek near the mouth? Everyone who had the same tumour as her could have experienced exactly the same things and no one would ever know, least of all the doctors.

Like the Earth itself, Nancy's head was made up of geological plates and the pain was a plate movement. That first tremor on a fault line. A tiny neurological California, waiting for the big one to leave her devastated. It was there, alive and waiting. The disease was sluicing her around, getting ready to spit her out. When she went, it went too. She knew the cancer was too stupid to realize it. Like the monkey's paw. It would kill her but in the process, it would kill itself.

It had been so easy to believe it was nothing. As the pains and then the numbness continued in the left side of her head, Nancy had tried to lower the stakes, telling herself it was earwax. She poked her finger in her left ear, and when that didn't help, she tried some cotton buds, pushing wax up into the canal and making herself deaf for four days. She bought ear drops and started swilling out, forcing her fingers in roughly, trying to create a generic pain, any pain, in her head, something to distract the attention away from what was starting to scare her.

Being terminal was how she imagined it would be to mistakenly drive a car off a cliff or be in an aeroplane when the engines cut out over a mountain range. Rapid descent. You knew it was over. What would it feel like to hit a wall in a car and break your neck? Those few seconds where you would get a sick feeling in your throat, knowing that you've really fucked up. A few moments where you felt truly real.

Naturally, she became an expert. If she knew more about it than it did about itself, she might win. In one brief, hot week Nancy read about invasiveness, escape into lymphatics and immunological circumvention. Carcinoma, sarcoma, leukaemia, metastases, antigens. None of it made much sense. Certainly, none of it made any difference.

Nancy picked the small scrap of paper off the floor and unfolded it.

Something very special and very nice.

Was that where the story would start or end? Whether she had to write away from it or towards it, there wasn't much time in either direction. Certainly less than a year, possibly six months if she were lucky.

The phone by the bed trilled. Nancy knew who it would be.

'Hello,' she said.

'Hi,' said Julia Summers. 'How you doing? Ready for Lee Mitchell?'

Nancy sat up to make her voice sound less like she were still lying in bed when she should have been up and about, getting ready. She had been deliberately staying in bed, the way she used to when she hated a job.

'I'm fine,' Nancy said.

'You have to be very up with him, Nancy. Be sunny and bright, not too English.'

'I will be, I promise,' she said, her stomach loose and rolling.

'Don't take Lee Mitchell too seriously,' Julia said.
'What do you mean?' Nancy asked.
'Nothing. Just go with him.'
'I don't know what you mean,' Nancy said, her inertia suddenly hardening into nerves.
'Don't worry, okay? Call me when you get out of there. I have to run,' Julia said, the line going abruptly dead.
If Julia's call was intended as a pep talk to lift Nancy's spirits prior to the meeting, its effect had been exactly the opposite.

Lee Mitchell looked older than her, but she doubted he was. His sparse and wiry beard, a mix of black and grey strands, stretched too far and squarely around a gaunt face. Dark, bespectacled eyes that had seen it all before were sunk into shadowy sockets. Even as he smiled at her and shook her hand, his facial expression was one of someone about to heave a sigh as though resigned but still fighting cynicism. In advertising, Nancy had come across account handlers like him, mostly maudlin but able to switch on like a light, so bright and dazzling it was impossible to see what was really behind it. Nancy wondered if he was doing drugs, too many and too expensive. His suit was improbably bright, a kind of sherbet yellow, and his hair had the look that took a lot of work just to be nothing special. As he drew his hand away from the shake, she noticed his dressy watch, the band and the face virtually the same wafer thinness and fitted closely to his wrist.
'Nancy, great to see you,' he said. 'Come on in.'
There was a tidy office somewhere beneath the surface, trying to fight its way through a sprinkling of scripts, and the walls she suspected contained every photo opportunity of his life. Nancy noticed how he looked much younger in most of the pictures and was almost always wearing a tuxedo and bow tie, as though attending a premiere or charity function, the sort of event she imagined would level the playing field enough for Lee Mitchell to hang on to the cuffs of the powerful and the glamorous. A pile of paper

and two empty glasses were on a small round conference table, a remnant of some previous meeting. The office did not make her believe this man could produce anything, let alone her non-existent movie. Stop looking for negatives, she said to herself at the same time as she noticed the room had the only bad light she'd encountered since her arrival in California.

'*Stolen Hearts*,' said Lee Mitchell, landing himself heavily into his chair. 'Tell me about it.'

'I started as a writer in England, where I had a novel published. Then I wrote a script, which my agent in England thought should have been a novel, but I didn't. He's very sweet and he helped me get in touch with Julia Summers, via a couple of people. She read it and then suggested I write something else, which was how the treatment for *Stolen Hearts* came about.'

Lee Mitchell stared at her impassively. He brought both hands to his face and ran them slowly down his cheeks, as though mopping himself with a damp cloth.

'You haven't done this before, have you?' he asked.

'What do you mean?'

There was silence again and she could see he was making his mind up. With any luck, in less than a minute she would be back on the other side of his door and free, able to run away from Hollywood, from Julia Summers, from cancer.

He sniffed. 'Can I get you something to drink? I'm about to have a Pellegrino.'

Please don't give me a chance, she thought. I've done my best just by getting here and trying my hardest to throw the meeting.

'Please,' she replied.

While he was standing, his back to her and fiddling with the refrigerator concealed behind a cupboard door, Nancy picked up her bag and rested it on her lap. At first she thought she was about to get up and run from the office, but instead she opened the clasp and looked inside. Crumpled and pushed into one corner was a piece of white towelling. It smelled of rusk, even from that distance, and of baby sick, milk warm from maternal breast and infant stomach. She frowned and massaged the temple nearer the tumour.

'Are you okay?' he asked, leaning over her and holding out a glass of water.

His arm seemed ten feet long, like a camera lens from *Citizen Kane* was distorting his image, holding him in a deep and distant focus. Nancy snapped her bag shut, a sickly headache descending.

'I'm fine,' she said, losing count of the number of times she had said it since arriving in America.

'Okay.' He returned to his seat. 'The way I see it, you have a hot idea. I read your book, which I didn't get, but I loved the treatment. What you do best is on paper, not in the flesh. I can live with that. Do you really want to see your movie up on the screen?' he asked.

'Of course I do.'

'You hesitated. Nancy. Look at all the scripts laying around here, finished scripts. You're sitting there with a six-page treatment, expecting me to make your movie without even having a script, or without having to sell me on the idea.'

'The ideas are there on the paper. Me telling them to you isn't going to change them. If you have questions, you should ask,' she said.

'It's a great treatment, don't get me wrong. Julia says you're already working on the script?'

'Yes. It's moving along quickly,' she said.

'No one with money reads scripts anyway. We wouldn't want to deal with them if they did. So, the script is moving along?'

Nancy did not reply. It was becoming clear to her that Lee Mitchell was keen to be involved with the project, that it might one day become a movie. He was putting on a front, trying to make her feel grateful he was even talking to her. Nancy would have happily turned and walked away from everything and it was as though Lee Mitchell could sense it and it made him anxious. She wondered how he was feeling inside, if he was nervous. Perhaps he had thought she was going to leave when he turned to see her holding her bag.

'Have you seen anyone else?' he asked.

'There are several people interested in speaking to me,' Nancy said, the way Julia had told her to in the event of such a question.

Lee nodded. 'I'd like to talk with Julia, see if we can strike a deal on an exclusive basis. How would you feel about that?'

'I leave it to Julia to have feelings about things like that. That's why I have her,' she said.

'Right,' he said, nodding.

There was a kick, from inside her bag, as though from a pregnant stomach. In a reflex action, Nancy grabbed at it, pulling it close to herself in a sudden and inelegant movement.

'You okay?' Lee Mitchell asked.

Nancy held the bag tight, but it was writhing against her grip, fighting to break free of it. There should have been something comic about it, a big laugh that would have come from the belly. The movement subsided and the bag pulsed against her stomach like a heart.

'Nancy?' she heard Lee Mitchell say.

Not wanting to, but unable to resist, Nancy opened the bag and looked down into it.

The brown lump of meat was seething, pores on it opening and closing like a live sponge. There was a dark sheen to the surface of the mass and it filled the inside of her bag entirely. The small holes covering it quivered as though the thing was breathing through them. Blood ran from several of the orifices and in one painful second, the block was removed and Nancy had a flash of memory.

Her knickers being removed. The feeling down between her legs. Full and then empty. Had that been how it had been put in her or how it had been removed? Both? The man she'd trusted.

'It's not going to end like this,' she said. 'My life is worth more than this. It's not going to end with a script or a film. There are more important words to be written. Grace is coming, Nancy. Grace is coming.'

The block fell back into place. Nancy snapped the bag shut and looked up at Lee Mitchell.

He didn't appear to have been involved in anything that had just happened, as though the needle had jogged over that part of the record for him.

'What was I saying?' Lee Mitchell asked.

'*Stolen Hearts*, the treatment.'

'Right,' he said brightly. 'I know exactly how to get it made. What are you doing a week today?'

Chapter 8

'Paul, I'm not convinced about the timescale for the deal with Trellis. It's ambitious and the Trust are pushing too hard,' Kavanagh said, not even across the threshold of Paul Baran's office.

'That's just what Alexander Cameron would have said about his father,' a voice from within Baran's office said.

Baran, who had met him at the door, stood to one side, a warning look on his face. Kavanagh saw a man fitted against the sofa as though he were part of the brown hide. The man leaned forwards and closed a thin paper file that was open on the coffee table in front of him, doing it with enough casual power to demonstrate Kavanagh would not get to see what it contained.

Kavanagh sucked in some silent air, bracing himself and hoping to recover, feeling on the ropes without even knowing who the stranger was.

'Mike, this is Andrew Mathias. Andrew, this is Mike Kavanagh, Sales Director,' Baran said, ushering Kavanagh in with an arm pressing on his shoulders, as though pushing him towards the man.

Andrew Mathias detached himself from the leather and stood – he was about the same height as Kavanagh. They met eyes, shook hands firmly and nodded, repeating each other's names like strangers meeting on a train in a mutually foreign country.

The three men remained standing.

'Andrew is a board member of the Cameron Trust. He's met Jack Burns and is here to help you out with some insights into him,' Baran said, as though introducing Mathias to a room of people in advance of a speech.

The first thing to strike Kavanagh about Mathias was how at home he was in his surroundings. He was more comfortable than Kavanagh, who had been visiting Baran's office in its various incarnations for the last ten years. The man might have been fifty or possibly sixty, falling into a category Kavanagh could still complacently think of as old. His neatly groomed hair was more grey than black, although it suited him, his eyes shining like a younger man evidencing wonder of some kind. The skin on his face pulled tight against the angles of his bone structure, the result lean rather than hungry. A yellowy tan, probably the combination of sun bed and vitamin pills, framed the smile he was giving Kavanagh.

'Sit down, Mike, please,' said Mathias, gesturing at the sofa opposite the one he had been occupying.

Kavanagh settled himself into the settee but it did not feel as comfortable as it usually did.

'We are moving too fast for you?' Mathias asked, in a manner so carefully designed to be neutral, Kavanagh was uncertain which way to jump.

'Mergers are rarely sprints,' he replied. 'I used to believe they could be middle-distance races, but they always turned into marathons.' Kavanagh wondered if Mathias was the sort who jogged, his frame waspish enough to suggest it. 'I can run fast, very fast when I have to, but it's knowing when to go for the line.'

'Agreed,' Mathias said, seeming to warm up. 'The Trust are stern trainers, always wanting you to go faster and longer.'

'Andrew is a relation of the Camerons,' Baran interjected, as though trying to get in between them.

'Not by blood,' Mathias said gently and Baran gave a warm smile.

'Andrew stepped in when there was no one to steer the Cameron Trust, when it went through the fallow period,' Baran said. 'Without him, none of us would be here. His affinity for maintaining the momentum of this business drove it through some hard times.'

Kavanagh hadn't seen Baran do as hard a sell since they used to go out in the field together, doing joint calls.

Baran was watching him, as though trying to gauge his reaction. Kavanagh had met several people from other companies in the Cameron empire at various social functions, treating them like distant cousins at a wedding, but the Trust people themselves never ventured out. Those who did get to meet them, people like Baran, were summoned.

The head office of the Cameron Trust was in the West End of London, one plaque among many at a serviced address. Mail was directed though a clearing centre and passed on. Anyone with access to an on-line credit-checking service could find out as much. It was what they didn't know that fascinated them, the people working for Kavanagh believing he knew more than he was telling them. Perhaps now he would have something to tell them. A real live member of the Trust, in the flesh – and a relative, of sorts, of the old man himself.

'I believe business is going extremely well at the moment,' Mathias said.

'We're on plan for the quarter, which is good. Normally you see a back-ended skew, whatever the plan, but we're looking good for the third quarter,' Kavanagh said, wondering if it would mean anything to Mathias.

'LKG was sizeable and a good margin, Paul tells me. Sounds like we have a rising star with this Carson,' Mathias said, pausing for half a second as he appeared to grope for Chris Carson's name.

'Is Chris in at the moment?' Baran asked.

Carson had not been in for three days now and Kavanagh had tried him at home several times. Yesterday it might have been a hangover from extended celebrations, but today Kavanagh didn't know where Carson was.

'He's out with clients all today,' Kavanagh said, stopping himself from touching his nose as he lied.

On the coffee table, to one side of the paper file, was a thin brown leather pocket-book, lines worn into it like on an old pair of shoes, and a streamlined gold pen resting at an angle across it. On top of the folder was a mobile phone not much bigger than a chocolate bar. Kavanagh glanced around Mathias's feet and saw no sign of a briefcase. It seemed right. Already, Kavanagh could tell Mathias was the sparse type, carrying a few accoutrements in the capacious pockets of expensive, elegant suits. Everything else he needed would be in his head.

'How do you feel about the Trust's offer, Mike? We believe you deserve a reward for your efforts up to now,' Mathias said.

'It's not the kind of offer you go around refusing. I'm pleased. It's always good to have recognition,' Kavanagh said, flitting his eyes from Baran and back to Mathias.

'If you wish to retain the equity position in the vehicle, you can. Please don't think we're trying to kick you with a golden toecap boot,' Mathias said.

'What Andrew is saying, Mike, is there is a place for you at Pendulum and in the venture. It doesn't have to be goodbye,' Baran said.

Kavanagh studied Baran. There were things he knew about Baran, times they'd spent together, that gave his words a currency he glibly assumed Mathias would not appreciate, but at the same time, he wondered what secret history lay between the two men sitting in front of him. Kavanagh caught sight of just how little he knew. What weight would Baran's words to him hold for Mathias?

'At the Trust, we like to think that history repeats, that things we've done well in the past can be used over and again, adapting to specifics. That's what the Trust has in terms of its global plan, an overall set of objectives we want to put into play.' Mathias had sat forward as he spoke, leaning into his words, and it was clear to Kavanagh that he and Baran were meant to listen rather than interact.

Chatter was over.

'Pendulum was the first subsidiary of the Cameron Trust,' Mathias continued. 'The two are inseparable. Pendulum is a company in its own right, but it is welded to the Trust.' Mathias clasped his fingers together, as though about to arm wrestle with himself. 'When Clough Cameron formed the Trust, he created Pendulum at the same time. The massive injection of capital enabled Pendulum to operate almost like a merchant bank. It was able to finance whole companies, lock stock. There was a two-pronged strategy in which Clough consolidated a business base in asset finance, one of the first, with Pendulum, while using the surplus to pursue other interests through the Trust. It was a slow process of diversification and, as you know, some of the businesses connected to the Trust were started from scratch, others were acquired.'

Kavanagh sat and listened. The story was familiar as far as it went. Where did the 'massive capital injection' always referred to come from? Kavanagh had thought no one really knew. No one except, perhaps, Andrew Mathias, and he showed no sign of elaborating. Clough Cameron and his son Alexander were enigmas in life and had remained so in death, lost in the intricate web they had created.

'The presence of the Trust was always there, behind Pendulum, even as it outgrew it. In many ways, by the end of the Seventies Pendulum had served its purpose and could have been closed down, yet it remained there like a figurehead. The eighties did us no harm, as you know yourself. Pendulum was, and is, well-poised to act as corporate lessor. There is a lot of tax capacity floating around the group and you have access to cheap money, be it from the Trust's own coffers or the brute power of our treasury operations. Even our interests in manufacture place Pendulum well to take risk on equipment we either make or understand.

'Much of the success of Pendulum, the thing that's kept it going beyond what, to be cynical, was its useful life, has been down to Paul.' Mathias paused and looked at Baran. 'He has invaluable links across the Trust and is able to play the politics as well if not better than anyone else. But it's you, Mike, that's been the front-end, the face Pendulum shows to the world. Pendulum and the Trust behind it, is the beast, the thing with appetite, and it's you who goes find it things to eat. That's why we value you.'

Kavanagh blinked and frowned. Mathias paused for a moment, as though logging the action before going on once more.

'Now, the Trust sits in its strongest-ever position in the UK and we're making forays into Europe, like most businesses. Looking for advantage and responding to customer-driven need. There are developmental strategies in other areas of the world. Look at what we've done in Africa, Australia and several of the South-East Asian countries. These will grow and we will wait for them to do that. That's not our concern, here today. America is. We have to make up for lost time and buy our way into a market that's already well-developed. It would have been possible to buy something off the shelf, ready-made, but that is not the way of the Trust, certainly not in the States. Trellis is a ready-made contact base and a perfect entrée into America. We want to plant a seed and become part of the fabric, not an embellishment.

'I can't over-emphasize that our plans are long-term but that we must also move quickly. You're the one that's going to plant the seed for us, Mike. History, as I said, runs round on itself. Using the finance company as a jumping-off point. The joint venture will be the way the Trust takes root and then diversifies. Once we're part of the fabric, that's what gives us real power. Otherwise there is nothing but the noise of too much information. We have access to more information than we could ever want. What we need is knowledge. Information is not power; knowledge is.'

All three of them were leaning towards the table, like boys round a campfire at midnight. There was something dark about the moment and Kavanagh realized his breathing had taken on the same pattern as the other two men's. The room was silent, as though holding its own breath in anticipation, and it took Kavanagh a second to disengage from the situation, to find his own stride. Mathias and Baran were staring at him.

'And what do we do with all this power?' Kavanagh asked.

Mathias sat back upright and smiled lightly. 'We look after our customers and the people who work for us,' he said.

Light flooded in and everything suddenly seemed banal. That was all it was really about, selling washing powder and aspirin? The older Kavanagh got, the younger and more inexperienced he felt. Whatever he achieved in business, whichever new plateau he reached, there was always one more rung to climb, somewhere else to be. Things weren't mundane, it was simply that Mathias and Baran were another rung away and had something he didn't. He looked at the two men and realized they were, effectively, holding out their hands and offering to give him a pull up to the next rung.

'How much do you know about Trellis, Mike?' Mathias asked.

'Just what I've read. They look impressive on paper and I can't see they're hiding anything away. Our issue here is that we're not buying what's on paper. When we've looked at acquisitions in the past, we've often had concerns when we find that seventy-five per cent of a company's net worth is intangible, made up of goodwill, but in the case of Trellis, that's what we're hoping to achieve, I assume,' Kavanagh replied.

'Precisely,' Mathias said. 'If we wanted a portfolio in America, we would have bought one by now. What we need is a presence, a way into some of the American corporates that isn't just us buying our way in. We need to look serious about it or they will see it from a mile away. I wouldn't want to take anything away from what Pendulum does, but there's no track record of it ever getting into the States via any European branches of big US corporates.'

'We've toyed with it, when the request had been driven from the client, but we've never been actively seeking it. I wasn't aware it was even part of the strategy,' Kavanagh said.

'At the Trust, one of the more pressing and time-consuming tasks is to find accord between our plans and the requirements of the individual businesses. We realize that can cause problems. It's one of the reasons we're willing to recompense you so greatly. The other is the speed with which we hope to conclude this. You say you run fast, Mike. You may be able to break a record of some kind.'

'How fast?' Kavanagh asked.

'A month,' Mathias said.

'No way. We couldn't even get through due diligence in that period. It will take me time to build Burns's confidence in me.'

'We have every faith in your ability to do that, Mike,' Mathias said. 'Try your best and keep in mind our desire for swiftness.'

'I will. What can you tell me about Jack Burns that will be helpful to that end?' he asked.

'The primary thing to keep in mind,' Mathias said, 'is don't try and play him. Burns is far too clever for that. He built Trellis himself, all by himself, even though he could easily have gone into the family textile business or sat it out until his trust fund came up, like his younger brother did. On his own earnings, Burns could have retired thirty years ago. Six years ago, his father died and left his remaining shares in the textile company to the boys. They both sold immediately. It's hard to put a precise figure on it, but our sources estimate his personal fortune to be in excess of three hundred million dollars, but you wouldn't be able to pick him out of a lineup.'

'So he's a man of the people?' Kavanagh asked.

'Not in an unpleasant way. He's self-made and self-effacing, very down to earth. The key point is that he absolutely doesn't have to do business with us if he doesn't wish to. It's purely down to his own whim, but let me stress he is not a whimsical man.'

Kavanagh had been in situations where he sold to people so powerful it was not an issue of money. It could make things difficult because removing a tangible like money focused attention on intangibles, but he could make it work once he found the way into the client.

'Paul tells me Burns is receptive to an approach?' Kavanagh asked Mathias.

'I met him at a function earlier in the year and, yes, he did seem receptive. He's been looking around for a while, casting about to find a way to be sure he's leaving Trellis in good hands. Burns has no one to pass it on to and he still owns ninety-five per cent of the stock – the other five is with a few employees. Burns wants to know Trellis will go somewhere in the future. A venture between Trellis and Pendulum, with the Trust behind it, would be ideal. He knows something of the Cameron Trust, but now it's Pendulum he needs to understand.'

'How old is he?'

'Sixty-four. No children, divorced thirteen years ago. He's a Harvard MBA, very bright with numbers. Likes to swim every day, plays a little tennis. Paul has a file covering everything we've spoken about and some more general information. I wanted to meet with you personally, Mike, because I feel it's time.'

'I appreciate it. When am I going to be able to meet Jack Burns?'

'He'd like you to go out next week, Tuesday,' Mathias said.

It was still sooner than Kavanagh had expected, despite all the talk of having to act quickly. He would need to make definite arrangements for Lucy.

'Fine,' Kavanagh said.

Mathias breathed out through his nose and leaned towards Kavanagh. 'A lot is resting on you, Mike. I know you know that, and I don't say it either lightly or to put pressure on you. I want you to know that we're here for you on this.' Mathias reached his right hand to the left breast-pocket of his suit and removed a small white card, handing it to Kavanagh. 'You can contact me directly on this number if there's anything you need.'

Kavanagh held the card so the pointed ends stuck into the fleshy tips of his thumb and forefinger, examining it with all the grace and interest he normally reserved for his

Japanese customers. It bore nothing other than the name Andrew Mathias and a mobile phone number. No name, no address, no company logo.

'You're living in one of the Trust houses in North London?' Mathias asked.

'That's right,' Kavanagh said.

'I was there myself, many years ago, when Alex stayed in it briefly,' Mathias said, enjoying the apparent warmth created by the memory.

'I didn't realised he had lived there,' Kavanagh said.

'Only for a very short while. It was such a lovely house. I'm sure it still is, despite what has happened there.'

Kavanagh felt uncomfortable, not certain how to react to such a personal line of conversation from someone so distant.

The phone on the desk trilled and Baran left his chair to answer it.

'Mike, there's a call for you, someone at LKG. Do you want to take it outside on Jean's phone?' Baran asked.

'Excuse me,' Kavanagh said, pocketing the card and leaving the room.

When Kavanagh reentered Baran's office, Baran was standing by his desk, on a call. There was no sign of Mathias, the folder and the accessories that had been on the coffee table nowhere to be seen. Kavanagh had been engrossed in his call, standing with his back to the office door, so Mathias could have slipped past him, but he was sure he would have noticed. Kavanagh put his hand in the side pocket of his jacket and touched the business card Mathias had given him, making sure it was still there. He was tempted to go and touch the leather where Mathias had sat, to check if it were warm.

Baran was still on the phone and Kavanagh left him to it. His mind was directed towards Los Angeles and Jack Burns, but first he had to make plans for Lucy.

Chapter 9

There were things she and Mum hadn't told Dad about.

Like the day they first saw the Lady, when Lucy was only five years old.

In the kitchen, Lucy Kavanagh stood on a box to bring her up to height with the kitchen surface, her arms reaching over the edge of a mixing bowl, hands burrowing into flour and butter and sifting them with salt and sugar, making them too warm. Beside her, her mother was doing much the same, but with fingers more deft and a bigger bowl.

They had been playing at baking for almost three quarters of an hour, the pre-heat of the oven raising the temperature in the kitchen pleasantly and wafting the smell of ingredients around them. It was half-term in Lucy's first year at Infants and Mum's turn to look after her. In the latter half of the week it would be Dad's and he would be out of the house with her, not wasting time there. But today Lucy Kavanagh and her mother Helen were whiling away the afternoon making cakes.

The Lady must have been standing behind them, watching them from the doorway of the kitchen for at least five minutes. Lucy felt her there and yet it felt more like Dad was standing behind them, watching his girls with a smile on his face. Once or twice, Lucy and her mum had looked up from a game or turned their heads to find Dad grinning at them, as if sharing a private joke between the three of them. That was what it felt like, as though it was Dad.

Lucy realised, or sensed, that it wasn't Dad. She moved her head up slowly and looked into the glass pane of the window in front of her, letting her eyes slowly focus and make out the geography of the room as it reflected against the early afternoon dark of the outside world. As her eyes adjusted, she could see herself and her mother in the foreground, the expanse of the kitchen in the middle ground and, in the background and in the doorway, a woman. It felt odd, but not dangerous. It would have been easy to turn suddenly and look, but she didn't.

'Mummy, there's a lady at the door. Behind us,' was all she said.

Her mother's fingers stopped abruptly and Lucy sensed a stiffening of her mother's spine. Lucy's mother inhaled a small breath and Lucy saw that she was almost relieved.

'It's all right, darling. I know. She won't hurt you, I promise.'

'Is she going to come in and help us?'

'No,' her mother said, fingers moving once more.

'Why not?'

'She never comes in here. I don't know why. Perhaps because it's the newest part of the house.'

'Does she live here?'

'Not any more. Not like that. I think she might have lived here once and now she just comes to visit.'

'Are you scared of her, Mummy?'

'No. And you shouldn't be either.'

'I'm not. Does Daddy see her too?'

'No. Daddy can't see her.'

'You can see her?' Lucy asked, flour and butter gathering in the joins of her fingers.

'Yes, I can see her.'

'It's just girls that can see her?'

Her mother smiled. 'Yes. Just girls. We should keep it our secret, otherwise she might go away.'

'And then she'd have nowhere to live.'

'That's right,' her mother replied.

Lucy was too young to fully comprehend the feelings she was having, but she knew her mother was right about not telling Dad. The presence of the Lady was nice and Lucy was sure it would feel different if Dad were to know about it. At five years old, Lucy Kavanagh was entering into the first important secret of her life, with the most important person in her life.

'I won't tell Daddy, I promise,' she said.

She looked at the window. The Lady was gone. Lucy carried on with her sifting.

And they never told Daddy. They seldom spoke about the Lady between themselves, although now Lucy wished her mother had said more, in case it might have helped. Lucy caught glimpses of the Lady every now and then. Even when she did not see her, she could feel her, as though the Lady's heart were inside her own chest, beating in time with it.

Between that afternoon of cake-making and first secrets up until her mother's death, Lucy only ever felt the Lady's presence or saw her as reflections; sometimes patterns in wallpaper that had always hung in the less used rooms; at other times, she could make out the lines of a face in the clouds of a busy watercolour leaning against the wall in the garage. Always reflections, images bounced off something else, as though the Lady were insinuated into the very fabric of the house; that or nascent feelings, intuitions that made her queasy; but never anything tangible enough to convince Lucy she was not imagining it all.

And she never told Daddy, as though to do so would alter something between them. Had still not told Dad. Not even about the day she found her mother. The only time she ever really saw the Lady. In the kitchen.

Something very . . .

Lucy sat up, her face muscles slack. The train was pulling out of Chancery Lane, ready to make the short journey through to Holborn. Something twinged in her memory, but the feeling was neither strong nor well-shaped enough for her to hang on to. A few words mumbled out and she put her hand to her mouth to cover the movements of her jaw, which felt like it had been to sleep and now had pins and needles.

Sitting across from her, a young man frowned in her direction, his eyes glazed and his hands perfectly still. Lucy averted her gaze to her lap and the Japanese paperback comic she had been holding but not reading as she stared into blank air. Rapidly she flicked the pages from back to front, the familiar and much-read story jerking past her eyes. In her bag was the copy of *Hamlet* she had intended to read in preparation for seeing it on stage. There would not be enough time now. Lucy looked up and saw the young man had gone, leaving unconcerned early-afternoon commuters behind him.

It was still more than an hour before Dad would be finished and Lucy knew she would be in the way were she to visit him. She strolled along Holborn, looking in the window of a camera shop and watching herself on video before making her way to the Pendulum building to call on the only other person she knew who worked there.

Tom used to be in charge of security at Pendulum, as well as all other aspects of the building's safety. Now the door security was contracted to a private firm, its employees showing only the minimal amount of deference to Tom's years with the company. In his late sixties, several inches shorter and many pounds heavier than Lucy, he was friendly and always smelled of too much aftershave. A large gold bracelet hung on his right wrist and he usually wore a short-sleeved shirt, the fat of his biceps straining the hems. What hair he had left clung to the sides of his head as though attached by static, thin black wisps that seemed to levitate a millimetre from his scalp.

At the very back of the building and down in the basement, Tom's room was a stark contrast to the open-plan office areas she had seen on the floors above. Instead of the rented-plant tidiness, his room was a yellowy mass of paper. Lucy stood at the door, Tom with his back to her and fiddling with some paper on an ancient fax machine. The office felt damp and the lighting was too bright. Lucy knocked on the open door and Tom turned slowly, his neck and shoulders looking stiff.

'Hello, Tom,' Lucy said. He was the oldest person she knew whose first name she could use.

'Hello,' he said, 'Your dad know you're here?'

'Not yet. We're going to the theatre tonight but I can't meet him until six. Probably later, knowing Dad.'

'Probably. Time for tea then?' he asked.

'Yes. Please.'

From the steel-framed chair that reminded her of something from a church hall, Lucy observed Tom's podgy fingers as he squeezed the tea bags and added milk to both cups. There was something about his office she liked. He had his own kettle, but wouldn't allow kettles anywhere else in the building for health and safety reasons. On her first-ever visit to his office, Lucy had noticed the stainless steel kettle standing on a brown cafeteria tray which had sticky ring marks on its finely woven surface. That visit had been almost six years ago and, she thought, it was the same kettle and tray.

Before Tom sat, Lucy noticed a large overstuffed cushion on his chair, foam poking from one corner. On the window ledge, a mostly eaten packet of biscuits.

'What's that?' Lucy asked, looking at the ornate piece of metal on his desk.

'One of the original door handles from before the Trust did the refit. There were over sixty of these and the builders had most away with them. I've got five in storage and I came across this one in a cupboard, at the bottom of a box.'

'It looks like it's made of gold. Can I pick it up?' Lucy asked.

'Of course,' Tom replied.

The door handle weighed about as much as a bag of sugar, its heft surprising given how small it was. The density of the compact globe was matched by the intricacy of the design that snaked around its circumference.

'Have you been polishing it?' Lucy asked.

'I used to go round and polish them all. Murder, all the little corners and hard-to-get-at places on them. One Sunday every month I'd come in and go from top to bottom with a rag and a bottle of brass polish. That one used to be one of my favourites, so I thought I'd give it a shine for old time's sake.'

Tom had been at Pendulum longer than anyone else and had known the original owners personally. Lucy suspected he knew more about the company than her father did, even if it were a different kind of knowledge. Given the choice between her dad's dry analysis of numbers and the life Tom breathed into the company with his stories, Lucy preferred the latter and had spent long afternoons listening to Tom.

The ramp into Pendulum's underground car park ran along the side of Tom's room and through the window Lucy watched people passing by, unaware they could be seen through the one-way glass.

'My dad's got to go away on business,' Lucy said, still looking out of the window.

She heard Tom move on his seat.

'For long?' he asked.

'Shouldn't be more than a week. He's going to America.' The long vertical slats of the blinds swayed gently in the air and Lucy let her eyes move with them. 'It's my mum's anniversary in three weeks' time.'

'I know,' Tom said, as though he wished he did not. 'You and your dad miss her. I see it in him every time I lay eyes on him. And you. There's nothing wrong with being upset about it, Lucy.'

What would now be like if Mum were here? Lucy wondered. Since she died, it was never just 'now' any more. All the moments were tainted with her absence. With no Mum, Lucy sent energy into nothing, no one to absorb it or react to it. Her death had cut into Lucy's life like a blunt axe, wielded ferociously and for no reason, gouging her mother away with no thought to what was left and how it would reassemble itself around the gap. There was no point in thinking about it, she knew, but it did not stop her. Lucy knew it would be possible to think about it until she began the kind of crying that would never stop, the sort of sobbing that would leave aches all over her as she heaved air out of her lungs. Even if she felt like that most of the time, she rarely did it, except on the odd occasion she turned it on for Kim and then it felt fake, as though it were doing her counsellor more good than it did Lucy herself.

'Are you going to stay with someone?' Tom asked.

'Do you mean am I going to be in the house on my own? I'm going to stay with my Aunt Karen.'

'You can always pop in here to see me, if you get bored,' he said.

'I'm supposed to be back at school. This is a big year. Everyone keeps telling me,' she said.

He batted the comment away with a hand. 'You're too clever for school. Me, I was too stupid. Hated it.'

Lucy wanted to tell him how much she hated it, too, but it seemed a heavy thing to say and would bring an otherwise light moment down. She stopped analysing, trying to switch off the internal voice, which sounded like Kim's. The one that asked questions of every interaction, looking for an agenda. In Kim's favourite terms, Lucy did for the old man what people often did for her. She threw him a bone to chew on.

'When did you start working here, Tom?' she asked, already feeling as warm as if she'd bought a copy of the *Big Issue* or signed a petition outside the Body Shop.

The old man's eyes shone, as though something in his head had been switched on.

'I first sat on that door in nineteen forty-eight,' he said, gesturing in a general way towards the front of the building. 'I wasn't much older than you are now. Nineteen. I'd already done a few jobs, mostly painting and decorating with my dad, but the work wasn't there. He was a master builder, had a lovely set of tools. I've still got some of them. When I landed the job here, I was glad because it took a weight off me and my dad. Clough Cameron wasn't much back then. His company had been in this building since the war ended, when the Trust was first set up.'

'He must have been quite old. What did he do before then?' Lucy asked.

Tom looked at her with a keen expression. 'No one

knows. Travelled. His family, more of a clan, were supposed to have owned most of Scotland at one time, but I never believed that. Over the years, I heard all sorts of stories about him. How he'd saved the life of an officer and two privates on the Somme. Became a hero by operating on them with a bayonet knife. His studies at Cambridge were in medicine and they were cut short by the war. He was supposed to have met people like Lenin. You never knew and he didn't often tell. When he used to arrive here some mornings, it was like the wind had swept him in and you thought he'd have to lean against the door to stop it blowing in after him. After the Great War, he didn't want to study medicine and he fell out with his father, over religion. Who knows? No one ever will now. One thing was true, though. His wife was only twelve when Mr Clough first met her on his travels in Europe, and I think they were, well, like man and wife from the first.'

'How old would he have been?'

'At least forty. He never married her until she was sixteen, mind. They travelled together, some time in India and the last two years in America. They got back to England between the wars and built a hotel in some little seaside town where they camped out for the duration, keeping to themselves and raising those children. By the time the second war came along, Mr Clough had gone from hero to pacifist. When the war was done, he set the company up and they moved into this building in nineteen forty-six. The Trust had only been running two years when I arrived.'

'What happened to the hotel?'

'Burnt down in the Fifties. The Trust still owned it. They had it built by architects he brought in specially to work on the design. One came from India and the other was from Hungary, which is where his wife was from. They were the same people who worked on the interior design for this building, turning it into a fucking maze, pardon my language.'

'Why do you think he decided to set the company up, when he was already so old?'

'I reckon maybe he was running out of money and they had the children to think about by then, not just to provide for while they were alive, but something to leave for them when they were gone. Those children weren't brought up ordinary. Private tutors, no school. There wouldn't have been anything they could have done in the outside world, so Mr Clough set to building a world for them. Clough Cameron was already a middle-aged man when he met Krista and perhaps he didn't expect to have children, thought he had enough money to last him. But then some say he wanted children and they tried hard. Couldn't hold her eggs, that one, and so young. When the triplets were born, Krista was just eighteen.'

Lucy loved the name Krista and the impossibly exotic feelings and thoughts it illuminated in her mind. What would it have been like to have babies at eighteen, such a short step in time from her own age? And to lose one straight away? Lucy knew the stories as well as Tom, had heard him tell them many times, yet each time he did, something new emerged. It was the first time Lucy had heard about the operation with the bayonet. Dad didn't like her talking to Tom, said he was full of ghost stories, but it was a more rewarding hour than she had ever spent with Kim.

'Alexandra, Camille and Alexander. Girl, girl, boy. That was the order they came out, the one in the middle dead,' Tom said with such conviction and sadness that it was easy to forget he only knew it secondhand and was now giving it third hand to Lucy. 'Maybe that little baby got the best of it, when you look at how the others turned out. That family came to a bad end.' He sighed. 'And that little dead baby, even she had a bad start.'

Tom leaned forwards, telling Lucy something she had never heard before.

'Krista told me this. She saw the body of that child before they took it away,' he said.

Lucy swallowed. 'And?'

'It had marks on its neck, like little hands had been round its throat and choked her.'

The knock on the door made Lucy's heart jump and her body followed, lifting an inch or so off the chair. Her cheeks were hot and a fast tingle spread over her back. She gave a small laugh to show she was embarrassed at herself. Tom's jaw had a grim set to it but eventually he managed a smile and looked towards the door.

A man was looking around it, not venturing into the room.

'I was just about to leave. Do you want a lift anywhere?' the man asked Tom.

'No, I'm fine. Have you met Mike Kavanagh's daughter?' Tom asked.

'No,' the man said, emerging from behind the door and into the room.

'Lucy, this my son, Garth,' Tom said.

Garth smiled, reached his hand out, shook Lucy's, retrieved his fingers and brought them to his nose.

Chapter 10

Nancy entered Forest Lawn Memorial at three o'clock, the weather the same monotonous, blanching wave it had been since her arrival on the West Coast.

Burn or bury had been a favourite phrase of Nancy's, mostly because of the effect it had on her mother, whose face would sour at the supposed blasphemy of such a dichotomy. There was always just a slight chance Nancy could wake up long after she had been declared dead, only to find herself flat on her back and her face a few inches from a piece of white silk, an inch or so of wood and six feet of earth. It wasn't being buried under the earth, it was the constrictive nature of a coffin that bothered her now. A mausoleum would be the ideal solution, so even if she did wake up, she could walk around while she waited to suffocate. Forest Lawn, she had read in a guide book, was big on mausoleums. How much would all the earth on top of her coffin weigh? Being eaten by worms, or whatever they were, did not worry her. Burning seemed cleaner, however, but suppose she woke up during that one?

Nancy had already decided she was the only suitable person to plan her funeral. Apart from the fact she was the only person outside of the medical profession who knew she was dying, there was nobody else to help. Four years of silence between her parents and herself was enough for her. They had not even responded to the invitation to her launch party, which had been far more important to Nancy than her death. Her parents had blown the chance to plan her funeral, she'd decided.

Julia Summers, her only friend in Los Angeles. Bad choice. Although it might have been nice to trundle up the runway towards the curtains accompanied to the trill of mobile phones and Julia's heartfelt assurances to Lee

Mitchell, the only mourner, that Nancy could still finish the script.

You needed help to die. It was the one thing she thought she might have been able to do on her own, but there were too many practicalities involved, matters which would survive her. She was only doing it alone to be stubborn, she knew. Her death would be a fabulous opportunity to say a final fuck off to her parents and to Colin. Only Malcolm, her literary agent in London, made her feel bad. She could already picture his weary sadness as he added her death to the weight on his shoulders, remembering over a lonely pint in a crowded pub. Nancy had already written him a letter which she had to work out a way of having mailed to him once she was buried, or burned, leaving him the task of breaking the news.

The only other cemetery Nancy had visited, apart from the three funerals she had attended, was in Hampstead. Then, she had upset the friend who accompanied her by walking round and making fun of all the stones, asking why a communal Chinese one didn't just number the people like a menu, asking who would put the last name on the stone for a family plot, suggesting the person with 'fell asleep' on their stone would be pissed off when they woke up. The trip had ended abruptly when Nancy's grave-side humour moved up a gear and she began to talk of a cemetery theme park, with embalming rides.

Forest Lawn had almost beaten her to it. Even if she was never going to visit Disneyland, this almost made up for it. She had wandered around, stunned into a silence that might have been mistaken for awe. A gigantic mosaic, 'The Birth of Liberty', depicted a group of solemn men and plain women, all diminishing in detail the further back they were in the crowd. When she saw the copyright notice on its bottom right corner she actually laughed out loud and was stared at. The Lincoln Terrace was a similar experience, the sixteenth president represented in a collage of small stones, showing him with one hand raised, the other on a book. The larger-than-life paintings and mosaics seemed to be running from the inevitable. The result was that the supposed timelessness of death was stuck in a sort of Seventies kitsch. It was the least deathly she had felt since finding out she was doomed.

The Church of the Hills was a little better and she liked the expanse of grass, especially as there were no grave stones, nothing upright to mar the landscaping. All memorials were on brass plaques set into the ground.

Crossing the road, she made for a small tree near the side of the path, avoiding all the plaques like cracks in the pavement. Beneath the shade of the tree, one plaque was buried alone like a small island in a sea of lush green.

Nancy stopped over it. The smooth brass was polished to the colour of pure copper, like a piece of paper yet to be written on. At its top was a pattern which troubled her from the second she laid eyes on it. She squatted to get closer.

The embossing was intricate, like nerves or a complicated roadway that went round and round on itself. The shape acted like a magnet, holding her gaze and not allowing her to look anywhere else. As she continued to watch, Nancy found she could not even blink, her eyes beginning to water and her pupils trembling from the strain of holding a stare. Similarly, the muscles of her thighs became more like jelly as she maintained the position on her haunches.

'It goes on forever, but you can see it.'

It was a man's voice, calm, confident and only inches from her ear. Nancy was certain she could feel the warmth of breath carried on the breeze.

'Sorry?' Nancy asked, as though not hearing him the first time.

'The knotwork goes on forever but you can see it. Infinite patterns visible to the eye. It's seeing forever.'

The man was behind her, she knew. Possibly squatting down in the same way as her, close to her, yet she was unable to turn around. Her eyes were welded to the pattern on the gravestone and the muscles of her neck were locked.

Nancy tried to move her head to look behind her and immediately nausea came over her. It was easier to remain where she was.

Nancy's lips dried out, the skin feeling cracked and in need of balm. Her tongue was like felt, stuck to the back of her mouth and tickling its roof.

'You could follow it around and around all day and never stop. Unless you got tired,' the voice said.

The man's hand extended over her shoulder and his finger made circles, not quite touching the brass as it mimicked the patterns of the weave.

'I could do this all day and my finger would never stop moving. Only when I got tired,' the man said.

The hand was solid and old, as if it had been well-made many years ago and weathered the passage of time gratefully. The voice had a brogue to it, a regional accent neutralized by distance from home.

'You'd have to stop somewhere. Back where you started,' Nancy said.

Her words did not belong to her, she knew. And yet they were familiar, as if she had spoken or read them somewhere before, almost as if she were reading a script.

'Besides,' Nancy continued, 'you can start anywhere you want. It's arbitrary. And it doesn't really go on forever, it's only a line joined up.'

'I agree. If you think of it as a line that only goes in one direction. When did we start doing that? Thinking of things as a line? Don't you find the pattern of infinity comforting?'

The dark lines of the knot gave a tremor and Nancy saw a glimmer of gold in the depths of its veins.

Her head twinged and she scrunched her left eye closed as a sharp bolt of pain forced itself through the eyeball. She shook her head as if trying to get water from her ears after a swim. When she looked back at the plaque, the knot seemed to be alive with energy, practically humming the way she imagined a high-voltage cable might as it made ready to kill her dead from the slightest touch. Carefully,

Nancy extended her arm, knowing it was dangerous but knowing also that she had to do it.

The smell of leather came into her head, as though stored somewhere within it. Her breath tasted of the hide and her nostrils were filled with the sweaty, cloying odour. The side of her head was burning with pain and sweat trickled along her temple, a salty drop stinging the corner of her eye.

If I put my hand into this, I'll die, she thought. It will be over now. As she reached out, she aligned her arm with the man's, moving her finger in time with his like a small child copying an adult.

Nancy felt a bewildering loss of gravity, as though she were nothing more than a pair of eyes floating in front of the plate. The rolling motion of the old man's finger was like the sea, waves lapping in the back of her mind as though heard in a shell. Through the whistling emptiness, words echoed, familiar and unsettling. Her finger stopped moving and her arm dropped loose to her side. As the wind subsided and the voices tuned in with perfect clarity, Nancy realised she was not going to get away with just killing herself.

What are you going to do?

Something very special and very nice.

What is it?

Do you trust me?

I don't know. Will it hurt?

Am I hurting you now?

No.

Or now?

Ah! No, I like that.

Something horrible was happening with the voices and yet she was impassive, like when she watched a famine report and switched her compassion off. Nancy knew what the voices were saying, who they were and what they wanted. She knew, but she could not access it. The finger moved on and on, going faster.

So you trust me then?

Yes.

Take off the rest of your clothes then.

Tears were running down Nancy's cheeks, out of her unblinking eyes, over her jaw and onto the grass.

'Don't you think . . .' Nancy looked up and over her shoulder. He was gone.

Chapter 11

Garth walked along a side road, contemplating patterns. For the last week, since The Book opened him, Garth had become aware of a unity, a sense of order he had not previously appreciated. There was a feeling that knowledge lurked just around a corner, the sort of knowledge that meant he could know everything. Would his body and mind be able to carry all that weight? Surely there always had to be something you didn't know, or else you'd be God? Garth was not certain he wanted to know everything, any more than he might want to live forever, given the chance.

The world slowed down in a way that he was now getting used to. He had been walking past the house for less than a second but the world was travelling much slower than that, enabling him to move through it and savour it with his newly heightened sensitivity. Looking through the curtainless window of the house and on into the back of the living-room, Garth saw a young boy, eleven or twelve, lying on a sofa, television flickering on his pale face. Several nights a week Garth would walk down this road and go past the river on his way home, and the boy was always there, part of a regular pattern. The boy was still wearing his maroon school jumper, grey narrow-legged trousers and white towelling socks that were scuffed with dirt on the soles. The white-clad feet tapped together in some unknown, boyish rhythm and Garth could smell sweat from between the toes. The front garden had been covered in cement to make a parking space which was at that moment empty, as usual. For the first time, Garth realized the boy was in the house alone, waiting for parents to arrive home from work. There was another smell of sweat, more profound and coming from the pressing together of soft pieces of flesh.

Garth's chest palpitated with a mixture of nausea and excitement as he felt an urge to do something.

The moment passed and Garth released the breath he had been holding as the world came back to speed and he was past the house, the disconcerting stiffness in his trousers already subsiding.

Garth turned left onto the towpath that ran along the side of the river, glad to be away from the houses and their rumblings, their mix of sound and smell that buzzed away as though there were a beehive inside his head. At work, there had been talk of this being the day the Indian Summer would end, where Autumn would wrestle it towards winter. It was colder than it had been for many weeks and the air smelled seeded with rain about to blossom into fat drops. The river was glutted, submerging the flora on the usually steep sides of its banks. It was as if something were waiting in the water, swelling it until it was ready to rise up. The low-hanging layer of vapour held down all the mossy smells like a blanket, dirt, nettles and pig parsley so pungent they could be tasted. The scent from the damp slats of a memorial bench rose up to him as he looked at it and Garth could feel the coldness of its stone frame even from ten feet away.

The clouds gathered and seemed to be moving faster than they should have, as if the rest of the universe were moving at a different speed over his head. Spring. Summer. Autumn. Winter. Garth felt as if he had been suddenly plunged into the coldest part of a dark Winter, his own weather in his own private world.

Squatting by the bank, the rustle of rats and squirrels whispering in the background, Garth squinted at a bunch of nettles. *Urtica*. That was the botanical name. Garth was absolutely certain. As sure as he was that he had never known that before. Pig parsley. *Petroselinium crispum*. Grass. *Gramineae*. Grass. Grasp. There will be things to do, Garth, unpleasant things. Grass. Nettle. Grasp. Grasp the nettle.

Garth reached out and closed his hand around a bunch

of the jagged leaves, feeling the stinging hairs find their way into the grooves of his palm. There was a sharp, burning jolt of pain but he did not flinch. All he did was bite down, locking his teeth together and freezing his jaw in one position as the heat in his hand cooled into a sensation of bleeding. He relinquished the grip and withdrew his fist to look at it. Already it was covered with blistering hives. Garth stared down at the tiny sacs of milky poison, wondering what they would smell like, if they would be hot, what they would taste like.

An ownerless dog came running by and Garth stood, putting his sore hand in his pocket. Labrador. *Chordata. Vertebrata. Mammalia. Theria. Carnivora.*

'Stop!' Garth shouted into the acoustic flatness of the trees and plants.

But it wouldn't stop. The voice droned on in his head, imparting information to him that he did not want, had no use for. He was capable of going directly to the root of any word that came into his mind, the etymology screaming out at him, reducing everything to basics but making no sense at all. It had no logic but it was still information. Once the pattern became clear, perhaps, there would be knowledge, but until then it was all a pointless knot of facts growing into each other. He was drowning in the world. All the information, the words, the sights, smells and sounds, the touch and taste, were burying him alive. It was like being possessed.

Garth stomped along the path so hard it hurt his knee joints. It was pointless to try getting away. There would be no running away from this destination, he knew. Garth opened his mouth and let it fill with the swarms of midges, fat with blood and dirty grey-green in colour.

He came to a stop at the playground, which was fenced in by waist-high green railings and overlooked by an unused cafe, its white metal roller covered in graffiti. Garth spat out a couple of stringy gnats, picked one from a tooth and wiped his hand on his suit jacket. In his pocket, his right hand wept with soreness.

A roundabout, two four-seater horses, two sets of swings in different sizes and a pit that had never been filled with sand. A mother was pushing a child on a swing, pram parked off to one side. Garth wondered why anyone would be out on such a gloomy evening, when it already seemed darker than it should have. He entered the playground and sat on its empty, lopsided bench, moisture seeping through his trousers until he could feel in intimate detail the pattern of the wood grain on the back of his thighs. Like an aftershave, there was a whiff of cinnamon in the air. *Cinnamomum. Kinnamon.*

Garth realised he was mumbling to himself and that the woman had noticed him. The swing was no longer moving and she held on to the chains protectively, as though ready to whip the child out of the seat and back into its pram. He saw fear in her eyes and he wanted to say something to her, but he could not. At that moment, The Book was merely browsing him, keeping him in its hold. If Garth had been fully aware of it, he might have realized he was not possessed. Rather, he was scripted.

The woman lifted the child clear of the swing, its fat legs dangling in the air for a moment before she fitted them into the pushchair like a peg into a hole. The sugar-sized granules of grit under the rubber wheels deafened Garth as the pram moved off. With a single look, Garth was able to take in the lives of the mother and daughter and he felt a depressing thud, like running into a wall. They both ended at the same time. The two people moving away from him were going to die together, possibly soon, although he could not be sure.

Garth watched the vacant swing as it continued to move in a narrow arc before coming to rest. Gently, and as though the force had come from within, the swing next to it began to move back and forth. Two swings, and then three, were swaying, gathering momentum. Garth stood engrossed, transfixed as if by a hypnotist's watch. Out of the corner of his eye, he saw that all the other swings were in motion. The roundabout spun lazily on its axis, a creak as it went into motion. By the time he turned to look, the horses were bucking away wildly, high enough in the air to reveal their greasy metal innards where springs stretched like oily sinews.

Laughing, he held his hand in front of his face and looked at the swollen lumps of nettle rash, the biggest, in the fleshy centre of his palm, looking back at him like a yellow eyeball. The full venom of the nettle beat away in it like a heart. In the depths of the malignant fluid, the truth was swimming about. He could feel it in there, throbbing away. The word *emetic* came into his mind. Perhaps that was the way to rid himself of the information. He had grasped the nettle and now it was time to see what it contained.

Garth opened his mouth and bit down onto the lump as though it could have been a juicy plum. Instantly his mouth was filled with steaming pus and he sucked hard on the toxin, his cheeks indenting from the pressure. The hole on the surface of his palm was sore and ragged, its contents now in his mouth and stinging it like acid, the fetid stench like a mixture of heavy bleach and garlic.

Garth flopped to the ground, hearing a tear somewhere in the wool of his trousers. In long heaves, the laughter became sobs and through the blur of tears he saw clearly what was going to happen to him, the burden of certainty heavy in his heart. In far greater detail than it had allowed with the mother and child, The Book gave Garth a taste of what was to come.

Alone amongst the empty horses, Garth Richards sat and wept for his future.

Chapter 12

From the moment Kavanagh heard Trellis would send someone to meet him at LAX, he had the feeling in his gut that it would be Jack Burns himself who turned up. Scheduled for five days, his stay had pushed his luggage requirement beyond the expansive nubuck bag he used for overnight jaunts into Europe and on into the medium-sized Delsey suitcase which now rested on the trolley he trundled up the long ramp leading from of the Arrivals gate, past a picture of the President smiling in Technicolor. The flight had left London at noon, was in the air for eleven hours, and delivered him to California at four in the afternoon. Kavanagh was wearing the lightest-weight, most crease-free suit he owned, having fumbled it on in the toilet of the plane before the seat-belt lights illuminated for final descent. He felt dirty and sweaty under a layer of clean clothing and the aroma of mint toothpaste, ready for sleep when it was not even dinner-time in Los Angeles.

A man stood about halfway along the barrier holding up a sign on which the word PENDULUM had been written in a fastidious hand. Kavanagh's gut hummed and he was sure it was Burns. He had tried to turn up a picture of Jack Burns but had failed. The passive manner of the man holding the card showed him to be neither bored like a professional driver might be nor anxious like someone of stature would possibly be.

'Hello. I'm Mike Kavanagh from Pendulum,' he said, holding out his hand and hedging against the possibility it wasn't Jack Burns.

'Mike, hi. Jack Burns. Good to meet you.'

Burns had a firm grip. He was short, his neck thick, his eyes small and his head bald. Kavanagh noticed Burns had small ears and that his chin had a slight upward point as though lifting towards the faint crook of his nose. There was something military about him, the way he held his head back to regard Kavanagh, inspecting him. You didn't get to three hundred million dollars being a pacifist, Kavanagh reasoned. The impression of the squat general was softened by an open-neck denim shirt and cool cream chinos. The common touch, Kavanagh thought, feeling over-dressed and recalling the meeting with Mathias back in London.

'My car is nearby. I thought I would come say hello in person and maybe I could drive you to the hotel rather than you searching for it. I'll arrange for a rental car to be brought by your hotel tomorrow.'

'Thanks. That's kind,' Kavanagh said.

'You must be tired.'

'Another hour and I'll switch out like a light,' Kavanagh admitted.

They moved with the flow of bodies, Burns to the front of Kavanagh, walking with his shoulders back and spine erect. If Kavanagh saw Burns coming towards him, he'd have moved out of the way.

'It's good of you to meet me like this,' Kavanagh said when they were in the car park.

'It gets me out of the office. Is this your first time in Los Angeles?'

'I was out here on business the year before last, closing off a few deals in a portfolio we inherited with a company Pendulum acquired.' Kavanagh didn't want to mention Pendulum so soon. 'And I came here on holiday as part of a tour of the West in my second summer at university. I didn't go near downtown that time.'

Burns smiled and Kavanagh was relieved, realizing it was the first time he had seen the man's teeth.

'My car is here,' Burns said, gesturing to a silver Lexus as he opened it with the remote, side lights flashing to life simultaneously and locks lifting with slick precision. 'Let me get that.' Burns lifted the suitcase as though it were empty, marooning it in the desert-sized boot of the car.

'We're starting to see more of these in London now,' Kavanagh said, looking at the car.

'I like it. Comfortable, but not too big.'

Kavanagh nodded, already imagining Burns swamped by the beige leather of the room-like interior, his head a good foot from the roof.

'What do you drive?' Burns asked him.

'I got a BMW 8 nine months ago.'

'Nice,' Burns said.

It was idle small talk, no sentence connected enough to the previous to end up as a conversation. During his early days in the field, Kavanagh had hated the pleasantries, always eager to cut to the business. Now he found the chatter a relief, was more interested to see if he could raise a laugh with the client. If the first ten seconds of an interaction really did decide a sale, Kavanagh felt good about Burns. There was a warmth to the man he could already feel from beneath the taciturn shell. The thick neck and seldom-blinking eyes had put Kavanagh off for a second, but, if Burns were going to be cold, he would have shown it by now, probably never even have come to meet him. It was a while since Kavanagh had analysed something so closely, but then no other deal had been worth so much in personal terms. The thought of two and a half million pounds, slim pickings to Jack Burns, shuddered through Kavanagh and he wanted to smile.

Sitting in the traffic, Kavanagh looked at the wide sky. Los Angeles was cut from a different cloth and very little had altered from his student perception of it when he and Helen had rode in on a bus in the late morning, crusty-eyed from sleeping on each other's shoulders.

'We don't have too much of an itinerary for you. There are one or two social events I'd be glad if you could attend,' Burns said. 'Mostly, you should come out to the office, meet people and get a feel for the sort of company we are. I'd like for you to meet Arnold Long, our Chief Financial Officer.'

'It would be useful if we could spend some time

together, so I can give you an overview of Pendulum, answer any questions you might have,' Kavanagh said.

'I'm at your disposal, Mike.'

The lilt of Burns's voice was comforting on top of the gentle roll of the car's suspension, the whirr of the engine almost electric. As they threaded their way across town, Kavanagh tried not to yawn, but it was hard work. He felt himself sinking like the sun.

Jack Burns was shaking him gently by the shoulder. Kavanagh's head lolled forwards and then he snapped it upright, as though catching it before it fell off.

'Mike, we're here.'

'Oh god. I fell asleep. I'm sorry,' Kavanagh said, snorting an exasperated laugh.

'You were out cold. It seemed rude to wake you.'

Burns was smiling but Kavanagh felt embarrassed. He let the moment pass, but knew it would niggle at him for the rest of this visit.

They had arrived at the Biltmore downtown. Burns's assistant at Trellis had told Kavanagh's secretary it was the most convenient for reaching the office. Kavanagh was too tired to be impressed by the building, but it did offer the promise of a hot shower and a comfortable bed.

'I'll look forward to seeing you tomorrow, around eleven,' Burns said as they stood by the car, a bell hop waiting patiently with Kavanagh's bags.

'Thanks for the lift. Sorry I slept for most of it.'

'Please. It's no trouble.'

Burns held out his hand and they shook.

It was too late to call Lucy and Kavanagh wished he had done it from the airport as soon as they landed, but the preoccupation of disembarking, baggage reclaim and Customs had sucked the precious and small amount of the London day away without him even being aware of it.

Kavanagh opened the window and listened to the traffic. Every city had its own tune, and LA was no exception. The heat brought back memories of younger times, times with Helen. They stayed in Westwood with someone a year ahead of them at college who was doing her American Studies year abroad. Still only twenty, he and Helen huddled together under a blanket on the floor, listening to their friend's breathing, waiting for it to regularize into sleep when they made the quietest love they could on the floor, the heat in the room and the restraint they had to use infusing the sex with a tense passion they both remembered and sometimes alluded to.

He closed the window, shutting out the clamour that sparked such a piercing recollection, turned the air conditioning up and went to shower the grime off himself.

Chapter 13

The offices of the Trellis Corporation were on Wilshire Boulevard. Kavanagh was used to awe-inspiring head office buildings, flashy shows of power and money intended to impress those who bought and intimidate those who sold. Grey marble and green glass formed the atrium, which was the size of a football field with a few palm trees and a lot of pebbles scattered precisely throughout its space. Even the air felt expensive, but in the most understated way Kavanagh had come across. Trellis was a company comfortable with its clout, not afraid to spend the money. Kavanagh had not been as struck by some of the basilicas he had visited on holiday in Rome. Glass elevators hugged the inside walls, lifting as though gravity were non-existent. Two people stood talking on a walkway across the middle of the atrium, framed by perfect sunlight as though in a brochure.

A receptionist entered details into a screen and a badge was printed bearing his name and Pendulum's. Kavanagh took a seat and craned his head up to look at the activity of the building, as though at the centre of a beehive. The panopticon openness, the glass revealing everything, and the antiseptic cleanliness had a hint of the penal, but the thought took more imagination than Kavanagh had to give at that time. From a high balcony, Burns looked over before entering a lift, and they smiled at each other across the distance.

Kavanagh felt inquisitive eyes on him as Jack Burns led him through the main office area. The open-plan floor was not so different from the one at Pendulum, similar people doing similar things. Back in London, people would most likely be at home in front of television sets or out in pubs, telling stories about great deals of the past, while here in

Los Angeles, a day was just beginning. If the merger happened, the combination of Pendulum and Trellis would be a company that hardly slept.

It was a familiar journey through a strange area and Kavanagh had lost count of the number of times he had made it. A stranger led through an open-plan area and on to an inevitably more cloistered and plush inner sanctum. Jack Burns' office was a combination of wood and glass, each with a shine several feet deep. Leather and light mixed, Venetian blinds dissecting the sun with not a trace of dust visible in the shafts that fell across the room.

'Have a seat, Mike. I'll call Arnold and let him know you're here.'

Most people would have had a receptionist or secretary summon someone to a meeting but Burns was completely unaffected in the way he looked after himself. Even the opulence of the office they were in did not really suit him and it looked unlived in, like a hotel room just serviced.

Kavanagh felt tired, still kicking against the time difference and worrying about Lucy. If there were times when he stopped and noticed the unreality of his life, the almost ridiculous nature of what he did for a living, it was never more so than when he was a long way from home and in another country. The fact of other people sharing his business interests across the globe ought to have made him feel better, more legitimate, but instead it all made less sense to him.

Burns was still dressed casually, as were most of the people Kavanagh had noticed in the office. The old man poured Kavanagh coffee with a steady hand and passed the cup to him.

'You could probably use this,' Burns said.

'Thanks.'

'Do you have family in England?' Burns asked.

Kavanagh shifted in the seat. 'Only my daughter. She's almost sixteen. Staying with her aunt at the moment. I spoke to her just before I left the hotel.'

'Next time bring her out. Has she been to the States?'

'No,' Kavanagh said.

'I bet she'd like to see the theme parks?'

'She's at that age where I'm not sure what she likes any more. Anything I don't. Mostly.' Kavanagh could sense a wife-question about to be asked and he jumped in. 'Do you have children?'

'No. Never did. Too busy, all the usual crap,' Burns said, no trace of bitterness evident.

'Well, you've built an impressive business,' Kavanagh said.

'Thank you. We're not much compared to the Cameron Trust, but I like to think we could be. We've always had incredibly good people at Trellis. That's been the key to it. I've seen corporations where they have to put on training to teach people how to answer a phone.' Burns shook his head in disbelief. 'My solution? Employ people who can answer a damn phone in the first place. We have two hundred and fifty people across the country and I've had some contact with all of them. Of course, that gets more difficult the bigger you get, so you try and put people under you who you're absolutely certain can do it right. That took a long time at Trellis, but we have it about right.'

'The Trust started in a way not dissimilar to Trellis and it might have followed a similar trajectory, but it diversified. There are a lot of ends to the chain and they all pull in the same direction,' Kavanagh said.

'And Pendulum was the original link in the chain, of course,' Burns said.

'I was speaking with Andrew Mathias and he tells me you met with him recently.'

'We met at a fund-raising ball. He'd been trying to make contact with me for several months before that but I was too busy to set anything up. I knew what it would be as soon as I saw his name on a message. Alex Cameron once promised me we would work together. I guess if he'd have made it, it'd be him sitting there instead of you today. You should feel honoured.'

'I didn't realise you knew the Trust back then,'

Kavanagh said, wondering why Mathias would have left something like that out of the meeting and the report he left behind him.

'There was no Trellis back then. It was the last summer of the Fifties and he and his father were out visiting my father at the house on Long Island. I was back from college, a hothead, still not certain about what I was going to do, except the opposite of whatever my father wanted. A bit like your daughter now, I expect,' Burns said, nodding. 'Alex was ten or eleven years older than me and I wasn't interested in the business they were there to see my father about. He told me we'd work together at some point, made it like a promise. Of course, four years later he was gone.'

'But you went on to create Trellis. Don't you think he would have approved?' Kavanagh asked.

'Yes. I think he would.'

The door opened and both men looked round. Burns stood and Kavanagh followed.

'Mike, this is Arnold Long.'

Long was boyish early-forties with a faint sneer. Skinny enough to suggest he might have been a geek in college, he was wearing a suit that seemed too heavy for him and a shirt that was an obvious nod towards England, with a bold stripe, the sort Kavanagh's people usually bought from Hackett or Thomas Pink.

After soft handshakes and hellos, Long pulled a handkerchief from his pocket and blew his nose weakly, his nostrils still quivering as he returned the white cotton square to his pocket.

'I'm sorry,' Long said in a tight New York accent. 'Allergies are giving me hell today.'

Long's skin was white enough to show it did not get on well with the sun. That together with hair which was almost red and the allergies made Kavanagh wonder what he was doing in Los Angeles. Would all the dangers of the world mean the one-time geek would pour his energy into one small area? Kavanagh wondered. He looked into Long's eyes, which were brown like leather, and tried not to make any snap judgements.

'That doesn't sound like a California accent,' Kavanagh said lightly.

'I used to work for a bank back East and then I came out here eleven years ago, trading people traffic for automobile traffic.'

'It's certainly different to New York,' Kavanagh said.

Burns poured coffee into a cup and slid it towards Long.

'I have a friend working at UBS in London. They tell me you were looking at a securitization?' Long asked him.

Long wanted to joust. Kavanagh sighed silently.

'We spent a long, long time looking at it. It got to be like something we wanted to have so badly, we forgot why we were doing it in the first place,' he explained.

'So it never happened?'

'It's still being talked about. We began the process nearly four years ago and now there have been a few others, so the chance to use an off-the-shelf structure is there. We're nurturing the rather naïve belief this will save on fees,' Kavanagh said patiently.

'Right now,' Long said, 'I'm talking to some companies in the monoline bond insurance business.'

'As a form of credit enhancement?'

'Previously, we used a senior/subordinate structure and split the securities into several tranches. Even when we had set up the bankruptcy remote special purpose company, to sell asset-backed securities, we still needed to make them more attractive to investors,' Long said earnestly.

Kavanagh went with the tussle.

'Those kinds of issues are usually over-collateralized or have a first loss protection fund that lifts the bonds to investment-grade quality,' Kavanagh said, making it sound like he was seeking information from Long.

Long nodded. 'There was still a danger of the securities being downgraded, but once the insurance was in place, we were uprated to triple-A and the bonds sold in a much broader market.'

'Neat and tidy,' Kavanagh said.

'We just used to finance stuff,' Burns said, cutting in.

'We still do, Jack, but we have to at least keep up with, even ahead of, everyone else. They don't just finance stuff any more,' Long said.

'Paul Baran sent me a copy of the last Pendulum report,' Burns said.

'We must like you. That's usually hard information to get. I'm lucky if I have one,' Kavanagh said with a smile.

'We're the same with our own financial information. How do you feel about the prospect of a venture, Mike? What does it mean to you?' Burns asked.

'I was expecting to ask you that question. To me, there seems to be a fit, a way we can weave together what we've got and have very little duplication.'

'Almost like we were meant for each other,' Burns said.

'Something like that. Across the portfolios, while there is a great deal of asset similarity, it's spread through different market places. We have deep penetration into industrials, for instance, whereas Trellis has a hold in the service sector. We're both strong on government.'

'I can take that to mean you think a venture of some kind is worthwhile?' Burns asked.

'I wouldn't be here otherwise. Part of the attraction is the fact we're separated by two continents. There's still a lot of room to do our own thing. We're just going home when you get to work.'

'But in the long term, a joining together is not really what we're talking about, is it?' This was Long, who had sat upright in his chair and was now leaning back a fraction. 'Ultimately, we will end up as a foreign arm of the Cameron Trust.'

'In so far as Pendulum is an arm of the Trust, then any merged company would be. That's logical. Commercially, and personally, I have no issue with being part of the Trust. It's one of the most successful diversified conglomerates of all time. That brings an awful lot of leverage,' Kavanagh said.

'And it brings no downside?' Long asked.

'I didn't say that. If you want the power that membership gives you, you also accept the limitations it occasionally brings.'

'I think what Arnold is saying, Mike, is that at Trellis we've always held on to a small-company feeling and the prospect of losing that identity is uncomfortable,' Burns said.

'I can understand that. We have a long-term view on this. In Europe, Pendulum and the Trust have been acquisitive, moving in and buying companies or portfolios where we've seen fit. It wouldn't have been so hard to do that here and it would have been my first instinct. We're trying to put roots down here and we're not trying to rush anyone.'

'You'll really spend two or three years talking about how we're going to form a joint-venture company?' Long asked.

'That's what this is about. No one is trying to make this happen overnight,' Kavanagh said, thinking about the cooperation document he needed to get in place to trigger his own pay-off in the deal and the timescales Mathias and Baran were trying to hit.

There was a faint knock at the door and a young male face appeared round it.

'Jack, I have CR on the line. Shall I put him through?'

As though disconcerted, Burns looked around.

'Do you want us to leave, Jack?' Long asked.

Burns thought for a moment. 'No. I'll take it in your office, Arnold. Instead of moving two bodies, I'll just move mine.' He rose and left.

There was silence for perhaps a full half minute as Kavanagh and Long were alone. It was easy to sense the attitude and Kavanagh tried to ignore it, but the sneer on Long's face seemed to be lifting his cheeks so that more of his teeth became visible.

'So, you boys think you're going to swing in here and buy up Trellis?' Long said, shaking his head.

'I've already been through this. There is no agenda here

other than the one I outlined just now,' Kavanagh said, keeping his tone friendly as though they might have been two good friends rehearsing a familiar and long-running disagreement.

'Jack may be putting on all the down-home shit for you just now, but he won't move without my support and I'm not the only one in here who's against this.'

'Arnold, Trellis is a privately held company. There is no way we can mount any kind of hostile takeover bid. You and I know Jack owns virtually all the stock.'

'You may not be hostile, yet, but this is a takeover bid as far as I'm concerned.'

'Then I'm sorry you feel that way.'

'I guess Jack's told you his Alex Cameron story, how he feels indebted to him because of what happened that summer day in 'fifty-nine?'

Kavanagh sat upright and was about to speak when Long leaned forwards and brought his face closer. The geek Kavanagh had imagined earlier was both gone and there at the same time, a sort of hateful core revealing itself as though the skin on Long's face were about to roll back in one disgusting leer.

'I'm going to fucking stop this, Mike. There will be no takeover, no merger, no nothing. There are people with too much invested in this company to let it get away from them.'

The door clicked open and Kavanagh looked round. It was Burns and by the time Kavanagh had turned back to Long, he was already sitting casually on the chair as though nothing had happened, the sneer settling back down to normal and a shine returning to his eyes. Innocently, Long removed the handkerchief from his pocket and blew his nose.

'How are you two doing? Merging yet?' Burns asked with a laugh.

'We're doing fine, Jack,' Long said, keeping his eyes on Kavanagh the whole time.

Kavanagh did not speak.

Chapter 14

Lucy slipped out the front door of the house and walked down the road quickly, guilt making her certain a teacher would be driving past at that precise moment and would stop to ask her why she was not in school. Lucy had left her Aunt Karen's house at eight-thirty, declining the offer of a lift and going straight back to her own house, where she quickly changed out of her school clothes, which were not uniform as such, but bland nonetheless. The house felt cold, as though the lack of her and Dad's bodies over the previous days had deprived it of energy. She changed into a long skirt with a bold sunflower pattern which almost reached down to her three-stripe Adidas trainers, their blue felt a pleasing clash with the sunflowers' background. Over the top of her black T-shirt she wore a blue jeans-jacket with the cuffs turned back. The moment she changed, she felt more herself. And she could now wear all her jewellery, not the minimum permitted at school.

The bus arrived and she headed for the top deck, glad the back seat was empty and installing herself in it. From her tan leather case, no bigger than the size of a magazine, she retrieved oversized headphones bought from a catalogue shop. Lucy smoothed her hair where the wide band of the phones ruffled it, left the wire trailing from the bag and clicked on the tape, fiddling with the volume until the sounds of the bus became no more than a vibration. The home made compilation of Britpop began to jangle in her ear, a nasal voice whining over acoustic guitar. Also in the bag were spare batteries for the Walkman, an apple, pieces of makeup required for emergencies and one of her favourite Japanese comics, which she pulled out and began to read.

There were days still when she could not face school. It

was one of Kim's greatest uses, being able to get her to phone the school and explain Lucy's absences away, playing the counsellor card. Lucy even had Kim talk to Dad on her behalf and the occasional absenteeism went mostly unremarked between them. She wondered how long such goodwill would last. With Dad and Kim, most likely forever, but at school it was becoming harder. Even if no one said it, Lucy could feel the questions, the comments. Her mother's been dead for three years. Isn't it about time she got over it? Other people have problems too.

Her lips moved silently and an observer would have seen just another teenage girl on a bus, noiselessly lip-syncing to headphones that were annoyingly loud, except in Lucy's case, the movements had nothing to do with the lyrics of the song.

Lucy stared down at the page which had been open for several minutes, ignored by her as she tried to plan the day. It was as though all the ink had drained out of the paper, the lines that made the words and pictures all dissolved. All that remained on the blank tablet were nine words written in a swirling script that appeared to be moving, as though the letters were arteries with blood flowing through them. Lucy gazed down, her eyes locked onto the gently writhing veins of the words. When she actually got past the movement, the odd geometry of the writing, and read the words, it seemed as though the voice in her head was not her own.

It goes on forever, but you can see it.

The words could have come out of the earpieces pressed to the sides of her head. Where had the music gone? Sometimes she could read and become so engrossed that the music she listened to would disappear, but it always came back the moment she thought about it, the hypnotic state quickly broken and impossible to get back to consciously. Lucy could hear no music, although the slightly nauseous trance was the same. All that remained was painful silence, throwing her off-balance even as she sat. Into the chasm the words repeated themselves, an echo behind them like a thousand other voices.

It goes on forever, but you can see it.

Before her eyes, the words on the page unfurled like worms and grew into each other, forming a mass that was like a pile of rope.

The knotwork goes on forever, but you can see it.

Lucy struggled to make her own voice be heard inside her head, shouting the thought.

'It doesn't really go on forever,' she thought. 'It's arbitrary. Only a joined-up line.'

I agree. If you think of it as a line that only goes in one direction. When did we start doing that? Thinking of things as a line? Don't you find the pattern of infinity comforting?

Sitting at the back of the top deck of a bus, hiding from school and the world, Lucy felt very small. The pulsing knot on the page in front of her was no bigger than a fist, yet she understood that it was vast, completely beyond anything she could ever comprehend. Lucy felt afraid, knowing that to understand the words in her head and to embrace the infinity of the knot would be to die. The notion of infinity stabbed at her, making her feel terribly mortal, and she could feel sick welling up in her throat. Looking at the page, she knew she was being given a glimpse of eternity and it was frightening. On the headphones, voices were speaking in the distance, getting louder by fractions as though approaching her. Even before she could hear them properly, Lucy knew what they would be saying and her lips began to move in time with them.

What are you going to do?

Something very special and very nice.

What is it?

Do you trust me?

I don't know. Will it hurt?

Am I hurting you now?

No.

Or now?

Ah! No, I like that.

Lucy put her hand to her chest, fingering the chain around her neck and feeling the palpitation of her heart, irregular and rapid the way it was when she drank adult amounts of coffee. It was happening in her head, the way it always did, except she felt closer to it than usual, almost as if she were a part of it. On the page, the knot was spinning so fast it made her eyes ache, every tributary alight with golden fire that raced round.

So you trust me then?

Yes.

Take off the rest of your clothes then.

A hand touched her shoulder.

Lucy shouted out. The voices snapped off and music flooded back in.

It was the bus driver, smiling because he had scared her.

'We're here,' she saw his mouth say.

Lucy just stared at him. There was no one else on the bus. She looked out of the window and saw they were at Piccadilly Circus. How long had she been sitting there?

'Are you all right?' the driver's mouth formed.

Lucy stood and pushed past him, clunking down the stairs on weak legs, pulling the headphones off and noticing how sweaty the cushioned black plastic was.

A day of truancy always began as an adventure that was normally over in half an hour as the rest of the day yawned in front of her, six or seven whole hours to fill. Going to Pendulum to see Tom would be too risky in case he mentioned it to Dad when he got back from America. And there was Tom's son. Creepy.

The pavement near Eros and past the Criterion theatre seemed too wide and she felt vulnerable on it, hurrying across and into the Trocadero. She hurried through and boarded an escalator, heading for the noisy anonymity of the arcade.

The words she had heard on her headphones, dialogue from a scene she struggled to recall, went back to their hiding place in her head, leaving their mark only on her lips, enough to create an annoying whisper that could never be caught in speech. Lucy felt tender, her stomach trembling as though upset. She wondered whether going into the arcade had been such a good idea.

It was bright and noisy. Noisier than it should have been since it was almost empty. Glass was made hot by electric light, all the plastic surfaces greasy with the fingerprints of past customers. Most of the machines were electronic but there were a few games where real balls were thrown into hoops, darts into playing cards. Money fell into metal with captivating loudness somewhere off to her right and then two voices cheered each other. The noise of the place gave her an instant headache.

Lucy walked round the rink of unused dodgems to the row of games machines lined against a back wall, the light they gave off the only illumination in the dark corner. On his own, moving energetically, was a boy playing a video game. She wondered what it would be like to be able to fill the day with someone else. What was he doing in the arcade at this time of the day? He wasn't a tourist. Even from behind she could tell he was London.

She scanned his attire approvingly. Nike boots – Air Mada. The sky-blue Umbro top had lines of silk running through it and the dark navy shellsuit bottoms lay on his boot-tops, gathered pleasingly at the ankle. A baseball cap topped it off, hair cut close to the back of his head. On top of the machine was a half-drunk bottle of Lucozade. He reminded her of some of the boys from school, the ones who wore the West Ham shirt on match days and played football at lunchtime.

Lucy stood and watched his arms move as his fingers tapped wildly on the buttons of a video game called The Palace. His elbows stuck out at the side and she noticed how broad his shoulders were and the way his hips narrowed nicely to his small behind.

She went and stood behind him, by his right shoulder. He didn't notice her at first, but then glanced quickly to his side as though afraid to lose his concentration. She could not tell if he had acknowledged her as he went back to the game and she eased herself near enough to see his reflection in the sloping glass of the machine. As she stood directly next to him, a computer-generated woman leaned out of the window of a high stone tower, boggle-eyed and arms waving, an evil ogre smiling in the background as it pawed her. A handsome blond prince was scaling the tower, dragons nipping at his feet. It was so corny, Lucy had to smile.

'Fuck,' the boy said as a spike came from the wall of the tower, ran the prince through and left him wriggling like a worm for a few seconds before retracting and letting him fall to the open jaws of the dragons below. A few seconds of muted red butchery and devourment followed.

The words GAME OVER flashed.

'Are you waiting to play this?' he asked, straightening and half turning to her.

'No,' she said.

Lucy absorbed as much of him as she could in the quick glance. He was tall without being especially solid, occupying the sort of tenuous place in the world where girls would want to protect him, boys to pick fights. Something about him suggested he had been caught in the middle of some mischievousness, violet eyes moving about innocently and mouth tightly closed, not about to give anything away. She rapidly processed all of the surmized information and generated a feeling towards him, trying to forge a connection to him just by her will. Lucy wanted to make this slightly older boy something to do with her.

Nonchalantly he turned and walked away. Lucy watched his shoulder-blades roll against the back of his shirt, the hard points of bone sticking through the shiny material. What would it be like to be with a boy? Any boy. This boy. Would he put his arms round her and pull her tight? What would he smell like? What would they talk about? What would the hairs on his arms feel like when she ran her hands over them? What would he be like without clothes on? Would he be shy, aggressive, both? The further away he got, the faster the questions came and she went into a panic. She grabbed the bottle off the top of the machine and chased him.

'You forgot your Lucozade,' she said, pulling up next to him.

He stopped and looked at her. 'Thanks,' he said, taking it and getting ready to go on his way again.

'My name's Lucy,' she blurted.

The knot tightened.

'I'm Nathan. Nathan Lucas,' he said.

Chapter 15

Nancy stood on the edges of a flotilla of people all competently socializing. She felt lost, wondering quite how she had made the journey from shabby North London eccentricity to this. At Lee Mitchell's increasingly whining insistence, she had agreed to accompany him to a party at the house of Alan Vishtar, the head of Conical. A talking-to from Julia that had verged on the testy was what finally convinced Nancy it might be in the general interest, even if not her own, to attend the party.

'It's about raising money by showing them what's on offer,' Julia's voice had issued across the mobile airwaves, its whistle sharpening further the already evident edge in her agent's voice.

'You mean me? I'm what's on offer?'

'Well welcome to Hollywood.'

The house of Alan Vishtar was more like a small art gallery or museum, the cool stucco of the walls pulling the strategically positioned lighting into itself so all the rooms shimmered as if they might have been filled with water. Art that was too grotesque to be fake and furniture too designed to be comfortable was dotted apologetically about the diamond-hard floor that Nancy was certain she would slip on at any second. She would not have expected to develop a sudden yearning to be near Lee Mitchell, but she felt like grabbing hold of his arm and clinging on to him, the only person she knew.

'I don't recognize anyone,' Nancy said to him.

'It's not that kind of party, Nance. These are the suits, the money people. There are investors here who could bankroll a small movie if they wanted, provided you let their kid be involved in it, the one that just graduated in film from USC and has great ideas.'

'These people don't look rich to me,' Nancy said, keeping her voice low.

'That's because they are.'

Nancy had managed to stay on the fringes of the group since their arrival ten minutes earlier, but she could tell that already Lee was anxious to work the room. That gave her the choice of staying alone on the borders or going with him. The high ceiling and the tall windows giving on to a pool bounced chatter off themselves. In the background, a melody not quite Muzak twinkled. There must have been thirty people in the room, casually draped in various layers of easy-breathing fabric, sipping Chardonnay and grabbing one-bite canapés from trays that circulated atop the arms of pretty young men. Woven between them were men in suits, more staid and stiff, but still California-cool enough not to look too businesslike. Nancy tried to tell herself it was no different from some of the parties she had attended in her advertising days, but her socializing skills still remorselessly eluded her.

'There are people here you have to meet,' Lee said, taking her arm and leading her into the fray. 'Just give them top line, okay?'

'Sorry?' she asked, stepping after him.

'Ivan, this is Nancy Lloyd. She wrote the script, *Stolen Hearts*, I mentioned to you. Nancy's in from London.'

Lee had been telling people? About a script? A finished script?

'Hi. What's your movie about?' the man asked in between chewing on what looked like mutant peanuts.

'Well. It's about . . . actually, it's hard to explain,' Nancy said.

'Bullshit!' Lee laughed. 'She kills me with all this English fucking modesty. It's about a woman professional thief who falls for one of the guys she robs. Got a twist that'll kill you.'

'I like the sound of it,' Ivan said, as though it might have been his own idea.

'We're thinking Michelle Pfeiffer or maybe Geena Davis. Matthew Modine or Jeff Bridges for the guy.'

'They're interested?' Ivan asked.

'Hey, this is a hot script.'

Nancy stood and watched two men bat an idea back and forth like a tennis rally, an idea for something that had once, in some way, belonged to her. If she stayed in Los Angeles much longer, she might not even have to write the script. As she watched Lee throw his head back and laugh through his beard, she tried to imagine how he would react if he found out what she were really working on and how little time she had left to do it. The moment of satisfaction, the feeling of superiority over him, quickly dwindled as it dawned on her that he wouldn't miss a beat. He would assimilate it in a stride of over self-confidence. All he needed was a two-sentence idea and he'd be out there pushing it on anyone who'd listen. He might as well have had a briefcase full of encyclopedias.

'You need to pitch yourself better than that, Nance,' he said when they were alone. 'I cut you some slack when we met last week because I could see something in you.' He touched her bare shoulder in a way that made her want to slap his hand away.

'Lee, you might not understand this,' she said, keeping her voice controlled, 'but back in London, things are different for me. I don't have to go through this, jump through hoops for people. Part of the reason I began writing was so I wouldn't have to do that.'

'That's books, Nance,' he said, scolding and scathing. 'Hey, there's – what – ten planes a day back to England. Either catch one or do what we're here to do, Nance.'

'Could you call me Nancy, please, Lee?'

'Sure. Hey, George, this is Nancy Lloyd. Nance is in from London and she's got a hell of a script. We've got people offering money just to read coverage.' Lee foisted her towards someone else.

By the seventh or eighth old man, their names all melding into one, Nancy was reciting the pitch and emulating all of Lee's enthusiasm for it. For a while, midway through all the grip and grin, Nancy knew she no longer cared if what she said were true and she knew these old men didn't. At the end, strangely, she actually found she did believe it. It was almost possible to imagine that back at the apartment, neatly typed and bound, was the finished script. Like a freed defendant who had got away with murder, the more she protested her innocence, the more she believed it.

'Lee, I need a break and I need the bathroom,' she said, her voice hoarse.

'Sure. I'll catch up with you.'

Nancy spent longer than she needed in the bathroom, leaning against the sink and looking at herself, breathing as heavily as if she'd just exercised. Always the same, she thought, putting herself through something when she didn't even have to. She needed another drink.

Back out there, turning from the bar, Nancy almost bumped into someone who did not look film industry. Judging by the suit, he was finance. Another rich man, just younger.

'Sorry,' Nancy mumbled, avoiding eye contact.

'That's okay. My fault for charging at the bar.'

The English accent made her look up.

'Mike Kavanagh,' he said, his hand held out.

'Nancy Lloyd,' she said, matching his firm grip for a second.

'Another stranger in a strange land,' he said. 'Unless you're a part of all this?'

'Not really. You're not, then?'

'No.'

'Thank Christ for that,' Nancy said conspiratorially. 'Someone I don't have to try and sell my script to.'

'So you are a part of the show?'

'It's more like a dog show.'

'So. You write?' he asked.

'I wrote a book, a while ago. Now I'm working on a script. If you listen to the people here, the movie's already a success. How do you come to be at a party like this?' Cringing as she realized it sounded like an all-the-gin-joints-in-all-the-towns kind of line.

They were blocking the area in front of the bar. He reached out and took a glass of wine and moved off to one side. Nancy went with him, only half consciously following the flow of his movement with her own. The slightly bemused look he wore, the amused glint in his eyes at the absurdity of it all, attracted her. Nancy was standing perhaps only two or three inches closer to him than she should have been, but it felt exciting, an interesting zone to be in. She flicked her hair and smoothed it across the left side of her head, taking a swallow of wine but barely tasting it through the sudden aluminium flavour nerves had deposited in her mouth.

'I'm out here on business,' he said, looking right at her. 'The guy I'm visiting was invited to this party and he asked me if I wanted to come along. It seemed impolite to refuse, and I was intrigued.'

Nancy could almost sense he wanted to append the words 'Now I'm glad I did' to the end of the sentence.

'What's his name,' she asked.

'Jack Burns.'

'I don't think I've met him yet.'

'He's over there,' he said, motioning with his wine glass. 'The one with the bald head.'

'I'd be too frightened to speak to him,' Nancy said.

'He's a charmer, really. Tell me about your script.'

'Please. Don't ask me about that. What do you do?' she asked.

'I'm in finance,' he said, as though apologizing. 'People normally walk off and leave me at this point.'

'You're a stockbroker or something?'

'No. I work for a company that finances assets for businesses. We lend them money but find clever ways of making it cheaper by playing about with tax and anything else we can legally massage.'

'But your company isn't about to go into Hollywood?'

'We're trying to expand our business over here and we're looking for a partner to help us. His company is the one we want to be our partner.'

He seemed distant, almost agitated to be talking about it. She decided to change tack.

'Have you been here before?'

He nodded and smiled. 'When I was in my second year at university, we did a tour of the West Coast. We'd done the Eurorail thing the previous summer and by that time we were getting more ambitious.' He paused and seemed to sense she was waiting. 'My wife and I. Well, girlfriend. We weren't married then.'

'Is she out here with you?' Nancy ventured.

'No. She died three years ago,' he said.

'I'm sorry,' she said, hating herself for the way she was feeling.

'Can I get you another one of those?' he asked, nodding down at the empty wine glass.

'Please,' she said, blinking slowly.

It's been so long, she thought as she watched him go. Nancy had met Colin, her most recent ex-lover, at a party. That time, from her first sight of Colin, she could tell he would be trouble and, she believed, that was why she had embarked on a relationship with him. This felt different. Come on, Nancy, she said to herself, you're dying. This is the last thing you need. She repeated the phrase again. The last thing you need. It might be the last thing you ever get. A sweaty, pornographic image flashed in her mind and she shifted her feet about on the hard floor.

Halfway across the room, and moving towards her, interrupted only by the occasional pause to grin and slap a shoulder, was Lee Mitchell. Kavanagh had turned from the bar and approached her with a full glass in each hand. Nancy flitted her eyes from one man to the other.

'Here you go,' he said, handing her the wine.

'I'm here with someone from the company that's hosting this. I really have to go and put my face around a bit to show willing,' she said.

'I understand,' he said.

There was a teenage moment between them and Nancy could feel words held back by both of them, blocked by anxious breath that stuck in their throats. Lee Mitchell was less than two yards away. Nancy breathed in to speak but Kavanagh beat her to it.

'I'm staying at the Biltmore. I leave Saturday but maybe we could meet before then, for dinner or something?' He handed her a business card deftly produced from the top pocket of his jacket.

'Nance, where've you been?' Lee asked, getting between the two of them and giving Kavanagh only a cursory nod.

'I'll call you,' Nancy said to Kavanagh, satisfied that even Lee had picked up on the ambience between the two of them.

'Alan wants to meet you,' Lee said, throwing a propriet-ary arm across her shoulder and leading her away.

As Lee guided her back into the throng once again, Nancy looked back over her shoulder at Kavanagh who was regarding them with the same wry expression he had been wearing when she had almost knocked him over.

The last thing I need.

Chapter 16

Ordinarily, Garth would have been extremely anxious to be sneaking off work on the pretext of a meeting. With Kavanagh in Los Angeles and everyone still preoccupied by the absence of Chris Carson, it was easy to go unnoticed. All Garth had said was that he had a meeting, from a cold call, no less.

It was nine-fifteen in the morning and Garth had decided to get off at Tottenham Court Road and walk the rest of the way to his destination, mostly to calm the nerves he felt. It was going to be a testing morning. He had felt that as soon as he opened his eyes, but he was also coming to understand that for The Book, it was not always enough to *do*. There were times when he would have to be done by.

'All right, darling!' a voice shouted from a strange angle, breaking his concentration and making him feel irritable.

Garth looked up at the scaffold around a building that used to be a bar and would probably be a bar again when it was finished and saw two workmen baying over the edge. One had long, badly cut hair that was yellowy brown and the other, older one had short black hair. He had arms like Popeye, manual-work muscular as well as manual-work stupid. Even from this distance the two smelled like old digestive biscuits and dog shit mixed together, he thought. Looking back down in front of him, Garth saw the focus of their attentions, a young girl not much more than fourteen and wearing a creamy pair of riding jodhpurs.

'Fancy a ride?' the black-haired one shouted at her.

Her backside did look very nice, held pertly by the fabric which gave off the faintest whiff of a damp crevice. The brown leather riding boots created a nice image of a thin riding crop that would whistle piercingly through the air and make a pleasing crack against the soft fabric and the virginal nates beneath. No. She was far too young, Garth thought with sudden indignation. How could they be like that to such a sweet young girl? Christ, he hated sexist bastards like that. She was just a girl.

Garth looked for a sign on the scaffold that would indicate the name of the company so he could write and complain about their behaviour. He found it just as the man with the black hair started to make neighing sounds like a horse. Garth had a better idea.

He took out his phone and dialled the mobile number on the sign. A phone trilled and the men went abruptly silent.

'Hello,' the voice of the black-haired man said.

'I really like your bollocks, darling,' Garth said.

'Do what?'

'Your bollocks. And your cock. It looks so big in those tracksuit bottoms. I'd love to suck you dry.'

'Who the fuck is this?' the workman said, getting angry.

'Would you like to blow your load in me?' Garth purred breathily.

'Steve? Is that you? Is this a fucking wind-up?'

'Steve? Is that your bloke's name? Does he fuck you up the arse or do you ride him like a horse?' Garth asked.

'You sick cunt,' the man said.

'Why don't you come and show me what a man you can be? I'm only down here.'

The man's head appeared over the side of the metal tubing and Garth waved jauntily, blowing a kiss at the same time.

'I'm coming down there and I'm gonna give you a fucking slap, you cunt,' the man said into the phone, loud enough for Garth to hear it forty feet below.

The Book spoke.

Why don't you jump off? It's quicker.

Garth had already rounded the corner before the man hit the ground, his scream muffling the dull thud his body made on the pavement.

By the time he arrived in Soho, Garth was whistling a tune to himself. Without having to look at a map, guided by

The Book, he found the doorway sandwiched between a taxi shop and a coffee bar. He pressed the bell once and was buzzed in without even being checked.

'You must be Garth,' said the man who waited at the top of the narrow staircase.

'Yes. Hello,' he said, shaking hands with the man and noting the pleasing strength of his grip.

'I don't usually see people this early,' the man said, closing the door of the flat.

'Your advert says twenty-four hours,' Garth said, looking around.

'Yeah. It does.'

The man was not unlike the one who had been shouting from the scaffold, his body rough-hewn and his face long in need of a shave. He could have been Garth's age or perhaps older. He was the sort of man Garth would be able to forget in an instant.

'It's through here,' the man said.

'Separate from the bedroom?' Garth asked.

'Yes.'

The man opened the door into a windowless room, its black walls and floor illuminated only by a dim red light bulb. Music pulsed from a portable tape recorder. The room smelled of Germolene.

'I need to get ready. Make yourself comfortable,' the man said.

Alone in the room, Garth undressed, looking at the things that lay around. Under the antiseptic was the smell of life, human smells mixed with leather and rubber, bound up with sweat. The odours echoed with cries of pleasure and pain.

The man returned wearing a leather harness held together by metal rings. He helped Garth get his wrists and ankles into the sling that draped from the ceiling. While Garth hung from the leather, hands and feet above him and his rear end drooping low, the man disappeared behind him and there was the sound of rubber being stretched, other noises he could not identify.

When he reappeared in front of him, the man wore an executioner's mask and a long rubber gauntlet that reached to his shoulder and gleamed with unguent.

'You just tell me when you want me to stop,' the man said.

'Don't worry. I won't be making any noise,' Garth said.

Chapter 17

There was, perhaps, one person in the world who could make Kavanagh feel nervous about a date and at that moment she was on the other side of it, asleep, he hoped. It was convenient to be so far away from his daughter as he contemplated the first real date since his wife's death. Helen, of course, was the only other person who had made him unsettled and he remembered vividly the cramped feeling in his tongue and the hotness on his cheeks when he had first asked her out. Kavanagh tried to measure that against the prospect of Nancy Lloyd, to see if he felt any butterflies about meeting her. If he did, they were minor in comparison to the jangling he had felt when he had called Lucy and not mentioned Nancy Lloyd.

Kavanagh picked up the phone on the bedside table and entered the long sequence of numbers that would take him home. He waited to be connected, across the satellite, through land lines and into the door of Pendulum in London, bypassing the switchboard and going directly into the private, secure line on Paul Baran's desk, a number less than ten people knew. From there, it was routed on to a number even Kavanagh did not know.

'Hello,' said Paul Baran, no hint of surprise at contact on the hotline. Baran never seemed to be caught in the middle of anything else, lifting the receiver promptly and speaking in a relaxed tone as though expecting the call.

'Paul, it's Mike.' He checked his watch. It was almost midnight in London. 'I tried to reach you yesterday. Sorry to disturb you so late.'

'No problem. I had to fly to Brussels middle of yesterday to talk to the Fortex consortium. The buying programme decision has moved into the European HQ, so there were new faces to see. It's under control,' Baran said.

'Did Chris Carson turn up yet?'

'No. His girlfriend called while I was away yesterday. I think she's ready to report him missing and I think she's right to. Do you know if they live together?'

'I don't think so.' Kavanagh was starting to worry about Carson too.

'How are things going over there?' Baran asked.

'I can't tell if my presence is extremely important or a complete waste of time.'

'How so?' Baran asked.

'First impressions are that Trellis is a homely, slightly wacky West Coast company, but I've met a few people at the account level and they're all well into their clients. They churn the base nicely on existing accounts and the business development team is very savvy. I just can't work out if Burns is serious about a merger or if he really believes we are.'

'Burns is the key. He's the one who needs to be onside,'

'I'm not so sure, Paul. Arnold Long, the CFO, is doing all this gladiatorial bullshit at the moment. I haven't risen to it yet. Until I get a feel for the relationship between Long and Burns, I'm staying on the fence. Long is being privately antagonistic to me and even though his holding is minuscule, if he's got some kind of sway over Burns, we could have a problem.'

'What have you floated past Burns? Does he have an expectation concerning the outcome of this trip?' Baran asked.

'I've laid it out that once I've done this preliminary fact-finding, I'll go away and rough up an outline proposal, nothing heavy or legal at this point, because I know he'll go cold on that. The proposal would then form the basis of a second meeting, most likely with me out here again. After that, I think you should meet with him, perhaps bring him over to London. Only then should we start the clocks running with the lawyers.'

'How hands-on is Burns likely to be at that stage?'

'Once we're rolling, I don't think he'll want to be. The

key thing is to bring his comfort level up to the point where he's confident enough to let go. I need you to check something for me,' Kavanagh said.

'Go ahead,' Baran replied.

'It seems Burns met Alex Cameron back in the Fifties. Burns mentioned it once in passing and I was going to ask him again but then Long said something strange about Burns feeling indebted to Cameron, almost like it was undue. I don't want to press it with Burns again until I'm sure it's not a hot button.'

'I didn't know anything about that,' said Baran.

'Mathias must have and he should have fucking told us. I don't want to get out here and upset Burns without knowing it. Can you chase Mathias for me in case there's anything to watch for?'

'Sure. What are you going to do on your last night, Kav?'

Kavanagh looked at the shirt on the bed, the new, hundred-and-sixty-dollar Ralph Lauren shirt purchased on Rodeo Drive two hours before.

'Nothing. Eat off room service, watch a movie on cable and sleep.'

'You're always the sensible one, Mike. Call me Sunday.'

Kavanagh put down the phone. The three casual shirts he had brought with him had been enough to encourage his venture into Beverly Hills. The subtle fusion of yellow and green on the button-collar shirt would match elegantly with the lightweight navy chinos he had with him. His green linen jacket fell agreeably into the blend of colours, more pleasing in effect than he might have expected.

There were a still few hours to pass before meeting Nancy. Tomorrow morning, Jack Burns had insisted on driving him out to the airport, rendering the car Kavanagh had rented practically useless except for tonight's jaunt. He had already showered and was clad in a complimentary robe. From the 110-volt socket and across the bed trailed the power convertor lead for his PC. On the bed, the laptop sat with its hard disk in sleep mode, a document containing his preliminary observations frozen in blue and yellow LCD. Kavanagh hit a key and the disk spun back into life, coming out of its dormant state with a comforting whirr. Kavanagh began to type, quickly absorbed by the task in front of him and quietly confident of his ability to handle himself with Nancy Lloyd.

She looked stunning.

Even more so than when he had first spotted her at the party and followed her to the bar, getting in her way so she had to notice him. As he climbed off the bar stool and stood beside it, Kavanagh watched her cross the room, her dress pulled close to the contours of her body, hips rolling suggestively and calf muscles tensed by the lift of high heels. There was something about the creamy fabric of the dress that suggested warm skin beneath. It was the kind of dress that was close to nakedness, a tight-fitting burden from which the wearer ached to spring free. So much for handling myself, Kavanagh thought.

'Hello again,' Kavanagh said.

'Have you been waiting long?' she asked, shaking his hand.

'Only this long,' he said, holding up a glass of mineral water from which he'd taken two small sips.

'This place is nice,' she said, delicately placing herself on the stool next to him and ordering a gin and tonic from the waiting barman.

'I read about it in a magazine at the hotel, so I can't vouch for anything about it,' he said.

'At least it's not a Hollywood place. If I hear Spago or the Polo Lounge mentioned one more time, I'm going to snap at someone,' she smiled.

'How did the party finish up the other night? Did it go well?'

'Well,' she said, digging at ice with the plastic stick in her glass, 'apparently we have a lot of people interested in giving us money of some sort for our project. It's always a project, there's always interest, there just doesn't seem to be any money. I think I could stay out here forever and it might never happen. I've only been here two months and it feels like all my life.'

'What made you come out here in the first place?' Kavanagh asked, trying to get film questions in while she seemed willing to talk.

'That thing you just can't seem to get hold of, I suppose. Money. I think my ego was strongly involved as well. Writing a film seemed more glamorous, to have more fame potential than just writing a book.'

'Couldn't you just write a book that gets made into a film?' he asked.

'You're starting to sound like my agent. Was the party a success for you?'

'I think it was mostly babysitting my host, which is odd because you'd expect him to do that for me. It's been that kind of trip, but this is only the first one.'

'Do you travel much in your job?' she asked.

'In Europe, mostly. This is a new venture for us.'

When their table was ready, they were led over to it and Kavanagh followed Nancy, the chivalry allowing his eyes to wander up and down her spine, switching between bare skin and fabric, and only occasionally sneaking a look at her behind. The way you used to with Helen, he said to himself. Apart from tonight, there had been only two other situations with women which might have qualified as dates and now, as then, he gave himself the same pep talk to try and beat down the feelings of guilt. Mike, it went, if it was you who had died and not Helen, what would you have wanted her to do? Give up her life and mourn forever? For a year, maybe? But then what? She'd need to get on with things, find someone else. It's a cliché, Mike, but she'd want you to do this, wouldn't she? After three years? It was a long string of questions, the answer to all of which was meant to be, it's okay to look for someone else.

They giggled over menus and eventually ordered, Kavanagh glad the atmosphere was so relaxed and easy. The light from a candle lifted the shadows of her cheekbones and shone in the green of her eyes. She did remind him of Helen, a little, but, as Helen had been, she was too much her own person to be a substitute.

'Do you write full-time?' he asked.

'I do now. I gave up the day job nearly two years ago. It was so nice to give up my job and then the first month I paid the rent with some money from my writing, it felt great.'

'Did you play a big scene at work, wreaking your revenge on everyone who'd ever upset you?' he asked, smiling.

'I worked in advertising, so it would have been easy, but I didn't. I just wanted to fade away with embarrassment at the thought of my book coming out.'

'Because people you worked with were in it?'

'Not at all. When people found out I was doing a book and that it was going to be published, they sidled up to me and asked in a really coy way if they were in it, pretending they were upset they might be, but also secretly flattered at the idea. I used to say one of the reasons I started to write was because real life was so disappointing, so why on earth would I put them in a book? That was never a popular approach.'

'But they weren't actually in it?'

'Not really. I've got two mercifully unpublished manuscripts in a box in London with all my friends and colleagues in them as characters. By the time I was published, I was over that. It was more about inventing something than reporting it.'

'Do you still have a house in London?' he asked.

'I hope so. I have a place in Islington which is rented. At this moment, for all I know, or care, it's being ransacked by my ex-boyfriend. He has keys,' she said.

Kavanagh was fazed by the mention of a boyfriend, even an ex.

'He didn't want to come out here?' he asked.

'He was the reason I came, really. Forget the money. I just wanted to get away from him before I killed him in his sleep. I'm sorry, I don't want to heavy this up.'

'That's okay,' he said, as appetizers arrived in all their translucent and parmesan-dusted glory.

'Colin, my ex, has a PhD in Medieval Literature and works in a secondhand bookshop. Don't get me started on him, please. He's a fucking nightmare. How did your wife die?' she asked, more gently.

Kavanagh looked down at the table.

'You don't have to tell me,' she said.

Kavanagh took a breath. 'She was murdered. An intruder got into the house, ransacked it and killed Helen. It was nearly three years ago. It got on the news for a day and then it was gone.'

'Oh my god,' Nancy said.

'My, our, daughter Lucy was thirteen at the time and she came home from school and found Helen. It was gruesome, really bad,' he said, deciding he might as well let her have it all in one go.

'It was a robbery, then?' she asked.

If it was, he didn't find it, Kavanagh thought.

'Yes. Helen and I married in our final year at university. She was pregnant with Lucy during her finals and I went on to do an MBA sponsored by the company I'm still working for. Helen was the really clever one, the one who could have gone on and done more than I did. I joined Pendulum, we moved into a company house and Lucy was born. I was at college, getting drunk on the weekends, then I looked up and Lucy was ten and I was in corporate finance, just like that.'

'A company house? Not bad,' Nancy said.

'Pendulum is owned by a large family trust that has an extensive property portfolio. Our house is just one of hundreds they own,' he said.

Kavanagh could see the question on her mind, so he decided to answer it for her.

'We stayed in the house, Lucy and I, even after Helen was killed. It was the only home Helen and I knew, and Lucy, and we saw no reason to leave it because somebody came into it and did something bad,' he said, perhaps a little too stridently.

'I'd find that hard,' she said.

'Sometimes it is.'

'How did your daughter, Lucy, cope?' she asked, frowning at him as though trying to feel his answers.

'At first, it was shock. A few months after the murder she had bad dreams, some turns. I was all for us moving out at that point, but it passed as quickly as it came. Three years is still not long and she has rough times, but she's a fighter like Helen was.'

'What did your wife do?'

'She ran her own jewellery design business, selling freelance to some of the big chains. She could do it all, from start to finish, right down to making earrings and things like that for her and Lucy. There were two years in a row where she made more money than me,' he said.

'Did you find it difficult to carry on working, afterwards?' she asked.

'Yes and no. I threw myself into it, just like you'd expect, but it lost any sense of meaning. It's ironic. I never worked so hard before the point of doing it went away.' He paused. 'If I can pull the deal off I'm over here to do, I'll make enough money to do something else. It's not that different from what you're trying to do.'

Main courses arrived and they fell silent, concentrating on the plates in front of them. Kavanagh was glad of the chance to take a breather, worried that he'd put a downer on the evening by being so frank about Helen. He hated the idea of coming across as self-pitying, because he believed he wasn't. Angry, yes.

'Can I let you in on a secret?' Nancy said.

Kavanagh was taking a drink as she said it and he raised his eyes as he swallowed and pulled his head back. 'If you want to. I can't think who I'd tell.'

Nancy put her fork down.

'I came out here because I thought I had an agent interested in a script I'd written only to find she wanted me to do something else. I produced a treatment, which is like an outline, of that something else and it looks like we're going full speed ahead.'

'Sounds good so far,' Kavanagh said.

'Trouble is, I haven't written a damn thing since then. I hadn't written anything after the first script and then the treatment came out of nowhere and I dried up again. I have serious, grade-A, deep-seated writer's block,' Nancy said, tapping the side of her head. 'And you are the only person I've told. I'm an impostor and I'm waiting for them to find out and send me home.'

'What stops you writing?'

She shrugged. 'If I knew, I'd fix it. It was getting so difficult in London, with Colin and a lot of other stuff, that coming out here seemed like a chance to leave it all behind. Like you say, not so different from you. It doesn't really worry me from the point of view of all the vultures out here. It's more about me. I'm happiest when I'm writing and when I dry up, I know it's because there's something on my mind. I can always go back to advertising copywriting. Maybe we should both just go missing.'

'Maybe. Pendulum would find me even if Lucy didn't.'

They both smiled.

The evening dwindled through dessert and into coffee, the atmosphere not as laden as it had been, Kavanagh glad to have started by setting things straight. It was the first time he had done that and he knew why he had done it. He could see himself spending time with this woman and there was no part of him that wanted to play games or hide things from her.

Outside the restaurant, they both lingered, each avoiding handing their tickets to the valets. Kavanagh was conscious of being watched, could see in the generous, smiling eyes of the boys who parked the cars that they sensed it was a first date. Traffic gushed past. Hot wind blew around them and Kavanagh moved himself closer to her, getting himself obviously into her space. All of the niggling feelings lifted themselves and then left him as he went for the moment, taking her hand and pulling her towards him.

Their mouths made contact and his hands rested on her hips, hers on his shoulders. Kavanagh worked his mouth lightly, tasting her lipstick and feeling the warmth of her tongue flicking at his. He put one arm around the small of her back and pulled her tightly, getting his body onto hers.

Abruptly he felt her tense, the stiffness beginning in her shoulders and ending up as a rigidity through the whole of her spine.

'What's wrong?' he asked, moving his head back from hers.

'Nothing,' she said quietly. 'It's just . . .' Her voice trailed off into the breeze.

'I'm sorry. I thought it was okay,' he said.

'It is, really,' she said, pecking him on the cheek. 'I had a nice evening, I really did.'

Their arms fell gradually to their sides and the contact was broken. She handed her ticket to a valet and turned to him.

Kavanagh looked at her for a second before he spoke and when he did, his voice felt small in the noise of the traffic. 'Will you call me when I get back to London? My home number is on the card I gave you. Do you have it?'

She nodded. 'I will.'

'I'm pretty sure I'm going to be out here again in a couple of weeks' time. We could meet up.'

'I'd like that,' she said.

Her car pulled up and the valet jumped smartly out, holding the door open for her.

'Good night,' he said.

'Good night,' she repeated, kissing him once more on the lips, the briefest brush.

Kavanagh watched her cross the pavement and he stood where he was for a full minute as the rear lights of her car got smaller and smaller. He turned and handed his ticket to one of the boys, who smiled sympathetically at him.

Chapter 18

Lucy entered the house in the same quiet manner the killer had, not quite three years earlier. She slipped the key into the lock, the grooves and teeth all fitting together with a pleasing solidity. The barrels turned smoothly and the hinges of the door swung with well-oiled ease, opening the house to her. Keeping the button on the lock twisted back as she stood in the hall, Lucy brought the heavy door to rest on its frame and eased the metal shaft back into its chamber. Executing a routine with such slow precision imbued the actions with new meaning. She rarely crept though her own house, certainly never when it was empty, and the experience was unsettling.

In her grandmother's house, clocks had ticked and chimed on varying fractions of the hour. In her own house, only the fridge or sometimes the central heating in the middle of a winter day would click into life intermittently and scare her. Even when she felt perfectly relaxed, Lucy could still be given a frightening jolt by the telephone or the doorbell. Until such surprises came, she did not appreciate how much tension she had been trying to smother. Nothing in her life had been that way, not until *that afternoon*. Even the Lady was silent in her movements through or appearance in different parts of the house. Where was the Lady now? Lucy wondered about where she went, if she had a continuous existence of her own or if she were real only at those moments when Lucy saw her. As if she were only in her head. Except for *that afternoon*.

Placing one tentative foot in front of the other, past her father's study, Lucy moved down the hall like a bullet travelling in slow motion, the way she knew the killer had. He had left trails of energy behind him like the white exhaust fumes of an aeroplane against a blue sky. The tracks were always there, sometimes strong and sometimes weak. On the second anniversary, the static they caused had been strong enough to lift stray hairs on her head, to give her a minor shock from the cold tap in the bathroom sink. The nearer Lucy got to the top of the house, the stronger the radiation of the footprints, buzzing invisibly through the calm air of the house, she the only one able to give it an earth.

Every stair leading to the top of the house, except for the last flight, was solid as stone, hard and noiseless. Would a creak, an old splinter of timber, have saved her mother as she sat in the attic room on top of the house, her steady hands fashioning raw metal into earrings? No. The killer had floated on light feet. Some of his excitement lingered near a tiny square picture, a framed rose, halfway up the stairs. The energy translated itself into a perfect feeling of anticipation for Lucy, but one that was lost on her, nothing for it to connect with. Lucy could not process the killer's excitement, her mind refusing to empathize and leaving her instead with a sense of sickness, as though she had overeaten. The feelings, however difficult, were all a necessary part of the experience and she understood that.

On the first landing, her heart began to pound. She paused and grasped at one of the killer's stray thoughts, trying to snatch it from the air, straining to hear through the locked door in her mind. He had gone straight to the attic room, with a clear sense of purpose. There had been no search for things to steal, no careful check to see if the house was empty. He had made directly for her mother.

In the hold of the unseen force, she ascended the final nine steps that led to where her mother would have been working. It was like standing too close to the roar of an open fire, the flames singeing the skin on one side of her face. The music her mother had been listening to filtered into her mind. Had she not heard him because of the music, would never have heard him because of it? Metal clinked against metal. The sound of a heavy tool being rested on her wooden table. The scuff of her chair on the carpet as she reached across for a bead from the fisherman's box containing thousands of them, all carefully arranged in the square compartments.

The world around her, the one beyond the walls of the house, might not have existed. It could have been any day, at any time. Even the day of the murder. There was nothing different about the moment in the physical sense, only that the world had continued to turn without her mother. For all Lucy knew, he could be in the house right now, following her, knowing she would be back because he had left the trail for her to follow, a powerful scent that sucked her into it.

Lucy brought her hand to rest on the door handle of her mother's workshop, seeing how much weight she could put on it before the spring would exert an opposing force. The gentle clicking of the handle as she pushed it downwards was like the joint in her right knee, the qualmish rub of bone rubbing bone, not enough gristle in between.

For nearly ten minutes, like the killer himself, Lucy stood in the open doorway of the work room, the overhead windows pushing a beam of light directly onto the bench. During the minutes, the power in the door frame grew stronger and gradually reshaped itself into something Lucy could neither avoid nor understand. She felt excited but in a way that was now underpinned by something darker and more specific. Methodically, she tried to cross-reference the feeling against experiences of her own, like a computer looking for a match. At school, there was a boy called Justin and, five weeks earlier, she had seen him in the park, lying on the grass in only a pair of grey jersey shorts. As her eyes had run over his profile, down his bare torso and quickly over the well-defined and obvious outline in the front of the shorts, the feeling had been similar to the one she was having now in the doorway. In some way, the killer had wanted, desired, her mother. Lucy mumbled quietly and incoherently to herself.

The noise came from the kitchen, just like it always did.

The Lady was trying to warn her mother, wanting her to look up and see what was waiting in the doorway for her.

Something very special and very nice.

As though there were a taut elastic cord attached to her back, Lucy was snapped away, pulled backwards through the slipstream of memory at the very moment she was about to encounter knowledge. All the stored passion and evil in the house rushed past her like wind and she was transported back to the front door of the house, as though she were stuck in an endless loop, forever denied the chance to find out what had gone on after her mother had looked up at the door.

In her mind, burnt into memory in a way that would never leave her, was one single certainty.

Her mother had known the killer.

Chapter 19

'Thanks for coming by. Sorry I wasn't able to see you earlier. Hell of a day,' Lee Mitchell said, holding the door of his office open for Nancy.

The outer office was empty, chairs pushed away from desks and left there, as though vacated gratefully. A tired pall hung over the scruffy surroundings, reminding Nancy of the morning after a party, the clearing up yet to be done.

'Julia said you might have some news for me, from the party the other night,' Nancy said.

'I have some Pinot Grigiot open. Let me get you a glass,' he said.

'I'm fine, thanks,' she said.

'Come on. It can't be too early. This is around the time you people eat in England, right?'

'Okay.' she sat in the chair facing his desk while he found her a glass. 'So, is there any news from the party?'

'I had a couple of meetings already this week. We can't look too hungry, so we wait for them to come to us. Most of the money in this town is tapped out. The guys with the cash get tired of watching it being poured away for them by kids like us.'

Lee poured a glass of wine and handed it to her. The green bottle had droplets of moisture on its side and as soon as her lips touched the glass, she could feel how icy-cold the liquid in it was.

'Is there any feedback, then, on *Stolen Hearts*?'

'Did you run into that guy again, the English one who was sniffing around you?'

Lee Mitchell was sitting on the edge of his desk, the wine glass hanging from his hand. His feet were close to Nancy's and she discreetly shuffled her shoes away from his before she spoke.

'No. He was like me, just a stranger in town pleased to meet someone from where he lives.'

'Did Julia talk to you?' he asked.

'About what?'

'I shouldn't tell you. Hell, maybe it's none of my business.'

'Tell me what?' she asked.

'I've known Julia a long time. She moves quickly and she moves on quickly. If you're one of her clients, it's up to you to keep up with her. That can take a lot of energy,' Lee said.

'And I don't have that energy?' Nancy asked.

'Julia and I go way back. We talk. That's not always good, okay? I'm telling you this because I like you and because I don't want to see you get fucked over.'

'What exactly did Julia say?'

He laughed. 'Julia's too smart to ever say anything direct. You have to put it together from what she says in ten or twenty different sentences. I just picked up a sense that she's losing patience with you.'

Nancy drank. Lee leaned over and topped up her glass, acting as though he might have been her only real friend in the world at that moment.

'The English guy was there with Jack Burns from Trellis, wasn't he?'

Nancy looked up at him, studying his pinprick pupils, wondering if they had been sharpened by something chemical, if that would explain the jumpy nature of their dialogue. It was the same edginess she had noticed in him at their first meeting but which had been absent at the party. Perhaps he was better when he was working a room.

'If Jack Burns was the bald man with the stare, then yes.'

'We could really use a run at a guy like that. No one's managed to get a cent of movie money out of him. He has no vanity. With the resources of someone like Burns, we could get your picture made.'

'I didn't think I even had an agent any more, still less a "your picture",' Nancy said, pointedly.

'Julia's not the only way to get your movie made,' he said, banging his leg against hers like a fellow plotter.

Nancy smiled, knowing how weak it would look from the slack feeling in her jaw.

'Maybe I should go back to England and write books, like you said I should.'

'Fuck. Don't listen to me.'

He paused. For a moment he looked away, his eyes seeming to focus on the pictures of himself on the wall. There was a low, comforting trill of a phone somewhere in the outer office, its placid tone cut short by an answering machine. Lee moved off the desk and sat with his back to it on the floor, elbows resting on his knees. Nancy had to look slightly down at him to meet his gaze which, even when it was on her, still seemed to be searching for a stable point somewhere far away.

'I was going to write once,' he said. 'I've even got a few finished scripts. I just had this other, bigger talent for talking people out of their money and into movies. The business goes round and round on itself forever. Nothing will ever be enough, even when the spiral is going up. How long ago was it we were saying there's never gonna be a twenty-million-per-picture actor and now there are, what, five at least?'

Lee shook his head, took off his glasses and rubbed his eyes. Replacing the silver frames on his face, he regarded her once again, now seeming to have found her. 'How much of the script have you really written?' he asked.

'It's all in here, really it is,' Nancy said, tapping the side of her head.

'It's no good in there, Nancy.'

'Stuff gets in the way of it coming out.'

'You just *so* don't want to be out here. It's too obvious. I'm surprised Julia doesn't see it like I do. Maybe she's losing it. You're not happy here, Nancy,' he said, knocking on the toe of her shoe as though it were a door. He reached his arm over his head and picked the bottle deftly off the desk. 'We should finish this. What stuff gets in the way?'

'Other stories. Ideas. Memories. Things that seem much more urgent and alive.'

'Tell it to me. Pitch it at me,' he said, his face resigned and tired.

'I'm working on a story about a woman with a brain tumour and a past, a nasty past. Bad things have happened to her.'

'What drives her on?'

'That time is going to run out on her. She's always known that, since she was a little girl. Since the first time . . .' Her voice trailed for a second. 'She never realized just how little sand was left in the top of the hourglass.'

'How does she beat the brain tumour?'

'She doesn't. She dies.'

'You should go finish your story. Clear your mind. Forget this picture, forget me, forget Julia. You don't belong here. What's that line? This place is bad.'

'I just can't face letting people down.'

'Go tomorrow morning and no one will remember you by lunch. I spent three months trying to attach River Phoenix to a project and the morning after he dies, six agents phoned or faxed me with details of clients who would be perfect for the project, ideal for the role, oh, and wasn't it all so terrible, and they'd settle for a point less than River would have got, a mark of respect.'

Nancy snorted, uncertain what to say.

Lee drained his glass. 'Shall we get a bite? Let's have a fuck-the-power-table-at-Morton's night and go to a Denny's or Roscoe's for waffles.'

'Well . . .' she hesitated.

'C'mon, Nancy. It'll be a blast.'

'I have my car outside.'

'No problem. I'll drive and we can pick it up later.'

He stood and put his glass to one side.

Nancy waited in the foyer as he went round shutting off lights and closing doors before he set the alarm. They rode in the lift down to the underground car park, Nancy wondering what Julia had really said to Lee Mitchell.

'Let me,' Lee Mitchell said, opening the door of the car after he had used the remote to unlock it. It was a long, dark-blue Mercedes with only two doors, each running almost the entire length of its body.

'Thanks,' she said.

'You'll need to put that seat back. I leave them forward when I'm parked in the sun. Habit.'

Nancy leaned over to lift the front passenger seat into an upright position.

Lee Mitchell's foot pressed into her behind and shoved her roughly forwards with its kicking motion. Nancy was hurled into the back of the car, hitting her head on the leather-covered seat post. She cried out, a mix of pain, surprise and fear.

'No one will fucking hear you,' she heard him say, his head close to hers.

The door clicked shut and locked. It seemed to change all the air that was in the car. There was no longer an outside, just the airless and tinted interior of the car. His leg was on her back and her face was pushed onto the upright of the seat, which smelled of polish.

'Lee!' she cried.

'Shut the fuck up. I told you, no one will hear you. Scream again and I'll cut your fucking tongue out.'

As soon as the knee was removed from between her shoulder-blades, she started to kick and struggle, spinning over onto her back and batting at him with her hands. He grabbed a wrist in each of his hands and pinned them down. Nancy wrenched one free and slapped him hard enough to make spit leave the side of his mouth. It hung there, drool on the end of his smile, and he slapped her back, the flattened palm stinging the soft flesh of her cheek. Holding both her hands down, he leaned over and made to kiss her. Nancy held her mouth closed, snorting frightened breath through her nose and swivelling her head from side to side.

There is more room in this car than there was in the other one.

A nauseating memory surfaced in her mind and radiated through her body in a wave of panic just as his open mouth closed over hers. It smothered her, foiling her attempts to open her own mouth and bite at him. Their lips were forced open and teeth banged against each other. His spit was hot, his breath fiery. He held her wrists a few inches down the arm, away from her hands which opened and closed into thin air, none of his flesh near enough to sink a nail into. She struggled against him and against her own fear, desperate to get out of the car, feeling as though she were suffocating inside it.

Don't fight it this time.

So, you trust me then?

Am I hurting you now?

Take off the rest of your clothes then.

'No!' she shouted when his mouth was gone.

Energy seized her and she sat up, but was quickly knocked back down with a hard punch, Lee Mitchell kneeling over her. The blow to her chest took the wind from her and she gasped, a burning sensation where her top ribs joined. Once again she was pinned to the long bench seat, her legs sprawled either side of him. His hand reached into her skirt and grabbed the front of her knickers. When he pulled, there was the sound of tearing fabric. Nancy cried out in pain as he took some of her pubic hair with the material.

'Don't fight me,' he said, pushing his fingers into her, fumbling to find the entrance to her. A fingertip probed roughly.

'Fuck you.'

Nancy sprang, throwing all the strength she had into getting herself upright, wanting her body to be higher than his within the enclosed space. The speed of her movements and the force behind them shocked Lee Mitchell as well as herself. While he was off-balance, leaning on one elbow, she pounced on him, throwing her weight at him so that he fell into the gap between the front and back seats at an ugly, awkward angle, one arm twisted under him.

'You bastard,' she spat.

Nancy pushed the bony point of her knee into the soft flesh of his side, applying her weight to his liver. When he began to wail, she calmly put her hands around his throat and began to squeeze, feeling the nub of his adam's apple under her thumb.

Lee Mitchell was unable to move and he began to gurgle, trying to force words past the obstruction she had put in their way. Nancy dug her fingers into his neck, wanting him to feel the hot, bloody sensation as her nails broke the surface while she continued to strangle him.

'I'm going to fucking kill you,' she sneered, her mouth next to his ear.

He flailed around, but it was no use. The position of his body made him like a tortoise on its back, disoriented and with no hope of regaining its balance.

The more noise he tried to make, the harder she closed the grip.

'No one will fucking hear you, remember?' she taunted.

There was a sudden vigour in his body and Nancy realized it was true panic on his part, a mixture of strength and stiffness as the real fear hit him, that he might be about to die.

'How does it feel? It's fucking scary, isn't it?'

The life-force began to ebb from Lee Mitchell's body, as though what little cowardly fight he had was gone already.

You're killing this man, she thought.

Nancy felt his life in her hands. She was poised, able to release her grip or to apply the final pressure which would finish him off. The muscles in her biceps ached and the bones of her fingers were fatigued. She drew a breath and readied herself for the last exertion.

She couldn't do it.

Nancy could not take the life of Lee Mitchell. With an exasperated sob, she released her grip and fell back onto the edge of the seat. She watched his body, trying to see if his chest was rising and falling. For a few moments she observed his motionless body, certain she had killed him anyway. She turned away from him and fumbled with the silver button that would unlock the door, reaching her hand over the top of the front seat. The door unlocked and Nancy found the lever on the seat, pushing it forward.

Lee Mitchell let out a roar as though all the life she had forced out of him had come back in one angry burst. Nancy screamed in a reflex reaction and grasped at the door handle. She was halfway out the car, her purse hurriedly scrabbled from the floor, when Lee Mitchell's hand clamped around her ankle. With one foot on the ground and her other leg stretched painfully out behind her, Nancy wriggled like bait on a hook, trying to break free of his grip. Unable even to see him, she kicked back with the foot he held, trying to connect to anything solid.

The hold grew stronger and she felt herself being pulled back inside the car. She held onto the door frame, letting her bag fall to the ground. Still he pulled her harder and she heard him struggling to move, repositioning himself. She craned her head round to see what he was doing and was scared by the hateful look on his face. She let go of the frame, swivelled round, and did something she never had before.

Nancy made a fist of her right hand and threw it into Lee Mitchell's face, driving it as hard as she could into his nose, immediately sickened by the crunching sound and the feel of something fixed suddenly becoming unhinged.

While he was still holding his face, bright red blood oozing from between his fingers, Nancy jumped from the car, picked up her bag and ran towards the exit ramp that led up to the street, the fading light ahead seeming brighter than anything she had ever seen. Her legs felt heavy and her ankles weak, as though sprained. Pain coursed through her limbs and she was limping slightly. Tears ran down her face.

The engine of the Mercedes fired into life and across the gloom came the beam of its headlights. Nancy sped up, almost at the ramp that would lead her to her car. Even when she heard the acceleration of the Mercedes, she could not look round, afraid to slow herself for even a second. The car was so near, she could feel the rumble of its engine.

'Nancy! Nancy! Wait!'

Lee Mitchell pulled the car alongside her and was calling out through the open passenger window.

'Nancy! Come on, Nancy.'

She did not look. His voice sounded scratchy, raw. Nancy kept running, struggling up the ruffled concrete of the ramp, one foot slipping on an oil patch. At the top, she was never so grateful to see the stupid rental car.

'Nancy.' It was an attempt to be more commanding.

Once on the kerb, separated from him by the row of head-in parked cars, she walked the final few yards to her own car, holding herself upright against the pain that tried to bend her.

'Fuck you,' Lee Mitchell called and sped away.

For a full twenty minutes Nancy sat with the doors of her car locked and cried, wanting nothing more than to be dead.

Chapter 20

'How would you feel about moving out, to a house of our own, when the deal happens?' Kavanagh asked.

'Are you going to give up work?' his daughter asked, keeping her eyes fixed on the chopping board rather than on him.

'I wouldn't have to work. If I wanted to, I could go as an independent consultant. I'd probably earn more than I do at Pendulum.'

Kavanagh watched as Lucy's swift hand reduced small ovals of garlic to granules, the knife moving down and across the white flesh. She was extremely proficient with a knife but it still scared Kavanagh to watch her.

'How much are you going to get for this deal, Dad?'

He had not told her how much, had never talked to her about money or how much he earned, and he wondered if she had a real sense of money's value.

'You're not to go flashing this about, telling your friends at school,' he warned.

'I wouldn't do that,' she said.

'Two and a half million pounds, give or take.'

It felt almost stupid saying the amount out loud but, for the first time since entering the kitchen fifteen minutes earlier, he had his daughter's full attention.

'God.' She shook her head and stared at him. 'That's a lot. What do you have to do for that, Dad?'

'Pull the deal together in America. Be the one who match-makes between the two parties.'

'And can you?'

'Of course.'

The sneer of Arnold Long and the high whine of his voice came back to Kavanagh, the same way they had when he said goodbye to Jack Burns at the airport in Los

Angeles. The day Baran had first floated the idea of a merger, when they had sat in his office in the middle of a frantic Monday morning, there had been a sense of unreality to the project. Now, after Los Angeles and meeting the Trellis people, the situation had become tangible, but at the same time there was the equally real prospect that it may fail. It was wrong to build up hopes, his own and Lucy's, but the time in America, away from the office, had demonstrated to him just how little he would miss Pendulum and the Trust.

'We'd be rich, then?' Lucy asked above the sizzle of the garlic as she threw it into a wide pan which had been heating olive oil as they spoke.

'As you're always pointing out, we were never poor. The money from Mum is in trust for you anyway, so you'll always have a good start, whatever happens.'

'Don't be morbid. So, the two and a half million is just for you? Shall I drop a crushed red chili into this?' she asked.

'I think there would be enough left for you after I've taken what I need to see me through to senility.'

'Yes or no for the chili?'

'Yes. When the deal happens and I have the money in the bank, we do need to think about what happens, where we go.'

'Can we stay here?'

'If I'm not working for Pendulum? I don't know. It's never occurred to me. Do you want to stay here?'

Lucy did not answer. Kavanagh saw the faintest of movements in her lower jaw. Of the two things he wanted to raise with her, he could not decide which to broach first. If he suggested the idea of Los Angeles as a holiday for the two of them and then told her about Nancy, he knew it would seem like he'd sweetened the pill in advance and Lucy did not like to be led on. However, telling her about Nancy might engender such a strong reaction that Los Angeles, together or alone, might be out of the question.

'I was going to put fennel and rosemary in this and some

small potato slices in the pasta water. Is that all right?' Lucy asked.

'Yes,' he replied, knowing she did not want to talk. He was due to go back to America in ten days and it would be best to tell her while he was fresh back, rather than looking like he had stewed on it. 'So, tell me what else you did while I was away,' he said.

'I already told you, Dad. Went to school, went home to Aunt Karen, who fussed over me. I saw Kim and we had a talk about exams and about the anniversary.'

'Luce. While I was in Los Angeles, I met someone.'

'Oh,' was all she said.

Kavanagh sighed. 'She's English. Her name's Nancy Lloyd and she's a writer.' He studied the side of Lucy's face, certain her eyes already looked glassy and hurt. How fragile was she inside, and should he have been telling her this?

'How old is she?' Lucy asked.

'A bit younger than me. Twenty-eight. I met her at a party I was taken to by the man who owns Trellis,' he said, really meaning, I didn't go looking, it found me.

'What's she doing out there? Does she live there?'

'She's out there trying to sell a film script. She's in the film business.'

The pan sizzled as if it was burning its contents. Lucy turned her back to him and began to scrape in an overwrought manner with a wooden spoon. Kavanagh watched her and hated himself for telling her and for being so excited about Nancy Lloyd. He walked up closer to her and rested his hand on her shoulder while she kept her gaze fixed on the spoon which she was jabbing into the over-browned garlic like a spade into earth.

'Luce, sooner or later, we both have to move on. You're just starting out and I have to start again. We both have to move on,' he repeated.

'I know. Me and Kim have talked about that. She said I have to be prepared for it because it's going to happen. I should rehearse the emotions, think about what it would be like for you to find someone else. Sooner or later. That's just what Kim said. It just feels soon, not late, do you know what I mean?'

Kavanagh was familiar with the therapeutic gloss his daughter's speech would occasionally take on. Sometimes it concerned him that a girl not quite sixteen should be so analytical and inquisitive about the foundations of her own and others' feelings. At fifteen, Kavanagh had not rehearsed emotions, or thought things through to the point where it stopped him acting. That was another thing the murder had taken away, robbing Lucy of the chance to be impulsive, every feeling now held up for scrutiny.

'When I go back to Los Angeles, I want you to come with me. We talked about a holiday and now would be a good time. I want you to meet Nancy, Luce. I want to see if you like her, because I like her. Is that okay?'

'When do you have to go back?' she asked.

'We have to firm up and I've got to draw up a preliminary document, but I'm still trying to move quickly. It's likely to be the week after next, for a week, but we might be able to stretch it to ten days.'

'That's Mum's anniversary. Aren't we going to the grave?'

Kavanagh had not quite forgotten the exact date. On both previous anniversaries of his wife's murder, he found that the closer the date got, the more blurred it became in his mind, like the same page studied so many times it became meaningless. He had known it was Helen's anniversary, it was just that his mind was skating around it.

'Luce, I'm sorry,' he said, not quite sure what he meant.

'It's all right. Mum wouldn't mind,' she said. Her voice quivered and then she spat out a sob, wrenching it from herself.

He put both hands around her and held her body, feeling it judder as tears took hold. Kavanagh smoothed his hands through her hair and planted a kiss on her scalp.

'It's okay,' he said.

Lucy turned and put her head on his chest. His shirt

quickly became wet and his shoulder muffled the crying. It had been a while since they cried together and Lucy's tears were always enough to start his own. It had not been long, only three years, but at such moments it felt as if time had made things worse instead of better. The whole stupid and pointless manner of his wife's death, the way it had gouged into their lives and changed them forever, hammered itself home to Kavanagh. For several months at a stretch he could almost forget about it by putting the feelings somewhere else, but then they would emerge uninvited in his mind, sharp and refreshed from their rest.

'I'm sorry,' he heard her say.

'You don't have to be,' he said.

'I wish I could have done something. Got home sooner. Helped her,' she said.

The thought-process was familiar to Kavanagh.

'How could you have?' he asked.

'I don't know.' She gagged and then sniffed wetly. 'Should. Have. Done. Something.' Each word was a self-contained sentence, fitted between heaves of her chest against his own.

'Lucy, don't. We've been over this. There was nothing you could have done.'

'If I'd come home earlier.'

'If you'd come home earlier, you might not be here now. I'd have lost you both. Don't be silly.'

'I miss her, Dad. So much.'

'I know you do. Me too. Let's reschedule America if you want to go visit the grave on the anniversary,' he said.

'No. It'll be all right. Mum would be pleased if we went on holiday, wouldn't she?'

'Yeah,' he said, his voice weak.

Kavanagh switched the gas off and slid the pan across to the back of the cooker, the metal base screeching on the hob. He hugged his daughter tightly, furious with himself, with Pendulum and Trellis, with Paul Baran, with the house, and even, he realized, with Helen for dying the way she had, leaving them this way.

They cried and, around them, the house was silent and indifferent to their pain.

Chapter 21

At seven-thirty a.m. Kavanagh swiped his card through the lock on Pendulum's front door and entered his personal six-digit code. As he entered the foyer, the security guard, who was only glancingly familiar to Kavanagh, looked up and back down to whatever he was reading in a smooth, unflustered motion.

'Morning,' Kavanagh said loudly.

The same nodding action was repeated but this time with a slight raise of the eyebrows. Kavanagh sighed and went to the corridor that led to the basement, hoping to find a warmer greeting.

'Morning, Tom,' he said, leaning against the frame of Tom's office door.

'Hello, Mr Kavanagh, sir,' Tom said.

The mock formality of the address was a running joke between them. Kavanagh was appalled by how rude other staff at Pendulum could be to Tom, the nonchalant way they asked him for things.

'I've just boiled a kettle if you fancy a cup,' Tom said. 'Lucy's bought me these green tea bags with mint in them. They're supposed to be good for me, better than coffee, at least.'

'A spoon of coffee won't hurt. How is she?'

Kavanagh sat. 'A bit rough lately. It's easy to forget how fresh everything still is for her. Did she come and see you last week? She skipped a couple of days of school.'

'No. Last time I saw her was the day she came in to meet you for the theatre. She seemed bright enough.'

He sipped at the coffee. 'The third anniversary is next week. I'm going to take Lucy away to the States with me. Part of me would rather be here with her, but if I have to be away, I want her there with me. She's unsettled at the moment. I can tell because she overcompensates to the point where everything seems too normal and then it just cracks. I worry about the pressure she puts herself under just to make it all seem okay.'

'She's a strong one, Mike.'

'What've I missed here?'

'We've had the police in. You know Chris Carson still didn't turn up?'

'I spoke to Paul yesterday. What did the police have to say?'

'They didn't really seem to think it was long enough to be worried. They were just going through the motions.'

'He'll turn up. I hope to Christ he does. I don't want to think I've driven someone away,' Kavanagh said, making lighter of it than he felt.

'How's my lad getting on?'

Kavanagh tried to fight the pause that inserted itself in front of any statement Tom asked him to make about Garth.

'He's doing fine. The cold-canvas campaign can be a bit gutty at first, slinging mud to see what sticks, but he's generated a few appointments. That's always a good feeling.'

'Keep pushing him, Mike. Don't let him get sloppy.'

Kavanagh drained the remaining half of the liquid in the coffee cup too rapidly, choosing to burn his windpipe rather than offer a further opinion. He looked at the old man who had been so kind to him and his daughter and wondered how someone like Garth could have resulted from him. Kavanagh remembered mentioning they were looking for new sales staff and the embarrassed way Tom had suggested his son. Kavanagh also recalled how he had felt as his resolve had slipped and he had employed Garth despite the strength of his instinct not to.

'Thanks for the coffee, Tom. Come up sometime and I'll make you a green tea,' he said.

They both laughed.

'Is Paul in?' Kavanagh asked.

'He was here when I got in at seven,' Tom replied.

The door to Baran's office was, like Tom's, open. Later in the day, Kavanagh knew, it would close and permission to enter would have to be sought. The pre-nine o'clock watershed was a time for easier conversations, a dress rehearsal. Kavanagh entered the office.

'Hey,' he said.

'How are you doing? You don't look jet-lagged,' Baran said, looking up from the pad in front of him and sitting back in his chair, at rest.

'Tom's been bringing me up to date.'

'He should be running this place. Andrew Mathias would like a conference call with us at three o'clock today. He's keen to hear good news about Pendulum and Trellis. You're in the diplomacy business, Kav.'

'Did Mathias know anything about Burns having met Cameron in the States?'

'If he did, he wasn't saying. I think he was as surprised as we were, but he just didn't want to show it. Mathias likes to be the man from the Trust, all seeing, all knowing and no telling. What are *we* going to be able to tell him at three o'clock?'

Kavanagh set his bag next to a chair and sat down.

'Burns want the merger to happen and he wants to see a good joint-venture operation first, a suck-it-and-see. If it works, there would be no barrier to an eventual full merger. He likes the idea of a strategic alliance.'

'Everyone does, Kav. Look at the computer industry. Everyone's allied with everyone else. It's like a fucking feudal system or a Latin American government. We can't have that. It has to be tangible.'

'It will be, Paul. Money will change hands. Commitments will be made. If the Trust really is serious about a long-term view on this, we should leverage off that gradualism. I'm going to propose we select five key indigenous accounts each from Pendulum and Trellis, ones that have international potential, and look at dealing with them through the vehicle. We'll have to pick carefully, going for places where the combination of Trellis and Pendulum can bring added value.'

'Agreed.'

'We have to think seriously, Paul. It won't be long before it all stops being theory and we have to face the practicalities of internationalizing Pendulum and inter-operating with Trellis. It's going to take resource, the need for Pendulum to go to the Trust for cash money, and to get it.'

'It's covered, Mike. I know there's a "we've been here before" feeling about it, times we were going to acquire portfolios and the Trust pulled the rug halfway through due diligence. It won't happen this time. They came to us with it. The Trust wants this to happen.'

'What about you, Paul?'

'I want it to happen, too.'

'Where will it leave you?' Kavanagh asked.

'If you want me to sing the Trust line, there'll be a place in the new company for everyone. At the grass-roots level, that makes sense. You need people in both countries, foot soldiers with their feet on the ground. It's comfortable to be a remote general, away from the battles, but the danger is they can get rid of you easily. I'm going to be okay out of this, Mike, and so are you.'

'Why are they really doing this, Paul?'

Baran picked up his pen and twirled it, the black barrel turning over in his well-manicured hand, the gold clip catching the light in sharp glints. 'I've given most of my working life to the Trust and I can't tell you why they're really doing it because I just don't know. They want it bad, believe me. Behind the scenes, at the Trust, the pressure is on. In this transaction, I see my role as shielding you from that and making sure you're properly rewarded for your efforts.'

'Two and a half million pounds is quite some reward.'

'They believe in you. Anyway, think how much money you and I have made for Pendulum and the Trust. It's not just about the margins and the fee income we generate individually. You and I set the course for this company and we steer it. You're getting no more back than you've put in.' Baran put his pen down and leaned forward. 'Take it and go, Kav. Let it go.'

'I'm still deciding,' he replied, knowing it was far better to keep everyone blind to his feelings. 'I don't know if I'm ready to believe there could be a place for me in the new company any more than I can imagine myself not being a part of it.'

'Andrew Mathias first contacted me about the merger five months ago. They wanted to suck me into the Trust and put you at the helm of the new company. That suits me fine and that option is still there on the table. It's rare for the Trust to come and hold its hand out with a lump of money, you know that. Once in your lifetime. They won't be doing it again. It's your one chance, Mike. I'd take it and go.'

'Lucy asked me yesterday if we'd be able to still live in the house if I wasn't working for the Trust.'

Baran smiled. 'She thinks like you, Mike.'

'It hadn't even occurred to me. If I do go, we'll go clean. Move. We should have done that as soon as it happened.'

'It's three years next week,' Baran said.

Helen's murder happened two days before Baran's wedding anniversary and Kavanagh knew the date stuck in his mind for that reason.

'I've promised Burns I'll be back in Los Angeles next week, so I won't be here for it. I want to take Lucy with me. It wouldn't be fair to leave her.'

'Is she going to be able to look after herself while you're doing business?'

'Yes,' Kavanagh said, thinking of Nancy Lloyd and a conversation he was yet to have with her.

'Fine. I think it would be good for the two of you to be away together.'

'Has any gossip started in-house yet, about Trellis?'

'No. It's too off the wall for anyone to make a connection

and the lid's on it too tight. There's been more talk about Chris Carson.'

'Tom said the police were in.'

'The Trust made a call, the usual secret-finger-wiggle masonic handshake, and we were visited. Where do you think he's gone, Mike?'

'He has plenty of money and enough of the maverick spirit to wander off. He could be anywhere. This sounds crass, but we should run an internal audit over his deals, just in case.'

'None of the sales guys are close enough to the green to pull off a fraud,' Baran said.

'I know, but let's run a check on it anyway. It would look bad later if we didn't. I'm going to go and run through my messages, catch up from last week, pick up on what I've missed. Should we get together around eleven? I'll give you a full update and show you the outline of the document I want to give Burns next week.'

'Eleven sounds fine.'

'One thing we should look into, before we go too far down the line,' Kavanagh said, getting to his feet and retrieving his bag, 'is the precise legal structure we want for the initial vehicle. I know there are different tax implications depending on the type of unincorporated association you choose, connected with partnerships and non-partnerships. It's worth doing some homework on.'

'Do you want to get Legal on it?'

'I was hoping for something in my lifetime. And that I could understand. We need a commercial take on it,' Kavanagh said. He paused and realized he must have been softening with age as he felt his resolve weaken in spite of his instincts. 'Garth Richards worked on a joint venture in his previous company. We talked about it at his interview. I'll have a word with him later and get him to do some digging. There's nothing too major about it. It'll give him a break from cold-calling.'

'If you think it's wise, Kav, go ahead.'

'Unless we use him, we're never going to know how he'll

really perform. He needs a chance. And besides, what can he do wrong on a bit of research?'

Chapter 22

The fatter of the two boys looked at Garth again and smirked. For the second time, the boy opened his mouth, proudly revealing its mashed-up contents. Pieces of bread and hamburger and lettuce turning over in a damp lump like a cement mixer making coleslaw. The fat boy turned to his friend and they both laughed, pleased at the look of disgust so obvious on Garth's face.

Garth looked away and round the burger joint. The bright fluorescence hurt his eyes and he rubbed them, feeling the itch on his eyeballs and using his lids to scratch it. Two girls of about fifteen were on a table several rows down and an aisle away from Garth, some doleful green plants with cigarette ends in their pot partially obscuring his view of them. He put two fingers to his nose, a digit resting lightly in each nostril, and inhaled slowly. He took another long draw on the banana milkshake, feeling the pressure on his ears because of its thickness – its triple thickness. He grabbed some more french fries and opened his mouth wide to accommodate them. Then turned his attention back to the rude little fuckers on the table in front of him.

The boys were eleven, perhaps twelve, years old. The fat one looked to Garth like the sort of person who would cheerfully and mindlessly eat, burp, fart and shit his way into a premature grave, a heart attack before thirty. His friend was not thin, but nor was he fat. The fat one was now sticking his fingers deeply into his nose and talking loudly about bogeys. Both of them whined a shrill laugh, its tone girlish, both making sure to catch Garth's eye as they did so.

Garth's straw made a slurping sound as the first large milkshake emptied. His thirst, like his sexual appetite, had become practically insatiable. Most of the time he was so charged up, he hardly felt the urge to snort any cocaine, despite the access to greater amounts of it his new-found prosperity allowed. What kind of power was running through him that made the previously scintillating white powder now so impotent? The Book was being strict with him, allowing him to take certain pleasures while denying others. It was a cruel balance and one that only excited Garth further.

Kavanagh had asked him to help on a project. It was, Garth realized, what he had been waiting for. It would be the thing that led somewhere, that took the path he was already on to its logical end. He had expected to feel enormous relief to be away from the cold-canvas campaign, but it meant nothing to him. His memory was burning up almost as fast as he could fill it, the sheer volume of virtually everything there was to know cramming him up and leaving no room for himself. There were long moments at a time where he could not tell his own voice from The Book's. Garth was unable to distinguish when he was having an idea of his own, when The Book was informing him of something or when The Book was instructing him.

It was thirty minutes until he had to meet David Roke and he had stopped off to get some french fries and a milkshake first. Garth had ended up ordering three extra-large portions of fries, two and a half of which were now gone, and two jumbo-sized milkshakes, one down and one to go. Later, he hoped, he'd be able to fuck with someone, anyone, again, if he had the energy. He'd masturbated four times so far that day and it was only just eleven-thirty. He started on the second banana milkshake.

Now the boys seemed to be talking specifically about him. They whispered to each other, their eyes darting towards him and then back to each other. Fatty started to blow down his straw into his drink, making a fizzing, frothy sound. He sucked some up and spat it out at his friend. They threw some food at each other and then Fatty was back doing his regurgitation trick, this time spitting some food out into his hand and making a ball of it that he threw at his friend, who didn't seem to mind that much.

Anger rose in Garth. He had been given permission by Kavanagh to hunt around Blackwell's for a few books on partnerships and joint ventures and it was irritating to have this stolen reprise before his meeting broken by the actions of two indolent little fuckers. There were so many things he could do with them, things he could make them do with each other, things he should not even let himself think about. They were not his thoughts and there was no OFF button, no way to stop them. Images glided through his mind and eventually he gave himself up to them, an upsetting stream of their potential suffering that soothed him.

Garth finished his fries, an erection calling to him from his trousers. The fat boy made a face at him and laughed. As Garth drained the last of the other carton, so the boy made the same slurping sound with his mouth and pretended to be choking.

Gathering the empty cartons and used serviettes, Garth stood up and put them in the bin. On his way out he stopped by the table with the two boys, both of whom went suddenly silent.

'Congratulations,' Garth said. 'We're running a competition today for the ugliest fat cunt in the shop and you've won. The prize is two free milkshakes and a portion of fries.'

The fat boy looked up in confusion as Garth vomited the fresh contents of his stomach over him, the cheerful yellow banana of the milkshake rendered slimy and bilious by only a short residency in his stomach. The boy's face was covered with the slime and it acted as a glue for the half-chewed fries, some of which still had Garth's teeth-marks on them. He vomited twice more, unable to force it all up in one go. The fat boy's bewilderment turned to tears as Garth left, touching his crotch and then his nose.

The purpose of the project, Kavanagh had told him, was to check out a legal situation before getting the lawyers involved. This Garth understood. In every company Garth had worked at, he had seen the legal department derail or at least slow down any process that came past it. That didn't bother Garth initially, who liked to think he couldn't give a shit about Kavanagh, even if he were busting, but the sense of higher purpose the project had imbued him with made Garth anxious.

Entering Pendulum, Garth retrieved the bathroom kit he kept in the bottom drawer of his desk – what he liked to think of as his personal drawer – and went to the toilets to brush his teeth, wanting to take away the smell of sick. He wet a paper towel and dabbed at some vomit on his navy-blue jacket. He looked at himself. His eyes looked tired and red. Too many late nights, he thought with lurid satisfaction. He reached for the hardening in his trousers, but something stopped him. He knew what to do.

David Roke was a year younger than Garth and Head of Legal Services at Pendulum. Roke reported directly to Baran, which Garth knew upset Kavanagh. David Roke had the look of someone who might have been a Scot ten generations ago, his hair black and slightly wiry, his eyes pale blue and his features made up of harsh Celtic lines. But these were only echoes of who he might have been. The reality was far from as grand.

'Garth,' Roke said, looking up from his desk.

'David,' he responded, surprised at the warmth in his own voice.

Garth was afraid of Roke. Despite what he thought about the man's lack of gravitas, Roke was still younger than him and senior to him. Mostly it was the age difference that troubled Garth, amplifying his discomfort with authority. Garth wondered if Roke, with his access to all areas of the Cameron Trust, knew about The Book? No, he comforted himself, Roke wouldn't even hear the voice of The Book, still less understand it.

'We don't often see you in here. Have a seat,' Roke said. 'I'm sorry we had to put a brake on that deal with Marinez, but we would have been unduly exposed by that structure. It's never one we've felt comfortable with.'

'I understand,' Garth said.

'You haven't come seeking redress, then?'

The thick carpet and lush wallpaper had no effect. Nothing in the room was warm.

'David, I came down because I wanted to have a chat with you. Concerning a legal issue.'

'Certainly,' Roke said, peering at Garth.

'This office is lovely. I should come down here more often,' Garth said, leaning back in his chair and stretching his legs out.

Garth could feel his doubts were about to be swept aside. The source of his recent power was going to show itself. Control of the situation would be taken away both from Garth and from David Roke as The Book wrote through them. Already Garth could pick up on the remnants of the other man's feelings, as though they lingered in the air and he could sniff them up.

The Book opened them.

Roke was nervous. In the balance of anxieties between them, the scale had tipped in Garth's favour. Garth felt the nerves, as though nervous himself, but knew they were not his feelings – they were Roke's. The Book tuned in like a radio station. Garth could not hear Roke's thoughts, but he had found a link to him at some emotional level.

The Book was reading Roke.

Garth sat back in his chair and let himself be the eyes of The Book as it read the situation.

'What can I do for you, Garth?' Roke asked.

'I'm in a bit of a legal spot, as it happens.'

'Really. Why?'

'I killed Chris Carson. I didn't really like him very much and I enjoyed doing it, but that doesn't make it all right. Just because he was a fucking waster, I assume I'm still not allowed to murder him. It doesn't make it legal.'

'It doesn't. There isn't really much we could do, unless you can make some kind of case for self-defence.'

'That would be difficult. He was tied up most of the time. And then there was the car battery he was connected to. It left some burns.'

'How exactly did you kill him, Garth?'

'I don't want to tell you that,' Garth replied, using his last reserve of free will against The Book.

'I'm not sure how I can help you.'

'There isn't any way. I think I'm telling you this because I want to kill you as well, David. That's my real purpose for coming here. How would you like to die?'

'What do you mean?' Roke asked.

'When you're a kid, you and your mates always talk about suffocating or falling out of a window and landing on a railing, how you *wouldn't* want to die in such a horrible way. When you grow up, there's all that laddish talk about how you'd want to go on the job, fucking a supermodel, how you *would* like to die in fantasy. What I'm saying, in seriousness, is how would you like to die? I'm planning to kill you, quite soon, and I wanted you to tell me how you'd like it done.'

The Book relinquished Roke to himself, letting go of the dialogue for a moment and allowing Garth to feel the younger man's reactions. He was scared. Roke understood what Garth was saying to him, knew it was true and knew he would forget it as soon as The Book was done. Garth savoured Roke's consternation.

'I'm going to do it, David, whatever happens. I want you to pick. If you really want it, I will throw you out of a window and onto a railing, or bury you alive. I'll even make it quick if you want. Break your neck or stab you.' Garth breathed out loudly. 'Now, if it was me, I'd go for something painful and terrifying, and long-drawn-out. You don't get to do this every day. Apart from those sad fucking suicides, who gets to choose? How many people? What's that saying? It's your funeral.'

'I'd rather not die at all,' Roke whispered.

'What, not ever? What things are you most scared of?'

He felt Roke try and pull against the question, as though not wanting to read what The Book was writing in him.

'Don't fight it, David,' Garth said.

'Dogs,' Roke said. 'And the dark,' he added, his throat sounding tight.

'See? There's something. How about I lock you in a dark room with a couple of dogs? Ones you might think would be cute, like Labradors. Be killed by an adorable version of the thing you're most afraid of. Wouldn't that be splendidly banal? Go out with a real bang. Imagine dying in the middle of pure fear. What's the thing you love most?' Garth asked.

The pull against the question was even stronger.

'You're afraid that if you say your son, I'll do something horrible to him, aren't you?' Garth asked.

Roke nodded.

'I won't. I promise. Not while you're alive, anyway. After that, maybe. It won't matter to you after you're dead, but at least in the middle of all that pain and fear, you'll die and never be quite certain what will happen to your boy. All this will come back to you, when you're in that room. How old is your son?'

'Nearly three.'

'Now,' Garth said, pulling out his pocket diary, 'we should set a date. When would you like me to kill you?'

Roke opened his desk diary, flicking through the pages, his attention distracted by them.

Garth felt his cock stirring. Troubling images formed in his mind, images of him and Roke, together. They sparked in his brain photographically, like subliminal frames placed between the action in a film. They came and went so quickly it was hard to make out what was going on in them. Unlike the earlier thoughts about the two boys, which he wished he could have shut off, Garth now wanted to hit a pause button and study the picture, make out what he and Roke were doing together. His cock pressed against the material of his trouser-leg and the strain was pleasant.

The flashes, Garth realized, were coming from Roke as he pretended to be interested in the pages of his diary.

'How about Wednesday?' Roke asked.

'Awkward. Thursday might be better. Come to my place. There's a lock-up garage I've taken on and it will be perfect, kitted out just right.'

'I'm supposed to look after Ben that night while Rowena's out with a client.'

'Bring Ben along. I bet he likes dogs. Or we could make it Friday.'

'Friday's good,' Roke said.

'About eight?'

'Eight's fine,' Roke said, lifting his pen.

'David, I'd prefer if you didn't write it down. You won't forget. I told you, this will all come back to you when it's too late. And you'll know where to come.'

'Okay. I'm looking forward to it,' Roke said.

Elation gushed through Garth and he struggled to hold himself in check. The full power of The Book was surging through him.

He watched Roke. Garth was dragging the physical sensation from Roke and filtering it through his own body, becoming the object of both his own and Roke's desire. It was a peculiar and appalling moment in which he knew himself and Roke far more intimately than he wished. It was slimy, neurological and synaptic all at once, almost a cannibalism. The weight of it made him feel sick, the sweltering intensity of it in such a plain setting. It hurt him.

The phone on Roke's desk trilled and Garth exhaled loudly under cover of its noise, not realizing he'd been holding in so much breath.

'Let's talk again, day after tomorrow,' Roke said, lifting the phone, no more feelings emanating towards Garth.

Garth nodded, stood and spun quickly around, heading for the door and trying to walk normally in his soggy underwear.

Chapter 23

If he did not arrive soon, she was going to leave. Lucy lifted the strap of her shoulder bag into her collarbone and sighed. On the way into town, the D-shaped ring which held the strap to the end of the bag had given way to metal fatigue and Lucy had made a hurried, bodged attempt at tying it back on. The material was too thick to make into a decent knot and she had already decided that were it to give, she would throw the whole bag away. The yellowing, knitted canvas sack, which had seemed damp from the day she bought it, was already well past its best. Perhaps the heat would end today, the sun seeming to burn harshly in a final rage before it would yield to the chill blanket of what should have been Autumn. Lucy had only just become used to under-dressing but she knew it would not be long before many more layers of clothing would be required.

She was standing outside the Trocadero, a few safe feet away from the people holding out benevolent leaflets. The last time, the first time, she had met him, Nathan was already on his way somewhere else and Lucy had badgered a few details from him, surprised at herself and her audacity. As a result, she had extracted an agreement to meet in the current place, at the current time, although the way his eyes continually shifted from hers to some point over her shoulder as they had made plans to meet convinced her he would not turn up. Another wasted day of absenteeism from school, all the time easing her nearer to the point where she would have to explain herself. It felt so safe to do it, to go into town and let herself disappear in the motion of other people. There was no Mum, no Dad, no Kim, no school, no *that afternoon*, just movement.

'Hi,' he said, walking up and standing close to her.

'Hello,' she replied.

He was wearing black jeans that were hoisted around him like sails on the mast of a boat, wide in the leg and tapering down to his thick-soled Converse trainers, in their turn as brilliant white as a coat of gloss paint. With his hands buried to the wrist in deep pockets, he leaned towards her and moved his shoulders from side to side, looking at her from under the honey-brown line of his eyebrows. Waiting for him had annoyed her, but the twitch in the end of his upturned nose made her want to smile broadly, even though she didn't.

'Sorry I'm late,' he said, shrugging and looking off to one side.

'I was just about to go.'

'The trains were really slow. And I left late,' he added.

'What do you want to do?' she asked.

'Don't mind,' he responded.

Lucy fingered the strap of her bag. She could feel lethargy about to immobilize them. She was carrying some cash on her but had resisted the urge to bring too much, wanting to play it at least a little bit cool rather than spending all her money on him.

'Do you want to go up to the arcade?' she asked.

'If you want.'

I want to know what you want, she thought. I want to do something because you want to. 'Let's cross over to Piccadilly Circus, look in Tower,' she said.

He kept half a pace in front of her, the pavement thickening with the onset of lunchtime tourists and a smattering of office workers, most without jackets because of the heat. Partly trailing behind him made eye contact difficult and she studied the back of his head, the collar of the untucked orange shirt contrasting with the gold hairs on his neck, skin darkened by the recent sun. Lucy could not tell if he was being sullen, shy or a mix of both. It would be disappointing if he turned out to be just another miserable boy, the sort that overcrowded her school.

'Where do you live?' she asked.

'Walthamstow. Whereabouts are you from?'

'North London,' she said, suddenly embarrassed to be from Hampstead.

'Do you want a fag?' he asked.

'No.' She paused. 'I don't smoke.'

'Let's go in here,' he said, making a sudden right-turn.

Surprised, Lucy followed his orange back into a Body Shop. It was crowded, sweat taking the sweet edge off the fruit aromas. Still in his tow, she followed him and watched his long fingers as they picked up bottles and tubes and unscrewed them, sniffing at their contents as though fascinated or occasionally repelled.

'Do you like the stuff in here?' he asked.

'Some of it. Well, most of it really.'

'I knew you would.'

'What do you mean?' she asked.

'It's the sort of shop you'd like, that's all.'

She could not tell if he was making fun of her in a nasty or a nice way. Either way, he hardly knew her. He smiled and she laughed. It felt nice, not nasty.

'If we go down that escalator and into the subway, we can get in through the basement of Tower,' she said as they stood on the threshold of the Body Shop.

Inside Tower Records, they spent time amongst magazines, books, videos and CDs. Lucy felt as though he was checking up on her by seeing how many of her likes and dislikes he could correctly guess. His accuracy surprised her and she wondered if she were really so easy to read. For nearly an hour they cross-referenced each other, finding many common areas and a few sharp disagreements. It was a gradual process, but Lucy felt herself relaxing with him, finding that her expectancy about the situation was calming down. He would be a nice boyfriend to have, she thought.

In Burger King, she watched him take large bites of hamburger, which made one of his cheeks look swollen, and then chew on it only partially before swallowing so strenuously she was afraid he might choke himself. He smiled knowingly when she ordered a bean burger, which she picked at, and gave him half of her fries. The tendons in his neck stood out as he sucked at a strawberry milkshake. He had been relaxed about her paying, although she wished he'd at least made the offer.

Lucy cleared her throat. 'Could we go to a comic shop?' she asked. Before she could think about it too much, she reached out and rested her hand on his forearm.

'Yeah, of course,' he said, no reaction to her touch.

It was late in the afternoon when she next looked at her watch. The hot sun made it seem earlier. Somewhere in the course of a walk that was aimless but nonetheless pleasant, Lucy had carefully put her hand on the back of his shirt, finding the waistband of his jeans through the fabric and clinging on to it. Now and then her hip knocked against his and it felt solid, bone near the surface.

Nathan stopped abruptly and turned to look at her. Lucy thought he was about to kiss her.

'Here you go,' he said, putting a hand into his shirt and removing a tube of shower gel from it.

'Where did you get that?' she asked, knowing it was a stupid question but wanting to react.

'You said you liked the smell of that one,' he said earnestly.

'I didn't mean you should steal it,' she said, looking around and feeling guilty.

'I'll pitch it in a bin if you don't want it,' he said nonchalantly, holding it out to her.

Lucy looked at it for a moment and then reached out to take it, shoving it quickly under the flap of her shoulder bag without bothering to undo it.

'I didn't see you take it,' she said.

'Tons of practice. That's why you wear baggies and a nice long shirt. Bulges don't show. My dad used to show me little magic tricks, how to make coins disappear, all that sort of stuff. Make people look in one direction and then do what you have to in the opposite one.'

He held up his right hand and wiggled his fingers. When he held up his left hand, it had a CD in it. Nathan gave it to her and then raised the front of his shirt higher. Tucked into the waist of his jeans, near his groin, was a magazine. He handed it to her. It was warm from his body.

'Nathan, don't they have security tags on this stuff?'

'No problem,' he said.

From the breast-pocket of the shirt he took a packet of cigarettes, removing one and placing it in his mouth. He flicked the button on a blue, see-through lighter that was half full and lit the cigarette. Lucy watched as he smoked with casual practice. He walked on and, once again, she was a pace behind him.

'Let's sit on the grass,' he said.

They were in Leicester Square, all the benches and most of the grass taken up. Lucy enjoyed moving in the small orbit, following her well-worn routes between Leicester Square, Piccadilly Circus and Soho.

They found a spot. Before he sat, Nathan reached behind him and produced a green bottle the same size and shape as a hip flask. It had an old-fashioned-looking red label and heavy white script. Nathan sat with his legs partly crossed in front of him.

'What's that?' she asked.

'Thunderbird,' he said.

The cap made a metallic tearing sound as it came away from its seal and he lifted the neck of the bottle to his mouth and took a long drink.

'Try it,' he said, holding the bottle out to her.

She took it and drank. It was like surgical spirit. Dad let her drink wine sometimes, usually a smooth buttery red, or white ones that smelled like cut grass and vanilla, but the liquid she had just consumed tasted of evil. It was like all the nasty things distilled into a potent solution that would stay on her breath for hours even after a single sip. She took another gulp, long enough to require two swallows, and her head already felt warm and buzzing.

Nathan undid the buttons on his shirt and let it fall open to his sides. His belly was flat, his navel protruding ever so slightly and the skin ruffled into several ridges. Lucy held on to the bottle and stared at the trail of hair that went from under his belly button down to the waist of his trousers. He reached and took the bottle from her, his hand brushing hers as he did.

'You don't usually drink, do you?' he asked, a half smile on his face.

'Not very often.'

'Don't your mum and dad let you?'

'My dad doesn't. My mum's dead,' she said.

He leaned back on one elbow, took a long swallow and rested the bottle on his stomach. Lucy saw a sheen of sweat on his forehead, one tear trickling from where his fringe started. She knew it was the alcohol, but she felt herself becoming too relaxed, too malleable. As he lay there on the grass, she was afraid that he would ask her to do something she didn't want to, and that she would find herself saying yes.

'I live with my uncle,' he said.

'What's that like?'

'He's a real bastard.'

'Why?'

'He just is, but he's getting too fucking scared of me now.'

'Where's your mum and dad?'

'They split up. Before I was even born. My dad went abroad and my mum never wanted me. Her mum made her have me and then she went back to Newcastle and they gave me to my uncle who was living down south.'

'Is he married?'

'No,' he said.

'But he brought you up?'

'Sort of. Come here,' he said.

'Why?' she asked.

'Come here,' he said, looking at her.

Lucy knelt up and moved closer to him.

'Why don't you sit on my lap?' he asked, although it did not sound much like a question as he set the bottle to one side.

She straddled him and he pulled her head down using a

hand on the back of her neck. Their mouths fused and his lips were hotter and softer than she was expecting. While they were still kissing, Lucy stroked his bare side with her hand, making him gasp into her mouth. Where she sat on him, she could feel a hardness pressing into her behind and it made her flushed, a little out of breath. She broke the contact with his mouth and eased herself off him, feeling light-headed from the kiss and the Thunderbird.

The bells on the Swiss Centre began the build up to their hourly chime.

'I have to go soon,' he said.

'When can I see you again?' she asked.

'I'm not around much until next week. What about Tuesday?'

A whole week away. No, more than that. 'I have to go to America with my dad next week.'

'Have to be the week after next, then,' he said.

It felt like the longest time she could imagine, making her infant anticipation of Christmas seem like no time at all. America was suddenly an obstacle rather than an adventure.

'Give me your phone number, so I can call you,' she said.

'Better not,' he said, frowning. 'My uncle gets funny. Write yours down and I'll phone you, I promise.'

'What if I want to send you a postcard from America?'

'I'll phone you, Lucy, I told you. Promise.'

As the bells reached full anticipatory cacophony, she scribbled her phone number onto a piece of paper, crestfallen he was not going to give her his, but petrified to push it in case she scared him off. Five days of waiting by the phone flashed in front of her eyes. She watched him button his shirt back up.

Nathan stood and brushed himself off, running his hand over the top of his head, pulling and lengthening the front of his hair between two fingers. He looked at her and then kissed her on the mouth, his tongue just pushing between her lips and the hand he rested on her hip slipping over one buttock and cupping it briefly.

'I've got to go,' he said.
'Which station are you going to?'
'I'm, ah, I've got to meet someone.'
His eyes wandered the same way they had when the first date was set. I could come with you, she wanted to say.
'Thanks for the CD and the magazine. And the shower gel,' she said, the polite girl saying thank you the way she had been taught.
'That's okay.'
A single bell began to knell the hour.
He looked up at the clock. 'I really have to run. I'll call you.'
Within a few moments even the dayglo orange of his shirt was lost in the swell of bodies. Feeling both elated and dejected, Lucy trooped towards Leicester Square station, already anxious to be at home in case the phone rang.

Chapter 24

Nancy tapped the nib of her pen on the page, speckling the paper with stubble as she listened to the phone ringing. The property manager had shown her the answer-machine and how it worked and there were even carefully written instructions in mauve biro, but she hadn't bothered to learn how to set it. It could only have been one of very few people calling her and Nancy did not feel like talking to anyone very much.

Her body still ached, two days after Lee Mitchell. Nancy's fingers felt like they had stretched and then not returned to their normal length, hanging too loose, the way a spring might if it were pulled over-hard. There was deeper pain, embedded further in her body, inhabiting organs. She wondered if the struggle was the only reason for feeling the way she did. Perhaps it was the onset of the cancer, the first sign of real sickness, the kind that would leave her flat on her back.

The phone stopped ringing. On the floor in front of her, where she sat with crossed legs and the writing pad on her knee, a pair of white baby socks were positioned as though they might have been walking along. The toe of the front foot was pointing up and the following one down, invisible legs taking a stride. The soles of the socks were greying, as though real feet could have been walking in them.

It had come back to her. The car. The locked doors. The feel of him rubbing inside her. The baby that never was. Mothercare. It really had moved, that washed-out red-brown piece of meat that was part of her and of him. There had been a life force in it, however brief. The same way his life had pulsed and expelled itself into her, living there until she had repelled it like the rubbish it was. She didn't want it in her, so she flushed it out, willing it to happen. Nothing had been special or nice. The thoughts were painful, but they were true feelings. What would she have done had she carried it to term? It would be twelve years old now and on its way to being an orphan.

Again, the phone.

Nancy wrote. Something was flowing, taking shape across the twenty-nine pages she had filled with her careful script over the previous two days. There was a pattern in the words, buried somewhere but getting nearer to the surface. It was as if the writing were gradually unearthing a secret, a structure she was not aware of but which had been there all the time. She had even been looking at the first paperback edition of her novel, ignoring the gaudy cover and going past the froth that fizzed from her words, examining the text harder and realizing she might have been trying to convey something other than what the words on the page actually said.

The phone seemed to ring harder and Nancy pressed more firmly with her pen, ignoring the pain in her fingers as she inscribed words deep into the pad. Nancy relished the sensation, one she had not experienced for so long, as the words became the only real thing for her, everything else forced into the background. If there was one way out of her predicament, a method for at least delaying the end, she knew it was to write.

Memory flowed from the pen, recollections formed into shapes, letters, words, sentences, paragraphs and, ultimately, a story. Nancy used to believe there was one story, one narrative so fabulous and so secret, it would eventually become accessible to her. The struggle to find it was like a race and, now, she didn't have much time.

Over an hour passed, Nancy lost in the exaggerated slowness of work that, paradoxically, made time go faster, when the doorbell rang. The buzzer rasped loosely, an electrical sound that grated at her. She made a token effort at ignoring it but, like the click of a hypnotist's fingers, the noise had brought her out of the trance. She straightened her back, stretched her spine and blinked, her eyes tired.

The buzzer went off again, held down for a more insistent burst. Nancy set her work aside, tidying it, and went to open the door.

'I've been calling,' Julia said before the door was fully open.

Nancy showed her in and Julia sat on an armchair near the window. She could feel irritation, possibly even anger, emanating from Julia. Nancy could tell it was not a time to either dress things up or skate around them.

'I'm not going to do this script. Not now. Not ever.'

Nancy waited for Julia to respond. She seemed to be measuring herself, thinking through the ways she was meant to react. Nancy could see the way Julia was trying to find the angle, to see what it was Nancy really wanted, what the purpose of such a statement could be. Julia was unlikely to see the real point ever, because it was contained simply in the words Nancy had said. There was no agenda to the statement. Nancy no longer wanted to do the movie.

'What happened with you and Lee Mitchell?' Julia asked finally.

'Nothing,' Nancy said, rubbing the side of her neck which was covered by a high turtleneck.

'Lee's been avoiding my calls since you saw him. Did you two have a falling-out?'

It was the first time since Nancy had arrived, since meeting Julia Summers, that her agent had been to her apartment. Julia had kept away from it. Now she was there, Nancy noticed how uncomfortable she seemed on the territory. It was the nearest place Nancy had to a home, a piece of ground to stand on.

'I have to tell you this before we get any further down the line,' Nancy said. 'I don't want to waste your time and I don't want any money to change hands. What I've given you so far, in terms of the treatment, is all I've written. It's all I'm ever going to write of that story.'

'You're blocked. It happens. There are ways round it. I know a good writer's block therapist. We'll get over this, Nancy.'

'I thought I was blocked. I am blocked with *Stolen Hearts*.'

'Nancy, we could sell them on just the treatment, it's so strong. How can you not write it? It's screaming for you to write it. If you don't think Conical are the right people for the project, I'll get through to Lee Mitchell, go sit outside his office if I have to, and tell them that.'

'It's not that, Julia. Stop trying to find ways to make this happen. It isn't going to.'

Nancy saw that her stubborn resignation was beginning to irk Julia.

'Take some time away from it. You've been working hard since you got here. Have a holiday and relax out here. There's time.'

'There isn't,' Nancy said.

'You're going back to England?' Julia asked.

'Before I came out here, I'd been getting bad headaches, attacks of nausea and some blackouts. I saw my doctor, had tests and then ran away when I knew things were bad. When I got here, it was almost like you couldn't possibly be sick in another country, especially this place. No one gets sick or even old. Then I went to a doctor out here. Nowhere to run, I guess.'

'What's wrong with you, Nancy?'

'I'm dying. I have a brain tumour.'

'Oh my god,' Julia said.

Nancy saw the jolt it gave Julia. She was the first and probably the only person Nancy would tell. Nancy knew barely anyone who had died, so death was not something she had grown used to. Having old parents, even as a child, stoked the worries for her, far more than it had for most of her peers, but no one actually died. She had anticipated becoming accustomed to it as time wore on and people around her began to expire. No one ever seemed to die and yet, eventually, everybody would. Maybe that was why Julia was so taken aback, because Nancy's imminent death was an unwelcome reminder of her own.

'There's nothing that can be done?' Julia asked.

Nancy shook her head.

'There must be,' Julia said.

Nancy smiled, watching the animation in her agent. All that vitality, waiting to burn itself out, Nancy thought. What's it all for?

'Julia, believe me. There's nothing.'

'How long . . .'

There was an unusual trail into wordlessness.

'Not long enough to write a script. Can you understand that, Julia?' Nancy asked. Her voice was quiet and sympathetic.

'Of course I do. I don't know what to say to you. You're going home to your family, I guess?'

'I will be,' Nancy said.

'I wish there was something I could do. Anything.'

The phone was ringing again and Nancy had begun to talk over it. Only Julia's stare and then words stopped her.

'Are you going to ignore that?' Julia asked.

Nancy went to the counter in the kitchen, hoping it would take her out of Julia's earshot.

'Hello.'

'Nancy, it's Mike Kavanagh. How are you?'

'Hi. I'm fine,' she said quietly.

She had been waiting for him to call since giving him her number.

'I promised I'd call once my plans were finalized. I'm going to be back in Los Angeles next week, another quick jaunt, but I'm hoping we'll be able to get together.'

'I'd like that. When do you arrive?'

'Monday. Lucy, my daughter, has been a bit down and I've been promising her a holiday. Don't get flustered by this, but I'm bringing her with me. This isn't a meet-the-family kind of thing. I didn't want to leave her here on her own next week.'

Nancy paused before speaking. How bad could it be, to be chaperoned by his daughter? 'I'd like to meet her. Where will you be staying?'

'Not in downtown this time. Somewhere nearer you, in Hollywood or Beverly Hills. Any ideas?'

'I'll call you if I think of somewhere, but don't count on me. I'm as much of a wayfarer as you.'

'Okay. We'll need to make reservations soon. As well as the business, I'm going to have to make time for Lucy. I'm not sure how she's going to be. I might have to be a bit flexible with her.'

His voice sounded repentant.

'Mike, don't worry about it. You sound apologetic. I understand. I want to meet Lucy and I'm looking forward to seeing you again. I want to make amends for the other night, running off like that.'

'Now you're being apologetic. How's the deal going on your script? Are you writing anything?' he asked.

The base of her stomach burned.

'So so. I'll fill you in on the details when I see you,' she said. She heard Julia shift in the next room, remembered she was there. 'If I don't talk to you again before Monday, shall I wait for you to call me once you're here?'

'Okay. I'm trying to keep Thursday and the weekend free for definite. We go back Sunday or Monday. You've got my number here and at the office if you need to call me?' he asked.

'Yes.'

'I'll see you next week,' he said.

Nancy stood with her finger holding down the button, the handset still pressed to her ear and with a broad smile on her face. The smile faded. I'm not going to tell him, she decided. Another thought occurred to her, connected to her writing. Replacing the handset, she opened the pad on the counter, ready to write something down. The squiggling doodle she must have drawn at some point was still there. She squinted at it.

It goes on forever, she wrote underneath it.

But you can see it, she added.

Closing the notebook, Nancy returned to the living-room and the company of her abnormally quiet ex-agent.

Chapter 25

Kavanagh sat behind his desk and regarded Garth Richards, who was seated at the other side of the wooden expanse.

It had been a while, Kavanagh realized, since he had really looked at Garth. So much of Kavanagh's recent time had been tied into the Trellis transaction that when he did see Garth, it was a nod across the office. Up closer, Garth did not look good, like getting too near a painting and seeing all the brush strokes. The rims of Garth's eyes were a sore red, the eyes themselves in need of rest as they darted about in their sockets. Several times, Garth had licked his lips and raised his eyebrows, bringing himself towards Kavanagh as though he was expecting some secret to be told to him. The thin grey chalk stripes of his suit were mottled by the occasional faded patch, as though food had been dropped on the fabric and wiped carelessly away. They were all small things, but they added up to a mess and telling an employee to sharpen themselves up was never an easy task. Kavanagh knew he and Garth did not have the kind of bond that would smooth such an exchange for either of them.

Kavanagh checked his watch, the day already beginning to slip away from him, and worked out the time in Los Angeles, wondering as he did what Nancy Lloyd was doing. They were good feelings to have and it made a change for him to feel pleasantly distracted. Even Arnold Long and all his negative input seemed far away and unproblematic for Kavanagh. Bringing off the merger with Trellis was going to be like docking a large ship, needing steady hand and nerves. Nothing would stand in its way. Kavanagh would not let it.

'How's the canvassing going, Garth?'

'Still slow, but I'm generating some interest.'

'And appointments?'

'Some on the way,' Garth replied.

Kavanagh knew when he was being lied to, the vagueness that set into phrases, the distant look that spread across faces. After the next trip to America, when things with Trellis were properly in motion, Kavanagh would have to do something about Garth Richards, even if it was just to liven him up. There was not time to do that right now.

'Did you dig up any information on partnerships?' Kavanagh asked.

'There were a couple of articles in the library and I found a very good book. I'm working through the information now.'

'Can you do me a paper that covers in detail the type of structures used for joint ventures with overseas companies and give it to me for a look-over before we get Legal to rubber-stamp it?'

'I shouldn't talk to Legal first?'

'No,' Kavanagh said. 'Do that and we'll have them taking the lead. This is a sales-driven issue, not a legal one.'

'What exactly are we doing?' Garth asked.

'There's an American company sniffing around a utility transaction and we might act on their behalf or look at ways of partnering with them that might give us some tax leverage.'

'I didn't know there were any good double-dip structures left. Which company is it?'

'I'm bound up by a confidentiality agreement, a really tight one. Can you show me the preliminary paper by end of today?'

'Yes.'

'Good. After I've seen it, let's have David Roke in here tomorrow and we'll bully him into agreeing with us.'

Garth laughed.

'Are things okay with you, Garth?' Kavanagh asked, hoping to latch on to the small amount of warmth created from the chuckle.

'How do you mean?' Garth's tone was defensive, not far from offensive.

'You just look a bit tired, ragged, like you've pushed the boat out a bit too far.'

'Just a bit too much partying lately, catching up with me.'

'Candle not long enough to burn at both ends any more?' Kavanagh asked.

'Something like that.'

'You're not going back to the bad old Eighties party days, are you?'

'I couldn't cope with that,' Garth said.

'Nor me,' Kavanagh said. For the second time, he was being lied to. Garth was not going to confide in him. 'Try and sharpen up a bit if you can.'

Kavanagh's phone rang, stopping words issuing from Garth's open mouth. 'End of today,' Kavanagh said as he picked up the phone. Garth nodded and left.

'Kavanagh,' he said into the phone.

'Kav, I just got off the phone with our Mr Mathias from the Trust. Can you come and see me?' Paul Baran asked.

'What's the story?' Kavanagh asked.

'Alex and Clough Cameron were at Burns' father's house in New England in nineteen fifty-nine,' Baran said. 'I even made notes to make sure you'd have the full story, such as it is. It was in the summer and your friend Jack Burns Junior was home from college. His father's business had been through a lean patch but it was recovering. Burns Junior was absolutely determined he wouldn't be going into the family business, any business for that matter. Alex and Clough had been travelling out East and had been to the West Coast before that, trying to do then pretty much what we're trying to do at the moment, get a toehold in the States for the Trust. Burns Senior had met with them and invited them out to a formal garden party he was holding, Americans pretending to be English by playing croquet, all that Gatsby crap. A big row breaks out between Burns

Senior and Junior, loud and embarrassing. Junior's drunk and going on about how he doesn't want to follow in Daddy's footsteps, calling the old man an evil bastard, the full number.'

'Ugly,' Kavanagh said. 'You wouldn't know it now. Jack Burns is very placid, from what I've seen.'

'People change, Kav. Clough, who neither Burns knew well, other than from one brief meeting with Senior, intervenes and calms them down. Mathias made it sound like he was this serene Gandhi-figure, getting between father and son, especially placating the old man. Clough and Burns Senior go off together and the party gets back into swing. An hour or two later, Clough and Jack Burns the first rejoin the fray, acting like old friends, but both quite subdued. Mathias got all this from someone who was there, says the older Jack Burns looked drawn, low in spirits. All's well because father and son make it up in public, good old Clough, but Burns Senior won't talk about what happened between him and Clough Cameron, what was said. Never talked. After the summer, Jack Burns went back to college and switched his major to economics, the MBA after that. Father and son followed divergent paths, one of which led to Trellis today, the end of the path for Jack Burns.'

'It's a nice anecdote, an after-dinner story, but I'm finding hard to believe it's not the sort of story that's got embellished over the years.'

'Mathias says a lesser Kennedy was there and a reference to this party and the fight turns up in a book somewhere, not in any detail.'

'Great, but what does it buy for us, Paul?'

'Nothing. But at least it doesn't cost us anything either. Arnold Long doesn't have anything over us. I suggest you sound out Burns innocently about meeting Clough and Alex, just to see where it goes. There must be a reason for him not mentioning it. It's been in a book for Christ's sake.'

'Agreed.'

'Are your tickets sorted, for you and Lucy?'

'Yes. Garth Richards is putting some words on paper for partnerships and JVC arrangements so we can get Roke's initial buy-in. Once we do, I'll incorporate it into the document I'll be giving Burns. I'll fax it before I leave, let him read it while I'm in the air, nothing too heavy. I'll leave a few blanks for him to fill in.'

'Good. Mathias was getting twitchy. They're waiting to open the cheque book. I can sense they've got the flavour for it. The iron's hot, Mike, let's get out there and strike. Make them happy. If they are, so are we.'

'Let's talk through the finals of the document after I've seen Roke tomorrow.'

'What are you doing for lunch today?' Baran asked.

'Meeting Lucy to look in a few shops for clothes. I've let her have the day off school and she's probably down in the basement with Tom now, getting her head filled with ghost stories,' Kavanagh replied.

Chapter 26

'My dad and me are going to America next week,' Lucy said.

Tom nodded, his lips pursed tightly as he worked the blade of an old screwdriver into the head of a screw embedded into the frame of a weathered chair.

'He told me,' Tom said, letting his breath out as he spoke.

The old man was exasperated. For the last five minutes, since her arrival in Tom's room, Lucy had watched silently as he had worked on the leather swivel chair that looked as old as he did. Up-ended and face down on the floor, the heavy mechanism looked ungainly and kept moving each time Tom tried to do anything to it. He gave up, leaving the screwdriver to one side on the floor and wiping his hand on the leg of his close-knit navy-blue trousers.

'Can I have a cup of coffee now?' Lucy asked, knowing better than to touch the kettle herself.

'You're allowed coffee but your dad isn't?' he asked, smiling at her.

Lucy smiled back. The interaction between herself, her father and Tom meant a triad of possible criss-crosses and that made for many trivial secrets and betrayals.

'I don't drink as much as he does,' Lucy said.

'Getting in practice for your holiday? That's all they drink out there, I hear. Looking forward to it?' Tom asked.

'I've never been before. You haven't either?'

'No. Couple of holidays in Spain when Garth was a baby and the one big trip to Australia, two years before my divorce. Most of the time, I take long weekends through the year. I'm never away from this building for too long.'

'I think we're going to Disneyland. That's all I really

know about it. There might not be anything else to do,' she said.

'Being away with your Dad, that'll be nice.'

'The man who works for Dad is still missing, then,' Lucy commented at Tom's back as he made coffee.

'Still no sign of him. I thought we were done with all that sort of thing here. I reckon he'll turn up. Chris Carson is young and he can be a bit of a show-off, rude to me sometimes. He's taken a fit in his head and he'll be back.'

'It's a bit creepy, though. How old is that chair?' Lucy asked.

'About thirty-five years. Left over from one of the refits. Our last head of the Tax Department was fond of it. Just gets in the way now. Are you going to be all right next week?' Tom asked.

'Because of my mum?' she asked, knowing it was what he meant.

'Because of your mum,' he repeated.

'I haven't told my dad, but something funny happened the other day.'

'What?' he asked.

'It happens sometimes, only now and then. I go into the house and I start to remember the way it was that afternoon. But it's different, because instead of how it was when I found her, it feels like she's still there and I'm the one that's looking for her.'

'Trying to save her?'

She shook her head. 'No. It's like the feelings, his feelings, are mine. I know they really belong to someone else. My counsellor would have a field day with this if I told her.'

'If that's how you feel, that's how you feel. What's that to do with anyone else?'

'When I walk through the house, I can feel it the same way he could. I remember finding Mum and how that was, but when I get this sensation, I know it's him. The excitement.' Her voice was almost a whisper.

Tom did not speak.

'Mum knew him. She knew who it was,' Lucy said.

'You can't know that, Lucy. Not for sure.'

Lucy looked at him. 'I know it more than if someone had told me, shown me a photograph of him.'

'It was a tragedy, Lucy. I don't think they'll catch him, not now. It was a one-off, horrible, but it's over.'

'Kim says that. It's about moving on and making new foundations. But, do you know what? It doesn't feel over. Inside of me, I can feel it's not right and I know Dad can too, even though he won't talk about it. I'm the one who gets to see someone once a week but Dad doesn't talk to anyone. You're right about it being horrible, though. Finding her was.'

Lucy wondered how she could be so detached from her own words, their real meanings. Kim was supposed to help her get closer to the essence, but Lucy had realized that all the talking served to do was bleed emotion from her utterances, leaving just empty sentences. All her words became like false smiles.

'I know a bit about what that's like,' Tom said.

'How do you mean?' Lucy asked.

'I've sat on that door for a lot of hours of my life. I've been here for all the big moments in this place's life, the good and the bad. I reckon I know more about this building than anyone apart from one man who's probably dead now. Here for everything, good and bad. The murders were no exception. I was here, the first on the scene and the one who found them. Like you, I wonder sometimes if I could have done more. It gets easier, trust me. It was me who walked into that room.'

'You've never told me that,' she said.

Tom stared at her and the wrinkled skin around his eyes tightened. 'Perhaps I didn't think you was old enough before. Now you're a bit more grown up, you should hear it. Might help you.'

Lucy saw his face alter as memory worked itself under the surface of his features. As she looked at him, she tried to imagine what he would have been like thirty years earlier. The fact of him being involved in something that had happened so many years before and now sitting in front of her in the flesh made him seem like some sort of artefact.

'The Trust was running into trouble, even before it happened,' Tom said. 'To the outside world, everything was successful. Even I could see that. There was a real buzz to the place, all sorts of different people coming in and out for meetings. Mr Clough said it reminded him of being back at the hotel. That was the way everything looked – good – but it wasn't how it really was.'

'Why not?' Lucy asked.

'Just like Mr Clough and his own father, Ellis, so Mr Clough and his son Alexander weren't getting on. There might have been things to do with the business, things I wasn't privy to, that they disagreed about, but you didn't need to be a genius to see something was going badly wrong. Alex and Mr Clough couldn't even agree what time to meet. First, they want to be in the building together, always watching each other and, next thing, they aren't talking and don't want to be here at the same time. I was on the door and sometimes Mr Alex would call me to see if his father was here and of course, an hour earlier, Mr Clough had arrived and made me promise not to tell Alex he was in the building.'

'Couldn't he just have got rid of his son?' Lucy asked.

'They were all dependent on each other, like they were tied together. Bloody children, the lot of them, and I felt like I was in the middle, some of the time. Of course, it was the women who got the worst of it.'

'Their wives?'

'Mr Alex didn't marry. His sister, Alexandra, was part of the Trust. According to Mr Clough, she was to be treated the same as everyone else, an equal partner, but it wasn't like that. Mr Clough's wife, Krista, might have been the only sane one between all of them. Some days, I'd see them storming in and out, shouting after each other, and you wondered how people like that could be in charge of such a successful firm. Nowadays, you look around and all the most successful people are a bit mad, on their own side. I wish I understood more about the real business of what was going on, the reasons Mr Clough and Mr Alex acted the way they did.'

'Did you prefer one to the other, out of Mr Clough and his son?'

Tom rubbed his chin and Lucy heard the scraping sound it made. 'Mr Clough was the one who employed me and he always treated me well, but he kept a distance. Mr Alex would be more sociable although that could make it awkward. You have your worst rows with people who are your friends. Give them enough rope and they'll come and hang you. On balance, they were both as good and as bad as each other.'

'But you still stayed working for them,' Lucy said.

'I love this place, I really do. Besides, you always do things you don't want to, work for people you don't like all of the time. That's being an adult, growing up.'

'School's the same, Tom. Even if you've done things you didn't want to, you're still happy here. What happened the night of the murders?' Lucy asked, afraid the old man would get off the track.

'I was tired. Been on a double shift, my third in a fortnight. The morning shift was due to take over at six and it was a bit after three in the morning when Mr Alex arrived. That wasn't so unusual as he kept odd hours. This building was like a home from home for them and that's the way they treated it. Why shouldn't they? It was theirs. Mr Alex being here made me sit upright, awake all of a sudden. "Evening, Tom. No interruptions, please." he said. Made his way through Reception like it could have been the middle of the day instead of the middle of the night. I thought it was a bit funny, him asking not to be disturbed. Who was going to come looking for him at that time of night? Anyway, he was in no mood for being sociable and he was right across the foyer and into one of the lifts. They were the old sort of lifts with brass plates and lots of woodwork. The floor of Reception was all inset mosaic, like something from the British Museum. Of course, that was torn up. In the lift and gone. The floor indicators were those pointers like you see in old films. They were out of date back then, but we kept them over the lift doors more for show.

'Over an hour passes and I'm starting to settle again when the door rings. It was Mr Clough, Krista and Alexandra. They said they didn't have any keys with them, which, apart from the time of night, was the first real thing that struck me as funny. You'd think out of the three of them, one would've had a key. When them three were together, it was like a royal visit and you didn't much argue with them. It was the same routine as with Mr Alex, straight in and up, Krista smiling and being polite, Mr Clough distracted and Alexandra with her nose in the air. I wasn't going to tell them Mr Alex was there and asking not to be disturbed, so I just sat back on the desk and kept thinking about those keys. They didn't find any keys with the bodies and there were none at any of the houses, so I reckon Mr Alex ran off with them. I don't know what he was planning to do that night or what was on his mind. I still don't think he meant it to turn out the way it did.'

Tom stopped for a moment, taking a long breath. There was a change in him as the recollection went sad.

'It was just like a bomb had gone off, but without the bang. When that IRA bomb went off in Long Acre a few years back, we heard the explosion and lost some windows, which is when I got the firm in to put big sheets of clear plastic tape over the inside to catch the glass. That night, the whole ground moved, like an earthquake. It's quite a thing for the earth under your feet to suddenly just move, like it's come to life. For the first few seconds, I just sat there like nothing had happened, or that it was just an ordinary thing to happen. The fire alarm rang and that was what made me jump up, like it was my clock going off in the morning. There used be a square panel, under the desk, with lights on that would show you where in the building the alarm had been triggered. None of them were flashing and I started tapping them because we'd had a problem with one of the bulbs not working a year before. There were thirty tiny bulbs with red glass, the size of Christmas lights, and I knew I couldn't stand there all night tapping them, not with people upstairs and the chance that the building was on fire.

'All of the lights on the panel flashed on at once. I'd never seen them so bright and it looked like they were about to blow from a power surge or something like that. Just like that, the fire bell stops ringing and the power goes off, the whole building dark. The lights on the panel all stayed on and made the skin on my hands look blood-red, like when you hold your hand over a torch. The only other light was coming from the overhead bulb running off the emergency circuit. The lift gears started to grind and one of the three bells dinged as its doors opened. It made me jump even though I knew the lifts were on independent power and were meant to come back down to the ground floor and sit there when the alarm was on. The fire alarm shouldn't have stopped ringing like that, though. At that moment, I was worried about the Camerons eight floors up. There were panic buttons that called into the police and the fire brigade and I couldn't be sure the station would have known about the alarm so I hit the button, grabbed a torch and made for the fire stairs.

'They had the whole of the eighth floor in suites of offices and there were so many passages and doors, you could get lost up there. When they first moved in, Mr Clough had the top floor gutted and redesigned. Someone told me it caused a lot of problems at first, safety and fire regulations, but Mr Clough got it sorted, one way or another. You've been up there and seen how open-plan it is now, but it used to be closed in, so much so it was claustrophobic. There were some outer offices, a small reception area beyond them, this sort of ante-room, like a waiting room, and three inner offices. If you looked at it from above, it was a bit like a spider's web, Mr Clough squatting away at the centre of it. I knew my way around it well enough, but I was in a panic because I thought the building was on fire. For five minutes, at least, I was twisting and turning and it seemed like there were doors I had never seen before. It was so dark and the safety lights were next to useless. All I was glad about was I couldn't smell any smoke. I had to use the torch to find my way about and when I came to the door of Mr Clough's office, which is where I thought they'd be, I tried the handle but it wouldn't move, not left or right, like there was someone on the other side, holding it really tight.'

Tom looked down and opened a drawer on his desk, fishing out something hidden from Lucy's view.

'Later on,' he said, 'I found out this was what was left of the lock.'

On his desk, Tom laid a tangle of melted metal, the part of the lock where the key would have fitted still just discernible, like the empty socket of an eye.

'So there was a fire and the lock melted?' she asked.

'It would have burned my hand off if there had been. There were no marks on either side of the door and the handles were untouched, like the ones I showed you in the box. The lock just gave way from inside and grew into itself. Mystery. Whatever, it meant I couldn't get into the room. Not that way.'

'There were other ways?'

'For them that knew. By that time, I could tell there wasn't any fire, that we weren't going to be burned alive, so my senses were coming back. I stood outside that door in the dark, out of breath and afraid, I don't mind telling you, and I knew it was much worse than just a fire. Something was wrong and I needed to get into Mr Clough's office. Even the downstairs of this building, the ground floor and the bit we're sitting in right now, was changed by Mr Clough. There were sets of plans kept, but then there were other plans, ones not many people got to see. Let's just say that once I got my bearings, it wasn't long before I was standing outside another door, well, entrance, that led to the office. I couldn't even be really sure there would be a way through, but, right enough, there was and, once I got in, I wished I hadn't.'

Lucy waited, her breathing short and the beat of her heart faster than normal. It had happened in the building, where she was sitting. The people Tom were talking about had moved through the rooms, lived and breathed in there. It scared her in a basic way that made her stomach loose. There was no point in asking a question. Tom was so enveloped in events three decades old that nothing would break his flow or change what he was telling her.

'Mr Alex had taken a blade to all three of them. Of course I didn't know that at first. I shone my torch around the room and there they were, the three of them sitting round that table, like they were having a seance. Mr Clough, Krista and Alexandra. There was a lot of blood, the beam from the torch picking it up. In some ways, I was glad the lights were off. It was like trying to make up one picture from all the bits I kept seeing. Faces were the worst, like I'd frightened them with the torch. There was something deathly about that room, not just the quiet in there, but a whole atmosphere that hung over the place. You could tell they were dead, even without seeing all that fear in the eyes, the faces twisted like they were in pain. When my Garth was a boy, we took him to Madame Tussaud's and he was petrified of the Chamber of Horrors and that's what Mr Clough's office reminded me of, one of them displays. I wondered how they managed to stay frozen where they were until I saw they'd been tied to the chairs, rope put around their middles. The nails were what held their hands to the table, long ones driven in so far you could only just see the flat heads, looking like a liver spot on the top of their hands. They were cut up bad, mostly near their stomachs where they were tied, and a few small nicks on their faces.

'A shock like that takes you back. I don't need to tell you that, Lucy. You don't ever expect bad things like that to happen to people you know and even care about in a funny way. A sick feeling came over me, knowing that I had to act, to do something, when all I wanted to do was sit down on that floor and cry my eyes out. All the while, you know how sad you're going to feel for a long time afterwards but that you have to do the right thing. The right thing was to find Mr Alex. Part of me was hoping that he'd be lying on the floor, dead, because that meant he wouldn't have done that to his parents and his sister. But he wasn't there. He was gone. Or somewhere in the building.'

Lucy swallowed. 'Do you think he was hiding?'

'There were plenty of places he could have been. If you ask me, he was here. I could feel it.'

'Did the fire brigade arrive?' she asked.

'Not long after. I checked the rest of the floor and then made a quick run through the rest of the building, just in case there really was a fire, then I set to getting the power back on. By the time the firemen got here, I knew it wasn't them we needed.'

'And nobody ever saw Alex again?'

'Lots of people said they did. Like Lord Lucan, he was always popping up somewhere. There have been plenty of sightings. Mr Alex was too clever for that. He was in here, that night, while the police were closing off the building and searching, but they would never have found him, not if I couldn't and, believe me, I checked everywhere I knew. But there were funnier things, afterwards.'

'Like what?' Lucy asked.

'He came back. I know he did. It's like what you were saying, about sensing things. I could feel when he was here, somewhere in the building, even in this room sometimes – I'd come in and it was like he'd been in here not long before.'

Lucy looked around the cramped office, seeing more corners and shadows than she had ever noticed before. All at once, she wished she could back against a wall.

'How long afterwards did you get the feelings?' she asked.

'Up until quite recently. Five years ago would have been the last time. I don't tell anyone about it in case they cart me off if I do, either for being mad or for being an accessory.'

'I knew about the murders, from Dad and you, but I never knew you were the one who was here on the night.'

'It's not meant to scare you, Lucy. It's meant to show you that horrible things can happen but you can still be all right. Unless you think there's something wrong with me,' he said, smiling at her. 'Go away with your dad and try to have a good time. Remember your mum but get on with it.'

Chapter 27

The knot, which for nearly three years and also for nearly thirty years had been the same shape, moved its tendrils around them in a way so seductive and so sly they were not even aware of it. Minds were distracted by the troubling surface, the membrane of actions that encased meaning. It was the beauty of The Book that it was able to refashion the knot through them, the shifting of shapes appearing natural in the midst of the exterior disturbances it created and their reactions to them.

The task was not straightforward, could not be. The Book could not issue the story in one single moment, every loose end tied off, because it would have been against its very nature. The knotwork was the story and it had to unfold in due course as a process, its meaning organic and unfixed. As powerful as The Book was, it could only circulate its words and let them play through the participants, only ever as good as the people it read or wrote.

In fact, that was what made The Book so powerful.

For The Book, closing the first knot was simple. It meant assembling the elements, the words and the speakers of those words. But, as it closed the first knot, so The Book had to leave the way clear for the second knot to fit into the pattern, the pattern that was visible yet went on forever. It was only ever about creating the potential for a story because The Book was ultimately indifferent to the outcome of what it wrote, its only purpose to write; writing in itself.

Some branches of the first knot were now fused because paths had irrevocably crossed. Others pointed in new directions, with new possibilities, ready for the second knot to open and ultimately close.

Without heed to anything except the process and with no

one to read it or to write it, The Book wrote on ceaselessly, searching for the point of entry into the second knot, readying itself for the painful work it would do there.

The Second Knot

Woe be to him that reads but one book.
George Herbert, *Jacula Prudentum*

Chapter 28

Kavanagh checked his watch again and looked back up at the road, wondering if he was going to find the cinema in time. It was hot weather and he had left his sunglasses behind at the hotel, making him squint to see the names of unfamiliar roads on unfamiliar blue signs. To his right, Lucy sat in the passenger seat, an elbow on the window frame, chin cupped by her palm, and looked away. A sheen of sweat, similar to the one on his own forehead, covered his daughter's face. Since their arrival in Los Angeles, Lucy had gradually withdrawn, words less frequent and her excitement no longer as visible as it had been in London prior to their departure. Something was on her mind, more than the fact that it was coming close to the day Helen had died. Lucy was not particularly prone to sulking. Her silences had more the tenor of introspection, as though the gears of her brain were all quietly occupied as they ground away to produce a single thought. Kavanagh gave her a quick sideways glance and watched her jaw working, chewing on unspoken words.

Westwood was chintzy, reminding him of the kind of roads that ought to lead to a beach. The lines of semi-rustic shops paraded an array of half-familiar items, many of them tourist-oriented. The breeze was not enough to cool them down and Kavanagh wished he had rented a bigger car with air conditioning instead of the recklessly expensive convertible in an attempt to please Lucy which ended up feeling like selfish and vulgar largesse.

Seeing a movie had been Kavanagh's idea. In all the thinking he had done, there was no easy way to introduce Lucy and Nancy to each other. The cinema was the easiest. They could meet shortly before the film was due to start, thus avoiding too much interaction early on, sit together in the dark for a couple of hours, getting comfortable with physical proximity, and they would have something to talk about afterwards in the form of the movie. To Kavanagh, it seemed like the best way he could attempt the fusion of two separate parts of his life, one extremely important, the other potentially so.

Of course, Kavanagh had not planned on being late.

'Do you know where we're going, Dad?' Lucy asked.

It should have irked him, but he was glad to hear her voice saying something other than yes or no. Perhaps the silence was about to lift, just in time.

'It looked straightforward on the map,' he said.

'We're going to be late,' Lucy said.

'No we're not.'

'You've been looking at your watch more than the road, Dad. You said we had to be there at half past two and it's twenty-five past now.'

'We'll be fine,' Kavanagh said, looking from side to side for anything that resembled a cinema.

'Dad, we're going to be late. Why can't you just admit it and start to get comfortable with it?'

'Get comfortable with it?' Kavanagh asked, his voice the closest he could make it to what he imagined a therapist might sound like.

Lucy smiled to herself. 'I sound like Kim. You are nervous though, Dad. Taking me to meet you girlfriend.'

'Luce, you promised me you weren't going to make this difficult,' he said, his chest aching to laugh, a way to relieve the tension.

'Should I call her Mum?' Lucy asked naughtily.

It was good to have her back. Kavanagh pretended to ignore her and kept his eyes on the road, lips pursed and jaw squared with determination.

'What about Auntie Nancy?' Lucy asked.

'Lucy,' was all he could manage before an exasperated laugh escaped him and infected his daughter.

'Over there,' Lucy said, pointing.

Nancy Lloyd was standing outside the cinema. The wind seemed to find her, trailing her fringe and the sides of her hair so that it rippled. She shifted from foot to foot and looked as nervous and alone as she had beautiful the night he had first seen her at the party. They cruised by in the car, Lucy craning her head curiously. Kavanagh was not sure she had seen them. He swung the car round a corner and into the parking lot, glad to find it first time, wanting to get parked and get the meeting over with. He fiddled with the handles that docked the electric roof into the posts of the windscreen while Lucy stood outside the car smoothing her hands over herself in the way Kavanagh knew she did to dry her palms when they were sweating.

As he and Lucy approached the short awning that jutted from the cinema box office, Kavanagh caught Nancy's eye. It made even walking a self-conscious activity, as though he were being filmed. Should he kiss her? In front of Lucy? After the way their last kiss had ended so stiffly? His stomach rolled. No. Let's get the meeting going, he thought. There had been managing directors, chairmen and chief executives, people Kavanagh had felt unsettled about meeting. None of them had made him feel quite the way he did now, awkwardly ambling across the sidewalk towards Nancy Lloyd, his daughter in silent step by his side. What it would have in common with a business meeting, or so he hoped, was that, like the nerves of an actor before the curtain rose, things would be all right once he was on.

Nancy's features illuminated with pleasure and it made him feel better.

'Hi, Nancy. This is my daughter Lucy. Lucy, this is Nancy Lloyd.'

'Hello,' Nancy said, holding out a hand to Lucy.

'Hello. Nice to meet you,' Lucy replied, taking the proffered hand.

'Good to meet you again,' Nancy said to Kavanagh. 'You found it okay then?'

'Eventually. I thought we were going to be late,' Kavanagh said, looking at his watch.

'I just love it in Westwood. It's one of the places I've spent most time in since coming out here. I've been to this cinema at least six times. There's a great place we can get coffee after the movie,' Nancy said.

'That'd be good,' Kavanagh said.

'This film won't be out for ages in England,' Lucy said, pointing to the poster.

'I know,' Nancy replied. 'It's brilliant. All I keep doing is going and seeing things I know I couldn't see back in England. It's the same with all the sitcoms. How do you like America so far?'

'It's hot and big,' Lucy replied.

'In the mornings, before about eleven, the weather is lovely, especially down on the beach.'

'Do we need to get tickets?' Kavanagh asked.

'Already got them,' Nancy said, producing them from her bag. 'In case you were late.' She slapped Kavanagh on the shoulder with the tickets. She turned her attention back to Lucy. 'They have fantastic popcorn that comes in a tub the size of a dustbin. And you can squeeze this liquid butter stuff all over it. I put a bag of M&Ms in too. Or we could try Reese's Pieces.'

'What are they?' Lucy asked.

'You're in for a treat,' Nancy said.

Kavanagh watched them go through the door talking and pointing at things. Nancy was slightly taller than Lucy. All the fraught images of Lucy screaming 'You're not my mother and you never will be' dissolved and Kavanagh wondered what he had been so worried about in the first place.

Kavanagh could hardly remember a line from the movie or a thing about it. He had sat between Nancy and Lucy, a monstrously large bucket of popcorn on his lap, and spent most of the film glancing at Lucy or trying to brush discreetly against Nancy, as though he were the teenager in the trio. Midweek, mid-afternoon, the theatre was dotted with only a few people, most with apparently nowhere else to go. Occasionally Kavanagh saw Lucy say something to herself, but he could not tell if she was reacting to the film, its actions a silvery flicker across her face. Each time he made contact with Nancy, he kept his eyes on the screen and tried to make the touch seem accidental or at least casual.

They were seated in a coffee bar only a short walk from the cinema, having elected to postpone the more formal business of dinner until later on. Kavanagh was glad and happy to be in the relaxed atmosphere of the shop. He and Lucy faced Nancy across the brightly checked tablecloth of a booth for four, a hefty lamp-shade looming not far above their heads.

'So, is your film going to be like that?' Lucy asked Nancy.

'I doubt it. It's the second time I've seen it. It surprises me how much is going on. I can't see me ever writing a blockbuster movie. My brain isn't right for it.'

'Dad says you wrote a book.'

'Yes. It seems like ages ago, but I did. I must have finished it about two years ago. By the time it comes out, you hardly remember it.'

'Was it exciting to get a book published?' Lucy asked.

'It got exciting for a while. When I wrote it, I wasn't really thinking about getting published. It was only when I found an agent. By the time the publishers picked it up, the writing was mostly done, so it was about the more fun parts. Writing the next book was what turned out to be difficult and a lot less fun. That's why I tried to do a script, for a film. Do you read much, Lucy?'

'A bit. Some for school, a bit of science fiction.'

'Lucy's big into comics,' Kavanagh said.

'Not that big,' Lucy said.

'I bet you've got one with you now. She likes American comics and Japanese ones,' Kavanagh said.

'I never really read anything like that,' Nancy said. 'I've stood and looked at them, the ones they have in bookshops.

The artwork on them is incredible, almost like watching a film.'

'So, will your film be coming out soon?' Lucy asked.

'I'm not sure. I don't really know what's happening with it. How's the deal going, Mike?' Nancy asked.

Kavanagh could sense Nancy's desire to shift the conversation away from herself, the subject of the script in particular. He stared at her for a moment before speaking, wondering if she looked a touch drawn, her cheeks just a fraction more hollow than when he had first met her.

'I have a meeting tomorrow morning to present an outline document for discussion. They're the kind of meetings where either nothing gets said or they last the whole day.'

'It's pretty diligent of you to come back and forth across the Atlantic like this,' Nancy said.

'We have to show them how serious we are. It's a measure of our commitment. Actually, I have a huge favour to ask,' Kavanagh said to Nancy.

'Ask,' Nancy said.

'My meeting is at ten and, seriously, it could go on most of the day. Would you have time to spend with Lucy?'

'I'll be okay if you can't,' Lucy cut in.

Kavanagh was not certain if Lucy was against the idea.

'No problem. If Lucy wants to,' Nancy said. 'We could do the beach, some shops, anything you want.'

'Okay,' Lucy said.

'Thursday, we'll do something proper.'

'Don't worry about it, Dad. You're supposed to be over here on business. Go do whatever it is you do.'

'Yeah. Leave us girls to it,' Nancy said.

The two women laughed and Kavanagh chose not to speak.

Chapter 29

Wadlow Grace sat and let his eyes cast far enough down on the page to make the kids who had just sneaked into his shop think he was sleeping. These were okay kids, locals with the hint of their parents and grandparents in them, people Wadlow had known for years. Friendly contact had ended with the previous generation and now that people were getting more similar to each other, not as different any more, Wadlow had become an oddity. These days, kids came to the store for dares, fraternity pledges, stuff like that. The local kids he could stand, saw it as his duty to be the local Boo Radley, but the out-of-town, snot-nose college kids were just rude and they didn't have any parent nearby enough for him to complain to.

The kids, three boys about eleven, were sneaking towards the counter, moving slowly and cautiously, looking like rabbits in the periphery of Wadlow's vision. Two in baseball hats, one turned backwards, all in faded sky-blue jeans. Wadlow breathed heavier, emitting a small snort that could have been a snore, and the three small figures froze briefly. He suppressed the smile that was trying to break out across a chin that hadn't seen a razor in two days, but there were other reasons for that. Wadlow was no greebo.

All three came a step closer, now about four feet from the low counter. They must be able to see my face, he thought, pressing his lids lightly together and switching to his ears as his radar. Only one was stepping forwards now. Wadlow doubted it was the ringleader, more likely the weakest of the three. There was always a ringleader, one who had sat around in the mall at the other end of town and talked the other two up into a frenzy about Wadlow Grace and what he did to small boys before making the dare. Over the summer, Wadlow had seen all three of them at various intervals, looking in the window and squinting at the counter, trying to get a good look at the bell on its surface.

A tiny footfall. Another. The light shuffle of nervous feet. Wadlow could almost feel the air move as a young hand reached out towards the button on top of the bell, ready to bang it down and be a hero for the remainder of the summer.

'And what can I get for you young gentlemen today?' Wadlow boomed, sitting bolt upright and showing all the teeth he had.

Three young mouths fell open at once.

Wadlow hefted his three hundred and twenty pounds out of the chair as fast as he could manage. Not many people saw him standing these days and he knew his height would scare them, the way he would suddenly fill their vision.

Three heads atop frozen bodies craned up to look at him. The noise finally started and it was a cacophony of pre-ball-drop fear, adrenalin spinning them round on the heels of hundred-dollar basketball shoes and sending them sprinting for the door.

'You have to ring the bell to win the dare,' Wadlow yelled, a shout propelled by a laugh as the door flew open and the kids ran out in single file.

Wadlow let out a long guffaw and went to close the door. Attached to a quivering band of metal screwed into the top of the door was another bell, one which had long since lost its clapper, but he left it there anyway. Maybe this year he'd put chimes on the door.

The Raynford Bookshop was at the slow end of the main street, the end only the footsore New England tourist or one of his many regular customers would stretch to. It meant things were peaceful and that suited Wadlow just fine. Two storeys and two shops wide, it was the last shop on the street and had barren, untended land that stretched off far behind it, all of it Wadlow's. His in trust.

Shelves ran all round the walls and rose from floor to ceiling, a rickety ladder on a squeaking rail the only way to the top. Across the floor, in library-like lines, were free-standing bookcases six feet high, set at an angle to create the aisle that led to his counter. Chalky dust drifted near the high windows, as though the books were shedding skin, and afternoon sun breathed through the misty cloud, creating a haze. The waft of paper, new and old, was the only ambience. The shop had been his home for thirty-eight of the fifty-two years of his life, the first ten of them shared, the rest alone. It was a long time and a long way from his home.

When the preacher found him in Memphis, Wadlow was fourteen years old and had been walking for nearly nine days. The once soft and pink skin of his feet had passed through a sore, weeping red into a hardened and callused yellow, traces of blood and the first look of septic tinging the outer edges of his empty blisters. The preacher took Wadlow's shoes off and washed his feet, between the toes and underneath, on the tender soles. Wadlow sat and wept quietly, keeping his mouth closed and letting his tears escape slowly, rolling down his cheek. With his feet in the bowl and the preacher kneeling at them, working methodically away, Wadlow sensed the kind of love he had missed in the previous days.

From the safe nestled under the counter, Wadlow took out a notebook that had belonged to his brother Randall. He kept it next to the box containing Pa's .45. The frantic drama of his older brother's long dead brain was splashed across its pages in ink. Phrases, doodles, words. Randall had been almost nineteen the last time he wrote in it, but the battered green notebook of just sixty-eight pages contained more than enough thinking for a whole life.

For thirty-eight years Wadlow had looked through the pages for clues. The few sentences that were in English held no meaning because they were wildly out of context. The Indo-European and Sino-Tibetan language families were the most prominent in the book, each line or word painstakingly formed, different languages sometimes coexisting in one sentence. Wadlow puzzled over some words, wondering if they were anagrams, words in more than one language, an unbreakable code. Arabic and Urdu looked more like drawings to Wadlow and it had taken him a long time to decipher some of it, still to find no real meaning. If Wadlow had learned anything from the process, it was the impossibility of finding meaning simply through translation. The dead or virtually unknown languages had been the hardest, mostly centred on a few pages of the notebook and predominantly Trumai, Bok and Lule, making the Italian, Thai and Tagalog seem mundane. In several of the aged leaves were marks which could have been drawings or the remnants of a forgotten language. Or one yet to be born. Randall had drawn things, doodles mostly, over some of his writing, obscuring the words beneath swirling patterns, as though capturing them in a net.

Wadlow would have given anything for chance to talk with Randall about it, to make his dumb older brother explain what all the inscriptions meant. Not one day had passed since Randall's death when Wadlow had not opened the notebook and looked at it in memory of his brother.

The wait was over.

The empty bell on the door rattled and Wadlow looked up, wondering if the kids were back, newly brave after regrouping round the corner.

Someone was coming into the shop but he could not see them. Wadlow knew they were entering and he could sense their passage down the central aisle, but he was unable to focus on them or make them tangible. It was as though all the energy of the person was moving towards him in a wave not contained by matter. Wadlow felt queasy, his big lunch grinding together unpleasantly in his stomach.

It was happening the way, thirty years earlier, the preacher promised it would as he lay on their bed in the back room and squeezed Wadlow's hand with the last strength he had, as though he had been saving it for him. There was a movement in the text and Wadlow Grace felt the energy bathe him, realizing the wait was over. The preacher's dying words came back to him. It was the voice

Wadlow had known better than any other voice, even Mama Grace's.

'It goes on forever, but you can see it.'

'Sorry?' Wadlow asked, as though not hearing him the first time.

The preacher's voice spoke the words in his head again; this time, as they were spoken, Wadlow's head lolled forwards as though his neck muscles had failed. With his head slumped down, Wadlow looked at the intricate doodle his brother had drawn on the ninth page of his notebook, a drawing that always reminded Wadlow of a nest of snakes, wriggling sweatily over each other like freshly spilled guts. There was something intrinsically erotic about the knot of lines, a sinewy sexuality that was both exciting and repellent.

'It goes on forever, but you can see it.'

Is this what the preacher had been talking about in a dying moment of insight? The drawing?

'The knotwork goes on forever but you can see it. Infinite patterns visible to the eye. It's seeing forever.'

Wadlow's lips dried out. Memories of the preacher came back to him, his smell and touch. Love.

'You could follow the knot around and around all day, Wadlow, and never stop. Unless you got tired,' the voice said. 'You could do it all day, move your finger around and it would never stop. Only when you got tired,' the man said again.

'You'd have to stop somewhere. Back where you started,' Wadlow said. 'Besides, you can start anywhere you want. It's arbitrary. And it doesn't really go on forever, it's only a line joined up.'

'I agree. If you think of it as a line that only goes in one direction. When did we start doing that? Thinking of things as a line? Don't you find the pattern of infinity comforting?'

Wadlow put his finger on the page and began to slide it around the pattern, the old paper becoming warm under his touch. Randall used to sit and do this, Wadlow thought, the weight of his own finger causing a sound that was almost like a hiss. Wadlow and Mama Grace used to sit and watch Randall make endless figure of eights on a greasy table top or in spilled salt. That was just a Randall thing to do, Mama would say. Anything slightly out of the ordinary, strange even, was explained away as just a Randall thing to do.

The preacher's voice was right. The pattern was comforting. The tip of Wadlow's finger was starting to tingle, the paper rubbing his skin smooth like a stone.

The arc of Wadlow's finger began to take on a pattern, as though discovering a secret route through the never-ending line drawn on the gray page. As his finger remained in motion, Wadlow became synchronized with it. It was like learning a new language, he thought. No. It was like learning every language. This was the secret. Even after his finger had stopped, movement continued inside Wadlow, the whole of his mind, conscious and unconscious, whirring like the mechanism of a clock.

Wadlow turned a page over in the notebook, already knowing what would happen.

Every page, each word and mark on it, was legible. Through the pattern of the knot, Wadlow had found his way into the text, into his brother's mind, as though the arrangement of lines had created a grid in his brain, one that would enable him to interpret what had for so long remained impenetrable.

Nine and a half hours later, when Wadlow had finished the reading, it was dark. His head hurt and he was sweating as bad as if he had run a race. For the first time in his adult life, Wadlow had gone more than three waking hours without eating or drinking and it added to the sick feeling his newfound knowledge had brought on.

Wadlow turned the key in the door and then the sign to closed. He put the long bolt into place and went behind the counter, shifting the blanket that served as a curtain so he could go into the back. Wadlow produced a key and opened a cupboard, empty but for a steel door in its back with a large wheel on it, like an airlock in a submarine. The key slid into the lock and well-oiled mechanisms tumbled against each other. Wadlow pulled the door towards him. A red light came from behind it, illuminating the top of a spiral staircase that wound quickly down into darkness.

He closed the door behind him and descended into the bunker that stretched deep into the ground and out across his land behind the shop.

Not quite a librarian.

The lights flickered and cast across the shelves, lines and lines of them. It reminded Wadlow of a military cemetery instead of a collection of over sixty thousand books amassed over almost forty years. He smiled and went to the computer console, running it through its boot sequence and staring around at the endless shelves as the disk clicked away. The collection was catalogued on CD-ROM and Wadlow had several versions of Books In Print.

Nancy Lloyd's name came up and Wadlow felt a rush in his chest. He brought his hand to his mouth, as though aghast. He had the book in his collection and its presence in the room was almost troubling.

In the dark, he sat and pored over the screen.

Wadlow Grace, the astronomer of books, had finally found the sign he had been looking for. Sitting under the compact circle of light created by the lamp, his hands shaking slightly, he opened Nancy Lloyd's book and began to read.

Wadlow was about to discover a new star.

Chapter 30

How many things, great and small, happened across a table? The hefty piece of wood separating Kavanagh from Jack Burns and Arnold Long had no practical function other than as an arm rest for the occasional note to be taken. It was a physical boundary with psychological implications, a sounding board and a barrier to prevent one party seizing the other by the throat. Kavanagh was a veteran of many long-fought campaigns where words were shaped, honed like fine instruments that would be used on the real world, slicing it up into acceptable chunks. He was also a veteran of about ten training courses on how to negotiate, knew all the tricks and also knew that, ultimately, it was not something that could be taught. Kavanagh was not expecting today to be a tough one.

Jack Burns was in a suit and tie, the first time Kavanagh had seen him in formal business attire, and he looked more comfortable than Kavanagh would have expected. The slight over-thickness of his neck was exaggerated by the shirt collar, making him resemble a bodybuilder working as a doorman. Arnold Long was almost an afterthought, appended to the side of Burns and wearing similar shades of washed-out autumn colours to those he had on at their first encounter. Kavanagh had yet to go beyond his instinctive dislike of Long and see in him whatever it was Jack Burns obviously did.

On the table in front of the two men was the fax Kavanagh had sent, hazy from transmission. It was like seeing an unexpected reflection of himself in a window, the way he could catch such a casual glimpse of the piece of paper that had been so much work to produce.

'You've done a good job, Mike,' Burns said.

'Thank you.' Kavanagh nodded and looked from Burns to the impassive Long.

'I've looked at the way you visualize the operating company working at the most day-to-day level and there are a few wrinkles, but basically it seems okay,' Burns said.

'We tried to set it out generally but also to give a flavour of the thing working in practice. It's still very conceptual and it's difficult because you don't always know how something on paper will turn out. The feedback of the people on the ground, in Trellis and Pendulum, will be of most value at that stage,' Kavanagh said.

'The timescales are vague, but I guess you're just trying to make me feel comfortable,' Burns said, smiling.

'I wouldn't want to make you feel otherwise,' Kavanagh replied, returning the smile.

Long had yet to speak and it bothered Kavanagh. It would be better to include him in the exchange sooner rather than later. Kavanagh assumed Long was serving some purpose by his presence. It might have been imprudent, impudent even, to canvas Long's opinion before Burns did, but he felt comfortable enough to try.

'Arnold, how do you feel about what's been presented?' Kavanagh asked.

Long glanced at Burns as though seeking permission to speak. 'All of this this-is-the-way-we're-going-to-do-it stuff is fine. I've seen it a hundred times. But the global perspective, the underlying logic of the transaction, still raises questions for me. Of course we're going to have an operating plan, of course there'll be a joint-venture vehicle, of course we'll globalize the sales resource, co-manage accounts across continents where appropriate. What else would we do? That's a no-brainer. It's the question of whether or not we want to do that in the first instance.'

Kavanagh at least admired Long for having the balls to be so negative, so far into everything. What was he clinging on for? Best estimates to the value of Long's shareholding was just over one million dollars. It might be enough to cash out his chips and go home, the same way Kavanagh planned to. The thought of throwing a personal sweetener in the deal for Arnold Long, stock in the vehicle, had already been discussed with Baran, but it was risky and hard to float in without it looking obvious. Perhaps Long didn't want to cash out, still enjoyed playing the game. Maybe that was the source of Kavanagh's dislike.

Long did have a point. Often it was easy to cruise along in a honeymoon attitude, fussing over the nuts and bolts, picking curtains without realizing they never should have married. It was usually easier to do that than to ask the bigger questions. Kavanagh had been involved in several large transactions where, down the line, variation clauses kicked in and it became obvious the client had no real understanding of what they had committed themselves to. Merging with another company was slightly different from a single deal, but it might still be a good time to check the fundamentals, now Long had thrown them on the table.

'If I can be very level with you both for a moment,' Kavanagh said, locking eyes with Burns to make sure he had his assent, 'my understanding is that for a couple of years now, Trellis has been flying a kite, looking for a potential buyer. Several large corporations have sniffed around and, again on my understanding, Trellis has shied away because they were looking for a certain kind of fit with whoever buys them. Unfortunately, when you're the bought rather than the buyer, you don't always get that luxury, least of all with the heavyweight corporates. When you're fucking a gorilla, it's not you who decides when to stop. Pendulum, and the Trust, spring from a very long tradition and, as far as I can see, have a certain symmetry with Trellis in terms of core values. What's on the table here is the chance for Trellis to shape its own future through a fusion with the Trust.'

'And you get?' Long asked, as though he had been waiting impatiently for Kavanagh to finish.

'We get what we want. The chance to build a base in America, something we've made no secret of from the start.'

If he were following his script, Kavanagh might well have been pushing for a close at that point, removing all the logical obstacles that existed and leaving the client in the harsh glare of the open, ready to run to him. But these people were adults too and the transaction had its own rhythm and pace, as well as a whole bundle of illogical baggage that might never be removed. It would close when it was good and ready to – Kavanagh's job to keep it on track, however quickly the Trust might have wanted it.

'You have a very accurate perception of what we're about here, Mike. More so than anyone else who's ever come looking. And the terms are generous.'

The terms had not been discussed, not the cash on the table. Burns knew that. Long knew it too and he wore the knowledge as a satisfied smirk.

'Late last night, Andrew Mathias faxed me with the hard stuff. A cash offer plus convertible preference stock in the vehicle, fixed to an agreed timetable.' Burns pulled a fax from the wad of paper in front of him. It bore the crest of the Cameron Trust. For Kavanagh, it was like being trumped by his own side. Worse, it left him wondering what side of the table he was actually on. There was no sense in trying to bluff it out.

'I've had no contact with Andrew Mathias unless his communications have slipped between time zones,' Kavanagh said.

'I guess,' Jack Burns said.

'Does the Trust do this sort of thing often?' Long asked.

Kavanagh ignored it. 'I'll need to speak with Andrew Mathias. Do you mind if I look at the fax?'

'Of course not.' Burns slid the document across the table.

There it was, like Burns had said. A cash payment, stock, a timetable. What the fuck was Mathias up to? It rode roughshod over what Kavanagh had been trying to achieve. Baran could not have known about it. At least, Kavanagh hoped not. There weren't many places to go from the piece of paper, not much to say.

'It's the sort of offer I'd find difficult to refuse,' Kavanagh said, pushing the fax back towards Burns.

'I think I might agree if it wasn't made in such a state of panic. Do you want us to screw you? This is with no disrespect to you, Mike, but what sort of show are you guys running? When this arrived unannounced from Mathias, I started to get nervous. This pace may be fine for you, but it's a bit too fast and assumes too much for my liking,' Burns said.

Arnold Long smiled surreptitiously, controlling his features in a way that made Kavanagh want to land a solid fist on his nose. Maybe the table did serve a purpose.

'Nothing changes as far as we're concerned. At some point, the Trust would have made an offer. We seem to be in agreement they jumped the gun. No offer, big or small, makes sense without the structure being in place. That's flying without a net,' Kavanagh said.

'Jack's right though, Mike. This is the kind of thing we wanted to avoid, the headquarters overriding the branch. How much power, autonomy does Pendulum have and what chance would Trellis really have of shaping its future in an alliance with the Trust? This whole thing could just run away from us,' Long said.

'Arnold, let's not run away from ourselves,' Burns said.

'I want to get us back on track. Let me put a call into Mathias, find out why they felt the need to do this. Then we can put the fax away and bring it out when we need it. You can even write in some bigger numbers as a penance,' Kavanagh said, wanting to take some of the lead weight out of the atmosphere.

'I agree,' Burns said.

Kavanagh could feel Burns's sympathy as readily as Long's hostility. Burns wanted to keep the ball rolling, Kavanagh sensed it. If he had wanted to, Burns could have made a pointless fuss. Kavanagh had seen deals wrecked on the basis of less. Kavanagh was furious with the Trust and Mathias, but it had flushed Burns out to some extent and shown the strength of his commitment.

'It's doubtful I can get in touch with Andrew Mathias now, but I'll try Paul Baran. He may be able to help. Can I suggest we take a break and perhaps I can get to a phone,' Kavanagh said.

'Do that, Mike. Then we'll get some lunch and this meeting can happen tomorrow. Today I'd like you to meet a few more of the people who head up the divisions,' Burns said.

As they stood, Kavanagh practically burned under the glare he was getting from Arnold Long. Putting it from his mind as soon as he was alone in the room, he turned his thoughts to Andrew Mathias. Retrieving the card Mathias had given him, Kavanagh counted to twenty before dialling.

No answer.

Kavanagh called Baran on the private line, which was picked up before the second ring.

'Paul, it's me. What the fuck are the Trust playing at?'

Chapter 31

Lucy kept her eyes on the road in front of her, wishing it wasn't so hard to maintain a sulk. The spongy plastic earpieces of her headphones were uncomfortably sticky, but to move her hands and adjust them would be a visual display of interest in herself, and she wasn't going to give in to that. It was not easy to be upset so far away from home when there was so much invested in this trip, financially and emotionally. If she and her father had been on a day out to, say, Hampton Court, stony silence and general indifference would have been an option.

And she didn't just have to perform for Dad. Now there was Nancy Lloyd to consider as well.

The simplest, most comfortable thing in the world would have been to hate her; on sight, on principle, in total and without reservation or reason. Instead, Lucy could not even feel neutral about Nancy. Kim had deftly eased her into comfort with the general prospect of a 'someone else' and Lucy had gone along with that, assuming no amount of therapy would soften her reflex reaction to whatever kind of bitch that 'someone else' would undoubtedly turn out to be. Not so. Lucy liked Nancy and could already notice a change in Dad, which was good to see even if it made her feel strange. Without Mum, it was like Dad kept a part of himself locked away, not necessarily a bad thing, but it was a part of him Lucy knew he needed to share with someone other than his daughter.

That was all right for Dad. What about me? she thought. Who was she really friends with at school? The thousands of miles from home were a good distance from which to survey things like that. Were there any people genuinely interested in her who were not paid to be? Mum used to be her only real friend. It was easy to feel sorry for herself.

Why shouldn't she? Wasn't she allowed to do that sometimes? Dad was her best friend now, but it was the same for her as it was for him – she had things inside her she could not share with her father.

Nathan. Lucy had been saying his name quietly to herself, getting used to it. She visualized situations in which she used his name casually, to him, to other people, in front of other people. In such fantasies, friends were mostly faceless composites, the kind of people she would like to know, like her and Nathan to know. A couple.

But Nathan wasn't that sort of boy.

He would want, demand, all of her for himself, the whole time remaining completely his own person. What would she have to give, just to get a little in return? Nathan had not called before she left England. The first thing Lucy ascertained on arriving at the hotel in Los Angeles was whether the phone in the room had tone dialling, enabling her to check the answering machine back in London. Across thousands of miles, almost every time Dad's back was turned, Lucy made the call, thinking of the sound the phone would make at home, ringing out into the emptiness. Perhaps the Lady would pick it up before the machine got to it. Each time, she listened to the even and practised tone of her father's voice, enticing the caller to leave a message. It had not enticed Nathan, if he had even called.

How much? What would be left for herself?

When the machine had a message stored inside itself, there was a whirr as the tape wound. Every time, Lucy held her breath, listening as hard as she could for the giveaway noise. Nothing.

How much? All of it? Would she give it all to him? Anything he wanted? Maybe. Yes. Isn't that what she wanted herself? Yes.

Thinking about Nathan was nice but it also brought about fear, about where he was, who he was with and what he was doing. Thoughts that created a panic impossible to quell. It was a hard trade-off, the niceness of the daydreams against the inevitable panic they led to. She was thankful for the shortness of the break in Los Angeles.

The car had stopped moving. Dad was looking at her and Lucy took off the headphones, letting the music escape for a few seconds before switching off her sulk and the tape at the same time.

'We're here,' Dad said.

They were parked on an upward slope in a residential street. Lucy had paid no attention to the journey.

'Right,' she said.

'I'm sorry we had to change plans. I really need to be at Trellis today,' he said.

Lucy could not get much sense out of him about what was wrong at work, but something was upsetting him.

'That's all right,' she said.

'I know we said we'd spend today together. If there was only a way to change it, Luce, I would. She'd understand.'

Mum's anniversary. Three years since she was killed. An anniversary in a different time zone.

'It doesn't matter. She'll understand,' Lucy said.

'You seem quiet. You'll be okay with Nancy?'

'Dad.'

'Okay.' He checked his watch. 'Do you want me to come to the door with you?'

'I can find it from here,' she said, knowing he felt better when she was cheeky.

'It's that one. Nine hundred and sixteen. Apartment Two. I'll wait here in the car until she opens the door, then I have to get away.'

With her father's eyes on her back, Lucy walked up the wide drive, blanched plants sitting in dusty earth, and found the buzzer with Apartment Two, the letters written on the tab with a scrawling felt pen. She pressed and waited. Nancy was at the door more quickly than Lucy was expecting, her smile wide and a bit nervy.

'Hi,' Nancy said.

Lucy repeated the greeting and stood to one side, an apologetic smile on her face on behalf of her anxious father, peering out of the convertible. Nancy waved at him and he waved back. Lucy gave him a quick wave and turned to Nancy, raising her eyes in her head. Nancy smiled and Lucy gladly crossed the threshold of the apartment.

'Something funny happened with this deal he's working on,' Lucy said.

'He said so on the phone. Is everything all right?'

'Dad'll work it out. He always does. I'm sorry about changing plans and him landing me on you like this. If you have work to do, tell me because I can stay out of your way. I've brought some comics.'

'No, of course not. I'm treating the next few days as a holiday. I haven't done that since I got here,' Nancy said.

Lucy looked around the living room which was like a scruffier version of their hotel room, everything makeshift but a bit more lived in. The television was oversized with a thick glass screen and large chrome dials and there were a few ornaments that could have belonged to no one, afterthoughts dotted around vainly to make the room more homely. The room was the first worn-down piece of America she had seen and she wondered if this sort of thing was hidden from tourists. The door leading out of the room opened to a passage that had several doors off it, stretching beyond where she could see, giving the impression of a cavernous space.

Nancy must have caught her stare. 'I know. Isn't it awful? I might take a few of these things back to England, just for the souvenir value.'

'Dad didn't say what time he'd be finished, but he expected it to be late this afternoon. He'll call when he's done.'

'Have you had any breakfast?' Nancy asked.

'Sort of,' she replied.

'I'm ashamed to say this, but the other thing I've hardly done since arriving is cook or shop. There are still cupboards in the kitchen I haven't even opened. Your dad says you're a demon in the kitchen. If you want, we could go to the local grocery store and stock up on some things.'

It did not sound alluring, but Lucy didn't want to appear reluctant, so she nodded more enthusiastically than she ought to have.

'I love all of your jewellery,' Nancy said, pointing towards her.

'Thanks. My mum made a lot of it.'

'Right,' Nancy said, seeming flustered to have touched on a subject relating to her mother.

In the supermarket, they wheeled a tarnished trolley around in turns and talked about the food on the shelves, some products totally familiar, some unrecognizable and others a variation on a theme they knew. Nancy talked about her time in advertising and some of the food products she had worked on. Lucy liked the variety but was surprised that the shop itself lacked the disinfected polish she was used to at home, with wide aisles and big labels. This was the shabby local corner shop multiplied by twenty.

'Dad says you haven't been writing a script, that you're writing something different,' Lucy ventured when they were back in the apartment.

Lucy sipped from a decaffeinated, cherry-flavoured, diet soda, wondering what could actually be left in the tin. It was too early even for an early lunch, and they had sprawled on the chairs in the living-room, the air conditioning turned to high while they waited it out.

'I never really started work on the script to have stopped it. For the last week I've been working on a new story, for a novel.'

'Is that why you're going back to England?'

Nancy nodded.

'What's the story about?' Lucy asked.

'It's not a very nice one. It's about a woman who's had bad things happen to her in the past.'

'Does she work it out in the end?'

'No,' Nancy said quietly and took a drink from her can.

'She could work it out if you wanted her to. You're in charge of the story,' Lucy said.

Nancy smiled and just raised her eyebrows. She was not going to respond.

'Do you have a boyfriend in England?' Nancy asked.

The question was so short and simple that it caught Lucy off-guard, so much so that by the time she was about to say no, Nancy was already asking another question.

'What's his name?'

'Nathan,' she said.

'That's a nice name,' Nancy said. 'Sexy,' she added.

Lucy felt bashful. 'I haven't told Dad anything yet.'

'I had lots of secret boyfriends when I was younger. I would have died if my mum and dad had known, and so would they. I won't say anything, I promise. When did you meet him?'

'Only a couple of weeks ago, while I was out in London, and then again just before we came out here.' Lucy remembered sitting on the grass in Leicester Square with him, watching him swig from a bottle with his shirt open.

'You must be so glad to be out here, then. Have you phoned him? You can call from here if you want.'

'He's away this week, anyway. I'll get in touch with him when I get back. You won't say anything to Dad, will you?'

'I promise. I told you. Shall we just make sandwiches now, forget the time. I only had half a grapefruit for breakfast.'

'Okay,' Lucy said.

They stood side by side, chopping tomatoes and cutting cheese. Lucy was overcome by a feeling of safety and security. It was a moment before she realized it was a recollection, an overpowering memory of some other time. Like a face without a name, she struggled to place it. Her knife stopped moving when she recalled the time and the place. She set the knife down, blade away from her as though she were taking safety precautions.

Lucy looked up from the counter top. In the window of the kitchen, half framed by shadow, half framed by light, was the Lady. Three years since Mum. The way she had been with Mum in the kitchen as a girl, making cakes when she had looked up and seen the Lady for the first time.

'Lucy?' she heard Nancy ask.

Her eyes were fixed on the window, trying to form the shape from all the tones of light and dark. When her concentration did break, it was as though her and Nancy's stares switched places, their heads passing each other as Lucy looked down to Nancy's hands and Nancy looked up from Lucy's hands and at the window. Whatever Nancy saw in the window, Lucy didn't know, but she saw its effects as the sharp-pointed knife Nancy held skidded over the wet surface of the tomato she held and the blade opened the damp and wrinkled skin on the fleshy part of her index finger, near the knuckle.

Nancy's hand flew to her head, gripping it and smearing a trail of blood over her brow. Lucy thought Nancy had cried out from the pain of the cut, but it became clear that the sounds were too deep and heartfelt for it to be just that.

Nancy bent double and went into a kind of squat.

'What's wrong?' Lucy asked, resting a hand on Nancy's shoulder.

'Oh! Jesus!' Nancy cried out and tumbled sideways to the floor, the knife spinning noisily on the tiles and Lucy jumping back from it instinctively.

From a foetal position, Nancy convulsed and held both hands to her head, blood covering her face and dripping onto the floor.

'Nancy? Nancy?' Lucy felt a panic setting in, not knowing how she was meant to cope with this in a foreign country.

Nancy gave one concentrated holler of pain and then it was quiet. Lucy stared, afraid she was dead.

'Oh,' Nancy muttered.

On the floor she looked ungainly, too big for the space she was in. There was something ugly about the way she had fallen, the blood.

'Are you okay?' Lucy asked, out of breath.

Nancy sat up and looked at her finger. 'I caught a sharp

pain in my head. It's okay now. I get migraines sometimes and they come on like this. It's nothing to worry about.'

'You don't need a doctor or anything? Should I call Dad?'

'No, don't,' she said quickly. 'Please, let's not make a fuss about it, Lucy.'

'Whatever. You need a plaster for your finger.'

'I just caught the pain and then bloody cut myself,' Nancy said.

Lucy couldn't remember if Nancy had screamed first and then cut herself or if it had happened the other way around. She was clear on one thing, however. Nancy had seen what Lucy had seen in the window, too.

Nancy had seen the Lady.

Chapter 32

Garth stood in the narrow gap of a passage separating Paul Baran's office from a room no one at Pendulum knew of. Almost no one. The hiding place in the cleft between the rooms, the public and the secret, was so enclosed that each of Garth's breaths brought his chest up against the wall in front of him. There were so many places like this to go in the building, slim margins that were interwoven into its structure like veins beneath the surface, a hidden part of the pattern that underlay the building more surely than any foundation could have. There was an intimacy to the subtext of the building that comforted Garth. For the last half of the day he had moved through ancient passageways like liquid through a pipe, unseen, unheard and unfelt by those he observed. Around whole floors, between whole floors, the intricacy of the Pendulum building enabled him to be certain the office was emptying of people, people pouring out gratefully onto the streets, another day of ignorance behind them as they laboured on for the Trust. That was the beauty of The Book, he was learning, part of the requirement of the knotwork that all the loose ends flow across and over themselves, sometimes in opposition and at other times in harmony.

Paul Baran did just as little as Garth had always imagined he did. For the last half hour of his day, Baran sat and shifted paper around his desk in a way not dissimilar to Garth when he was in the hold of deep-seated boredom. Through the small chink, Garth trained his eye and watched Baran pore over his schedule time after time, fingering the effete leather pocket-book he kept it in. As impressive as Baran might have been, to Garth he was nothing more than yesterday's man. Whatever events were contained in his calendar, one must have been for that evening because Baran made a polite phone call confirming the time and place of the meeting and then began to tidy his already tidy desk, sweeping it clean of paper then locking anything with a keyhole.

With a folder in his hand, Baran turned and approached the wall Garth was standing behind. Garth froze, his breathing interrupted. Baran seemed to be looking straight at him, as though making eye contact. When Baran took a step nearer, Garth drew a sharp little breath through his nostrils. There was a clinking sound to Garth's left and he realised Baran was putting the folder into a safe. Garth let out a cautious sigh and in less than a minute Baran had left the office as orderly as if he had never been in it.

There should not have been a way for Garth to enter Baran's office and yet he knew he would be able to, knew what lay in wait for him and had been calling him for so long.

The wall dissolved and the panel in front of him became like fluid, held together only by his fragile imagination. In the moment it took for him to be the other side of the wall, Garth wondered if he were imagining everything, the whole world around him conjured chemically, all of his life merely a tale told by his accelerated brain. Like when he used to wonder if awake was really dreaming and dreaming was really awake. Was he making it all up, every last part of it, as though writing a story?

The Book was in the middle of the floor, occupying the centre of everything the way it had been the first time Garth had seen it. Its physical form brought memories and different feelings. It was happiness, a simple and untainted layer of it underpinned by inevitability and sadness. Garth was not making it up. The Book was where it began and ended, and began again.

Its presence in the room was akin to another person being there. Garth could feel himself being watched, pored over; read. It wanted nothing from him and yet he would give it everything. The Book reached deep within itself and into Garth, illuminating a pattern in everything that had ever happened to him, from the simplest, most random of words to the immeasurable convolution of his whole life.

This would be his last-ever time in the building, Garth knew that. There was a melancholy in him he would not have expected as the sense of last things pervaded him. There were two things he wanted to do, neither of which he would have considered pleasant a month earlier. Things changed. The first act was for himself, to bring closure to his time at Pendulum. The second was for The Book and promised to be even more personal.

Baran's office reminded Garth of the lobby of a hotel, oversized and well-placed furniture ready to catch anyone falling towards it. The atmosphere was like an operating theatre, washed through the filters of air conditioning, light evenly painted onto surfaces by a range of bulbs and tubes. When Garth stopped looking at his surroundings and turned his attention back to the centre of the room, The Book had gone, physically at least. He could feel its pulse within him.

I want them to know it was me, Garth thought, or at least heard the voice say inside his head, the voice that used to belong to him and whispered his thoughts. Garth removed his employee identification badge from the side pocket of his trousers, the swipe card with the frowning passport portrait of him. From his other pocket he took out another card, the one that had belonged to Chris Carson, his picture full of hope, happiness and enthusiasm. It was a picture that showed someone with more of a future than Garth himself could ever have hoped for. Garth laid the two cards on the closed leather covers of Baran's blotter, resting one on each half of the gold-trimmed and cushioned hide as though setting them out for a game of cards. In the space left between the cards, along the join of the blotter's door, Garth positioned the ragged remains of one of Chris Carson's index fingers, which no longer looked as though it had ever belonged to anyone. Garth laid it so that it pointed absurdly to the empty space on the front of Baran's desk.

Let them know it was you, he thought. Mark out the

territory. Make it your own. There was something he had often joked about doing to the boss when he had left other companies, the thing to do when you get fired.

Standing on the desk, Garth dropped his trousers and underwear into an unruly pile around his ankles, squatted over the empty space and strained, a rasp of gas escaping him before his muscles found something solid to push against.

His father would not be as easy.

'Who's there?' Tom Richards called.

Garth suppressed a giggle. The silly old bastard might as well have said, Halt, who goes there? All of his life emptied into looking after a collection of bricks, glass and wood, haunted by its ghosts and telling its stories to anyone who would listen.

The Pendulum building was, Garth knew, the only thing his father truly loved. More than his ex-wife, more than Garth and more than himself. Bad feelings towards his father were easy, little or no analysis required. There had been happier times, made sweeter by their rarity, when his father had cheated on his true love. Days out to the museum, the seaside. As a boy, sitting in the room his father was about to enter, listening to his yarns about the place, he never imagined he would work there one day. Before Baran and before Kavanagh, Garth had been here learning about things. Yes, there had been good times, but they stopped one night nearly thirty years earlier, when Alex Cameron took a knife to his family and wiped them out before disappearing. The idea was appealing, Cameron slicing through his father, mother and sister. What order had he done it in? Garth had no brothers or sisters. Of his father and mother, father was the obvious place to begin.

Garth rattled the handle of the slightly ajar door to his father's office once again.

'Who is it?' There was a quiver, close to fear, in the old man's voice.

'It's me,' Garth said, remaining where he was and making his voice deep and sonorous.

'What are you playing at?' His father had half opened the door. 'What's the time?' He looked at his watch. 'You're here late tonight, boy.'

'I wanted to see you, Dad.'

Garth saw the curiosity desert his father's face as the impassive and familiar stare ousted it. How long had Garth felt the force of that stare, dropping his head or turning away to avoid it? Tonight he held his father's gaze, feeling his eyes begin to water. I will not turn away. I will not blink.

'You'd better come in then,' his father said.

The office was a room Garth knew mostly from memory, rarely venturing into it since joining Pendulum, happier with his head poked round the door.

'Do you want a cup of tea or coffee?' his father asked.

'Which one do you think I drink, Dad? Have a guess.'

His father sighed. 'Don't be awkward, son.'

'So, you don't know?'

'No. I don't know. What do you want, tea or coffee?'

'Cappuccino?' Garth asked mockingly. 'Nothing for me.'

Garth watched his father shuffle nervously, his hands reaching to any available item on the surface of his desk, visibly finding comfort when he latched on to the long-bladed screwdriver, one Garth had seen first when he had been just a boy. His father was not comfortable and it gave off him like an odour.

'Why did you leave Mum?' Garth asked, regarding his father across the desk, his voice that of a job interviewer.

His father continued to look at the screwdriver, turning it around in his fingers.

'Why did you leave Mum?' Garth's voice was slightly louder the second time, a touch more shrill, and he saw his father flinch.

'Garth, we've been through this. It was between me and your mum. It had nothing to do with you.'

'Nothing to do with me?'

'You know what I mean.'

'That it was none of my business?' Garth asked.

'That we didn't separate because of you. It didn't have anything to do with you in that way.'

'Why didn't I come and live with you, instead of staying with Mum.'

'It was practical at the time. Garth, what's wrong? You haven't been like this for a while. Why now? I thought we'd sorted it all out, son.'

'I wanted to hear it from you, the words. They're only words. Just say them. Tell me the reason why you left Mum.'

'Garth.' There was more of his father's weight pressing down on the word, trying to give it some authority.

'When I was a boy and you used to bring me here, to see what you did, you used to talk to me. You haven't said a word that meant anything since I was seven. Now you say it all to that little slag that comes here, Kavanagh's daughter.'

'Don't say that about her. It's not nice,' his father said.

'Does she turn you on? Coming in here with those T-shirts that show off her tits, her jeans pulled up the crack of her arse? Would you fancy giving her one up there?' Garth asked.

'You're not too old for a wallop,' his father warned.

Garth leaned over and moved his head close enough to feel the warmth of his father's breath, the remnants of a microwave meal on it. Gently, he took the screwdriver from his father's hand.

'Do you know what?' Garth whispered. 'I think I might just be a little too old for a wallop.'

Lifting his hand high in the air, Garth brought the screwdriver down onto the back of his father's hand, putting his shoulder into the action to give it force. He felt it glance against a round bone. He grabbed his father's fingers to prevent the recoil of his hand. The square-ended blade of the tool pierced through flesh, moved bone and sinew, split the soft skin of his father's palm and came out against the wooden top of the desk. His father's reflex cry of pain lingered on as a howl. Garth picked up the old phone – receiver and cradle – and cuffed his father across the temple before using the ancient Bakelite as a hammer and the screwdriver as a nail, hitting it so hard the plastic shattered.

Garth's father wriggled and was struggling against the pin the driver made. Soon, Garth knew, his stubborn father would wrest himself free. There was probably a hammer somewhere in the room and Garth could easily nail the old bastard to the table and have his way with him there, but he wasn't sure he wanted to kill him. Not until he had what he wanted. He dragged his father over the desk, pulling the screwdriver out, causing him to mewl from the soreness. Garth hefted the dazed old man to the far end of the office, dropping him onto a swivel chair and sending him on his way with a punch in the stomach.

'Garth, what are you . . .?'

It was all his father managed as Garth hit him across the side of the head as hard as he could manage with a full tablet of paper, five hundred hefty sheets bound by a wrapper with a zebra pattern. As his father sat in a stupor, Garth began to unwind a roll of gaffer tape around him, attaching his torso to the chair with it. The roll was almost new and Garth used all of it, dancing around his father as though he were a maypole. When the top half of his father was firmly attached to the chair, Garth took the old man's shoes, trousers and underwear off, baggy yellow-white cotton. For a moment he stared at the genitals, surprised how much they resembled his own. That's where I came from, he thought.

The second roll, a brand new one, he used on the legs, ensuring they were nicely apart to allow him access in between them. Finally Garth secured his father's arms. Placing a short piece of tape over his father's mouth, reaching from ear to ear, he went and boiled the kettle while he waited for his father to come back to consciousness.

Garth found his father's tool box and opened it out on

the desk, which had a smear of his father's blood across the surface. The office was a trove of things he could use on the old man, the tool box its crowning glory. There were two Stanley knives, three pairs of pliers, some wire cutters, an adjustable spanner, drill bits, a wood rasp, more screwdrivers, nails and countless other things which all had sharp or rough edges that could be brought into contact with soft, fleshy parts of the body.

'You're back. Hello,' Garth said, peering into his father's bleary eyes. 'I've got something for you. Something very special and very nice.'

Garth held up the saucer as though proffering milk to a reluctant cat and chopped away at the white powder with a razor blade. His father's eyes became more focused and Garth wondered if he knew what was on the saucer. His father looked down into his lap, as though just realizing he was naked below the waist.

'It'll loosen you up. Help you to talk more easily.'

His father's breath rasped through his nostrils, the silver gaffer tape painted across his face like a smile preventing any flow of breath. He tried to speak and made a snorting noise through his nose.

'That's the idea,' Garth said.

Bringing the saucer to eye-level, Garth reached between his father's legs, took hold of the two soft rounds of flesh and closed his hand tight. As his father drew breath with the pain, Garth shoved the saucer into his face, watching the powder suck up unevenly. Garth released his father's balls, licked his fingers, which tasted of sweat, daubed them with cocaine and stuck them up his father's nose. Garth was fascinated to see the effect of the drug on the old man. At first it was hardly perceptible, but soon it was as though everything inside him had sped up by a ratio of ten, its evidence the wildness in his eyes.

'I'm not certain you believe I'll hurt you. I can tell you think that because I'm your son and I love you, I won't do anything bad to you.'

Garth fetched the freshly boiled kettle and took its lid

off. He immersed the dessert spoon his father used to measure out coffee and left it in the boiling water until he could feel the heat spreading up the handle.

He put the spoon between his father's legs and rested the concave side of it against his scrotum. The old man struggled against his shackles, trying to get away from the pain. Garth pushed the hot metal further into his father's delicate and wrinkled sac, knowing it would be burning. A while longer, enough to bring a tear to his father's eye, and Garth relented.

'Time to talk,' Garth said.

He took a Stanley knife from the tool box and cut a slice into the gaffer tape which opened like the skin of an orange, his father pulling away. He must have cut into some flesh.

'Tell me where it is,' Garth said.

'What?' His father's voice was slurred, the tape not allowing much movement.

'Tell me where it is,' Garth said.

'Tell you where what is?' There was spit and other gooey stuff gurgling in the voice.

'I'm going to make myself a cup of coffee, which is all you ever seem to do, as I recall, and then, when I've finished it, I'm going to ask you again where it is. You're going to tell me where to find what I'm looking for. If you don't, I'm going to use that wood rasp to give you a pedicure. Then, the adjustable spanner will make that spoon seem like a jockstrap. You're a stubborn old fucker, so I expect then I'll use the wire cutters to take a finger or two off and maybe put them in the toaster.'

His father did not reply. Garth knew The Book would make him kill his father if that was necessary. Could he do it? he asked himself as he looked at him, helplessly bound to the chair, his eyes shrunken and blood seeping from his mouth onto the gaffer tape. Looking at the fear in his father, the adrenalin and self-preservation that was struggling against the drugs, Garth wondered if he would be able to finish the job.

Garth took a long swallow of coffee.

The decor of his father's office had changed little over the years because old Tom had got round people, ever keen to keep things the same in his little home from home, his only home. Somewhere in the building was what The Book had been waiting to retrieve. Garth had been unable to track it down on his own, but he knew his father would know.

He drained the cup of its remaining liquid.

'You know what it is I want, don't you?' he asked his father. 'But you're not going to tell me where it is, are you?'

His father said nothing.

Garth sighed. He retrieved the wood rasp and knelt. Grabbing his father's middle toe, he set to work.

Chapter 33

There had been a time for waiting and a time for reading. Now, those times were past.

Wadlow Grace gathered together the things he would need for his journey, things that would get him there, other things needed once he was.

Pa's gun had been in the Grace family pretty much since they started making .45s and Wadlow kept it in a wooden case he had made specially for it, the lock too big and too strong for the fragile joins of wood, but he wanted to store the weapon this way, as though it were a caged beast. Wadlow knew, deep down, that he would need it and reluctantly maintained the piece in a state of readiness, firing off one clip of ammunition each week to keep the parts moving in the right direction, the killing direction. Guns scared Wadlow in general and Pa's old gun in particular, always had, as if it knew the things it had done, or would do, keeping the secrets locked in its dark metal. Mama Grace never approved of it being in the house but Pa insisted on it, and on his boys knowing what it was and what it could do, even Randall. The first time Wadlow fired it, his hand had been shaking so much and his grip on the butt so weak, the end sight wandered around everywhere except on what he was meant to be aiming for. Pa laughed as loud as Wadlow screamed when the gun went off, his hands disappearing behind the left side of his head. Wadlow had been eleven then.

Randall stood there as if the pistol were just a part of his hand, growing out of its end. His arm was perfectly still and the shot seemed to come out with one of his breaths, straight along the barrel, freed from the muzzle and into the middle of a paper target Pa had drawn in thin pencil and pasted to the back of an old door. The next bullet barely had a chance to lift from the magazine and into the hole before Randall put it right into the perforation made by the first. Randall had been learning for three years before Wad had been allowed to pick up a gun.

Every lesson would end with Pa's favourite warning: 'Don't be pointing no gun at anyone unless you plan on using it.'

The gun was now secured in the box once again, but, the night before, Wadlow had taken it down into the sound-proofed depths of his bunker of books, the place he always took it to fire it. Instead of a target, he lined up his favourite hardcovers and put a bullet through the heart of each, the shake in his hands gone, the fear in his heart still there. The hardcovers were ruined, but that didn't matter – Wadlow was done with books for now.

In a protective plastic bag, packed next to the gun, were Randall's notebook and pen. Pages of the notebook had once again become senseless, while others were still painfully intelligible. Randall's old pen still refused to write, but Wad tucked it into the notebook in any case. A casual flick through the pages had been like the flashes of a bad dream lingering on into the day.

Life in the little town of Raynford was over for Wadlow Grace. All the years spent there with the preacher, learning, watching and waiting. Just as the preacher had, Wadlow had waited for a sign, knowing that it would come, knowing that he would recognize it once it arrived.

Upstairs he gathered the few remaining things from his first years in the store, when he was still a lean, toothily attractive teenager. The room was tiny, constricting his current size as much as it had his youthful frame. Wadlow knew, even then, he would soon outgrow it. One night, three months before his seventeenth birthday, Wadlow rose from the narrow single bed, removed his nightshirt and quietly walked along the hall to the preacher's room. Naked as the day he'd been born, Wadlow slipped silently into the bed, finding space on the mattress and fitting himself carefully into the shape of the preacher's sleeping body, clinging on tight. And they'd stayed that way, boy and man, man and man, until the preacher died.

In 1931, through a network involving eight companies and an unspoken agreement between people whose existence Wadlow knew nothing of, Clough Cameron acquired the land on which the store, and most of the street, now stood. Wadlow heard a few local stories about it, but they were never more than small rumours, not enough fire in them to break out of the confines of Raynford. How and when exactly the bunker had been hollowed out, Wadlow didn't know and neither did anyone else for that matter, apart from the preacher, and that secret died with him. It's a mystery, like the pyramids or the catacombs, Wadlow, the preacher told him.

Clough Cameron and his son Alex had been travelling in America in 1959, spreading some strange gospel. While they were in New England, staying with Jack Burns and his son, who would later go on to form Trellis, they sent the preacher out to Memphis to find Wadlow, as though they had known, precisely, where he would be. The preacher had his own theory of predestination and he told it to Wadlow. He also told him about The Book.

As Wadlow stood at the door of their old bedroom, the cardboard box was now fuller with bits and pieces of their life together and Wadlow's alone, but it did not have the kind a weight a life should have. This had never been a place to stay, to make a home. It had been somewhere to wait. Of course, for The Book, waiting itself was a part of the process. With more haste, Wadlow moved through the other rooms, wiping himself and the preacher from the house, leaving only traces of where they once were.

It was not really a bunker.

The cavern that stretched far down into the ground and out beyond the back of the shop was created for a final purpose. The technology involved in it was similar to that once used for terrible, terrible things. The bunker was conceived, designed and built to be a massive incinerator. On this day, it would be a crematorium for the books he had spent so long amassing with the money that still arrived each month, its source undoubtedly the Cameron Trust, but its trail untraceable. It was a bunker for a short time only, somewhere to store things before this fire, and the final fire, whenever that came. There was only a single book he needed from the collection, Nancy Lloyd's, and that was already packed into the small bag he could keep close to him at all times, along with the gun and Randall's notebook and pen.

Wadlow spent a further hour shifting his old life underground. From the PC, he down-loaded several files onto floppy disks. Wadlow once bought a scanner and used it to try and suck the words from the pages of Randall's notebook, converting them to electricity, but, in the same way Randall's pen would not give of itself, nor would the pages yield. He had tried to photocopy the notebook with the same result – just blank pages as though the marks on the page might actually be a figment of his own mind. Even though he knew it stood no chance of surviving the heat, Wadlow erased the entire contents of the hard disk, a tingle of excitement running down his spine as he did, the feeling of the purge enjoyable.

The preacher had shown him the procedure for starting the incinerator and they had practised it numerous times, always as though they might be in a rush when the time came, rather than the leisurely pace at which Wadlow was now moving. Unlike Pa's old gun, the incinerator required no maintenance to keep it on standby. The technology was simple and built to outlast them all. It would work when it was required to. Wadlow studied the instructions, admiring the preacher's neat hand as it described which levers to pull, which buttons to push and where to light the first small flame that would grow into a consuming blaze. He knew all the directions by heart, but wanted to look at them one more time, to say goodbye to the preacher. Wadlow placed a gentle kiss on the page.

With most of everything he had ever called his own stacked in the centre of the bunker, Wadlow stood at the bottom of the spiral staircase, wanting one last look. All those books, and in them so many stories, realities and fabrications. A vast knot of stories, interweaving, criss-crossing, finding opposition and balance. And, in every one, The Book. That was the first thing the preacher had taught, the first article of faith. Every story is not in The Book. The Book is in every story.

The time for waiting and the time for reading past, Wadlow Grace closed the door and left the words to the succour of the flame.

Chapter 34

Kavanagh, Lucy and Nancy spent an easy day together. Lucy had chosen the venue, Disneyland, and although it was the most obvious place to go, it pleased Kavanagh that she had involved herself in a decision connected with the holiday. He still felt bad about having had to cancel the previous day's plans. Kavanagh was angry that Pendulum, as always, and Trellis, in this instance, had come between himself and a private occasion – one connected with Helen, at that. Lucy, for her part, seemed to be taking it well and he even thought that, possibly, it had been a good idea not to spend the day of Helen's anniversary together, silently mulling over the past. Things moved on.

Nancy sat in the passenger seat, her hair tied back and her eyes hidden by sunglasses. A trace of makeup gave her features an inviting outline, her lips covered in a matt pastel shade of pink almost invisible against the tone of her flesh. Her white sleeveless blouse fitted close at the waist, high shoulders revealing a lot of arm and ragged cutoff jeans showing the skin of her legs turning from white at the top to a tanned gold on her calf muscles. Nancy looked dressed for a day at the beach, the clothes and the makeup making her appear young and relaxed, more like a friend of Lucy's. Each time she threw back her head and laughed and the clear sky reflected on the lenses of her glasses, Kavanagh found himself looking at her and laughing along.

The drive out to Orange County was wild and windswept, their voices carrying on the speed and swallowed by other traffic. Kavanagh began the journey worried it might be hard work for all of them, but, as with their first encounter, the three of them fitted together with no discernible effort, even Lucy participating in the conversation. Disney turned out to be a fast-food leisure experience, designed to slice their time and extract money from them with deft precision. Moving through the fabricated world, they had the opportunity to take part, laugh or be indifferent, as the mood took them. Kavanagh took some photographs. The one he knew would stick in his memory was of Lucy standing in front of giant teacups, in her black T-shirt and jeans, the sun in her eyes making it impossible to tell if she were smiling, scowling or squinting.

Late in the afternoon, as Lucy and Nancy walked ahead of him towards 'It's a Small World', a memory of Helen, a sense of her being, came back to Kavanagh in a way so profound it stopped him moving. Kavanagh would not have believed things could shift in a single moment, but as he stood on a counterfeit street, surrounded by parents, children and adults in costumes, the feeling came to him that he could be with Nancy Lloyd in a way he had with Helen. The awareness of it made him sad for Helen and happy for himself. Is this what would be beyond Pendulum and Trellis, a way out and someone to share it with? Kavanagh regained his stride, afraid to think about it too much.

As they pulled up to the door of Nancy's apartment, still full from dinner, it was after ten-thirty and there was the first moment of palpable awkwardness in the whole day, no one speaking.

'Why don't you come in for coffee?' Nancy asked. 'It's still early.'

They had drunk several cups in the restaurant. Kavanagh was trying to force a no from himself when Lucy spoke.

'I'd like that,' she said.

Kavanagh and Nancy were out of the car almost as soon as his daughter's words were spoken.

This shouldn't be difficult, Kavanagh said to himself, as he nursed a cup of coffee and they indulged in subdued conversation, mostly revolving around a gentle ribbing of him for being so stiff in Disney. We're both adults. My daughter is practically an adult, more so if you count her therapy. This should be easy. I want to stay here tonight, I think Nancy wants me to stay here and Lucy can tell I want to stay. How best to manage the economy of emotions and desires between them, to achieve a satisfactory balance?

Again, Lucy was ahead of him. She drained her coffee cup and gave a dramatic yawn, stretching her shoulders into it.

'Do you want to go?' Kavanagh asked, looking at his watch.

'Can't we stay?' Lucy asked, distilling into a few words all the tension in the room.

Lucy looked away, so he could not make eye contact with her, and he glanced at Nancy, who seemed to nod with the slightest movement of her eyes.

'I can make up beds for you, in the spare room. It'd save you driving, Mike, and then you can help me out with the duty-free Jack Daniels.'

Kavanagh noticed how well Nancy had accented the plural, beds.

'If it's no trouble,' he said.

'Of course not. Do you have meetings tomorrow?'

'Not until just before lunch,' Lucy chimed in.

Twenty mostly silent minutes later, Nancy had made the two beds in the scantily furnished spare room and Lucy had retired to one of them, complaining of extreme tiredness, the effects of the day and delayed jetlag.

'She's a smart one,' Nancy said.

'Believe it,' Kavanagh replied, his voice a note lower despite his daughter being behind closed doors.

Nancy fetched the bottle of Jack Daniels and they sat on the sofa with tiny amounts of the brown-gold liquid filling cheap, thin glasses.

'Today worked out fine,' Nancy said, clinking her glass against Kavanagh's.

'Lucy was no trouble yesterday?'

'No, none at all. She administered a bit of first aid,' Nancy said, stroking a plaster on her finger.

'How have things been going?' he asked. There had not been much chance to talk during the day.

'I've finally told my agent I'm not doing the script and that I'm going back to England. She took a lot of convincing. Even more than I did.'

'Are you going to write anything else when you're back in England?'

'This last couple of weeks I've been writing like mad. Today was the first day away from it and it's made me anxious, itchy. A new story just started to flow and it's surprised me because it's so much darker than the frothy stuff I usually do.'

'What's it about?' Kavanagh asked.

'I usually hate that question.'

'Sorry.'

He watched her expression shift to something more serious. Gently, he reached out and touched her knee and she looked down at his hand.

'It's a story about a woman trying to dig back to one key moment in her life, something that's made her the person she is but also something that haunts her. It sounds very specific, but that's the way this one's unfolding. They do that sometimes, start with a minor event,' she said.

'Do you plan it all out from that?' he asked.

'Kind of. I like to have a grand plan. Something to write towards. I don't really know where this is going, but at least I'm writing again.'

'What's the significant event?' Kavanagh asked.

'Not the one she thinks it is. When she's sixteen, she meets an older man and falls for him, literally. He's about thirty and charms this girl, who comes from quite a strict family, the sort that never let her feel as though she might be attractive to anyone, the kind of people she won't get on with in later life. The girl sees the man a few times and they don't really do a lot, but he likes to listen to her and she finds that flattering, that someone will listen to her. Of course, it's all a bit too good to be true and anyone except her could have seen where it was going and, eventually, she realizes she should have known that too. One night, late and in the winter cold, they are on the dark edge of a common and he talks her into the back of his car and he's doing things to her she doesn't like and he's so strong and there's so little space in the back of the car. When he's starting, about to do something she doesn't want him to, she asks what he's doing. *Something very special and very nice*. That's what he says and it's the line which haunts her. One small piece of dialogue that goes round and round in her head like a chant. By the time she realizes she is pregnant, he's long gone, as though he might never have existed. For as long as she can, she hides it from her parents and thinks they are hiding it from themselves. When none of them can do that any longer, there's a dilemma – a baby out of wedlock or an abortion. God seems to intervene for them and they don't have to make either choice because she loses the baby, what there is of it. It takes her a while, but she makes the kind of recovery that leaves her fragile, feeling like she can never hold on to another life, that she doesn't have it in her. *Something very special and very nice*. Round and round. It troubles her because even when he said it for the first time, she knew it had been said before, as though the words had been branded into her and he is touching something familiar, that is already there. For a while she thinks about it, but her mind is blocking it out, until she realizes what really happened, what the truly significant thing was.'

Nancy paused and took a breath, refilling her glass with a more substantial amount of whisky and doing the same for Kavanagh, clinking the neck of the bottle against his glass. Was she going to stop? Kavanagh wondered. He allowed the hand he had kept rested on her knee to brush at her hair and she moved closer to him on the sofa, sitting back against him so he could see only the side of her head and bringing her shoeless feet up onto the couch. Hesitantly, Kavanagh nuzzled the hair at the back of her neck, smelling her and feeling the warmth of her body. He wanted to grab her and crush her into him and it was difficult to let such strong desire show itself as gentle caress.

'Her mother,' Nancy continued, 'a very proper church-going woman who can see nothing outside the most narrow periphery, bitter in her core and withering on the outside, had an affair when the girl was very young. Five years old. The father never found out but the girl did. The man was someone living in the town, a stranger passing through who got to know the family through the church and because her father, an accountant, did some work for him. It meant that the man was around from time to time, usually with the mum and dad there but then with just the mum, who could always find a way to explain it to the dad. The man was somewhere in his forties and the girl always found him friendly, very friendly. Although she's only five at the time, she can still get a sense of something unspoken passing between the man and her mother. One day, when the man comes over, the girl's mother sends her to her room so she can discuss church things in peace, which pleases the girl because that bores her anyway, even at that age. Her room is a bright yellow attic at the top of the house, one that always seems to let the sun fill it.

'She sits in the middle of the floor, playing for a while, and then she looks up at the door. The man seems to fill it as he stands there and the girl stops what she's doing with her toys.

' "Hello," says the man.

' "Hello," the girl repeats and goes back to her rag doll.

'The man sits down on the floor with her and starts to idle with some of her toys, building a tower from square wooden bricks, taking the lids on and off and rearranging some blue and green plastic saucepans. All the time, he's doing it as though he's just playing on his own, not interested in the girl being there. It makes her feel jealous, left out because he wants to play on his own, and she just sits and watches him, her mouth slightly open. He reaches over and takes the dolly from her hands and she lets him, staring up at him again because even when he's on the floor, he's so much bigger than her. The doll is one of those classic rag dollies, long spindly legs with striped socks, knitted black hair and a funny sort of crocheted dress. The man holds it upright and pretends to make it walk along, the round feet padding on the carpet from the ends of gangling legs. Neither the man nor the girl have spoken other than saying hello. She feels like she should not speak and, already perhaps, knows that something is not right.

' "Is this your favourite?" he asks.

'The girl just nods. The man strokes the hair on the doll, as though he's fixing it up. He picks it up high in the air and looks at it closely, staring in its face before giving it a kiss. "It's my favourite, too," he says, and, as he does, he touches the girl's hair and smiles. The man lays the dolly out on the floor, lifts its skirt up and laughs, trying to get the girl to laugh as well, but she won't. The loose knitted dress lifts off over the doll's head quite easily and the body beneath is naked in some way, the torso yellow-white and a pair of blue knickers that could be swimming trunks actually forming part of the body, unremovable. The man strokes the doll's hair, then the girl's. The doll's foot, the girl's foot. The doll's leg, her leg. The doll's calf, her calf. Higher up her leg.

'The girl's dress doesn't come off as easily, but he manages it. The girl wishes her own underclothes were sewn on, like the dolly's.

' "What are you doing?" the girl asks.

' "Something very special and very nice," the man says.

' "What is it?"

' "Do you trust me?"

' "I don't know. Will it hurt?"

' "Am I hurting you now?"

' "No."

' "Or now?"

' "Ah! No, I like that."

' "So you trust me then?"

' "Yes."

' "Take off the rest of your clothes then." '

Nancy's body was pressed tightly into Kavanagh's, tension obvious in it, the slight shake of tears.

'The mother knew,' Nancy said. 'She knew what had happened, what he did to her, and she made the girl promise that it would never be spoken about. There would be no words said about it, that's what she told the girl. At that age, the ferocity of an experience like that, connected with a promise to her mother, is enough to seal the event in her head. What happened to her is not only locked inside her brain where no one else can get to it, she hides it from herself as well. She realises she can't live with it in her head, so she puts a block in front of it, out of sight even if it's not out of mind. The only thing that seeps through and, eventually, provides the key is the phrase that goes round and round. *Something very special and very nice*.'

Nancy took a long swallow from her glass, Kavanagh doing the same from his own. They passed some time in silence and Kavanagh felt her body relax, its warmth pleasant against his own.

'I'm glad you decided to stay,' she said.

'I thought after last time . . .'

'Don't,' she said.

Kavanagh brushed a few stray hairs from the back of her neck and ran his fingers over the smooth skin. She wriggled her spine in response and it sent a small shiver through Kavanagh. He took the glass from her hand and set it down on the floor along with his own. With both hands free, Kavanagh put his arms around her and let his fingers roam over her, touching the fabric of the white blouse and the denim of her jeans, venturing to the skin. Her hand did similar things, but was more bold, lingering only briefly on his inner thigh before it was massaging the front of his trousers.

Nancy let her head fall back and he put his mouth onto her waiting lips. He kissed her in the way he had wanted to that night outside the restaurant and how he had imagined all day. The alcohol hummed in his head and he was clumsy and inelegant, but it worked. She turned and sat in his lap, straddling him and probing his mouth with the tip of her tongue, their breath clashing as they panted hotly.

He trailed on the end of her hand as she led him to her room. Kavanagh undressed her quickly, pulling at the buttons of the blouse and fitting his hands into her torso, pressing her hip-bones and tracing the tightly stretched skin of her abdomen, wanting to take her shorts off. He knelt and licked at her navel as he unzipped and unbuttoned them, pulling them to her knees along with her underwear, burying his face into her, smothering himself with her.

When they were both naked, they landed heavily on the bed, clambering and crawling to find a comfortable position.

It had been a long time and there had been no one except Helen. It made him cautious, nervous. She seemed to sense it and pushed herself out at him, grabbing him hard and shoving their bodies together. They coupled fiercely, Kavanagh feeling the painful strain, barely able to contain himself. Nancy moved beneath him almost as hard and fast as he did on top of her. In a few excruciating strokes, he was there, staring wide-eyed at her as he came and she gripped and grunted in time with him.

They lay entwined, not speaking, their limbs knotted together into one.

Chapter 35

Nancy jumped when the doorbell buzzed. Kavanagh and Lucy had left ten minutes earlier, so she assumed it must be them. Kavanagh had moved from her bed into the spare room at some point towards the morning. However bright she felt inside and however cheerful the three of them tried to be at breakfast, there was still an atmosphere floating. Nancy's mind tingled with thoughts. Where next? What now? How long do I have with him?

The bell buzzed once more.

Nancy's expectant smile faded as soon as she opened the door.

Standing on the step was a large man, packed with the kind of body weight it took years to acquire. Under the podginess of his face, she could detect a handsome man, dressed smartly in beige, as though about to attend Sunday service. Over his shoulder and destroying the cleanness of the image was a yellow canvas shoulder bag, one of his hands gripping the strap as though it would be snatched from him at any minute. Nancy looked down at his feet. Next to his highly polished loafers was a large holdall.

It felt as though death itself had donned a smart suit and decided to come calling at her door.

'Nancy, my name's Wadlow Grace and you and me have some talking to do. A lot of talking.'

Chapter 36

The day was bright and he didn't have much time. Even in the random and meandering nature of his heightened consciousness, Garth was well aware that there was a trail behind him, one which would soon be picked up. The previous week had been the most testing – so far. It had been a continual, waking anxiety-dream, his nerves on edge and every thought transformed into a fear.

There was unfinished business, things to take care of. One more straggling end to snip and he would be complete, or at least ready for completion. When The Book sent him out into the world, it wanted him to be alone, to have no ties in the knot other than to itself.

'Garth? Is that you, Garth?' his mother asked, her body divided into small diamonds from behind the stained glass of her front door.

'Of course it is.'

The door opened and he licked his lips.

Chapter 37

When she was fourteen, before trouble really began and she was in the first flirtatious stages of friendship with a boy at school, Nancy remembered one happy and sunny Saturday morning. It had followed from nothing more complicated than a trip to a bowling alley, some tentative hand-holding and a rushed goodnight peck on the cheek, but the morning after had been spent lolling on a giddy wave – until she opened the door to a pair of Jehovah's Witnesses. Fifteen minutes of doorstep sermon about the failing state of the world and the impending apocalypse placed a cloud so large across the face of the sunshine that the subsequent gloom extended itself uninvited into most of the next week.

The man who had introduced himself as Wadlow Grace was occupying more than the third of the sofa a normal-sized person would have and his presence in the room replicated with perfection for Nancy those Saturday-morning feelings of so long ago. His physical immovability was like the tumour in her brain, not about to go anywhere. The stories of a thousand true-crime reconstructions replayed themselves as she imagined how she would be found murdered in an apartment in Hollywood, someone almost famous in England who had lost her way and, by allowing a complete stranger in her house, become another anonymous victim in a big country.

But there was no danger in this man. Certainly, he was unwelcome and he seemed to sense that, although his expression was of someone on the verge of saying, I told you so, and wagging their finger. Nancy sensed he was obdurate to the core, wherever that lay. Nancy felt a reluctance with him, the way she had with her doctors, knowing they had bad news, not wanting to hear but unable to resist knowing.

Then he did something that troubled her, scared her, even.

As he reached into the stupidly tiny knapsack, she stiffened, wondering what murderous implements were poking through the canvas.

It was a copy of her novel and the sight of it at first made her want to laugh with relief.

He set the book on top of a wide thigh and said nothing. Nancy inspected it from a distance, her eyes darting over the cover and then down the spine. It was well-read, the pages rippled in a slight wave as if damp had taken hold at some point. Too much attention had been paid to her work, unwanted commitment lavished upon her words until they meant things far different from what she had ever intended. The grubby state of the tome put a chill through her. Was Wadlow Grace the fabled 'someone'? A man who had moved beyond being a fan and into something more demanding and complex? Did he want something back? Three thoughts, nauseatingly related, went through her head. Mark David Chapman. *The Catcher in the Rye*. John Lennon. What if he has a gun? she thought, fresh sweat moistening her brow.

When he cleared his throat to speak, it made Nancy flinch.

'There's some fine words in here, Nancy,' he said, the drawl in his accent softening the blow of word against word. 'And, there's a lot of words not in there, words that have been swarming inside your head, trapped and trying to get out. Of course, when they do break free, you lose them, make them prisoners on the page for everyone to come and look at. Passing sentence.' He smiled.

Nancy was desperate to find some kind of proposition in his words, something to grip on to that was rational and safe.

'Do you want to ask me something about the book? Sign it?' she asked.

'You start with a clean, blank page, a few lines to keep the words straight, maybe. A couple of marks, squiggles, each with their own shape and some spaces in between. A letter, a word, a sentence. A paragraph, a page, a chapter. A story. All those scratches in the paper, making up a pattern, intertwined and going on forever. Specks that become a mass, whole worlds created just by some words.'

He seemed calm and it made her feel worse. His speech, the ideas it expressed, were ordered but they made no sense. Was he ticking? About to go off having burned a long and bitter fuse for her? While keeping her eyes on him, she plotted the quickest route out of the room, surprised at her resourcefulness. How fast could a fat person move?

'Sorry. I'm not sure I understand,' Nancy said, trying to placate rather than patronize.

'Why did you write this book?' he asked.

'I don't know exactly. I'd dabbled with a few things and it was the one that came together best, fitted.' She hated herself. She could not resist a chance to talk about her work.

'But there were other stories? Things you might have written about?'

'Of course.'

He looked at her. 'You wrote it to get away from something, somewhere. To become someone other than who you were at that time?'

'It was a way of getting out of my job, which I hated. Writing allowed me to do that.'

'But, like I said, you also wrote it to become someone, inside, I mean, other than who you really were.'

'The book's not about me,' she said, frowning. 'How did you find me?' she asked.

He touched the book, tapping the cover with a fingernail. 'And now you're writing something to become who you really are. I imagine that's a story been rolling round inside your head for a long time.'

Nancy did not answer.

'A story,' he continued, 'that's been in there for as long as you can remember.' He touched the left side of his head.

'Seems like it might be that story you've been looking for, the one that started you writing in the first place. Perhaps.'

Once again, Nancy did not speak, but felt the whistle of breath through her nose, underlining the silence. How was he managing to get so close to the truth? Closer than her. How did he know? How much did he know? How?

'Perhaps. I'm going back to England soon, very soon, hopefully to finish it. If you leave me an address, I'll make sure you get a copy. Now, I have a lot of things to organize before I leave.'

'You're here, Nancy, specifically to finish something, a thing that started long before even you did. That's not necessarily fair, but that's your destiny, your place in the story that's still being written. Your future is out here, not back there. So is Mr Kavanagh's.'

His name made her sit up straight. 'Who sent you? Was it Lee Mitchell? My agent? Is this some ploy to get me to stay on out here?' Irritation prickled on her like a rash.

'You think that would be your future? A film? Once again, writing away from yourself, trying to beat the tumour to the finish line.'

'Now just . . .' she began.

He held his hand up, gently rather than harshly. 'I have a story I need to tell you. It's a simple story about me and my family and I think it might mean more to you than it does to me. After that, if you want, I'm gone. One story. It's all I have and I want you to have it too, because it will help. You're not the only one, Nancy. You're not alone.'

Shifting his position slightly on the sofa and mopping his brow with a clean handkerchief pulled with a flourish from a jacket pocket, he seemed suddenly dainty, dandyish almost. For a second, the weight of whatever he carried seemed to lift from him and Nancy caught sight of a happier person. He put the handkerchief away and once again he seemed sad. Nancy could tell he was not going to speak again.

She simply nodded.

With obvious relief, he began searching in the bag and

pulled out a heavy wooden box, some folded papers that looked like maps, a notebook with a cover chewed up by time and an antique pen. He laid them out on the cushion next to him in a way that seemed rehearsed. When he was done, he turned his attention to Nancy.

'Tell me your story,' she said.

Chapter 38

Kavanagh had called Paul Baran as soon as he and Lucy had arrived home from the States. There was nothing surprising in the conversation, nothing they had not already talked about. The only odd thing was Baran's request for a seven a.m. meeting with him at Pendulum.

A uniformed guard Kavanagh did not recognise was on the street, blocking the doorway. The badge on his epaulette looked official without being specific, the mark of private security. He asked Kavanagh to show his identity badge and then checked him against a list pinned in a file Kavanagh could not see inside the door. Two more uniforms were squashed into the space by Reception and they asked him to sign in, polite but distant in their manner. The building felt even emptier than usual as he rose to the eighth floor and went straight to his boss's office.

'Paul, what the fuck's going on?' Kavanagh asked, only halfway through the door.

Baran and Mathias were both standing there, as though expecting him. They looked grave.

'Mike.'

It was Mathias who spoke, as bereft of accoutrements as the first time Kavanagh had met him, dressed in the same kind of dark suit and carefully matched tie. There was something funereal about his attire and the posture of the two men, reminding Kavanagh of the afternoon the news about Helen had been broken to him by Baran, who had pulled Kavanagh out of a client meeting.

'You'd better sit down, Kav,' Baran said.

He did, the pervasiveness of memory giving him a sick feeling in his stomach.

'What's with the heavies on the door?' he asked.

Baran moved to face him and spoke. 'I was going to tell you this yesterday, when we spoke, but it seemed best to wait until today.'

'What?' Kavanagh asked, his stomach still loose. It couldn't be Lucy. She was in bed sleeping when he left. Kavanagh had checked.

'While you were away, Garth Richards went missing,' Baran said, clearing his throat. 'He left his ID badge on my desk, along with Chris Carson's and what is being assumed to be one of Carson's fingers. To make the point, he also took a shit on my desk. I left on time that Friday to attend a meeting in the early evening and I came back here late, around eleven. My office door was locked although we now know the lock had melted into itself. My first instinct was to go see if Tom Richards was still about, if he could open the door. Tom wasn't there, but his office was a mess, like there'd been a fight in there. And there was a lot of blood.'

'Jesus Christ. Are you sure? Garth Richards?' Kavanagh asked, screwing up his nose.

'We went to Garth's house. There was no sign of him,' Baran said.

Mathias took over. 'Garth's father has been missing since Friday. The only person listed to contact in the event of an emergency is his ex-wife.' He paused. 'He had been there too. It wasn't pretty.'

Something about the tone of Mathias's voice unnerved Kavanagh. 'Are the police involved?' he asked.

'Paul had the foresight to call me first. We have to be extremely careful who is involved in situations like this. A degree of public relations has to be balanced with our own options for security,' Mathias said.

'Are the police involved?' Kavanagh repeated.

'Yes.' Mathias nodded firmly. 'The Trust has certain contacts and we are managing the situation. They'll want to talk with you, of course.'

'And there's absolutely no sign of Garth, his father or Chris Carson? They haven't turned up?' Kavanagh asked, fully cognisant of the question's stupidity but his head reeling from the attempt to assimilate all the information.

'The Trust, as you know, has been through these kinds of tragedies in the past and we pride ourselves on our ability to handle them. We will not be tainted by the actions of one warped individual,' Mathias said.

A sudden heavy wallop of fear hit Kavanagh, moving him upright on his chair.

'What if he comes after me or Lucy? Why didn't you tell me yesterday, Paul? Warn me?'

Baran looked on helplessly and it became obvious to Kavanagh where control lay.

'Two people have been watching your house since Saturday. Before you arrived back, we took the liberty of checking it. You'll be covered around the clock, Mike, although there's no reason to expect he'll try anything,' Mathias said.

'There was no reason to expect he would have done as much as he has,' Kavanagh responded.

There was a pause.

'This comes at a very bad time for us. We've kept an extremely tight lid on it so far and can probably do so for another week,' Mathias said.

Of course, thought Kavanagh. 'You're worried this is going to affect the Trellis deal?' he asked.

'There is more than just that particular crease in this,' Mathias said. 'First, let me apologize for appearing to undercut you with Jack Burns last week by being so preemptive.'

It hardly seemed to matter in the light of what he'd just been hearing, but Kavanagh went with the tiny, pointless piece of sanity to cling to, the cup of tea made after the death.

'I'm assuming you have a good reason for acting the way you did,' he said.

'I've had word another party has expressed an interest, not that different from ours although they are going for a rather more direct money-talks approach,' Mathias said.

'That won't work with Burns. It'll have precisely the opposite effect,' Kavanagh said.

'You may be right. I hope you are, but we have to treat it seriously. My source tells me it was Arnold Long who initiated the contact some time ago, secretly of course, although he had Burns's full blessing. Trellis may not have been entirely open with us, as is their wont, but once we moved into action, I think Long was trying to steamroller something through before we had the chance to make an offer. It was felt that Burns may have had the perception we were not prepared to make a real offer when it came down to cash, that our ideas about a venture were simply a way of talking the price down. You have to understand that this all broke very suddenly and I took the decision to act quickly,' Mathias said, no contrition in his voice, simply a stating of facts from one powerful person to a less powerful person.

'Then why send me in to do the upfront stuff? Why not just fax him with the biggest number you can afford?'

'Come on, Kav, it doesn't work like that, you know it. You can kiss their ass forever but it has to be the money that does the talking,' Baran said.

'I agree,' Kavanagh said, 'but don't send me to kiss their ass and then slip them an offer while I'm not looking. That damaged us. It underlined the very thing that concerns Trellis most about us, a lack of coordination and autonomy.'

'You're right,' Mathias replied, 'but we could not have come this far without your efforts and the context for an offer was set by your presence. Don't underestimate yourself, Mike.'

'If you're not giving me the power to deal, at least keep me informed. Who's the other bidder?' Kavanagh asked. The name did not surprise him. 'Any indication on the size of the offer?' Again, no surprise. 'Is your cheque book up to that?' he asked.

Mathias gave him a long stare. 'Is yours? You want the power to deal, you can have it, but you take the responsibility as well, Mike. You're the one that brings this home.'

'That's the way I like it,' Kavanagh said.

'You'll have something in writing from me by lunchtime, giving you full authority to act solely on behalf of the Trust. I'll ask Legal to draft a letter for Burns, informing him of this, to make sure he understands you are empowered. That will give you all the clout you need. This deal can't fail, Mr Kavanagh.'

'It won't,' Kavanagh replied.

'With regard to the other matter, Garth Richards, I'll arrange for the police to talk with you, but I must stress again the need for it to remain under wraps for as long as possible,' Mathias said.

'What are you going to tell people here?' Kavanagh asked.

'We've made arrangements to minimize the fuss,' Mathias said, looking across at Baran.

'I'm going to make an announcement about Carson and Richards, along the lines of them having moved on, possibly under suspicious circumstances, get the gossip going the other way,' Baran said.

'You're going to lie to them?' Kavanagh asked.

'We don't know what the truth is yet, Mike,' Mathias said. 'We have a serviced office in Bishopsgate, fully kitted out. You'll have access to everything you need. I want you to move down there until the situation here stabilizes.'

'Is that really necessary?' Kavanagh asked.

'I think it is for now, Kav,' Baran said.

'A car has been arranged for seven forty-five to take you down to the City. I'm sure, as I've already said, that you have no worries in this respect, but try to stay sensible and we'll keep an eye on you at the house and your daughter in school. We can put someone inside the house with you, if you wish,' Mathias said.

'No,' said Kavanagh. 'I don't want Lucy upset or involved in this. She's very close to Tom Richards. Let me break the news when the time's right. Promise me that.'

'Promised,' Baran said.

Kavanagh looked at Mathias who eventually said, 'Promised.'

Mathias became even graver, which Kavanagh would not have thought possible until that moment. 'The power to deal, Mr Kavanagh. To close down this transaction. You'll have the full weight of the Trust behind you. Use it, but don't get crushed by it.'

Twenty-five minutes later, Kavanagh was in the back of a dark windowed Jaguar, two hastily gathered boxes of paper and his laptop on the seat next to him. As the car moved throught the gradually thickening early morning traffic, Kavanagh felt like someone who'd been fired and asked to clear his desk.

Chapter 39

The phone rang and she knew it would be Nathan.

Dad had left early for a meeting at the office and Lucy was mustering herself for another day at school, feeling as though her life was back on the same motionless, directionless track, floating and waiting for something to happen. Something like the phone to ring and it to be Nathan.

'Hello,' she said, looking at her watch. It wasn't even eight o'clock. Early.

'It's Nathan. Can you meet me today?'

Straight away, he wanted something. No questions about what America was like.

'When?' she asked.

'I don't know. Soon. Ten?'

'Where?'

'In town. Where we met before.'

'I should go to school,' Lucy said. 'It's my first day back after the holiday.'

'We can leave it, if you want.'

'Ten o'clock by the Trocadero,' Lucy said.

The phone went dead.

She took the school clothes off, wondering if she ever intended to go there at all. Looking at herself in the mirror, she ran her palms over her body, turning side on and viewing herself in only her underwear, trying to imagine what he saw. Selecting clothes in lighter shades of black and grey than normal, she dressed quickly after a spurt of extra deodorant and an uncharacteristic dab of perfume.

On the train, she let her mind go blank, genuinely thinking of nothing as she was packed into the car with work-bound commuters, the roll of the carriage occasionally bumping her against other bodies.

He was on time, there before her. His hair had been cut

short, clippers run around his skull leaving only a Tintin quiff at the front. It was sexy, gel separating the already fine strands, setting them close to his head and making him look harder than she thought he really was. His jeans were tight, dark blue denim and the T-shirt was purest white, a fine logo embroidered onto the breast in silky cotton, barely visible except at close range.

They kissed, deeply, and his hands touched different parts of her, never quite becoming intimate.

'Hi,' he said.

'Hello. I like your haircut. How are you?'

'I'm all right,' he replied, taking her hand.

They began to walk.

'What've you been doing?' she asked.

'Bits and pieces. Not a lot really. Did you have a nice holiday?'

'It was all right. Short. My dad was busy a lot of the time.'

'Did you miss me?' he asked, grinning.

Lucy looked away, but gave his hand a squeeze.

They passed away a morning like teenagers falling for each other, an irregular rhythm between them, sometimes halting and at other times flowing. All the shops began to look the same and she found herself keeping an eye on him most of the time, having made him promise not to take anything. She was afraid to express a liking for anything in case he stole it. By lunchtime, tiredness had set in, Lucy more interested in being with him than where they were.

As they sat on the edge of a kerbside bench in Oxford Street, eating big slices of cheap pizza, he said, without looking at her, 'Can we go back to your place?'

A bus went by, choking out a grimy cloud and smothering every other noise, including Lucy's voice. It was a question she had been anticipating most of the morning, but hearing it made her uncertain of the answer, or where the response might lead.

'Okay,' she said.

Lucy gave him a tour of the house, a perfunctory one.

She felt tense, the fact he was so relaxed and confident only serving to make her more nervous. It was the middle of the afternoon, the point in the day where the house seemed to admit too much light, providing no safe shadowy corners in which to hide.

He didn't want anything from the kitchen, nothing to drink or eat. He didn't want to watch television, a video, or listen to music. He didn't want to go out for a walk. Lucy knew what he wanted.

They sat on the sofa, near the join of the cushions, tipping towards each other, gravity pushing them together. He put his arm around her and she nestled against the downy brightness of his shirt, feeling him breathe. It was nice, safe. Lucy wondered how long it would stay like that before he wanted something more unknown from her. The silence bulged with words, Lucy feeling excited and sick at the same time, a shiver trembling through her as though a fever had taken hold.

When he moved closer and began to kiss her, she felt as ready for him as she could be. It wasn't as though it was their first kiss, but the posture of his body in relation to hers placed him in charge and the touch of their lips was imbued with something that implied the contact was no end in itself. His mouth was hot and watery, his tongue licking at her lips, flicking against the ridge of her teeth before probing in and meeting her own. It was an overwhelming sensation, the way he filled her mouth with himself and she found it hard to breathe.

Tickling the back of her neck, his hand shifted her forwards and traced along the bumps of her spine through the cotton of the over-washed plain black T-shirt.

She wondered what they were doing, hard London boy and nice Hampstead girl, groping round on her father's sofa in the middle of a schoolday.

The skin at the small of her back was exposed, lightly goose-bumped. For a moment, his finger followed the line of her skirt where its waistband separated upper and lower, bare and clothed. Lucy shuddered when he reached up her back and slotted his hand under the elastic strap. Moving round so he almost faced her, kneeling on the sofa, he made his other hand join the first and she felt the constriction around her chest disappear, her breasts falling free in the shirt.

Lucy wondered if that was what he wanted, to remove any tightness. She stared down at him as he moved to the floor, still on his knees, and put his hands up her skirt, bringing her tights and knickers off in a single movement that allowed no time for teasing her. Lucy lifted herself with her hands, silently helping him by raising her behind.

Who was giving and who was taking? she asked herself as she fell back on the sofa. She straightened her spine and let her legs part as he gently worked his hand in between them. Lucy had not known what he would do and she certainly had not expected it to be so artful, pumping her fuller and fuller with each ministration of his fingers. As a digit startlingly entered her, she bit down on her lip and looked at the movement of his hand beneath her skirt.

At first she tried to remain still and silent, but she ended up writhing on the settee and calling his name with increasing intensity as a jolt of pleasure released the stifling tensions he had so diligently built within her.

Before she could recover, catch a breath even, he was up and next to her, brushing her head with his own and pecking her with kisses. She felt flustered, her cheeks burning as though with embarrassment and her eyes wet as if with the approach of tears.

Nathan stood and took a step back. As Lucy looked on, he peeled the T-shirt off, bringing it over his head with both hands. A fine gold chain lay against his collarbone and the muscles of his stomach were perfect bumps, a symmetrical line flowing from the gentle definition of his chest. With his eyes on her, he undid the belt and buttons on his jeans and slid them down, standing before her in just underwear, the fabric as white as his shirt had been and clinging to the outline of him, prominent and urgent with desire. Fine tubular veins made his gold skin seem like a thin sheen of silk. With a stare and a blink, he tugged his underwear off, the first show of boyish awkwardness when he lifted alternate feet and fiddled with socks and shoes.

Lucy held her arms out to him as he approached her. He was big, even though, again, she had not really known what to expect. When he was near enough to her, she reached out and took him in her hands, squeezing.

His hand returned to her, where it had so recently been, a touch more insistent, harsher and deeper. Not just a single finger.

'What are you going to do?' she breathed.

'Something very special and very nice,' he replied.

'What is it?' She swallowed.

'Do you trust me?'

'I don't know. Will it hurt?'

'Am I hurting you now?' he asked.

'No.'

Another finger. 'Or now?'

'Ah! No, I like that,' she said, struggling with the words.

'So you trust me then?'

'Yes.'

'Take off the rest of your clothes then.'

He made love to her in what seemed to be the most restrained manner he could manage under the circumstances. His body was live with energy as it moved on top of her, coiling and uncoiling with each thrust he made. Lucy held his head in her hands, gripping his fringe, pulling on it until he gasped. At first, it was painful, a kind of strain she knew she would come to accommodate and, eventually, did. For all of that, it was his moment, and she knew it. What they were building towards would ultimately belong to him alone. As he banged harder against her, she smoothed her hands over him and felt the flexing muscles in his back. They kissed, a kind of frantic garnish to their thrashing, desperate to connect as much of themselves to each other as they could.

Lucy watched him, the sudden frown and the distance in his expression, his eyes on her but also somewhere else. If he was going to take this moment for himself, she was at least going to see it.

Nathan shifted and his body jerked. A noise spat from him, coming from his gut, chest and mouth, every part of him that could make noise seeming to do so. As the painful wave seared through him, Lucy held on to him, trying to contain him, all the while studying the grimace on his face and feeling the odd warmth he seeped into her.

Still hard, he withdrew abruptly. Lucy was about to speak when he gripped her hips and rolled her onto her stomach, face down into the arm of the sofa.

'Nathan?' she quizzed as he lifted her to a kneeling position, her behind in the air.

'Shush. Don't worry,' he said.

His finger touched a strange and sensitive part of her and she recoiled. She heard him spit, then the finger was back and she gave a groan.

'Uh. Nathan. Please.'

'It's all right,' he said soothingly.

As he became a different part of her, Lucy dug her nails into the upholstery and bit down on a knuckle to save from crying out for the next twenty minutes.

Chapter 40

'In Tennessee, about fifty miles north-west of Memphis, in Tipton County, five miles outside of Covington, is a town called Gift.'

The map was opened out on the floor and Wadlow Grace was leaning forwards, reaching over the rolling fat of his stomach to point his home out to Nancy. She followed the line of his finger as it scratched over the surface of the map and homed in on where he was talking about, off to the right of the map of America, just where the states of the West started to look larger. He leaned back and sighed.

'My Mama Grace was a singer. She was big, like I am now, although when I was younger, I started out slim like Pa and like my brother Randall. Started out looking like him, ended up looking like her. Mama had a square chin that jutted out of the fat on her neck and made her mouth look thinner and more severe than it really was. She always wore bright colours, and her hair was grey like steel. She usually pulled it back into a tail behind her head, showing up the few strands of black left in it. Some said it made her look like a native and she'd never do anything to dispute that. Mama Grace loved to let people run away with all manner of ideas about who she was supposed to be.

'She sang and played the piano and gave lessons to some people in Gift as well as her recitals where she'd sing some godawful tunes no one had ever heard of but came to listen to all the same. Mama even showed Randall and me how to play but I was no good, not as good as Randall even if he didn't have the application. In the garden out the back of our house, Mama Grace grew herbs from all over, some for cooking and some for medicine. There were ones you ate, some you smoked and others you took in teas, Mama's infusions. She was proud of her emetics and enemas and me and Randall only had to have so much as a cough or cramp and the hot water was on, the rubber tube out, and you'd be over the bucket, shitting and puking for the next three days. I know that people in Gift thought Mama was a witch and she used to say her own mama was, but Pa'd tell her off, say she was frightening us boys.'

'What did your dad do?' Nancy asked.

'Pa? He was a carpenter, could build most things from wood, right from a spoon for Mama to the house we lived in. Most of the time, he was building bookshelves, treating doors, that kind of stuff. Pa worked with his hands, like his own pa had, but he had a good brain too, knew things, remembered things, read books. His family had been rough and were known for it too, so when a chance came along to pull himself up, he wasn't going to wait for it to pass him by. He wanted to make something out of everything. Pa was a hard-looking man, like he'd cut his face from a block of pine with one of his chisels. Even when Pa laughed, which was more often than you thought, he just never seemed happy. He was a serious man who worked hard and we never went short. Course, we weren't rich either. Mama was pretty and her family had made some money out of growing things, and her family were as much against her marrying Pa as his were, but they loved each other from the first.

'They were sweethearts for a short while and then they married, when he was twenty-two and she'd just turned twenty. On a piece of land that belonged to Mama, Pa built the first-ever house of his life and that's where Randall and then me were born. It was such a beautiful house, sitting there on its own. All the passages connecting the rooms were long and smooth, like you could run down them forever and then take off so you were gliding, like when you dream about flying. They must have been so happy for the first years of their marriage.

'Randall came along in the second year. Four years later, I arrived.' Wadlow paused. 'Something wasn't right with Randall. They knew that by then.'

'What was wrong with him?' Nancy asked.

'He didn't speak much. In fact, he didn't speak at all. Now I know that's what they call aphasia, which is just a fancy word for someone that don't say anything. Gift was a small town and they said all the things about Randall you'd have expected, that he was backwards, a half-breed, inbred – pick one. No one in Gift, not even Ma or Pa, ever heard Randall speak. The only person who did was me, and that was the night he died. Backwards. That was the favourite. Randall Grace was backwards. It pains me to say it, but Randy did look strange. Whatever clothes you put him in, from beat-up old overalls to Sunday best, he still looked kind of weird, like you couldn't get round it by dressing him up. People saw him as just a tall boy who stared, never involved but always watching, like he was recording everything in his brain so he could play it back later. People didn't take to that. I might not look it now, but I was Mama's angel, beautiful.

'Do you know what? I think Randall might have been one of the most intelligent people ever to have lived on this planet. Just because you don't talk, that don't mean anything. Why was it wrong for him to keep all of that inside his head? Randall was twisted, but not in the way people mean. It was as though something had twisted Randall out of shape, on his inside, so that he didn't fit into the world. His brain was the wrong shape. Randall had the wrong sort of thoughts and I think he knew that.

'He read books, though. Book after book after book. It was all that would keep him out of trouble, or, more like, stop trouble finding him, and it meant he'd stay inside the house, where Mama could see him. She told me the first time she saw him with a proper reading book was when she was pregnant with me, couldn't even tell if it made any sense to him, but he studied it, every muscle in his face frozen while words echoed round in him, if they were really going in. I think Mama hoped one day he would take to reading aloud, that his lips would quiver, form some words and then burst into speech. He didn't. The only time his lips ever moved was when he sat staring at space, nothing in front of him but the mobile over the kitchen table or just a plain wall. His jaw would crunch away like he was eating but you'd realize he was almost mumbling, no sound coming out, just some conversation he was having with himself. Mama and me tried to read his lips, like they were a book, but there were no words in Randall's mouth for us.

'One night, we thought we heard him. Sitting round the table and about to have dinner. Me, Mama and Pa used to joke about the idea of saying Grace before meals, on account of it being our name. Then, as clear as anything, we heard the word Randall. It happened so quickly, we couldn't tell if it was a man's or a woman's voice. One thing, I was looking right at him and it wasn't him that spoke, whatever Mama and Pa thought. The word, his name, came out plain, but not from him. It was like there was someone else in the room. There shouldn't have been any ghosts in that house, unless they were our own, because, like I said, Pa had built the place himself. Maybe it was Mama's land that was haunted with all those pretend witches in her family.

'There shouldn't have been ghosts – but there were. Middle of the night, when I was eleven, I woke and heard noise downstairs, like chairs being dragged across the floor. That sort of stuff was usually a Randall-thing to do but when I went down, there was no one there and no furniture had moved. The dogs were out back, where they were meant to be, Randall was in his room and so were Mama and Pa. I was more frightened once I got back upstairs, knowing I'd been down there. And there was other stuff. Little objects disappearing and turning up days later, somewhere else. There was a corner in my room where the clock would never run to time. That feeling someone just walked past the open door of a room you're in, but you know you're in the house all alone. The faucet in the kitchen that would be on when you went in there, even though you remembered shutting it off because it always happened. There were ghosts in the Grace house, all right.'

He stopped, seeming to know he'd rambled away from wherever his point lay.

'Forgive me. It's such a simple story and I've been thinking about it since it happened and here I am, can't get the words out.'

'Your brother never spoke, ever? How did he get on? How did he and your family cope? With school? Just with communicating?'

'You would be surprised at how you can get by without using words. Gift was the sort of place you could fall into yourselves, if you wanted. Mama coped. Taught him what she could, looked after him. She was the one. I used to think she could read his thoughts.'

Nancy tried to imagine it. 'It's hard to picture.'

'I know. It's like he was sulking. A sullen boy who didn't speak. It's not so far to go from not speaking much to never speaking at all. Think about it that way and it doesn't seem so strange.

'He read books, which he may or may not have understood, mumbled, but spoke no words. Where did it all go? How did he die?'

Wadlow picked up the notebook from its place next to the box and held it up as if he were about to swear on it. When he opened it at a page near the middle and handed it to her, it was like a magician passing her an envelope that contained the card she originally chose.

Nancy looked down at the page and saw a painstakingly drawn knot, spinning eternally round on its own axis, going on forever but visible to her eye. Underneath it were the same six words she had written in her notebook at lunch with Julia Summers, the same six words that had removed the block and allowed the slow trickle of words to become a flood once more.

Something very special and very nice.

She thought that was where it would end, but, as she turned to the next page of the notebook, she realized it was only just beginning.

Chapter 41

Kavanagh found Lucy sitting in Helen's old workroom at the top of the house, twirling a string of frosted blue beads through her fingers as if they were a rosary. On his way up the narrowest staircase in the house, he was reminded of the time he climbed them the night of Helen's death, to see where it had happened. The house had been buzzing beneath him with the activity of people used to emergency and tragedy. When he reached the top, a police officer a discreet step behind him, the lifeless silence had been so disturbing and final, it was the moment, more than identifying her body, when he knew it was over and Helen was dead.

He had made enough noise for Lucy to know he was in the house, so he would not scare her.

'Hello,' he said.

She looked round, her fingers still moving over the pearls.

'What time is it?' she asked.

'Just after six,' he said, wondering how long she had been sitting there.

'You're early.'

'All I'm working on now is the deal with Trellis. They've finally given us access to the whole portfolio, so I've got the accountants crunching the numbers and I'm just in the way. How have you been?'

'All right,' she said, nodding and turning her attention back to her hands.

'I'm also back early because we need to talk, Luce.'

'What about?'

There wasn't an easy way. 'Tom Richards went missing last Friday, while we were away in America.'

'Like that salesman who works for you?'

Kavanagh had already decided he wasn't going to tell her everything. There would be no talk about Chris Carson, Tom's ex-wife or that David Roke was the latest person not to show up for work. Kavanagh would, as much as he disliked lying, keep Lucy in ignorance, his main concern to tell her about Tom in case she were to go seeking him out at Pendulum, looking for someone to chat to and finding he was not there.

'I don't think it's quite the same as with Chris Carson,' he said.

'You mean they're not connected?'

'I doubt it.'

'What does his son think, the creepy one who works for you?'

'Garth? We've given him a few days off,' Kavanagh said, unable to keep from looking around, as though he might be hiding in the room.

Stacked in corners and along one wall were cardboard boxes containing Helen's things, what was left after a few mementoes had been sent north to her family. Kavanagh wanted to keep it all, unable to select just one or two items that would distil her personality, condense it into an object. She had been more complex than that. The top of one carton was flapped open, revealing a pair of her gardening gloves, the mustard yellow suede pricked and torn, earth worn into the wrinkles. The sight of them jabbed at Kavanagh and he wanted to look away.

'Do you think he's all right, Dad?'

'Knowing Tom, yes.'

'But he hasn't been in touch?'

'It's not been that long.'

She said nothing, laying the beads in a bowl containing others, dragging her fingers through them as though they were water.

'You really should think about making some things,' Kavanagh said, motioning to Helen's work bench.

'She was teaching me,' Lucy said.

'I know. You were getting good.'

'I might,' she said.

Kavanagh cleared his throat. 'The school phoned today.' He waited to see how she would react to his lie. The school had not phoned. Paul Baran had, calling Kavanagh at the City office with a report from the person watching the house.

There was no response from Lucy.

'They phoned and said you'd been missing time, off and on. They were expecting you today. Kim's spoken to me and the school about this before, Luce. I left it because it didn't seem too out of hand, and because I've been so busy.'

Her fingers stopped moving and her lower jaw shifted from side to side, but she was trying to stifle the mumbles, he could tell. She rocked gently from side to side.

'Lucy, you're almost at the age where you can leave school if you want to. No one's going to make you stay. If it was that bad, they'd let you leave now. The downside to that is it's easy for them to just give up on you as well. I'm not saying you have to go to school if you don't want to, but we have to understand what's involved in that.'

'Some days are better than others,' she said.

'I know. Me too. I get the same.'

'I do want to go, but sometimes I can't. If I just hated it, things would be easier.'

'If there are problems, Luce, you'd tell me, wouldn't you?' he asked.

'There's this boy I've met,' she said, almost coughing out the words.

Kavanagh knew because Baran had told him she had been seen. It pleased him she was being honest with him, even if he was not with her. Kavanagh did not want to tell her about the security arrangements the Trust had made.

'Who is he?' he asked.

'He's a friend,' she said.

'From school?'

'No. Not from school.'

'From where then?'

'Just someone I met, okay?'

'Do you know much about him?'

'A bit. I met him a few weeks ago, when I was out in London.'

'He's a stranger?'

'No. I told you, I met him a few weeks ago in London. I'm still here, Dad, I'm all right. I didn't go to school because I wanted to see him.'

'Why didn't you say anything about him?'

She shrugged. 'Because you're not here very much.'

'I'm here now, Luce.'

'Only because you've got bad news. Tom's dead, isn't he?'

'Lucy . . .'

'People don't just go missing, not at his age, or at the same time as that man who worked for you. He's dead. They both are. You wouldn't have given his son the time off otherwise.'

Kavanagh sighed. She was probably right but he had been trying to avoid the worst for his own sake as much as hers.

'Things will be all right. Does this boy have a name?'

'It's Nathan. Nathan Lucas,' she said.

'And should I call him your boyfriend, or just "this boy"?' he said, smiling and hating being a parent at the same time as he loved it.

Lucy shook her head and grinned. 'I don't know. What should I call Nancy?'

'Touché. Touché.'

Lucy picked a large bead the size of a cherry from the bowl and concentrated on it, as though it were a tiny crystal ball. 'Do you ever get the feeling Mum's still here sometimes?'

'You only have to look around this room, at all the furniture, your jewellery, you even,' Kavanagh said.

'Not like that. I mean that she's here, physically, even though you can't see her. I was up here once and I was sure

I felt her lay her hand on my shoulder, like she used to when I sat doing homework at the kitchen table.'

'Memories are powerful, Lucy. Look at how we both get every time we smell that old tea chest in the garage, the one from my mum's house.'

Lucy dropped the bead, the sound of glass against glass. She frowned.

'You're going away again, aren't you?' she asked.

It was difficult to look at her. 'This should be the last time, for a while. You have to promise me that you'll go to Aunt Karen's and stay this time, and that you'll go to school. I've already spoken to her. I can't concentrate while I'm away if I have to keep worrying about you, Luce.'

'Aunt Karen gets on my nerves, Dad.'

'Mine too, but it'll only be a few days.'

'I can't come with you again? Stay with Nancy?'

'Not this time. She's getting ready to come back to England herself.' He paused. 'I might ask her to come back with me, stay here a while, until she gets herself sorted out with her flat. What do you think?'

'Why not? When do you have to go?'

He drew breath sharply. 'Wednesday.'

'So soon? You've only just come back.'

'Things are hotting up. It's the one last push and then we're done. It'll be over. Then we should really talk, about what we want to do.'

As they made their way down the stairs, a feeling he had experienced the very first day Baran had mentioned the merger came back to him as a thought recaptured in new words.

Getting away is not meant to be this easy.

Chapter 42

Kavanagh sat in the familiar plane, even the crew recognizable, and flicked through the sheaf of papers he had with him. There would have been nothing to stop him faxing it all to Jack Burns and discussing it over the phone, except it was Kavanagh's function to put breath into the dead words on the page. They were approaching a moment where all the paper, past, present and, potentially, in the future, was set to one side and a basic, instinctual decision was made. After that, the lawyers and accountants could do what they wanted to it, shroud it in arcane language. Kavanagh would have little involvement in that, but at its centre would always be that cardinal moment when the deal was struck. The time was close and Kavanagh brought with him the power to deal. He had a good feeling, quite literally in his gut.

He had brought a more detailed operating plan of how the joint venture would work, putting names from Trellis and Pendulum into boxes on an organization chart, setting realistic timescales which saw eighty per cent of Trellis and its business invested in the vehicle two years into the next century. It was too gradual for Kavanagh and probably not gradual enough for Burns, although he expected him to like it. In collaboration with one of the brighter, more recently qualified accountants at Pendulum, Kavanagh had worked some start-up cashflows and projections, the slide from modest to aggressive once again enough to keep Mr Jack Burns happy. The general structure of the transaction, how they would get from where they were to where they wanted to be, was alluded to in another document, which covered the monetary aspects and laid out a timetable for the subsumption of Trellis into the vehicle and Burns out of it, making careful mention of the walk clauses that applied in the first two years, the ability of either party to get out of bed under certain conditions. By the year 2002, Trellis and Pendulum would be gone, replaced by a still as yet unnamed joint-venture company.

Two other documents related to the deal, but were far more personal. Rather than Pendulum's crest, they bore that of the Trust. One was what Andrew Mathias had referred to as the power to deal. It gave Kavanagh parameters, how far he could go. The Trust knew he needed a degree of autonomy because the timescale of the deal meant linking the merger to performance and other variable factors. Kavanagh knew there were still people at the Trust who could authorize him to go higher, or give on a certain point, but he was happy to have as much power invested in him as he had. The final document would only be seen by himself, Baran and Mathias. Once the deal was struck and the JVC became a legal entity, the letter of intent signed, the Trust would make a capital injection into the vehicle, making Kavanagh, for a short time, one of its largest shareholders. Under the agreement, the Trust would purchase the shares from Kavanagh for the sum of two and a half million pounds. One of the tax lawyers at Pendulum had been given the task of finding an efficient way of sheltering capital gains from such a transaction, her brief vague enough not to point anywhere near Kavanagh's transaction. And then it would be over. Kavanagh could pull it off, he knew it, making up the lost ground from last week and bringing the deal together on time for the Trust and himself.

The last serious trip to Los Angeles, he hoped. There would be some social stuff, handshakes and smiles, but that would do it. In the normal manner, the publicity machine of the Trust would manage the fallout from the deal, ensuring it had the desired, precisely measured effect. After that, Kavanagh just had the rest of his life to concern himself with.

Before leaving England, he hand-delivered Lucy to Karen's door, feeling as though he wanted to walk her into the house, lock her in a room and tell her not to move until he got back. There was no trace of Garth Richards and the Trust was making a good job of watching the two of them. However many times he had told himself since taking off that she would be all right, it did not assuage Kavanagh's fears or feelings of guilt. He had put a lot of faith in Baran and Mathias, coming back to Los Angeles and leaving Lucy the way he had. He wished she were by his side, like last time, but that was not practical.

In a halting, transatlantic call, Kavanagh had agreed to see Nancy on his second night in Los Angeles, after his final meeting with Burns. Not seeing her on his arrival was an odd and self-imposed action, but he was determined to keep focused on Trellis and, at the same time, not to smother her. In his own mind, he wasn't sure which was more important to him, the need to concentrate on Trellis or the desire to take a step back from the situation with Nancy. Since their last encounter, their few phone calls had been perfunctory, the nervous chat of people whose only closeness sprang from the physicalness of sex, neither of them knowing enough about the other to pass time as breezy chat. They were both in a kind of waiting state, she on the verge of going home to England and he anxious to close Trellis. Kavanagh had forgotten the changes sex brought about between people.

Looking out of his window, he wondered if, up here, he were any closer to heaven and what Helen might think about the direction of his life following its derailment by her death. He shuffled the papers into a neat block and closed his eyes to a light grey doze.

Kavanagh's case was still beside the bed, unopened, when the knock came on the hotel door.

'Hello?' Kavanagh asked, aiming his voice at the door jamb.

'It's Arnold Long, Mike.'

Kavanagh opened the door.

'Hello, Arnold.'

'Mike, I'm sorry to disturb you like this. You must be tired. Might I have a brief word?'

'Come on in.'

Long went and sat on the edge of a high chair near the square, unisex dressing table. Wearing his usual colour suit, he perched as though about to stand and leave at any moment. Long was not settling himself in. He was here for a purpose. He dabbed his nostrils with a pure white tissue and Kavanagh noticed how puffy his eyes looked. Kavanagh had never seen Long in casual attire and it was hard to picture, even if it was likely to be the usual corporate away-strip of checked shirt and chinos. Kavanagh sat six or seven feet away, on the corner of the bed.

'I want you to reconsider this deal, Mike,' Long said.

'Arnold, even in such a short space of time, we've gone a long way down the road.' He sighed. 'There's no reason not to go ahead.'

'What would it take for you to think again?' Long asked.

'There's no compelling reason, Arnold. If it's not us, it'll be someone else. Look at how we've accommodated the wishes of Trellis so far. I don't want to pre-judge anything in advance of our meeting tomorrow, but you'll like what you see.'

'What's your interest in this, Mike?'

'The same as everyone's, I hope. To put the Trust and Trellis together in a way that's acceptable and beneficial for all of us.' It sounded prepared, but it had come straight out.

'I meant your personal interest.'

'That's not a relevant factor,' Kavanagh shot back.

'Meaning there is one?'

'Meaning, I'm given incentives in my work, just like I'm sure you are.'

'As you've said in the past, you know that other parties have expressed interest in Trellis, some more serious than others. At the moment, one such party is very serious and they have also expressed a desire for your involvement.'

'I'm flattered,' Kavanagh said, keeping his tone neutral, verging on the deadpan.

'I've known Jack long enough to recognize when he's sold on something. What I'm afraid you may be missing here is the fact that he's more sold on you than he is on Pendulum or the Trust. I've spoken to him about this. Now, the other party, in view of this, is willing to let you be in the vanguard, if you will. Can I ask you to reconsider?'

'Can you tell me who this "other party" is?' Kavanagh asked.

'It isn't who you think it is, I can tell you that. It's very private, a consortium of associated individuals. We're moving more quickly than we would like, which was why I had to leak certain information back to the Trust and throw some spin on our last meeting.'

'Be more specific,' Kavanagh said.

'I can't right now. What we need is some time. There are people willing to meet with you.' Long stopped for a moment and seemed to change tack. 'Back East, when we were still in our raiding days on Wall Street, I saw enormous amounts of fee-income pumped around for mergers and acquisitions. Whatever they're paying you at Pendulum for engineering this, it's not enough. Believe me.'

'Come to your point, Arnold.'

'If it were to cost our party five, possibly six million dollars in cash to win this, that would be seen as a wise investment against the downside cost of losing it. Even if that sum were to be rested with a single individual. Am I being clear on this point?'

'You are.'

'Our meeting tomorrow is significant, but it doesn't have to be final. The only person who can ensure that, Mike, is you. This factor is essential to our party,' Long said.

'It's not our party, Arnold, it's yours.'

Long stood. 'Again, that's a factor only you can ensure. You have a few hours to consider it. It won't take much to put a brake on during tomorrow's meeting. Sleep on it and I'll see you tomorrow. Let's not talk again before that. I'll know which way you're going early on, I assume.'

For a long time after he'd left, Kavanagh stood in the middle of the room, feeling like a boxer who'd just been asked to throw the biggest fight of his career.

Chapter 43

Something very special and very nice.

It was all there, her story. Not just the story she had written down on paper over the last two weeks, but *her* story. Nancy was reading a story that had been written about her. When she was a girl. A teenager. The man. The baby. The tumour. Kavanagh. Lee Mitchell. Lucy. As if someone else had planned her life. It was all there, and reading it, seeing the words on the page, should have made the story seem more real, but instead it felt like it might never have happened. Where did it all spring from? Did it come from her, or did she come from it? It made her nauseous, gave her a grave sense of doubt about her own existence.

Nancy had looked at the pages that followed the drawing of the knot and was able to follow what she herself had been trying to commit to paper for as long as she could remember. If they really *were* memories and not just events and feelings she had imagined, or which had been written into her by the hand of another, she was not sure. The world no longer felt stable under her feet.

Wadlow was watching her as closely as if he had been reading her like a book. He wanted to see her reaction to what was in the notebook. Nancy realized that he could not read what was in there, that it was a foreign language to him.

Looking down at the notepad again, it was like seeing into a mirror that reflected her thoughts in words.

'You don't need the page, Nancy, it needs you,' Wadlow said.

'What do you mean?'

'There's no need to see things in words to make them real. You don't need them verified. Don't you write your own life in any case, just through living? Isn't that what it's about, for everyone?'

Nancy flicked through some more pages, the words sliding away into something foreign until there were no longer even words, just lines that joined each other, no beginning or end apparent.

'Why do the words run into each other the further I go?' Nancy asked.

'For the same reason there's the knot at the start.'

'Which is?' she asked, her eyes making trails over the lines on the page.

'The knotwork is a story in itself, the stray ends of our lives criss-crossing and folding over each other, some touching, others never getting near, but all connected in the eternity of the knot.'

Nancy scanned back until she found words she could read once more. They led her right to the current moment, from where Wadlow had walked up to her door and knocked on it. There were quotes around speech and more quotes around those, and then more quotation marks still. It was like a complex mathematical equation where she had to work from the centre to the outermost bracket, looking for some key term, the brackets that would put a closure around everything, like a fence.

'The structure of our lives,' Wadlow said, 'the things we do or say, are all like stories, Nancy. I used to think that God had one big book and in it he would keep all the stories of our lives, of the world, of all worlds. Then I realized it was the other way round and that the search for a book which contained every story was a waste of time. The Book was in every story. It's where it begins and ends, and begins again, Nancy. The Book.'

'This book?' she asked.

'No. Randall was a loose strand in the story, but even that can turn out to be important.'

'Tell me what happened to Randall.'

Wadlow handed her a pen. 'This only ever wrote in one other hand. My brother Randall's. Lord knows, I've tried to make it write, to unlock the secrets of the ink. Why don't you tell me what happened to Randall?'

The pen fitted her hand, the balance of it pleasing and the barrel near the nib falling perfectly into the groove of her middle finger. Nancy placed the pen on the page, near where the text stopped. As she applied the first tentative pressure, not sure where it would lead, Wadlow drew a breath. She moved the pen. Wadlow began to speak.

'The night Randall died, my parents were out. Mama was singing and Pa had gone along to watch. Randall had shut himself in his room, which wasn't so unusual. There would be whole long periods when he would stay in there and we wouldn't disturb him. I was fourteen then and allowed to look after him, even though he looked after me most times. I was down in the kitchen, reading a book, when I heard a noise coming from upstairs, like something heavy was being dragged across the floor. I ignored it the first time, then it seemed heavier the next time. Before I knew it, there was all sorts of noise coming from up there, things being thrown around, hefty things.

'I ran up the stairs saying hellfire to myself and started banging on the door, calling out to see if he was all right. The noise just went on like I might not have even been there. I tried the handle on the door and it almost burned me it was so hot, as though it was about to melt. "Randall. Randall." I called him. Then, I heard this big shout, someone calling out in pain. I'd never heard him speak in my life, even when he'd cut himself or banged a toe on a wall, but I knew it was Randall's voice I heard. All I wanted, right then, was for Mama to come home and take care of Randall. He was a quiet boy, not someone who had fits. It was out of the ordinary for Randall and I don't mind saying it was scaring shit out of me.

'Mama would be gone for a good while yet and I was too scared to leave, almost as scared as I was of staying. I did the only thing I could, which was to start throwing myself at that locked door. They were strong doors, Pa'd built 'em that way, and I could feel the bone in my shoulder knock into the wood each time I ran into it. After a few tries, I heard the timber in the frame splinter and the door gave an inch. Three more times and I had it open. Would have taken a couple less if I'd been the weight I am now. I fell into the room as the door swung back and I stumbled onto my knees, trying to get upright.

'The room was pure dark. Randall must have closed the shutters. The only light was from the hall behind me. I reached for the switch and flicked it, but the bulb was out. The room had gone quiet, although I hadn't noticed it on account of the noise I'd been making on my own. The furniture, what I could see of it, was a mess, fallen about into unfamiliar shapes so I could hardly recognize it. I stood upright and listened, knowing there was the sound of breathing coming from somewhere inside that room.

' "Wadlow." My name, one word, and it felt like it had risen in a wave from under the house, right out of the foundations and on up through my feet and round my insides. The word made me throb, like my brain had got bigger in my head for a second or two.

'I tried to find where the breathing was coming from, looking round into the dark as my eyes got used to it. Randall was near one corner, behind the bed which had been pulled across the floor. I walked to it, real slow, stood on the mattress and looked over into the gap. Randall was there, curled up like a baby, shivering and breathing real heavy. He was buck-naked and you could see his muscles, writhing like they were doing all they could to keep his body from coming apart. I reached my hand out to him and, as I did, he sprang before I'd even touched him. He leapt almost fully upright and it made me yell. I jumped backwards off the bed and started inching out the door, keeping my eye on him.

'Randall looked at me, half-bent and clutching his sides like he was about to throw up. His eyes were looking right into mine and I knew he was trying to speak, could tell from the set of the muscles in his face. He looked like I'd never seen him before, the expression. His lips trembled and at first I thought he was going to cry. Then, he spoke.'

' "Kill me, Wadlow. For God's sake, kill me now." '

' "Randall?". That seemed a funny thing to say, like I was asking if it was really him. I said it again. "Randall?"

' "If you don't kill me, Wadlow, I'm going to kill you."
' "Randall," I said, holding my arm out to him.

'He let out a scream and pulled his arms tight, trying to restrain himself. Randall looked down at himself and I lost sight of his face. When he looked back up, it wasn't Randall any more. Something had changed and I knew he meant it. He was going to kill me. It was like he was thinking about how he was going to do it as he looked at me, his mind working out ways for finishing me off. For a second or two, we faced each other off like animals, one about to leap and the other ready to take flight. We'd played chase games, but not for a long time and never for real. I rested all the weight I had on my front foot, ready to spin on it and then run.

'I hollered as I turned and began to run, hearing Randall taking off after me almost at the same time, so I knew I didn't have much of a start. The floor on the landing was slippery and I almost went over. I was too afraid to look back, so I kept on looking ahead of me, trying to make it to the stairs and start going down them before he got to me. I must have been near the bottom before he jumped after me, because that was one of Randall's favourite things to do, take the stairs three or four at a time, going up or down. Something in me couldn't stop me turning to see, when I was at the very bottom, just like when we played and he always won on account of my curiosity. I always peeked to see if I was going to be found and that was how he always caught me. I wish it had just been a game.

'He was gone, like he'd jumped off the stairs and into nothing, a black hole that had swallowed him. Pa sometimes made jokes about how he'd built secret passages into the house, ways of moving round it without being seen. It was quiet again. It was like everything might just have been going on inside my head, not even real. It started to feel like the whole thing was dreamed up by me and I'd wake suddenly to find myself back at the kitchen table, head resting on the table and drooling over the book I'd been reading.

'He was behind me.'

'I don't know how he'd done it, but I felt him there. I

turned and he was standing at the end of the hall, his chest heaving up and down and his eyes fixed on me again, like they were transfixed by me. There were sinews and veins all over him, ones I'd never seen, like he was tied up by them. I was used to seeing Randall with nothing on, but I couldn't remember him looking so, so, tight, I guess.

'In his hand, hanging at his side, was the big blade Mama used for her herbs. Even when we helped her, we were never allowed to use it and she spent most of the time telling you off about it. I was scared of that blade and I knew Randall was too. Sometimes we'd open the drawer and look at it together, laying there next to all the others, both too afraid to touch it.

'He was excited too, if you catch my meaning. Big. He stroked himself with one hand, looking at me all the while.

' "Stop it, Randall. Don't. You'll get in trouble with Mama. I'm gonna tell on you." Several times lately Mama Grace had walked into a room and found Randall there touching himself. Of course, I'd taken to it myself at that age, but didn't talk to anyone about it, still less do it where Mama could catch me. It was difficult because I think she knew Randall was never gonna to find no lady being the way he was, but that didn't stop him wanting things. He was eighteen then, at the right sort of age for it.

' "Stop it, Randall or I'll set Mama Grace on you. Stop!"

'He didn't.

'As simple as if it were a side of pork, Randall ran the knife over the front of his thigh and I could hear the sound the metal made as it tore a strip into his skin. It was like he was testing the sharpness on himself and a thin line of blood appeared on his flesh right away, even though Randall just stood there like nothing had happened. Not a cry out of him. I looked down and saw a flap of skin the knife had flayed off.

' "Kill me, Wadlow. Please."

'He moved a step towards me, blood running down his leg. He was holding the knife out, pointing it at me, getting ready to stick it in me. I was convinced he wouldn't, that he'd never do anything to hurt me, his little brother. I wiped my hands on my pants, nervously, and stood right where I was. "You're not going to hurt me, Randall. I'm your brother. I love you." I thought the word love would be a good thing to say, might wake him up to himself.

'Turns out, he would hurt me. He lunged the knife and the tip of it went through the cotton of my shirt and just stuck into the skin of my belly. It was like a needle prick, more of a shock than a pain. I yelled and then Randall lifted the knife back and took a swing at my face. I jerked to one side, but I swear I felt the wind from the blade as it whistled past my cheek. I don't know where the next slash might have gone, because I was on the move again.

' "Come back, you fucker," Randall said.

'Pa's gun.

'That was when it occurred to me, as I headed to the back of the house, towards his workshop, where it was kept. I fumbled with the door handle and then I fumbled with the drawer in the bench, where he kept it. Mama said it should have been kept locked away, but Pa wasn't interested. It was there, like it always was, the clip out and next to it. I picked the two pieces up and made them one, pulling the barrel back, getting one in the hole, ready.

' "That's a good boy." It was Randall. Standing there, knife in hand and blocking the doorway.

' "Don't come no closer, Randy. I'll do it. I swear to God I will." My hand was shaking as bad as the first time I ever held the damn gun. I hated it. As best I could and trying to remember what Pa'd shown us about gripping the butt and holding the thumb of your other hand down to keep on target, I pointed the gun at Randall.

' "You know what Pa's always saying, Wadlow. Don't point no gun at anyone unless you intend on shooting it."

' "I know that, Randall, and I will. I will."

' "Do it."

'I just stood there, trying to keep my arm still, the gun feeling heavier and heavier every second longer I held it. I'd started to cry somewhere along the way, but they weren't boy tears any more. It felt like I wasn't a kid any more. From the first moment I heard that dragging noise upstairs, I wasn't a boy.

' "Do it."

'Randall gave off a scream so shrill, I thought it was going to burst my ears. He came at me, fast, with the knife. It was watching death come towards me, the point of that knife was going to enter me, open me up, and take my life away. There was more force behind Randall than just his own and he wasn't going to stop. The only way to stop him was to send something back towards him, that was travelling harder and faster than even he was.

'I snatched at the trigger, forgetting all the stuff about breathing and squeezing it. I hit Randall square in the chest. I don't know if you ever heard or seen a gun fire, but it's a sick feeling, the way the bullet flies off down the barrel, that kind of controlled explosion on the end of your hand. All the concentrated power held in check by a trigger. I'd heard all that before, but I'd never heard it hit a human being. The sound was almost like he'd sucked the bullet in. The moment it touched him, Randall wasn't coming towards me any more, the bullet sending him towards the door and over onto his back. He wriggled and tensed on the floor, the knife still in his hand.

'Randall pulled himself up onto his elbows and tried to get his palms onto the floor, as a way of getting himself upright again, I guess. He was still intent on getting to me. The knife made a scraping sound on the floor as he struggled to get himself upright.

'The second shot wasn't as bad as the first, like I'd already gotten better at it. It made a mess of his stomach, like a mosquito bursting when you squash it with a thumb. There was more blood this time. Randall started to writhe, the knife gone from his hand. He convulsed on the floor like he was having a fit, his body jerking, stiff and in pain.

'He let out a long groan and I'm not really sure what happened next, or how it happened. First, Randall was rolling about on the floor, blood spilling out of him. Next thing, he was sitting half up, supporting himself on his elbows. It was as if he was about to give birth, the position of his body. He gave three loud shouts, groans as he forced something from inside himself, trying to push it out with his voice.

'Then, it was there, like his guts had spilled onto the floor of Pa's workshop. Except they weren't like guts. You could tell it didn't belong to him, this big brown mess. The fucking thing was moving about in between Randall's legs. There wasn't much left of Randall down there, like it had taken him with it.

' "Finish it," Randall cried out. Or I think he did, although sometimes I wonder if I didn't just say that to myself. It might have been the last thing I ever heard him say, less than five minutes after the first.

'I went closer and emptied the rest of the clip into him and into that thing. I was standing almost over him when the hammer clicked onto nothing and there was real silence, perhaps for the first time ever.'

Nancy put down the pen and Wadlow Grace stopped speaking.

Chapter 44

The Power to Deal.

Jack Burns was dressed as though for a vacation as he sat impassively at the huge oval table in the main boardroom of Trellis. Kavanagh knew they could as easily have done this in his office, but the sombreness of the room gave the moment a seriousness that at the same time was instantly defused by Burns's attire.

Arnold Long kept staring at Kavanagh as though he wanted to lick his lips or make an inappropriate gesture with his eyes. Kavanagh had hardly slept the previous night, Long's words spinning around in his head, giving him fraught dreams. Long wanted to know which way Kavanagh had decided to jump and he was anxious enough for it to show, although it was doubtful Burns would have noticed as he seemed preoccupied with the piece of paper Kavanagh had put in front of him.

The sums were all but done. Buying a company was a simple process that became complicated as soon as people were involved in it. You looked at the value of everything tangible, the people, the buildings, things that could be manipulated, a price-tag hung on them. That was the simple part, although it could be controversial. Then there was the next step, slightly less tangible. The value of the business as a going concern, the quality of its portfolio and its ability to keep performing out into the future. In some cases, it could be a cash cow to be milked happily, in others, a millstone. Either way, it was hard for seller and buyer to convince themselves that bad was, actually, good. In the final area, nothing was tangible. It was a value judgement, quite literally. It was referred to as intangibles, or goodwill. At the extreme end of the scale, it would be easy to see how the right to use a name like Disney, McDonald's or Coca-Cola would carry a price far in excess of acquiring the name and reputation of Trellis, but the name was still valuable, not least because Pendulum wanted it and Trellis had it.

All the previous weeks, while Kavanagh had been fronting things with Jack Burns and Arnold Long, people behind the scenes at Pendulum had been putting numbers and cashflows through spreadsheet models, analysing all that was tangible and speculating on that which was intangible. The net result of all the work was a number and the prime function Kavanagh served was to sell Burns on that number. It was the moment where the lines became blurred, where it was difficult to remember who was buying and who was selling.

Burns spoke, his eyes still surveying the numbers.

'The value of our assets, against book value plus what you've seen for additions since we last filed look close enough. There are one or two holes in the portfolio, areas where I think you could benefit from a closer look, something we'll be happy to give you, but this number seems close. Now, how much am I worth?' Burns asked, looking up and meeting Kavanagh's gaze.

Burns was no fool. He knew as well as Kavanagh that they could haggle over the tangible net worth forever, but the slice on top was where Pendulum basically said what it thought Trellis was worth. Since Trellis equalled Jack Burns, they were essentially hanging a price-tag on him. Kavanagh had spent time on the drive over working out a line to slide him into the number.

'I've been involved in a number of purchases and the hardest part to quantify is this. We've taken a look at how both we and Trellis think the future profit forecast looks, that's to say the ongoing benefit of being involved in a joint venture. That's been set against both the value we bring into the merger and your ongoing equity holding in the vehicle until 2002,' Kavanagh said.

'That's one hell of a drum roll, son, but why don't you just give me the number?' Burns asked.

'One hundred and thirty-five million dollars,' Kavanagh shot back.

It was far too much. Kavanagh knew it and, back in London, Baran knew it, but Mathias wanted it that way. The power to deal, Kavanagh thought, and wanted to laugh. How could it be the power to deal when he was offering twenty million dollars more than he thought they should? Ten million more than Mathias's absurd and pre-emptive offer that had so nearly halted the whole process. Kavanagh and Baran had argued with Mathias, wanting to start at just under or over a hundred million. Kavanagh sat back and waited for Burns to react, wanting to at least take satisfaction from Burns's pleasant surprise.

Burns said nothing. Thirty seconds passed in which still nothing was said and the silence began to feel drawn out. Kavanagh glanced at Arnold Long who seemed to be glaring from behind an impassive mask. The size of the offer must have been a fairly clear indication to him of which way Kavanagh was jumping. He would stay loyal to Pendulum, pleased that he knew he could do no more with five million pounds than he could with two and a half. Kavanagh knew when enough was enough.

'I don't know.' It was Burns.

'I'm sorry?' Kavanagh asked, unable to keep shock from his voice.

Long twitched and leaned forward.

Burns rubbed his chin and sat back, disengaging himself from the piece of paper, from the whole situation. Kavanagh wanted to reach out and physically pull him back, to involve him. This wasn't supposed to happen. He hadn't rehearsed anything for this scenario.

'It's a bit short, plus there are still unresolved issues,' Burns said.

'Let's solve them then. I'm surprised, Jack. I thought we'd be picking names for the venture, naming the baby. If there's still a way to go, show me where and we'll try and get to it.'

'We know what the baby will be called. Always have,' Burns said from his position on the outside of the interaction. 'I need time to think before I can go any further. Arnold, I'm taking the Lear to Taos, spending some time on the ranch. I'll be back after the weekend.' Burns stood, as did Long. 'Thanks for everything, Mike. I'll be in touch.' He held out his hand.

Kavanagh gripped it loosely. He had expected the meeting to culminate in a manful grip across the table, where they remained seated and sealed all their fates. Instead, he was being shown the door, like a junior salesman on his first call, and there was nothing he could do to recover the situation. The power to deal.

Awkwardness filled the scene and Kavanagh stood to gather his papers while Burns looked on and Long sat back down.

'I look forward to hearing from you soon, Jack,' Kavanagh said.

'Gordius,' Burns said, when Kavanagh was about to open the door.

'Excuse me?' he asked, turning back.

'The name for the baby. Gordius.'

Chapter 45

Lucy moved carefully across the bed and rested her naked body against Nathan's, who was sleeping peacefully on his side, his back to her. With her chest against his back, she could feel the contented thud of his heart and the steady swell of his chest with each breath he took. It had been more gentle this time, more for her than him, and it shocked her how that had made her feel towards him. She laid her hand on his hip where the bone was closest to the surface. His back was broad and the tan on his neck was gold in the glow of the bedside lamp, the hairs on his neck bleached by the sun. Lucy traced a finger down the ridge at the base of his skull until she came to the first bump of his spine. With more caution, she returned the hand briefly to his hip before stroking the taut curve of his behind. With the stealth of a snake, her hand prowled over him and into his groin, her fingers eventually finding what they were looking for and holding him.

Nathan sputtered slightly and she felt consciousness fill his body. He turned so he was facing her, grinned and kissed her on the lips. The taste of him was still unfamiliar but Lucy found herself growing used to it.

'What's the time?' he asked.

'Nearly half-nine,' she said, lifting her head to see the red digits on the clock.

'Won't your aunt be worried?'

'Probably,' she replied.

'Are you all right? You were quiet, before.'

'I'm okay.' She pulled him closer. It had been on her mind all night but she hadn't wanted to mention it. Now she did. 'Before my dad went away, he told me someone I know where he works had gone missing. He's a really good friend to me and I'm worried about him.'

'You mean he's just run off?'

'He's too old to do that, Nathan. That's why I'm worried.'

'You don't know. I look at those missing-person pages on Ceefax sometimes, when I'm really bored, and there's loads of old people go missing. For years sometimes, they've been gone.'

'He's not that type of man.'

'How'd you know that? Who knows? Until they're gone.'

'If he was going to do that, he would have contacted me first, I know he would.'

'Where d'you think he'd go, then?'

'I haven't got a clue,' she said.

'If you know him so well, surely you know where he'd go if he wanted to run away and hide.'

Lucy sat up. There was only one place he would go to do that. One place where he could hide and not be found. A place where he could hide without ever having to go anywhere.

Pendulum.

'Get dressed,' she said, standing. 'We're going out.'

Chapter 46

Kavanagh was about to pick up the phone and call Nancy when it rang.

It was Arnold Long.

'Mr Kavanagh, today didn't really seem to go either our way or your way, whatever side you've chosen to be on.'

'You know what, I'm starting to think maybe I should just be on my own side.'

'A good place to be, but don't isolate yourself. What happened this morning could open up opportunities for you. I've fed details of the meeting back to our colleagues. I have a proposition I think you'll find difficult to refuse.'

'I'm listening,' Kavanagh said.

There was the smallest of laughs at the other end of the line. 'Not on the phone, Mike. I'm still here at Trellis. Can you swing by and see me?'

'Working late, Arnold?'

'Round the clock on this one, if I have to. How soon can you be here?'

'Half an hour.'

'I'll tell Security to expect you.'

Kavanagh recognized the guard, who seemed to do likewise. While he signed the book, Kavanagh made polite chat. The computerized visitor system and pre-printed badges were operated by receptionists and evening visitors had to revert to the old-fashioned logbook.

'Mr Long's in the main boardroom. You know where that is?'

'I certainly do, thanks,' Kavanagh said.

Long was seated at the head of the table, papers surrounding him and illuminated by a desk lamp whose cord trailed perilously high across the room on its way to the plug socket. Arnold was wearing the same outfit he had at the ill-fated meeting earlier on.

'Hi, Mike,' Long said, getting to his feet.

'Where's Jack?' was Kavanagh's first question, guilt already starting to gnaw at him. They sat.

'Where he said. Took the Lear down to his place in New Mexico. It's where he goes to be left alone. If there are telephones or faxes there, I don't know the numbers. He could die out there and it would take us days to find him. I'm told instructions are lodged with his lawyers to cover that eventuality.'

'That would suit you, wouldn't it, Arnold? Get Jack out of the way and leave it clear for you and your friends to take over the asylum.' It was refreshing to talk in such an unvarnished way, no need for pleasantries.

'We need Jack very much alive, and so do you, Mike. I'd hate to think what instructions exist in the event of his early demise.'

'Tell me about this morning. What do you make of his behaviour?' Kavanagh asked.

Long shrugged it off with a fey movement of his shoulders. 'I've seen it before. He gets scared the nearer the moment comes when he might let go of Trellis. I'm convinced he sits at home and imagines in fine detail what it will be like not to have Trellis. It's like watching someone on a high board, afraid to jump,' he said. 'Or in a burning building.'

'He's not going to come back from his ranch and tell us the deal's off?'

'That's the way it's happened every other time. The same balk, the trip to Taos and back to business as usual. This time, I don't think so. It is a minor derailment, one we can use to our advantage. He'd give you fucking Trellis if you asked, Mike. Now, I'm assuming you don't actually want it, and that's where we can help each other.'

'By being a clearing house. Let me take it from him so I can give it to you. Suck all the trust he has in me out of him and then spit it in his face like it was poison?'

'You're happy enough to do that for the Cameron Trust. I know you don't like me, Mr Kavanagh, but don't let that get in the way. If it makes you feel better, I don't care for you either.'

A moment of silence beat in Kavanagh's ears.

'The devil you know,' Kavanagh said. 'I'm going to make enough money, doubling it shouldn't be worth any more to me, not in the final analysis. I want to play the zero-sum game, Arnold. I'm going to do well out of this from the Trust and I know what their plans are for Trellis. All you've done is made vague allusions to your consortium and beef up the lack of content with offers of manna. That makes me nervous. I'm going to go with the devil I know, Arnold.'

'And you're one hundred per cent you really know that devil? What do you really know about the Trust, people like Andrew Mathias, or their plans for Trellis? If you were going to tell me the absolute truth, Mike, you'd have to say you know next to nothing. And, again being honest, you'd have to say you don't really care. Do you?'

'Not caring is a powerful thing, Arnold. It gives me choices and it takes away the hold other people have over me.'

'I'm not meant to have this information, but I hear that your remuneration from this is going to be near three million dollars. I've already said we'll double that.'

'And wire it to a European bank and then on into an account in the Caymans to make it more glamorous? I've already said, there isn't much more I can do with six that I can't do with three.'

Long stared at the papers on the table, although his eyes did not seem to focus on them. 'You're a man who likes zero-sum games. There are three scenarios here, Mike. The worst case is that the merger with the Cameron Trust goes ahead. The best is that our side concludes an outright purchase of Trellis. If necessary, there is a compromise of sorts and that is that neither deal happens. Of course, there is a common element in all of these, Mr Kavanagh.'

'Which is?'

'You. If you aren't coming onside with us, we would rather nothing happened. If that means taking steps to remove you from the equation, that's what will happen.'

'Am I really hearing this?' Kavanagh asked, the pitch of his voice rising in disbelief. 'Jesus Christ. Who the fuck are your backers?'

'A group of good men who are trying to prevent a bad thing from happening, whatever the cost,' Long said quietly.

'I've heard enough,' Kavanagh said, pushing his chair away as he stood.

'Don't leave,' Long said.

Kavanagh turned and made for the door.

'Don't leave, Mike,' Long said.

He kept on walking.

'Mike.'

There was a sound of papers rustling and then footsteps. Kavanagh turned to look and Long was no longer in his seat. It took a few moments to register that Long was actually up on the table and heading for him, the heels of his loafers sharp on the wooden surface. Long hurled himself from the table and, in mid-air, looked like the bookish nerd about to score a touchdown. The momentum of Long's body as it made contact with Kavanagh carried the two men along. Their skulls banged sickly together and they fell over the arms of a stray boardroom chair. Long was on top of Kavanagh and the two men flailed as one of them tried to find an advantage.

'Arnold,' Kavanagh shouted, as though to a child.

Long ignored him and Kavanagh felt his weight pin him to the floor, surprised at Long's strength. He began to pummel at Kavanagh's face, blows landing on his cheek-bones near his eyes.

'I won't let you do this,' Long said hoarsely.

The spindly fingers of Arnold Long found their way to Kavanagh's throat. They seemed to fit perfectly, as though they had been made for his neck. Something was familiar about it, a kind of déjà vu as though Kavanagh might have been strangled in some previous, sinful life. Long's grip tightened and some body-weight came to rest on Kavanagh's adam's apple

'I won't let you do this,' Long said again, sounding like he was crying.

This happened to Nancy. The thought flourished in Kavanagh's head, perfectly and completely sensible in the midst of the madness. Air could now go neither way, in or out. He could feel his face burning and imagined how red it would be. Long showed no sign of letting go and Kavanagh felt weak and light-headed. He's not going to stop and I'm going to die, Kavanagh thought, as his vision started to blur. He realized he had been making tight, strangulated noises.

Kavanagh's eyes must have been closed when the first blow hit the back of Arnold Long's head. He opened them in time to see the desk lamp strike Long once more. The tightness around his neck went and air seemed to flood in, blinding him. Through it, he heard several more blows and a yelp from Long, terrified like an animal. Then silence.

Kavanagh pulled himself to his feet, leaning on the table, and tried to see what was going on. His vision focused.

'You?' Kavanagh said, holding out his arm.

Without speaking, Garth Richards landed a single heavy punch into Kavanagh's face, knocking him back into a sudden and all-encompassing darkness.

Chapter 47

Lucy and Nathan walked briskly past the Pendulum building.

'Keep looking in front of you,' Lucy whispered to Nathan as she stole a sideways glance through the smoked brown glass. The security guard had his head nodded down towards some reading matter. Above his head and to the right, four screens flashed alternating black-and-white images of different parts of the building. Lucy had spent time with Tom watching the cameras change all around the building, the halting half-speed images of people unknowingly filmed.

When they were beyond the window, they stopped at the marble outer wall.

'There's a door down the side, by the ramp for the car park.' Lucy pulled out her father's spare swipe card. 'The buzzer for the entryphone doesn't work on the side door, so he'll have to come and open it. Stand on the other side of the camera, give the bell a good push and then get back here. When he goes round to open the door, we can go in the front and up the stairs.'

He pulled a face. 'Are you sure about this? Breaking in seems a bit dodgy to me.'

She held the card up. 'We've got a key, so it's not really breaking in.'

Nathan shook his head and set off down the side of the building. 'You're sure that card will work?' he asked, turning back when he was at the corner.

'Yes.'

At least she hoped so. It was almost eleven o'clock and there were only a few people about. Pendulum was situated at the edge of the West End that merged into Bloomsbury and attracted few tourists. The odd after-work drinker sauntered along, uninterested in what she might be doing. It seemed like only seconds before he was back, and as soon as he was, her heart began to palpitate and she knew it had begun.

They inched towards the window and Lucy waited a moment, trying to judge how long it would take the guard to rouse himself, if he even bothered. He wasn't there. Lucy grabbed Nathan's arm and pulled him along. She swiped the card through the slot and the light went from red to amber. She took a breath.

'Three nine seven one eight six,' she said to herself.

Her fingers shook and the plastic number pad felt slippery. Lucy pressed each number more firmly than she needed to, making the point.

The light changed to green and she pushed the door open.

They were hardly inside, the door clicked shut behind them, when she heard the door to one side of Reception move.

'Shit,' she said.

There was a toilet down that corridor, she knew. One the guards used. They had roused him, but from the toilet. The foyer seemed instantly large, nowhere in it to hide. Lucy pulled Nathan once again, heading for the small seating area where visitors usually waited, pushing them both against its far wall, the blind side of where the guard would be.

The reception area was like a Swiss clock with doors either side of the lifts. The guard was about to emerge from where they wanted to go and walk across Reception, to the door on the other side of the lifts. All he had to do, for Lucy, was not to look to his right.

The door opened and footsteps followed. She and Nathan pressed themselves together. She was sure their heavy and irregular breathing could be heard. The guard was muttering something and then he walked across Reception towards the passage leading to the side door. Don't look this way, Lucy thought. The guard broke wind loudly, the effort echoing around the deserted foyer. Lucy heard Nathan suppress a giggle and it made her want to laugh as well.

When the guard had gone through the door, Lucy and Nathan ran to the one he had just emerged from. They went to the end of the hall and down the flight of stairs that led to Tom's office.

'What do we do now?' Nathan asked, his voice hushed as they entered the room.

She was going to find him. She knew it. She just needed a moment. Lucy put her finger to her lips and he went quiet. In the near-dark, the only light coming through the blinds from street lamps outside, she tried to calm herself. The time she had spent in the building, in Tom's room, the stories he had told her there, came back to her, filtering through all her senses. The experience was similar to the ones she had at home and, gradually, Lucy picked up the trail of energy in the room, the sense of what had happened. They were bad moments, upsetting. The smell of disinfectant hinted at something unpleasant beneath its surface.

Lucy opened one of the tall grey steel cupboards, the door sharp and flimsy. She lifted a cardboard box from the shelf and set it down on the floor, crouching to rummage in it. The six door handles, the original ones Tom had kept and was so fond of polishing, were in the box. Lucy switched off her conscious mind and let her left hand roam in the box, not enough light for her to see clearly what she was doing. Her hand lighted on one of the handles and she pulled it from the box and then stood.

Nathan was looking at her as though she were mad. She looked at the handle and the careful engravings on its surface and it seemed to throb.

'Come on,' she said.

They used the back lift, which put them on the landing above the eighth floor, the same floor as her father's office and Paul Baran's. Lucy led the way down the few stairs, out across the deserted floor of the open-plan office, glancing at the half-open door of her father's room, and round to Paul Baran's office. She switched on the light and their glow was softer than she was expecting.

The office was tidy, all the furniture set at perfectly square angles and nothing to excess. One of the walls was halfcovered by an oak panel, the timber carved with grooves and bumps like veins traversing the surface. Lucy walked straight towards it and stood in front of it as if in a moment of silent prayer. Back to running on pure instinct, she reached out with the handle and placed it against a random part of the panel. It grabbed on as though a magnet were concealed behind the wood and Lucy felt a tingling jolt of static up her arm. Gripping the handle tightly, not sure she could let go even if she wished, Lucy turned her wrist.

There was a click and the panel swung back like a door, opening to a room beyond, a space normally concealed by the ancient panel. She crossed the threshold and peered into the gloom, Nathan a step behind her as she tried to make out what was in there.

'Oh no,' she said.

Chapter 48

'I left the house. Took Randall's notebook, Pa's gun, and some things of my own and got the hell out of Gift. Headed for Memphis. It was the longest nine days of my life and things nearly happened to me that I don't even care to think about, still less mention. Then, in Memphis, I met the preacher and he took me back to Raynford, and the bookshop,' Wadlow Grace said.

Nancy had closed the notebook. She wanted to hear what came after. 'Weren't you worried about what had happened, that they'd be looking for you?' she asked.

Wadlow nodded. 'Petrified. I was still a kid, however much I thought I might have grown up. Things had changed after that night with Randall and my head was heavier on my shoulders, but they were still a boy's shoulders. I spent the whole time waiting to be picked up, beaten up by the sheriff and thrown in a jail to rot in some small town on the road to Memphis. I slept rough, spent what little money I had, bummed food and some lifts to get nearer to the city. That's where a country boy goes to hide, lose himself in all those people.'

'What about your family? Your mother and father?'

He sighed. 'The preacher had contacts. When I was sixteen, he sent for local records, newspaper cuttings, parish registers. They all arrived, don't ask me how.'

'And?'

'There was no Grace family in Gift, not mine anyhow, or records of any Jacksons, Mama's people. It's like someone went back through my life with an eraser and removed all traces of me from the world. I didn't believe it, set on the preacher over it, said the records were fakes, accused him of doing it to keep me with him. He took me back to Gift, simple as that, and told me to look with my own eyes, said that it would make me believe all the crazy things he'd been telling me for almost two years. I said we couldn't do that since people would recognize me. Told me not to worry.

'The house wasn't even there, Nancy. Oh, there were things I recognized, people even, but it was all ever so slightly different. The names, the layout of the place. No one even blinked at the sight of me, Wadlow Grace, the one who murdered his backward brother Randall, walking down the street accompanied by a preacher. It was like looking through a blurred lens. The basic shapes were there, but you couldn't focus on anything special.'

'I don't understand,' Nancy said.

'It's as though my life was made up. That I have no real existence outside of that notebook of Randall's. I could be no more than a character in one of your books,' he said.

'Where do you come from, then?' she asked.

'It begins and ends, and begins again, in The Book. I learned this from the preacher. Behind the words of people passed down across centuries, in the meanings of the words and in the gaps between the words themselves, The Book existed. The Book has always existed. Before the syllable, the word or the sentence. Before writing, speech or symbols. Before paper or papyrus. Before thought. Before you. Before me. The Book.

'If it was bound, had a cover, a spine and pages and you could just pick it up and open it, things would be simple. I'd be able to tell you right now, Nancy, how it all begins and ends. There would be no need to read and no need to write. It doesn't work like that, Nancy. You have no more power to read it than I have to write it. The Book reads you. The Book writes you.'

Nancy listened, the rhythm of every phrase synchronized with her thoughts. 'How do you make any sense of it?' she asked.

'The knots of our lives, the tangles we embroil ourselves in, the twists, turns and intertwined moments are its text. It puts words into our mouths, thoughts into our heads. The only way to see the story is in the knotwork. It goes on forever but you can see it. From The Book come the intricate knots of a story, endless paths crossing each other at different points. If stray ends fray from the knot, splitting the infinity, The Book will search on until all the loose ends are tied up. This is what The Book reads and what The Book writes.'

He stopped.

Nancy ventured a question, gently. 'You believe this? Because the preacher told you?'

'I spent a lot of time trying not to believe it, finding other explanations. Then there came a time when it was no longer a question of belief, just one of truth. Look through Randall's notebook again, read what's in there. Pick up his pen and write with it, and then explain to me how that can be.'

'I can't,' Nancy said. 'If it does go on forever, why Randall? What brings you here? All the things you've been saying sound like they happen beyond our control. Why now? Why me?'

'The preacher used to say the story began as a small dot of light, no bigger than a full stop on a page of complete darkness. In that tiny speck was everything you could ever imagine, infinite. Something fell towards that light, something from outside of everything. It dropped from the sky, long before you, me or anyone knew there was such a thing as sky. It landed just where it was always meant to, at the precise moment planned by itself.'

'What was it?'

'The preacher used to say it was the touch of God's Gift, and that its secret was the only thing held in The Book.'

'And the preacher had The Book?' Nancy asked.

'Never saw it in his whole life, but then how many preachers have seen Jesus? The Book will have physical form at some points, but that is not The Book. Think of it as a mystery of faith, a trinity almost.'

'And the knotwork?'

'The Book is the process, the movement behind every

story, like an unseen motor. The knotwork is like veins, through which the life-blood of the process flows.'

'I don't understand. Be more specific.'

'Us. You, me, everyone, are part of the knotwork, the pattern that is made by the stories. Simply, you can think of it as a line that is joined up as though it's infinite.' He clasped his fingers together and made a tangle of them. 'Like this. It can be very hypnotic, just to look at this sort of pattern, to lose yourself in it. It's seeing forever.'

Nancy felt a hum of memory, like a voice whispering just below audibility. It goes on forever, but you can see it. These were things she had been working towards, in her writing.

'Why me?' she asked again, but it sounded more like a plea.

'You're part of a bigger story, you and Mr Kavanagh. Whether or not you chose to be or even like it. You can't run from it. If you run, that's what the story intended. If you stay, the same again. It's like death. You can run and run and run, but it will still be there, waiting for you.'

'So what's the point in doing anything?' she asked, annoyed by the fatalism of his words.

'Look at some of the amazing things that come out of the stories of our lives and how, even when bad things happen, we go out and carry on scribbling our lives. We go on because that's all we can do. If we stop, that's the way it's written.'

'And there's no way to take control of the story, to make it come out the way you want?'

Wadlow rejoined his hands into the twist and Nancy looked at it.

'If you have the knot, there's a chance.'

'And do you?'

'No. But there is a way we can get one. This might be your last-ever chance to influence the outcome of a story, Nancy. I need you to help it along, however much you might want to kick against it.'

For all the thinking she had done about death, the clever

intellectual word games, inoperable and inoperative, it was the first time mortality had felt so tangible and so imminent. One last story. She looked at the entrancing pattern of his fingers, feeling as though her whole body could as easily slip into them as into a spider's web.

'What do I have to do?' she asked.

Chapter 49

Lucy stood at the doorway of the concealed room, her eyes still fixed on what she had first seen, the detail clearer as she became used to the dark.

'What is it?' Nathan asked, a step behind her and apparently unable to see as well as she did.

'Tom,' she said, stepping into the chamber.

The old man was on the floor in a corner, naked. His back was to the wall, hands behind him. As she approached, he seemed to stir from a daze and become aware of her presence. There was fear in his actions, as though something unwelcome was approaching. When he moved his slumped head upright, he winced as though it caused him pain. Lucy realized his ankles were bound together. Looking down, she saw thick wire, wrapped several times round, twisted shut and chopped off into a menacing-looking point. Tom's toes looked bloody, one or two of them frayed. His nudity was embarrassing for Lucy. The floppiness of his stomach, the silver hair around his womanly chest and the wrinkled sag between his legs, resting on the closed join at their top, were not things she should have seen. Looking at his face, she saw dried blood and a cut in the soft flesh of his top lip.

Nathan was squatting next to her. 'Fucking hell,' he said.

'Where are you going?' she asked when he stood.

'There's a tool box over there.'

She looked at Tom while Nathan opened and searched through the tool box, the sound of metal against metal. 'Tom,' she said, more softly, trying to wake him. He no longer seemed even partially conscious of where he was or who he was. Lucy felt her face muscles weaken and a wetness wanted to run from her eyes. She resisted it. 'Tom, wake up.'

Nathan came back with a small pair of wire cutters, the red handles looking lost in his bony hand. The light from Paul Baran's office was barely enough but Lucy was not sure she could stand to see Tom in bright light in any case. There was a grunt from Nathan then a snip as the wire around Tom's ankles was cut. When Nathan pulled the wire away, she saw its thickness was akin to that of a coat hanger and she could also see the indentations it had made in Tom's skin, breaking it at some points. With a gentleness that surprised Lucy, Nathan eased Tom forwards into Lucy's arms, murmuring encouraging words, and cut the bonds that held his wrists together. When he was done, Nathan leaned Tom against the wall, removed his own coat and scrupulously covered the old man with it.

'There might be some water or something in that office,' Nathan said.

When he had gone, Tom's eyes flickered open. 'Who's he?' he asked.

'A friend,' Lucy said, relieved to hear Tom's voice, even if it did sound like a bad, ancient recording of the real thing. 'What happened to you?'

'My boy,' Tom wheezed. 'Garth.'

'Here's some water. And I found a box of tissues.' It was Nathan.

'Can you move?' Lucy asked Tom.

He shook his head mournfully. 'I think he broke my legs. And this.' He held up his right hand as though it might have weighed as much as his whole body. Around it, a rag was tied tightly. Lucy had not noticed it when they freed him. Now she could see he was missing a finger. Tom began to cry, quietly and with tears that slipped out from under tight eyelids.

Lucy poured some water out of the glass and onto a clump of tissues, dabbing at Tom's face and wetting his lips. His tongue poked through the cracked and bloody skin around his mouth. Lucy lifted the glass to it and he took a small sip, a tear of it running down his chin.

'Why did he do this?' Lucy asked.

Tom stretched his good hand towards her and, for a second, she recoiled. His bloody fingers touched her throat and she cringed, wondering what he was going to do. He grasped the chain around her neck and used the dead weight of his arm to slide his fingers along it until he came to the pendant on the end.

'Because of this,' Tom said, grasping at the metal knot which hung from the chain. 'Where did you get it?'

'My mum gave it to me,' she replied instantly.

Tom shook his head and smiled. 'No, she didn't. Not by my reckoning, at least. It was in your house all right, where Mr Cameron had put it for safekeeping and it's likely your mum found it, or, rather, it found her.'

'What's the matter with him?' Nathan asked. 'He's rambling.'

'I don't know,' she replied. 'Tom? Tom? My mum made this for me. She used to make jewellery, don't you remember me telling you that?' She could feel the chain digging into her neck. He pulled on it harder.

'By the time he came back for it, over twenty years had passed. He was looking for this knot, Lucy. That's why your mum got herself killed.'

'Tom,' was the only word she could find. The old man was dying. Lucy could see it in every half-filled action, death spreading through him like lethargy.

He opened his eyes wide and stared at her. 'You would have died too, if it hadn't been for the Lady.'

Lucy stiffened.

'Mr Alex gave me one of these for safekeeping. Told me to look after it for him, put it somewhere safe. That was two weeks before what happened up here. I never knew there was another one of them. He must have put it in the house at the same time. I never knew.' He sniffed. 'After the murders here, I hung on to it. I was too afraid to throw it away. Thought he'd come looking for it one day, but he never did.'

Tom let the knot go and put his hand out for water.

Lucy gave him some and he waited a moment before he went on.

'I remember still the first time I saw you, after your mum was killed. My heart stopped in my chest when I saw that thing around your neck. First thing I did, afterwards, was make sure my one was still safely locked away. This building's made for hiding things in. It was still there all right. There must have been two. I knew, as sure as anything, that your mum had died because of it. I wanted to tell you, make you take it off, but I could see that it was making you feel better, keeping you safe, perhaps. Until now. For this last three years, I've been keeping my eye on you.'

'What's he on about?' Nathan asked.

'Shush,' she said to him. Her mind raced, trying to find the exact moment her mother had given her the pendant. She could not. 'My mum gave it to me,' she said again, but the words were hollow, no longer filled with truth.

'I never knew. If I'd known there were two, I might have been able to stop what happened to your mum.' Tom winced as though something inside him was tearing.

'What happened to the other one?' Lucy asked.

'My boy took it off me. That's how I ended up like this. He had the same look about him, Lucy, the one I saw on Mr Cameron when he arrived here in the middle of that night. I held out for as long as I could before I told Garth where it was.'

'What does he want with it?' Lucy asked.

'I don't think he knows that himself, not really. I'm not even sure he is himself.'

'Where did he go?' Lucy asked.

'It took me a while to work out where he would go, sitting here in the dark. I shouted for help at first, but no one can hear through these walls. Garth said things, babble mostly, but I know where he's gone.'

'Where?'

'To America. To find your dad.'

Lucy gripped the knot around her neck so tightly, its ragged ends dug into the smooth skin of her palm.

Tom gave a cry, small but louder than any he had emitted so far. There was a noise somewhere behind them, distant, but a noise nonetheless. All three of them looked to the door of the chamber.

'Go,' Tom said.

'No,' Lucy said. 'I'm not going to leave you here.'

'It'll be Security. They're supposed to do a walk-round every three hours to check the offices. They'll find me if you leave the door open. Go and call them from outside if you want. There's nothing you can do here. Go and help your dad, Lucy.'

'How are we going to get out without being seen?' This was Nathan.

'There's an opening in the middle of the wall. You'll have to feel along to find it because the wall's painted black and there are two baffle screens. It's like a little maze. There's a lift that takes you down and a passage that leads to another lift. Go up in it and there's a set of steel doors, like fire doors. They open onto a side street three roads away from here. Push the bars. You won't need a key to open it from the inside. It's the way Trust members come in and out of this building without being seen.'

'Tom . . .' Lucy began.

'Go. Phone the police or do whatever you want, but do it once you're out of here. Your dad needs you.'

'He's right, Lucy,' Nathan said, holding her arm.

'Look after her, son,' Tom said to Nathan.

'I will,' he said.

Lucy leaned forwards and planted a kiss on Tom's cheek, on the least sore patch of skin she could find. As she did, the knot swung from her neck like a pendulum and touched Tom's throat. As it did, she felt a burst of energy through him. He whispered in her ear.

'Go find your dad and you'll find out how you got the knot. And what really happened to your mum,' he said, gripping her weakly.

She looked at Tom for one last time, trying to freeze a good picture of him, knowing she would not see him again.

'I've found the gap,' said Nathan. 'Come on.'

Chapter 50

Kavanagh stirred, coming into a consciousness disoriented by new experience. His wrists were sore and there was tightness around his waist as though he were wearing a belt pulled in two holes further than it should have been.

That wasn't the worst of it. There was something covering his head, a hood that was full of his hot breath and wet with his drool where it touched his mouth.

Feelings and sense spread beyond the immediacy of his body and he heard the sound of running water, close by. He was shivering with cold and fear. He kept his head slumped forward, neck muscles slack. While his brain worked away, placing himself in space and relaying body sensations, he struggled to fit himself into time.

A sound. A foot on a floor. Close, as though someone had been standing and watching him for a long time, only just deciding to move forward.

Who?

Garth Richards.

The hood was yanked from Kavanagh's head at the same moment Garth's name came into it. He expected to be blinded by a flash of light, but the illumination around him was only dim. He took some time to get used to breathing fresh air rather than his recycled breath and pulled against the cord that bound each wrist to the chair behind him. It still took a few moments to adjust to the gloom. If he was going to be killed, it would have happened by now. Perhaps it boded worse to still be alive. No, he thought, I'd be dead by now if he didn't want me alive.

'Not necessarily,' Garth said from behind him, startling him. 'No, you haven't been gibbering your thoughts out loud, Mike. The Book hears you and it tells me.'

Kavanagh tried to twist his head, his neck muscles

hurting, but the voice came from a blind spot. His body was aching, he realized, as if he had been in a rough soccer game or done a new work-out. He looked at the tiled floor and the walls rising around him, what light there was coming from small portholes along the wall that glowed like cats' eyes. The floor sloped up away from him and a few puddles of water hung stagnantly near drain holes.

He was in an empty swimming pool. He would have killed me by now. He hung on to the thought.

'Yes, that's right. I'd have killed you by now and you're in an empty swimming pool.' Garth walked round and stood in front of him. 'No, don't think about that or I'll have to tie your legs to the chair as well and I don't want to do that. I like to see a bit of movement. That's an interesting thought. Would you like me to torture you? With a small knife or a stapler? A soldering iron? You really are scared, aren't you?'

Kavanagh's hands were numb and his wrists tender. Lucy, he thought, and quickly smothered it.

'She's all right, Kav. On her way here as we speak. I'm looking forward to seeing that nice little pussy of hers. I expect it was bald the last time you saw it, unless you've been peeking.'

'What the fuck are you doing, Garth?' Kavanagh asked, shocked at the sound of his own voice echoing round the empty pool.

Garth brought his fingers to his nose and sniffed deeply as though inhaling the perfume of a flower.

Kavanagh looked around him. He was about halfway down the pool, the five-foot part, facing the shallow end, tied by his hands to a wooden chair. The ladders on the side were eerie without water refracting their image. They all stopped short of the bottom of the pool. Green mould grew in the spaces between the tiles, the fungus more heavy and moss-like near the water inlets. The inlets. Surely he wouldn't fill the pool, the crazy fucker. Kavanagh wondered whether it was day or night.

Once more, his thoughts turned to Lucy, and to Helen. Don't let Lucy be alone, he thought.

'How sad,' Garth said. 'Don't let me get into those thoughts, please. They make me so fucking angry. I might just . . .' He reached out his hand.

The lights in the portholes went off and Kavanagh sensed the tension come over Garth, the way his muscles froze.

'No,' said a voice that came through the dark from every direction, the bass in it rumbling Kavanagh's guts.

The remnants of the word oscillated through Kavanagh's organs as though it had come from inside him.

In the darkness, there was a bright burst as Garth ignited a lighter. It threw Kavanagh's night vision off-balance.

'You won't have long to wait, then you'll see things. Very special and very nice things. While we wait, maybe a few burns won't hurt. Well, will hurt,' Garth said as he approached Kavanagh.

Chapter 51

'No,' said Nathan.

'I didn't say anything yet,' Lucy said.

'You don't have to. You've tried how many times now to get through to your dad and I know what you're going to say next. No.' His tone was firm.

'What am I going to say?' she asked.

'That we should go out there and look for him. That old bloke was delirious. You could see that as well as I could.'

'But he might be right, Nathan. I can't remember exactly where and when I got this.' She held up the pendant.

'How come you've spent loads of time thinking your mum made it for you, then this old guy tells you it belongs to someone else, that your mum got killed because of it, and you believe every word of it?' Nathan shook his head and snorted.

His attitude made her angry and she felt like slapping him on the arm. They were back at the house, it was late, and Lucy had to decide what to do next. The decision fell to her. Despite the apologetic, placating phone call, Aunt Karen would be getting more and more worried and might come looking. Earlier, she and Nathan had cautiously emerged through the secret doors that led out of the Pendulum building. The first thing she did, from a phone box, was call the number for Pendulum. The night service rang out and was eventually picked up by the flatulent security guard. With luck, Tom would now be being looked after, although the state they had left him in scared Lucy, and she was uncertain an old man like him, however wilful, could take what had been meted out to him. She wanted to do more, but now there were other people to be concerned about.

A sheet of paper by the phone in the living-room listed all the numbers where she should have been able to reach her father in an emergency. The list, which was pressed into her hand each time Dad went away, had always seemed absurdly cautious, long even. Now, it looked stupidly short. His hotel. The number for Trellis. Paul Baran's home number. Lucy tried the hotel twice, leaving a voice message for her father on the second occasion, trying to keep the quake from her voice.

The receptionist at Trellis was friendly, remembering her father. 'You're the second person that's called today for him,' Lucy was told. The receptionist was kind enough to put Lucy on hold while she checked with Mr Burns's personal assistant. Mr Burns was out of town for the next few days. Nothing was scheduled with Mr Kavanagh after that. Then she tried the hotel again. Lucy was not going to call Paul Baran's number. Not yet. The second person who's called today, Lucy thought, knowing there was one other person who might be looking for her father.

Lucy punched the long sequence of Nancy Lloyd's phone number into the keypad, no longer enthralled by transatlantic telecommunication.

The phone was picked up after the first ring, the rattle as it was snatched off the cradle communicating nothing to Lucy other than anxiety.

'Mike?' was the only word Nancy Lloyd said and it made Lucy swallow hard.

'Nancy, it's Lucy Kavanagh.'

'Lucy, hi,' Nancy said, sounding as though she were trying to smooth her voice out, massage the tension from it. It was no good. Nervousness was stretching it thin.

'Is my dad with you? I've been trying to get in touch with him.'

'I haven't seen him yet.'

'Not since he arrived?' Lucy asked.

'There was a meeting yesterday and he wanted to spend the day before preparing for it.'

'What time is it there?' she asked, even though she knew.

'Four in the afternoon.'

'What time was his meeting yesterday?'

'I'm not sure. In the morning, I think.'

'And you haven't seen him since then? Didn't you see him last night?' Lucy asked, aware of the accusation in her voice.

Nancy was silent and it made Lucy feel nervous and guilty at once.

'You dad was supposed to see me last night.' Nancy spoke slowly. 'He didn't arrive and I haven't been able to reach him. I phoned Trellis and even went by his hotel, got them to check his room. Nothing.'

'He's left the hotel?'

'No. He hadn't checked out.'

'I'm coming out there,' Lucy said.

'No. Let's wait, Lucy. He could be on his way home to you, for all we know.'

'You said he didn't check out. Dad wouldn't come back early without letting me know. Something's wrong, Nancy.'

'Stay calm, Lucy.'

How much should she say to Nancy on the phone, about the things Tom had told her? She twisted the pendant between her fingers, the metal becoming warm and moist from her sweat. Already she could feel her mind on the threshold of something troubling about the knot. It involved Mum and now it involved Dad. Lucy knew, was certain, she needed to be wherever Dad was. Dad needed her and Nancy could prove an obstacle to that. Doing a quick breathing exercise Kim had shown her, Lucy composed herself.

'Nancy, if something's happened to my dad and I'm not out there, I won't ever forgive myself. You can help me get out there, or I'll just go ahead and do it myself. One way or another, I'm not going to sit around here and wait for news.'

She heard Nancy sigh at the other end of the phone. 'You can't come out here, not on your own. Your dad will go mad if he finds out I helped you do that.'

'I'll bring Nathan,' she said, ignoring the face he was making at her.

'Let me call the airport, sort out flight times and arrange for tickets, then you can pick them up. I'll come out and meet you at LAX.'

'Can you do that?' Lucy asked.

'We used to do it all the time at the agency. What's Nathan's surname?'

'Lucas.'

'Does he have a passport?'

Lucy asked him and he nodded, reluctantly, still protesting with his face.

'I'll call you back. Are you at home?' Nancy asked.

'Yes.'

Fifty-five minutes later, Nancy called back with flight details.

Lucy put the phone down and looked at Nathan.

'You'd better get that passport,' she said. 'We're going to America.'

Chapter 52

For almost two hours Kavanagh had sat tied to a chair watching Garth Richards burn himself with a lighter.

At first, Garth had taunted Kavanagh with the flame, standing behind him in the blind spot again and swinging the lighter past Kavanagh's ear, the smell of petrol in the air and the warmth of the fire just discernible. When he had heard clothing being removed, Kavanagh tensed. Several minutes of complete silence and total darkness followed, leaving him disoriented and afraid. Sweat formed on Kavanagh's body, the most obvious parts of him dripping with it, while areas such as his lower back were sheened with moisture. His crisp cotton shirt was damp with sweat and marked with sooty patterns of dirt.

Then there was a movement, a scurry like a rat.

Garth Richards stood in front of Kavanagh, four or five feet away from him. Through the dimness, Kavanagh could detect his nakedness. When the lighter ignited, it threw light into the small area around the flame and cast pointed, elongated shadows. The flame was blue-yellow, flaring occasionally. Garth pushed his arm out towards Kavanagh, bringing the lighter nearer to him. Just fucking do it, if you're going to, Kavanagh thought.

Kavanagh lost sight of him again and then felt heat on his right hand. Garth must have been holding the flame close to him. The heat grew more intense and Kavanagh was rigid. Just as it felt about to burn, it was gone. The heat was now on his left hand and Kavanagh clenched his fist. In a quick touch, less than a second, Kavanagh felt the hot metal of the lighter on the back of his neck. He cried out in pain, but said nothing.

Back in front of Kavanagh, Garth, with slow and obvious relish, reignited the lighter and carefully brought the flame to his own nipple, howling when the tip of it made contact with the raw and fleshy point. Kavanagh cringed at the sight and the sound. He wanted to enjoy what the mad bastard was doing to himself, but he did not. There was something in his cries which made them sound almost involuntary, a pleading to his moans.

It began with the extremities of sensitivity. Both nipples, then the tip of his tongue, the flame hissing as it vaporized saliva. Under his arms next, the smell of burnt hair. Behind his knees, the soft baby flesh searing quickly. Squatting, the blue tip of the flame grazed along his perineum. There were screams as it burnt his phallus, the flame as close as he could get it. Tears and sweat were mingled on his face.

'Oh, that felt so good,' Garth said when he was done. He disappeared from Kavanagh's vision and returned, still nude, dragging a chair similar to the one Kavanagh was bound to. He set it down four or five feet away and sat.

Since he had been sitting in the chair, with nothing to do but look at Garth Richards, Kavanagh had been studying him and had noticed there seemed to be moments of extreme clarity when he could recognize the person he knew as Garth Richards whereas at other times he felt he did not know the person he was seeing. Kavanagh didn't know Garth that well, but the excessive, frightening nature of his behaviour was far beyond anything he would have predicted.

'You think I'm mad?' Garth asked.

For the second or third time, Garth was reflecting Kavanagh's thoughts back at him as though they had been words in the air rather than in his brain.

'They're still words, in your head, in the atmosphere or on the page. It's not the context that matters, it's the text,' Garth said.

'Garth, what the fuck are you talking about? Get a grip, mate.'

'I'm your mate now, am I, Kav?' Garth said, bitterness putting a sharp edge on his tone. 'You sit there thinking I'm mad and there you are, the Trust's golden boy, Mr

Pendulum, working his fucking balls off for them, and all for what? In a million years, even in a hundred, who'll give a fuck? They'll look back at us in a few centuries and wonder what the fuck made us organize our lives like this. We're all dead, Kav. Don't you get it?'

'If this is something to do with Pendulum or the Trust, we can sort it. I can sort it, but I can't do it sitting here,' Kavanagh said.

Garth's laugh was on the verge of tears. Burn marks covered him, wilting and bloody. 'You're not going to negotiate your way out of this one, Mike. They've sold you down the river here, mate, Paul Baran and Andrew Mathias. I hate your guts, personally, but I bet that's a more honest emotion towards you than either of them have.'

'I've known Paul Baran a lot longer than you have, Garth.'

'Yes. And he's known Andrew Mathias longer than that. And they've both known the Trust and its secrets for even longer. They think they do, but if they'd even glimpsed the things I've come to know, their heads would crack open from the pressure.'

'Tell me what you've seen,' Kavanagh said, trying to engage him, afraid if he lost him, Garth might go further over the edge.

'I know why the Cameron Trust was first set up and I know why they want the merger with Trellis to go ahead. And I know who killed your wife.'

Kavanagh felt himself stiffen in the chair.

'You don't believe me, do you, Mike? Do you want me to tell you what's troubled you for so long, that you've never told Lucy?'

'Shut up, Garth.'

'You still don't believe me, do you? You think I'm making this up.'

'Don't,' Kavanagh said, feeling Garth's probing questions invading his mind.

'They found semen in her rectum, Mike, didn't they? It

wasn't yours and they couldn't confirm for certain the sex had been forced. You wonder about that, don't you? Was she seeing someone else, someone you knew nothing about? Perhaps they were in the early stages of the affair, ready for a bit of daring up-the-arse sex. What do you think, Mike? Does that sound like Helen? You'd rather think she was buggered against her will than she was having an affair, wouldn't you? Weren't there moments when you thought she deserved what she got? And you hated her for letting Lucy find her like that, didn't you? You keep all of that buried under that thick skin of yours, ploughing on and being good old Kav, ready to do the Trust's bidding.'

Kavanagh hated Garth at that moment, more even than the man who had taken his wife from him.

'You can't even start to understand,' Kavanagh said, slowly and definitely. 'You've never had anything in the first place, so you wouldn't know what it was like to lose it.'

'Nothing happens for nothing, Mike. The Trust, Pendulum, Helen, Lucy, Helen's death, the merger with Trellis, Nancy Lloyd. It's all tied up in the same knot. Even me. You're going to find things out, Michael Kavanagh, and it's all going to make sense.' There was satisfaction in Garth's voice. 'And then you'll end up dead.' Garth held up his hands. 'Me too.'

'Garth, I don't know how you know what you do, but we're still not too far down the road on this to turn back. Help me out here.'

'I'd love to stay and chat, but I have some errands to attend to. You won't have long to wait, though. I can promise you that. I've got something for you to look at while I'm gone, so you don't get lonely. Something to look forwards to, perhaps.'

Garth stood and approached the chair. Going behind Kavanagh, he seized him by the shoulders and turned the chair around, its legs making a jarring screech on the tiles.

There was a burst of light brighter than sunshine.

On the floor, sprawled in a depressing and lifeless mess, was Arnold Long. His head was to one side, as though looking up at Kavanagh, and his lips were mauve. An arm was pushed away from his corpse at an odd angle and Kavanagh could count only two fingers on the hand.

'He was your only friend in this, Mike. You should have paid more attention to him,' Garth said. 'But that isn't what I want to show you.'

Next to Arnold Long's body was a television set on a stand, like the one back in the boardroom at Pendulum, a shelf beneath holding a video player. Garth switched the television on and pressed the *play* button on the video.

'A bit of a cast of thousands in this. The man in the leather outfit you won't recognize, but then nor will anyone else now. The old woman is my mother, never the most photogenic but she goes out with a bang. There's a lovely surprise around the middle, especially if you love dogs and hate lawyers. Arnold's the big finale, my best yet, and I'm not going to spoil that.'

Garth was climbing the few steps up the side ladder that led out of the pool.

'Wait,' Kavanagh called.

'Enjoy!' Garth cried from a distant point. 'They tell me there's a demand for these sort of videos over here,' his voice echoed. 'Personally, I think there's already enough sex, violence and death on the television, without me adding to it.' He sounded like he was talking to himself rather than to Kavanagh.

The black of the video lead-in disappeared and there was a close shot of Chris Carson, his head occupying the whole frame. As the camera pulled back, fear was evident, as were several wires attached to his temples with black insulation tape. Once his whole body was in view, Kavanagh saw his legs were taped together and his feet were in a bowl of water. There was an audible crackle, like static, and Chris Carson emitted a scream which, even through the small speaker on the television, reverberated with pain and desperation.

Kavanagh closed his eyes, wishing he could put his fingers in his ears.

Chapter 53

The morning after a late arrival at her Aunt Karen's house, followed by an argument and a mostly sleepless night, Lucy left the train at Heathrow and made her way to the end of the platform, hefting a bag containing a surprisingly small amount of luggage and looking for Nathan. He was so set against the whole idea, Lucy was afraid he might not turn up. More than anyone, she needed him now.

The crowd thinned, filtering off into exits, and she saw him, standing there looking not much different from the first time she had seen him that day in the Trocadero. The sight of him created the need to be close to him and she began walking faster, dropping her bag on the floor next to his when she reached him and grabbing on to him, wanting to hug him more than kiss him. His body was solid and comforting, warm and fresh in the early morning.

'I missed you last night,' he said. 'Did you get a bollocking from your aunt?'

'A bit, but she's too scared of upsetting me.'

'Your dad never called, then?'

'No. I know you think we shouldn't be doing this.'

'I'd probably do the same if it was me and I had somebody buying the tickets.'

'Thanks,' she said.

'Let's get a move on,' he said, glancing over her shoulder.

The platform was empty, the sound of the next train whistling like breath in a bottleneck as it approached.

'You've brought your passport?' she asked.

'Yes. Come on.'

He was walking fast, carrying her bag as well as his own. A whole night had passed, as would the whole of the current day, and she would still be no nearer to Dad. Lucy rubbed the knot, letting its veins ripple under her thumb. She was trying to get used to it again, now it had become a stranger to her, its origins a mystery.

Using her best sensible-and-firm attitude, coupled with the familiarity of her recent trip to Los Angeles, it was less than an hour before Lucy had them in the departure lounge, free of luggage and waiting to board. She had dreaded taking the knot off to pass through the metal detector, remembering it had set it off on the last trip. This time, she left it on and the bell on the detector was silent, making her check it was definitely there.

'I thought you didn't even want to come and now you're more jumpy than me,' she said. Nathan had been as keen as her, if not more so, to get through the checkpoints and into the lounge.

They were sitting side by side in the felt-like upholstery of the bucket seats in Departures, surrounded by adults. Lucy could smell aeroplane fuel and the light in the building seemed unnatural. In between flight calls and announcements redirecting passengers to different gates, a plane would roar as it thrust itself into its journey.

'I think some bloke was watching us,' Nathan said quietly.

'Where?' she asked.

'When you got off the train. And the other day, when we were out. It was the same guy.'

'Are you sure?'

'Not totally. I didn't want to scare you and I didn't know for sure, anyway.'

Lucy fidgeted and looked around.

'Relax. He can't come in here unless he's bought a ticket and fuck knows what else it took to get us through that gate. I've been keeping an eye out and there's no sign of him. Can I have another mint?'

She gave him the half of the pack that was left. 'I told you something weird was going on.'

'There's some fucking weird people about, Lucy, but I'll look after you, help you find your dad if I can.'

Lucy took his hand and squeezed it. She whispered to him, letting her lips touch his earlobe as she did.

'I love you,' she said.

Chapter 54

Alone again, for a short while at least, Wadlow Grace sauntered into the middle of a Californian afternoon, relishing what little breeze there was. Memories ran amok in his head, about the family he might never have had, the preacher, the book store and his fabulous collection of books, reduced to nothing more than cinders and ash. But he put the past in its correct place and concentrated on the present and the future. And The Book.

You made a good decision. That was what he had told Nancy Lloyd before setting off for his walk, as she was leaving for the airport. Helping the girl come over here. There were still more things he wanted to tell Miss Lloyd, but he knew she would never believe him. Wadlow had stretched her trust and understanding as far as it would go and he knew she would find them out for herself soon enough in any case.

The artful contrivance of The Book, the subtle insinuation of the knot into all their lives, left Wadlow walking a tightrope. He was afraid to move left, right, forwards or backwards, not knowing which way was correct. But since it all took place within the context of The Book, whichever way he moved was always in some sense predetermined, written for him.

Wadlow found a phone and took a few minutes to compose himself, then dialled.

'It's Wadlow,' he said.

'How is everything?'

'Set. She's on her way to get the girl.'

'Good.'

'Are you sure she has one of the knots?' Wadlow asked.

'Yes. It is what propels her here. We are at a critical moment.'

'I know.'

'Are you ready, Wadlow?'

'Yes, I am.'

'You know what time to call Nancy Lloyd? Where to send her?'

'Yes.'

'She absolutely has to come alone to meet you. I must get the girl on her own.'

'I understand. Trust me. She trusts me. She'll come.'

'The preacher would have been very proud of you, Wadlow Grace.'

'Thank you.'

'There is a chance we may not see each other again, Wadlow.'

'Yes.'

'Be ready for what you have to do.'

The phone went dead.

Chapter 55

They wandered through the Arrivals gate like dazed soldiers returning from some sort of battle. Nancy spotted them straight away and wondered if they would have stood out so prominently had she not been consciously looking for them. Lucy looked tired, over and above the wearying effects of the plane. The boy was attractive in a hardened, London way, a bit too lean for Nancy's liking, but she could sense the fusion between the two young people as they came towards her, Lucy trying to smile.

'Hi,' Nancy said, gripping Lucy weakly in a loose hug. It was hard to be light-hearted. 'Hello,' she said, turning to the boy.

'This is Nathan,' Lucy said.

'All right,' he said, his eyes drifting around the interior of the Arrivals Hall, just above head level.

'Any word from my dad?' Lucy asked.

Nancy shook her head. 'No. I called his hotel and Trellis twice today.'

Lucy touched her hand to her chest and Nancy watched it, disguising a hard swallow and wondering if the knot Wadlow had talked about was beneath the shirt. She had not felt it when they hugged.

'Let's get you back to my place. You could probably do with showers.'

Back at the apartment, Nancy settled them in, taking their luggage and piling it in the living-room, which seemed empty without the imposing presence of Wadlow Grace. She felt awkward about where they were going to sleep. It was fairly obvious to her where they would want to sleep, but she was a having a hard time envisaging herself explaining it to Mike. If they all made it as far as bedtime.

Guilt tugged at her for leading Lucy on, however reassuring Wadlow had been. Once again, she missed him.

She showed Nathan the bathroom and found herself giving a California-style lecture on water conservation. He was indifferent, so Nancy left him to it and went to see Lucy, who was sitting on the sofa, staring into space and chewing unspoken words.

'He seems nice. Quiet,' Nancy said.

'I'm glad he's here. What if we don't find him, Nancy? What if he's gone, just like Mum?' The words were spoken casually and Nancy wasn't sure of the emotions underlying them or how she should respond.

'Don't say that, Lucy. It hasn't been long and your dad's a sensible man. He's not the sort of person bad things happen to.'

'My mum was sensible too. So was I. Look what happened. No one ever thought I'd walk into the house and find her in the attic with her guts all over the floor. She was opened right up.'

'Lucy . . .'

'I'm able to talk about all of this, of course, because Kim helps me. We've been through that scene a thousand times, finding the body.' Lucy smiled. 'I'm like someone who's watched so many video nasties, they don't scare me any more. It should be scary, don't you think? How can it be right? Why should I fucking accept it? I think it's my fault she died and Dad thinks it's his fault. What did she think? When the screwdriver went into her stomach and ripped her right up the middle? Did she think it was my fault? Dad's fault? Her own fault?'

'It's no one's fault in terms of your dad or your mum. Did something happen in England, before you decided to come out here?'

Once again, Lucy rubbed her chest.

'Lots of things have happened.'

Nathan returned, barefoot in jeans and topless, rubbing at his short hair with a towel. The two women stopped talking but were unable to fill the pause with idle chatter, making the silence seem conspiratorial.

'What?' he asked, as though he might have done something.

'Nothing,' Lucy said, standing. 'I need to shower. I feel really tired.'

Wadlow Grace called while Lucy was in the shower. Nathan was sprawled across an armchair, flicking through a comic of Lucy's. Nancy went to the kitchen and answered the phone there.

'Nancy, it's Wadlow.'

'Hello,' she said, trying to sound casual rather than relieved, in case Nathan was listening.

'Has she arrived?'

'Yes.'

'Does she have it?'

'Yes. I just saw it.'

'I need you to come and meet me, alone.'

'Where?'

He told her.

'Where?' she repeated, the same word now suffused with incredulity.

Chapter 56

'Where did she go?' Lucy demanded.

'She said she had to go out, that she'd only be a couple of hours and that we should stay here in case your dad called,' Nathan said.

'Why didn't you come and get me?'

'She was on the phone, off it and then on her way out. She was in a rush and she probably knew you'd be leading off like you are now.'

'You should have got me out of the shower,' she snapped.

He moved closer to her and stroked her hair. 'Two hours,' he said.

Lucy wanted to bat his hand away, to keep being annoyed at him for no real reason. It didn't seem right to be doing this, she thought, not with Dad missing. But it felt so right and it was a way of not having to think about anything, abandoning her mind to her body – and his.

He was still without a shirt, his skin clean from the shower, the sweat on his body fresh and sweet. Lucy kissed him and rubbed her hands over his bare torso while his own cupped her behind as he pushed his groin insistently against hers. Lucy pulled at the buttons on the front of his jeans and pushed them over his rear. He wore no underwear and she nudged him back until he was sitting on the edge of the sofa. As she knelt and worked the jeans down his legs until he was naked, he looked straight into her eyes the whole time. The rawness of the moment was already obliterating her. Greedily and without his encouragement, she leaned forwards and took him into her wide-open mouth, forcing in as much as she could, until it pressed against the back of her throat. Lucy wanted to choke herself on him, using him like a gag to block out all her thoughts. She made almost as much noise as he did, doing something she had never imagined she would. It was over quickly, his hips lifting his behind clear of the cushions and his whole body convulsing as it gave itself away through the deep-seated fluid it pumped into her. As though it might give her life, Lucy pulled at him with her mouth until he had nothing more to yield and was begging her to stop.

'Christ almighty,' was all he said, when she was sitting next to him.

Nathan stood and pulled on his jeans.

'Where are you going?' she asked.

'Just to the kitchen. Don't worry,' he said, tapping her nose with his finger.

'Fuck,' she heard him say.

'What?' she called out.

'There's all these fucking fruit juices in here,' he said.

She heard the sound of things being moved impatiently around the fridge.

'Bollocks,' she heard him mutter as something fell. 'Doesn't she ever eat?' he asked himself.

He returned to the room and pushed his bare feet into his basketball boots.

'What are you doing?' she asked as he slipped a navy-blue Fred Perry over his head.

'I need something fizzy. I can't drink that crap. There was a shop just down the road. I saw it as we drove in.'

Lucy felt a rising panic. 'Don't, Nathan. Nancy said to wait here.'

'You are here. I'll only be ten minutes. Give me that money you had.'

'Nathan.'

'I'll get some crisps and stuff, if we're gonna sit here and wait.'

She fetched the few dollars she had in her bag.

'How much is this in English money?' he asked.

'About ten pounds. Don't be long,' she said.

He made a face and kissed her.

Chapter 57

Nathan bounded down the drive of Nancy's apartment block, clutching the money Lucy had given him. He turned left at the end and headed towards the small square of shops that reminded him of some near the flats at home.

He passed an electrical shop, the window display looking a few years out of date, cardboard faded by the sun and dust gathering unpleasantly on black plastic. Nathan stopped and looked at his image on a television screen. The first glimpse of himself had made him double-take. There had been something familiar about the gait of the person he had seen out of the corner of his eye and when he turned to look, the image followed him as surely as if it were in a mirror. Nathan giggled, impressed by something as silly as a camcorder in the window of a shop. As people passed behind him, he watched them on the fluid fuzz of the screen before turning quickly to see what they were like in the flesh.

As he watched the screen, the area around his shoulders and behind his head started to change, becoming almost like a halo. A bleariness appeared as though the channel were going out of tune. At first, Nathan thought the interference must be coming from inside the television, something wrong with whatever made the picture real. As he stared harder at the glass, he realized the shimmering movement was coming from behind him. It was like the very fabric of everything was being wrinkled or ruffled, making the world distorted.

Nathan wanted to turn and see it for real, if it was real, but something made him keep looking ahead. The whole area behind him, the very tiny piece of the world he was inhabiting, had begun to swirl around in a long and graceful loop. It reminded him of long spaghetti all tangled together on a plate, or the way someone's insides looked when they had their belly cut open. It was as though someone had come and taken a scalpel to a bit of the world and revealed all the oozing nerves and organs underneath it.

There was the heavy press of a hand on each of his shoulders.

'It goes on forever, but you can see it,' a voice said, so low and comforting it could have been in his own head.

'What?' Nathan asked.

'The knotwork. It goes on forever, but you can see it. Infinite patterns visible to the eye,' the voice replied instantly.

A long arm extended over his right shoulder, the hand straight in front of it and the finger pointing at the glass window and the television screen behind it. Nathan looked and found it hard to see himself in the middle of the vibrant arc. The long finger began to trace the pattern of the arc, making figures of eight and speeding up until Nathan was sure he could feel the air moving near his face. The pattern of the finger and the throbbing of the shape on the screen made him feel sick.

'I could move my finger around all day and never stop, unless I got tired.'

'It doesn't really go on forever,' Nathan said.

'I agree. If you think of it as a line that only goes in one direction. When did we start doing that? Thinking of everything as a line?'

'What do you want?' Nathan asked.

'I think you know what I what. I think you know better than even I do,' the man said.

Nathan felt the hands slip from his shoulders, over his back and down onto his hips, finding their way round to the front of his jeans.

'What are you going to do?' Nathan asked, swallowing.

'Something very special and very nice.'

'What is it?'

'Do you trust me?'

'I don't know. Will it hurt?'

'Am I hurting you now?'

'No.'

'Or now?'

'Ah! No, I like that.'

It was later, he realized. It was dark and they were somewhere else. In the space of only a few sentences, words that were not his own, they were in another place.

'So you trust me then?'

'Yes.'

'Take off the rest of your clothes then.'

Chapter 58

'Didn't you take the key?' Lucy snapped, pulling back the door of Nancy's apartment.

The sight of a strange man standing in front of her brought Lucy up short. It embarrassed her to be so ratty in front of someone she did not know, to give a small glimpse of her true self to a stranger.

There was something familiar about the man. In England, he might have been the caretaker. He was old enough for Lucy to guess he was in his seventies, dressed in an antiquated way. The man and his clothes were both faded with time, neither of them as smart as they perhaps intended to be. He looked as if he had been journeying for days, years even, so driven that he paid no attention to himself. His clothing must be hot in this climate, she thought, realizing how out of place he was, but definitely familiar to her. Like he had been blown in on a wind.

'Hello, Lucy,' the old man said. 'I'm Alexander Cameron.'

Chapter 59

The screams emitting from the television had long since subsided, but they rang on in Kavanagh's ears. It had been hard to watch the grisly collection of Garth's achievements. Hard not to. Each time there had been a new sound, Kavanagh had to look, if only to satisfy himself of one thing – that Lucy was nowhere on the tape. She was not, and he guiltily found himself thankful, although watching brought its own penalties. Kavanagh wondered how long it would be before the memory faded of what he had seen Garth do with a hammer and chisel to an anonymous man near the start of the tape. The screen was now blank and Kavanagh was left in the dark with the troubled stillness of his thoughts. Where was he? What had happened to put him there? Arnold Long was sprawled ten feet away, still freshly embarked on his journey into eternity. The bindings on Kavanagh's wrists were sore, the muscles of his arms aching from his efforts to free himself. Pendulum, Trellis, the power to deal and two and a half million pounds all seemed like absurd memories of a different life, fear and jeopardy placing a new value on everything.

Light crept under his feet like mist, coming from somewhere behind him, casting his shadow down towards the nearest wall. Noise followed, slow footsteps heavy on the tiles of the swimming-pool floor. Kavanagh moved his head from side to side but could not see behind him.

'Hope you enjoyed the show, Kav.' It was Garth.

'Fuck you,' he spat back, wishing he'd thought of something better to say in the stretch of time he'd had to sit and ponder a response.

'Whatever. I'll be right with you. I've brought you some company. Sit down. Good.'

There was some shuffling and then Kavanagh felt

Garth's approach. His shoulders were grabbed and he was spun on the chair. Garth switched on the lights and they hurt. A boy was sitting in a chair facing him, bound to it like a mirror image of Kavanagh.

'Mike, this is the boy who's been fucking the arse off your daughter, quite literally. To tell the truth, I don't think she's a virgin anywhere, if you know what I mean. Maybe I should let you loose on him, Kav. Make you keep kicking him until we really do see shit come out of him. Or I could force you to do things to him, give him a taste of his own medicine. What about I roll the camera and you can watch me give him a bit of a seeing-to?'

The boy looked on in a daze, a dark weal under his left eye from a hefty blow.

'Where's Lucy?' Kavanagh asked.

'I really couldn't say, Mike,' Garth said.

'Not you,' Kavanagh said to Garth. He tried to direct his voice at the boy. 'Where's Lucy?'

'She was at the woman's house.' His speech was slurred. 'Your girlfriend, Nancy. I just went . . .'

'Quiet now.' It was Garth. He had walked round behind the boy and placed his hand over his mouth. 'We wouldn't want to spoil any nice surprises.'

'What's Lucy doing out here?'

'Looking for you, Mike. Doesn't that touch you? And she brought her boyfriend to keep her company. I can smell her mouth on him.' Garth leant in and smelled the crotch of the boy's jeans. 'Oh, you're a lucky boy. What do you think, Kav, did she spit or swallow? I'm guessing swallow.'

'You'll get yours, Garth,' Kavanagh said, trying to ignore the taunts.

Garth planted a kiss on the boy's cheek and disappeared behind Kavanagh once again.

'Is Lucy all right?' Kavanagh whispered sharply at the boy, whose head was lolling about. 'Is she?' he rasped.

'Mmm.' The boy nodded lazily, 'I just went out . . .'

Kavanagh tugged hard once again, the pain in his wrists now extended to most of his arm, pulsing through the numbness. He ignored it and tried to spur himself on with the thought of being able to lay his hands on Garth Richards if he broke free.

'There's no need for that, Kav,' Garth said. 'You'll have your chance soon enough. Always so impatient.'

'What's that?' Kavanagh asked.

Garth had set down a square object between his and the boy's chair.

'Time for a story,' Garth said.

It was a book, a fat volume like an encyclopedia or a telephone directory. There was an unnerving atmosphere that seemed to hang over the book, but Kavanagh could not understand why. It was not possible to see all its sides at once and it was frightening, as though something unpleasant was waiting in its shadow. The longer Kavanagh looked at it, the more anxious he felt, as though an unexploded bomb had just been set in front of him.

Garth squatted by the volume, facing Kavanagh.

'What are you going to do?' Kavanagh asked.

'What I've been waiting a long time to do. Something very special and very nice.'

'Don't,' Kavanagh said, the word coming to him instinctively, as if it had been planted there.

Garth opened the book, the strain in his arms evident, as if the pages weighed tons. As it fell open, there was a thunderous thump and Kavanagh was certain he felt tremors reverberate through the stone floor.

At first, Kavanagh thought nothing was going to happen. In the silence, across the gap, he and Garth Richards regarded each other. Garth's face had an expectant look, like a child unwrapping a present and hoping he is right about what will be inside.

Light began to flow from the pages of the book. Out and over the edges, it spread out across the whole floor of the pool, like a laser. When the glow reached the sides, it began to rise up evenly. The silent yellow light was going to fill the pool.

'Close it, Garth,' Kavanagh said.

'Didn't I tell you? I've resigned. I don't work for you any more. You can't tell me what to do.'

The light was up to the level of Kavanagh's ankles and he could feel static tickling him.

'We're going to fucking drown in this,' he said.

'Better hold your breath then. Or close your eyes.' Garth laughed.

The brilliance still gushed from the tome, up to Kavanagh's knees, over his lap and towards his lower chest.

'Close the fucking book. I'll kill you if you don't. I swear to God.'

'Up to your neck in it, Mike?'

The top of the boy's head was just visible for a second before dipping below the surface of the illumination. Kavanagh felt the light under his Adam's apple and then over all of his throat until his chin was dipping into the radiance.

The light covered him. It did not drown him, but it blinded him. He could no longer see or hear Garth or the boy, as though the intensity of the light had overloaded one sense and wiped out all the others, leaving him in the dawn of his own world of illumination.

Kavanagh's fetters dissolved, as though melted by the light, and as he stood, he realized the floor was at a different angle from the one he had expected. Losing his balance, Kavanagh toppled forwards for what seemed like forever, into the fabrication.

Chapter 60

Nancy sped into Forest Lawn, parked the car on a skew and ran all the way to the Church of the Hills.

Wadlow Grace was standing by a hedge to one side of the church. The clock tower showed only forty minutes until the park closed.

'How did you know about here?' she asked.

'How did you?' He smiled. 'The preacher is buried out here. It was in his will. Surprised the hell out of me. If we had the time, I'd take you to where he is.'

'We don't have time?'

Wadlow looked at her, a sad cast in his eyes, and his earlier smile faded to nothing.

'It's time for letting go, Nancy.'

'Please don't tell me it's going to end here,' she said, looking around exaggeratedly, surprised at her own mordant humour.

'This is where it will begin. I don't know where it's gonna end.'

'Is Lucy safe?' Nancy asked.

'As safe as she can be. She's in good hands now. Lucy has her own things to do, things she needs to know. Just like you did. Remember, this is only the beginning, Nancy.'

'What do I have to do?'

'You have to get yourself to Mr Kavanagh.'

'How?'

'Right now, he's somewhere unreal. A fabrication. You need to get to him the only way you can. By writing yourself into it. You're the only one who can do that.'

The hedge rustled in a low breeze and the sun was hidden by the church as it began to wane into the horizon.

'You say that it begins here, but, for me, it's also the end, isn't it?'

Wadlow nodded. 'I'm not going to lie to you about that.'

Nancy let out a breath.

'Are there things you need putting in order? Things I can do for you?' Wadlow asked her.

'No,' she said. She wanted to see Kavanagh. He was her only piece of unfinished business. Her life had all but ended the moment she had stepped on the plane to Los Angeles. 'You're not coming with me?'

'Nancy, if I could go instead of you, I gladly would, but I can't even accompany you.'

She knew exactly where to go.

Wadlow followed her as she crossed the path, walking fast. Nancy looked around, back in the sunlight for a moment, feeling it warm on the back of her neck. Birds were singing and she could smell grass. All the most obvious and grotesque imitations of life surrounded her in a moment so utterly filled with death, her death.

Nancy made for the tree by the roadway, past the stump and on to the brass plaque set into the ground. She looked down at it and it was blank, just like the first afternoon she had seen it. Blank except for the pattern of the knot, embossed on its top like a crest on notepaper. Nancy looked at it only briefly, afraid of being sucked straight in.

The swirling and infinite pattern had come to symbolize only one thing for her. An end.

'Is this goodbye?' she asked, turning to Wadlow.

He reached out and stroked her hair, brushing it from the left side of her face. Nancy planted a kiss on one of his puffed pink cheeks. Wadlow went bashful for a moment and she saw the slim and pretty teenager he had once been surface in the oversized and sad shell.

'Thank you for telling me your story. I hope you find out who you are,' Nancy said to him. 'Will I see any of this again?' she asked, gesturing to the world in general.

He shook his head. 'Not quite in this way.'

'Wadlow.'

'Yes?'

'I don't want to die, not yet.'

'I know, child. I know.'

Breath heaved from her once again. 'Goodbye, Wadlow Grace. I wish I could have known you longer. I would have written you such a wonderful life.'

'Don't be starting me,' he said, his eyes glassy.

Nancy gripped his hand for a moment, as though she could hold on there forever and not have to go. Inoperable. Inoperative. It didn't make much difference. She let go of Wadlow.

Turning, she squatted to get close to the plaque. The knot had been expecting her, remembered her from before. Immediately, her eyes were baffled by the shape, no one point on which her gaze could come to rest. The pattern was tiring. Nancy fell to her knees and looked more closely, seeing the knot glow as though becoming molten. It was as if her life really were passing before her eyes, but not in the detail of specific events. Rather, the unseen and unknown pattern of the knot was like a secret lock to which she was the key.

'It goes on forever, but you can see it.' Wadlow Grace was reciting the words, a true prayer in an unreal cemetery.

The hot shine of the knot had grown to a more potent brilliance, as if she were staring at a bulb in its socket. No heat came from it, just light filled with energy, so much life it could wipe her own out, or absorb it into itself.

'The knotwork goes on forever, but you can see it. Infinite patterns visible to the eye. It's seeing forever. Don't you find the pattern of infinity comforting?'

Nancy stared at the brass plaque and saw words develop on it like secret writing.

Nancy Lloyd

1969 –

She was coming into the text . . .

Nancy peered hard at the metal, aware that it was fading in the light. She was just able to see the final numbers develop before sight went.

1997

And out of it . . .

The light was now so bright, even the knot could no longer be seen. Nancy was washed in the brilliance, no longer certain she was even in the world, if she was even alive. The side of her head hurt, as badly as when she had first been prompted to go to a doctor. It didn't matter any more. The world had slipped away from her and she was left in light.

A hand, Wadlow Grace's, pushed her between the shoulder-blades and she toppled forwards, through the light and into the fabrication.

Chapter 61

Lucy slammed the door as hard and as fast as she could, expecting a foot to block it and a hand to slide through the gap, making a grab for her.

Instead, there was a polite knock from the man who had just introduced himself as Alexander Cameron. The man who had gutted his own family and returned to kill Lucy's mother for what was now hanging around her own neck. The knock came again.

'Lucy, I must talk to you.'

'Go away,' she said, slotting a bolt across and looking for something to lean against the door.

'You don't have to lock the door. I won't come in unless you want me to. I promise.'

'I know what you did,' Lucy said, beginning to hyperventilate. 'To your mum and dad. And your sister.' A few tears came. 'And my mum.'

'I swear, Lucy, I had nothing to do with your mother's death. I almost lost my life trying to save my own family.'

'You're lying. I know all about you,' Lucy said through the door.

'How do you know?'

'Because Tom Richards told me.' She was having to shout to make herself heard. It was like the times when, as a small child, she would have sullen and sulky conversations with Mum through the closed door of her bedroom.

'Tom is a good man.'

'He's probably dead now, because of what you made his son do for you.'

'I have no control over that, Lucy. Tell me what Tom told you.'

'You gave him one of the knots and hid the other one in our house, probably while you lived there. When you went missing, after the killings, Tom said he knew you were still around somewhere. He never realized there were two knots, but why should he if you didn't tell him?'

'It was safer for him not to know how many there are.'

'He never knew until you came back looking for it,' Lucy said. She saw a picture of her mother, opened up on the work-room floor, and a realization came to her. 'You were looking for it inside her. That was why you cut her the way you did.'

'None of this is true, Lucy. I can explain to you how I came to be what I am, the things that happened on the night I lost my family, and, I can help you see what happened to your mother.'

'No,' she said.

'I can give you those few minutes you want so badly, let you arrive home earlier. You will see for yourself, there was nothing you could have done. You have to trust me.'

'I'm not opening this door. I'm going to call the police,' she said.

'Do you honestly think any of this can be sorted out by something so simple as involving the police? What will you tell them? It hurts, Lucy, I know it does. I've been waiting, watching, anticipating. It has been so tempting to make contact before now, with Tom, or possibly even with you. I would have stopped your mother's death had I known it was going to happen. Now it's time to try and put things in order, to make some sort of amends.'

Where was Nathan? 'You killed my mother for some stupid piece of metal and you'll do the same to me if I give you the chance.'

'I saw you and your boyfriend at Heathrow. I was watching you and so was someone else. I would have had ample chance back there if the knot was all I wanted. What I want, Lucy, isn't that bit of twisted metal. It's what you can bring to it. I need your help.'

'How did you know about the flight?'

'One of the last friends I have left in the world has been here with Nancy Lloyd. It took us a long time to find her and realize how important she was to the story. We knew what flight you would be coming on. I wanted to make sure you were safely on your way here. I need your help, Lucy, and so does your father and your boyfriend.'

'Where are they?' she asked.

'Nowhere I can get to without your help. Nowhere you can get to without mine. We need to trust each other.'

'Tell me where they are.'

There was shuffling sound and a bump. He had sat down. Lucy's legs were aching, so she did the same.

'My father, Clough Cameron, was a clever man but also a vain and stupid one. For all the things he had accomplished in his life, in Scotland, at Cambridge, during the war, with the hotel, the single thing he most wanted was children. A fertile mind and a dead body. My mother Krista was like the child he never had, only a baby when he first met her and the man he foolishly believed to be her father. This man gave him Krista and the way to have the children he was desperate for. The granting of that wish did not come without a cost, but it was a long time before any of us realized the true price.'

Lucy pulled her knees up, rested her chin on them and continued to listen, the sound of the man's voice dulled by the door but still holding the ring of truth.

'At first, it did not seem much to pay. The man helped my father in business, provided money and was instrumental in the founding of Pendulum and the Cameron Trust. What more could my father have hoped for? Children and success in business affairs, the burning down of the hotel now just a bad memory. I was pulled along by it, too; even my sister was, and we became focused on nothing but the Trust, as though our lives depended on it. Once we began to fathom the true purpose of the Trust, its driving force, we understood just how much really depended on it. Are you listening to me, Lucy?'

'Yes.'

'My sister and I were only a little younger than you are now when we first saw the knots. One for each of us. My father made it sound like a fairy-tale, the end of which was a gift for us. Not a very exciting present when you are thirteen, some dirty old metal knots. It was later, much later, when he showed us The Book. So late, in fact, that it was too late. My father must seem like a disappointing giver of gifts, first the bits of metal then an old book?'

'What was in the book?' Lucy asked.

'That was the same question I asked my father. Nothing, he told me. There were no stories in The Book, but The Book was there in every story. You could not read it because it was reading you. You could not write it because it wrote you. The endless flow of all our lives connected together, like knots that went on forever. That was what came out of The Book, the knotwork.'

'There was nothing in the book?' she asked.

'There was one thing. A secret. My father called it the touch of God's Gift.'

'What is it?'

'Some are touched by God's Gift, Lucy. You are. So is Nancy Lloyd and, to an extent, your father. Your mother was. You are extremely close to the central strand of the story and you have important work to do in it, in its text. I must speak with your father if any of this is to be of use.'

'What's the secret? God's Gift?'

'If you don't let me in, you will not see your father again, I can guarantee that. Your mother really will have died for no reason, the way she always seems to have in your mind. I can help you make sense of what happened, stop the unspoken words that run from your mouth. Your mother, Tom Richards, Nancy Lloyd and your father will perish for no reason.'

She snapped out of the thrall of his words. 'No. You killed your family and you killed my mother. You can't get away from it by telling stories,' she said.

'My family were killed and I was lucky to get away. There is no way I can make you believe me, I can see that. Believe yourself, Lucy. Hold the knot. Look at it and feel its power. Has it steered you wrong so far?'

Lucy instinctively touched the knot through her top. She pulled the chain and lifted the pendant, cradling it in her palm like a bird as she stared down at it. The metal appeared brighter than it had previously, as though recently polished. She tried to let her feelings meld with the shape, using the knot like a tuning fork to see if there was harmony around her. The metal hummed contentedly, no danger apparent.

'It will lead you to your father and to the truth of your mother. Open the door, Lucy.'

'No,' she said, kicking against her desire.

'I don't mean this door. Open a door in the story, find a different part of the text.'

Lucy carried on looking at the configuration of lines. The secret was there, held within the shape. Following the lines around with her eyes was making her feel drowsy. The world around her became less solid, dim against the increasingly bright glow emanating from the knot. There was no longer a chain threaded through the metal and she was left with the knot resting on her open hand. Lucy put it down on the floor and knelt over it, staring intently at the sheer white that now bathed the area around the pendant.

'It goes on forever, but you can see it.' Alexander Cameron's voice sounded close, as if the door were no longer there.

The light was complete, tranquil energy.

'The knotwork goes on forever, but you can see it. Infinite patterns visible to the eye. It's seeing forever. Don't you find the pattern of infinity comforting?'

Lucy was swathed in a sheet of sheer, luminous power, floating on it as though in water. The world had slipped away from her and she was left in light, the knot nowhere to be seen.

A hand, Alexander Cameron's, pushed her between the shoulder-blades and she toppled forwards, through the light and into the fabrication.

The Third Knot

There is nothing outside of the text.
Jacques Derrida, *Of Grammatology*

Chapter 62

As she had done so many times in dreams, both asleep and awake, Lucy found herself standing at the door of her house. It was the same day as it always was, the day her mother was killed.

With one tentative foot in front of the other, past her father's study, Lucy moved down the hall like a bullet travelling in slow motion.

On the first landing, her heart began to pound. He had gone straight to the attic room, with a clear sense of purpose. There had been no search for things to steal, or a careful check to see if the house was empty. He had made directly for her mother.

She ascended the final nine steps that led to where her mother would be working. The music she was listening to filtered into Lucy's ears.

Lucy brought her hand to rest on the door handle of her mother's workshop, seeing how much weight she could put on it before the spring would exert an opposing force.

She stood in the open doorway of the work room, the overhead window pushing a beam of light directly onto the bench, lighting her mother as though in a film. Tears welled up in Lucy's eyes at seeing her alive once more. 'Mum,' she said. Her mother continued to work. She's alive and I'm dead, Lucy thought. She can't see or hear me.

The noise came from the kitchen, just like it always did. The Lady was down there, trying to warn her mother, wanting her to look up and see what was really waiting in the doorway for her. Her mother turned and smiled and it chilled Lucy. She was looking right through her, to someone who was also standing in the doorway.

Lucy watched as her mother began to speak, but there were no words, just the movements of her mouth. Her mother looked happy, but concerned, Lucy thought. She has no idea she's about to die. It made Lucy feel more sad than she ever had before, as though it was worse to think her mother's death had come so suddenly and in the midst of a kind of happiness.

Helen Kavanagh stood and walked directly through Lucy, who felt a shudder run over her body and wished she could hold on to her one more time, before she died.

Lucy floated along the corridor to her mother and father's bedroom. Down in the kitchen, she could hear the Lady frantically throwing things around, trying to make as much noise as possible, as a way of distracting her mother. She could not hear it. They were on different wavelengths. Lucy realized why she sometimes saw the Lady when she was in the house. Because she was able to tune into her. So could her mother, but not this time.

Her mother was kissing the man who was going to kill her and there was nothing Lucy could do. The man had his back to her and Lucy struggled to identify him, certain she knew him as well as her mother did. Lucy tried calling out again, but her words were useless, unheard and without context.

Helen's lips started to move again and Lucy heard a distant whisper that approached as she tuned into the sound.

'What are you going to do?' her mother asked.

'Something very special and very nice.'

'What is it?'

'Do you trust me?'

'I don't know. Will it hurt?'

'Am I hurting you now?'

'No.'

'Or now?'

'Ah! No, I like that.'

'So you trust me then?'

'Yes.'

'Take off the rest of your clothes then.'

With the dispassion of a ghost, dead and without feeling,

Lucy watched as her mother was cajoled onto all fours and used roughly, the tension of the sex evident in the strain on her face. Lucy tried to see who it was kneeling behind her mother, but she was unable to come to rest on his face, like a word she could not remember.

The time passed with painful slowness, Lucy floating through it and powerless to do anything. When her mother was on her back, Lucy began to panic, desperate to break free from the bondage of silence.

The screwdriver came from nowhere. Her mother barely had any time to register it before the blade was inside her.

'No!' Lucy screamed as loudly as she could and knew her mother had heard her.

'Lucy?' Her mother looked up from where she was on the bed.

Lucy knew there was danger and turned to run for the stairs. She could feel him behind her, moving faster than her and closing the gap too quickly. Lucy willed herself to go faster, jumping the last four steps and feeling the strain in her ankles as she landed.

In the kitchen the Lady was standing in the middle of the room. It was the first time she had ever seen her face on and it had never occurred to Lucy that she would be so beautiful. The Lady's face could have come from an old photograph, her top lip almost a straight line, no bow, the fulsome bottom lip cupping a generous smile that seemed to weigh down her whole jaw. The Lady's hair made Lucy want to reach out and touch it, to see if it were real, the long sheen of black set in a single wave sweeping off one side of her head. All of the partial glances, the peeks and glimpses she had snatched of the Lady were all represented in what stood before her, as much a spectre in the scene as Lucy herself. Lucy understood what it felt like to be the Lady, buoyed about on the sea of someone else's reality, watching them drown in it and powerless to act. Lucy's eyes fell to the Lady's neck and she saw the bruises. Strangled in the womb.

'Who are you?' Lucy asked, already certain of the answer.

'I am Camille Cameron.' She handed Lucy the knot. 'The man chasing after you is seeking this. It has been in this house since my brother Alexander put it here, until I give it to you. It is the only way you can save yourself.'

'Is this happening now or is this what really happened to me on the afternoon my mother died?' Lucy asked. 'Was I in the house when it happened?'

'This is both. There is no way to separate the events,' said the Lady. 'I have had the knot under my protection and your mother never knew of it. This is a fabrication of sorts and that means you are still in danger. You are like a child to me, Lucy. I've spent so much time watching over you, more since your mother was taken.'

'Have you seen my mother?' Lucy asked.

'It doesn't work like that, dear. You must have faith in the things my brother told you. He will be a good man, eventually, regardless of what he may have done in the past. There is danger here,' Camille Cameron said.

'What should I do?' Lucy asked.

'Turn around and see what's standing in the doorway. You have to do that, because you need to understand who killed your mother before you can understand why she was killed. Then you should try and get out of here, if you can.'

'How do I do that?'

'Let the story fall away from you. Let yourself forget everything. If this is a story, a fabrication, try to go outside of it. He's waiting for you, child,' the Lady said.

Lucy turned, looked at the doorway and straight into the eyes of her mother's killer.

Chapter 63

Kavanagh was no longer alone in the sea of noiseless light. As certainly as he had sensed the departure of Garth with the boy, so he could feel other bodies around him, their images eclipsed by the illumination which was far too brilliant to be anything so simple as real.

In the far distance of the glow, on an horizon of some kind, Kavanagh saw the smudge of a figure, daubed into the luminous canvas and getting larger, approaching. Off to the left of the speck, another was moving more quickly, getting closer and closer to him. Kavanagh continued to look at the fastest-moving of the two, watching as its proximity allowed him to discern the figure of a man.

None of it was real. That was the thought Kavanagh tried hardest to keep a grip on. The hushed intensity of the experience was such an overload for his senses, it seemed to leave no room for ideas of his own or for free will, as though they were being purged by the whiteness surrounding him. None of it was real. All the sensations were false. Made up. Not real.

'Fictional?' a voice asked.

Kavanagh stared, just able to see the features of an old man. His face was red, almost wind-burned, and his straggling grey hair needed a wash. There was something altogether unkempt about him despite the tweediness of his clothes. His skin was artificially brightened in the bath of light, making him seem alien.

'Fictional. As though written by someone else. A little bit like a story. Someone is coming who I know you will want to see,' the man said.

Nancy Lloyd, the distant spot, came into sharp focus, as though through a lens, a microscope that allowed Kavanagh to see each pore in her body. She was smiling sorrowfully at him, her eyes dark under the rims, as if she had been crying. He could find no words for her and just observed her through the silence, framed by the incandescence.

The old man squatted, there was a thump like a box-lid falling, and the light was gone.

Kavanagh moved his head around, surveying the scene. He was no longer in the empty swimming pool. Instead, he was seated at a table, a circular one, with the old man off to his right and Nancy to his left. There was something familiar about the room, at a level in him he found hard to reach, like a long-forgotten odour invading his nostrils anew.

'This is a fabrication,' the man said. 'An environment conjured by words so powerful they are able to make matter. This room is how part of my father's office looked on the night my family was taken from me. My name is Alexander Cameron.'

'What's going on?' Kavanagh asked, fidgeting, but still as rooted to the chair as if his bonds remained.

'Listen to what he has to say, Mike,' Nancy said.

The walls of the room were covered in painstakingly carved panels stretching from floor to ceiling. There was a single, similar panel in Paul Baran's office, the same ancient oak with white scars marking it, like birds in flight. The chairs were also oak, heavy and deep-cushioned, the upholstery an extreme shade of blue. Light came only from an elaborate fitting suspended over the table, swinging slightly from side to side, like a pendulum. The majority of its illumination was pointing down on the centre of the table, spotlighting the book which sat there.

'There is much to explain and, naturally, so little time. I am going to take the liberty of a shortcut. Would you be so kind as to open The Book for me, Mr Kavanagh?' the man said.

'Where are we?' Kavanagh asked.

'Mike, please,' Nancy said, pushing it towards him.

Kavanagh shook his head sadly, convinced it was all still false. They were talking to him as though he were a child.

Fictional. Made up. Fabricated. What if it was? he wondered. Could it be made up and still real at the same time?

The Book seemed old and new all at once, brimming with ancient energy and full of youthful vitality. A shine came from the tome, warm on his cheeks, and he found himself smiling. Kavanagh put his fingers on the pages, somewhere near the middle, and flipped The Book open. The pleasing thump it made against the surface of the table was the same noise it had made when the old man had closed it to shut off the light. Kavanagh wondered if he would be blinded once again.

The pages in front of him were blank. Holding his place with a finger, he looked at some pages nearer the front and then nearer the back. They, too, were clean.

Kavanagh was about to look up from the page, to ask them what he was supposed to be looking at, when he felt The Book grab him. He realized he was not looking at it; it was looking at him. Information was flowing in the wrong direction. The Book was reading him. It was like a sounding board for his soul, something that was able to suck from the marrow of his bones every thought, feeling or word that he would ever call his own. Any trace of doubt Kavanagh might have had about who he really was or his place in the world was erased. The Book defined him with absolute clarity. Held in its gaze as it perused him, Kavanagh felt shaken, violated but complete, able to give himself so totally to something that it might, in return, provide the very definition of himself.

Then, for a second, he caught a glimpse of The Book. The flow was reversed and The Book allowed him, fleetingly, to glance into it. Kavanagh slammed it shut.

Sick in his throat, his stomach whining, Kavanagh looked up at Alexander Cameron. He wanted to ask the old man what it was he had just seen.

'I know. An answer or two and, then, so many more questions. You have just seen where it all begins and ends, and begins again. And, it has seen you. You have taken the measure of each other. There are very few who could look into the abyss in the way you just have, Mr Kavanagh. Take Garth and how twisted he has become through his reading of The Book and, more so, its reading of him,' Cameron said.

'He was here. Before the light came and before you arrived.' It was coming back to Kavanagh as though he had been in the hold of amnesia. 'He brought a boy here he told me was my daughter's boyfriend. Garth said they were out here, together.' He thought harder. 'Where is she? Where's Lucy? Is she safe?'

'Your daughter is as safe as she can be, for the moment, but we do not hold the balance of that moment,' Cameron said.

'Lucy's at my house, Mike. I helped her come over here because she was worried about you. You've been missing for nearly three days,' Nancy said.

Cameron put the small metal knot down on the table.

'I'm afraid she is somewhere rather different from your house, Nancy.'

'Where?' Kavanagh demanded.

'Your daughter is finding the truth of her past. Of what happened to her mother.' Cameron gestured to the knot. 'How she came to acquire this. As I speak, she is reliving a moment, somewhere utterly fabricated although it will seem real to her. She needs to go through that in order for me to get here to you, Mr Kavanagh.'

'She insisted on coming, Mike. Lucy said she'd get out here whether or not I helped her. It seemed easier to help. I didn't know where you were,' Nancy said.

Pendulum. Trellis. The merger. Arnold Long. Garth. The video. Lucy. Kavanagh was disoriented, his head painful. There were questions, hundreds of them, but he could not formulate a single one. He wanted to get up, but knew he could not. He was imprisoned by ignorance, the only escape from which was words. Kavanagh regarded the knot and The Book and tried a single word, hoping it was the key to the linguistic prison.

'Explain.'

'As I've said already, it begins and ends and begins again, in The Book. The Book gives us the ability to write the stories of our lives. It is, quite simply, the process by which all stories are told, the engine behind them. I don't mean writing in the narrow sense of words on a page, but the way we go out into the world and live, or write, our lives. The Book is the life-blood of all those stories,' Cameron said.

'This book has all the stories of the world in it?' Kavanagh asked.

Cameron held up his hand. 'No. Every story is not in The Book. The Book is in every story. You cannot read or write The Book. It reads you and it writes you. The Book is at the heart, is the heart, of every story. Let me give you an analogy, with religion. If we were to allow ourselves to imagine, just for a moment, that there was a God, and that this deity was a he, what would be his motivation? What is it that would get him up from his bed each morning? It seems to me that God could only sensibly be a writer. What else could he possibly do? Now, religious people don't tend to believe that God makes every decision of their life for them. They assume God gives them a context of some kind, creates the conditions for their existence, and lets them get on with living.'

'So?' Kavanagh asked.

'So, The Book *is* the process, the facility to write our lives. Imagine how boring it would be for God to have to keep track of all those individual stories. That is why, I repeat, The Book contains no stories.' Cameron lifted the knot and showed it to Kavanagh. 'Think how simple your life is, when you are born. Then think of the way it becomes more and more complicated, intricate and overlapping. When you die, that knot of your life goes to rest. But then, even as a newborn, you are still connected to the people who came before you and at the end of your life you will be a part of many other things.'

He placed the knot in front of Kavanagh.

'Don't think of it as a line that only goes in one direction.

Think of it as going on forever, a process. It goes on forever, but you can see it,' Cameron said.

'What's the point of all this?' Kavanagh asked.

Cameron laughed. 'How long have you and men like you been asking themselves questions like that? The big question. What is it all about? Recall what I said about the notion of God being a writer. What would his only point be, ultimately?'

Kavanagh did not speak.

'To get to the end of the story.'

It was Nancy.

'Precisely. The Book contains no stories. The Book is in every story. It has only one thing in it, one secret. The secret of God's Gift. How the story ends. You are correct. It is that simple and that dangerous.'

'How does it end?' Kavanagh asked.

'If I could open that book now, go to its last page and show you how things end, it would be easy. Unfortunately, it is not that easy.'

'But you know something,' Nancy said.

'All three of us here have, in some way, been touched by God's Gift. Your daughter has a penchant for Japanese comics, doesn't she?' Cameron said to Kavanagh.

'Yes,' he said, uncertain where this was leading.

'We think too much of our stories as lines that only go in one direction. It amused me to picture your daughter so casually wearing this small knot of eternity and flicking through the stories in her comics, back to front. Consider Arab cultures and the manner in which they write. The text can go in any number of directions.'

'I think I understand,' said Nancy.

'God's Gift comes into the world complete. He goes from end to beginning. He leaves it as nothing,' Cameron said.

'He's backwards,' Nancy said.

'A person?' Kavanagh asked.

'That is the secret of God's Gift,' Cameron said.

'Retarded?' Kavanagh asked, feeling lost in the exchange.

'Not exactly,' Nancy murmured, recognition dawning on her face.

'What then?' Kavanagh asked.

'The story comes to an end because its most central character is travelling in the opposite direction to the rest of us,' Cameron said. 'When he gets to the end, the stories end. In the beginning, back in infinity, he sets out as a number so large it cannot be counted and his only purpose is to reach zero.'

'Oh,' Nancy said, rubbing her head sorrowfully.

'Think of how the universe expands and may one day contract, time going backwards to nothing. That's when, and how, the story ends. Getting to zero. It is a journey to innocence, the progressive forgetting of evil. He begins with the story of his life already written and goes through it backwards, getting to zero. From man of some kind through to child and then to nothing,' Cameron said.

'Who is he?' Kavanagh asked.

'When my father encountered him, he was over a hundred years old, young when you carry the experience of forever with you. By the time I first laid eyes on him, knew what he was, he was in his seventies, around the period he got to the young Randall Grace. In his late forties, not happy with the way the Cameron Trust was developing against his wishes, he took my family away from me.'

'The Trust?' Kavanagh asked.

'Of course, the Trust. What do you imagine the real purpose of a corporation such as the Trust would be? When my family was erased, I lost control of the Trust to men like Andrew Mathias. But there is much more. The first time you met him, Nancy, he was forty-two and you were only five. The next time, you were sixteen and he was thirty-one, catching him up. He killed your wife, Michael, when he was twenty. At this moment, he is eighteen and your daughter is very much in love with him.'

Nancy gave a huge sigh and Kavanagh looked at her. He looked at The Book, there on the table as a continual reminder that he had seen something he could not comprehend, as though it were in a language he did not yet understand.

'I appreciate this may be hard to come to terms with. The boy calling himself Nathan Lucas will gladly kill all of us to get this.' Cameron held up the knot.

'But he's just a boy. He was helpless,' Kavanagh said.

'Perhaps he is just a boy, in some ways. Possibly even helpless,' Cameron said. 'You have to take that much about him on faith, his duality. It is almost a mystery of faith, the father and the son being the same. Nathan Lucas is a character in the story he has written.'

'Just a boy,' Kavanagh said again, almost whispering it to himself.

'Yes,' Cameron soothed, 'he is just a boy and he may even be innocent, but the path he has carved for himself through the story is far from innocent. It is conceived with only a single purpose.'

'To get to the end?' Nancy asked.

'That is the purpose of The Book, the secret of God's Gift, but I don't believe that is his motivation. It is completely the opposite. To stop it. He doesn't want it to end. The original purpose of the Cameron Trust was as a vehicle that would allow him to change the logic of the story.'

'How?'

'You should know the answer to that better than me, Nancy. Isn't it a favourite cliché of writers to talk about the way the characters in their stories take on lives of their own, do unexpected things and begin to make demands? All those characters running away with the story. It is no different for him. He is attempting to reverse his decline.' Cameron touched the knot. 'All the stories, intertwined. Imagine the potency of them all pushing in a single direction, committed to something far stronger than the most powerful religion. The knotwork would have the potential to overpower The Book, to kill its own god. It might stop him reaching zero.'

'Why didn't he just take the knot from Lucy?' Kavanagh asked.

'Because that is not the way The Book writes it. He was looking for this when he took your wife's life, and when he murdered my family. He has one of the knots, given to him by Garth Richards who, previously, had taken it from his father. He has a knot and he has your daughter.'

'Where's Lucy?' Kavanagh asked.

'Outside of the text. He has removed her and himself from the text. The only way there is to take The Book and face him, Mr Kavanagh.'

'We have one. He has one,' Kavanagh said, looking at the metal on the table.

'No,' Cameron said. 'One will be unable to take you there. My father had one for each of us, his little fabrications. Alexandra, myself and Camille. There are three knots and we have two.'

'Where's the other one?' Kavanagh asked.

Cameron looked at Nancy.

'How many times, since finding you have a tumour, have you thought it was all in your head? All in your head. You are carrying something of great value in your head. It was put in there through what he did to you when you were a child. The seed was planted and growing from when you were young, even when he came back and you were older. It was already there.'

Nancy looked at Kavanagh. 'The story I was working on, the one I told you, was mine. You knew that anyway. This is where the meaning comes from, the point of the story for me.' She tapped the left side of her head. 'All in here. For months now, I've been getting myself ready to die, even before I met you. When the knot goes, I go with it. It's a part of me, embedded in me.'

'Is she right?' Kavanagh asked Cameron.

The old man nodded.

'There's no way other way to get to it or for me to get Lucy without it?'

'He has used his power to write the story in this manner.

What is the thing you value most in the world now? Your daughter. What is the next most valuable? This woman. The things he values the most, you have two of in your possession. If he has judged it right, you will lead them to him through the story he has constructed. It can never be as simple as just taking. It works itself out in the process and that is what he has used to lead us all to where we are now. The stories are all he has.'

Kavanagh looked at Nancy, already feeling her slipping away. It was cold to look at her and have to place such a clinical worth on her, to weigh her against the value of Lucy. There should not have been a choice of one or the other. The dichotomy angered him, the precise way it would force him to choose.

'It has to be this way?' Kavanagh asked.

'I can think of no other,' Cameron said.

'Nor can I,' Nancy said.

'Mr Grace has told you what to expect?' Cameron asked Nancy.

She nodded.

Kavanagh rested his head in the heels of his hands and closed his eyes, rubbing his fingers through his hair. When he looked up, Cameron was holding Lucy's pendant and fitting it into the cover of The Book. Immediately, the veins of its cover shone silver, gold somewhere deeper within. Kavanagh stared at the cover, the perfect fit of the knot into its surface, two other cavities waiting to be filled, to join all the arteries together, making the knotwork complete. Seeing it before his eyes, he gained a sense of the power that could come from completing the knotwork.

Cameron and Nancy were standing and it brought Kavanagh to his feet as well. Nancy came round the table and stood in front of him. They looked at each other and he tried desperately to smother the hurt.

'You have to go find her,' Nancy whispered, making the moment theirs, despite Cameron's presence. She kissed him and he held her, not wanting to let her go. The walls became light once more. The feel of her lips, the pulse of her body against his, were so full of life he could not imagine it any other way. 'I love you, Mike Kavanagh. Goodbye.'

'We need to press on,' Cameron said, breaking into their space.

'How do we get . . .?' Kavanagh asked, his voice trailing off as Nancy backed away from him and took Cameron's outstretched hand, allowing him to lead her to his side of the table, as if he had asked her to dance.

'I'm afraid there is no elegant way. He would not allow us that in his story,' Cameron said.

Kavanagh thought Cameron was about to kiss Nancy as he put his hand behind her head. Kavanagh was looking directly at her when Cameron swiped her head down towards the table with a force that seemed to expend all the energy in his body. Her forehead made a crack on the edge, sick and heavy, and Kavanagh could not distinguish which part of the sound was the splitting of bone. The ferocity of the movement left Kavanagh aghast as Nancy's body crumpled and disappeared from view, hitting the floor.

'No!' Kavanagh shouted.

Nancy was out of view, obscured by the table. Cameron was standing over her, stamping his foot, his hair flying wildly. There was the sound of something giving and then Cameron seemed to topple forward slightly.

'I won't let you do this,' Kavanagh said.

The knot on The Book throbbed and Kavanagh felt it in his chest. The Book was calling him, giving him the chance to try and change it, to take control of the text.

Kavanagh pushed Cameron away and looked down at Nancy, a long trail of blood spreading from the crushed bone of her skull, white foam bubbling. He stared at her and let The Book send the same palpitation through him, pulling it more actively this time, wanting to take control.

Heat, singeing and raw, blasted out from Nancy and he thought she was about to explode. Instead, she reformed, becoming a collection of lines as though Kavanagh were looking at her through the slats of a blind. The bits of her he could see suddenly lost their solidity and wavered like a television set where the horizontal hold had broken. Kavanagh made to speak but the heat was so intense he imagined it would char the inside of his mouth. The chopped lines of her face obscured the damage done, allowing him to imagine her as she should have been. Nancy smiled at him and just before the flames engulfed her, Kavanagh was sure he saw her mouth the word 'Go'.

The fire was gone and so was Nancy Lloyd. Kavanagh had watched her disseminate into lines before his eyes, leaving no trace of herself other than what she had carried for so long inside her head.

Cameron stooped down and picked up the knot, handing it to Kavanagh.

'You have just made the first step towards taking control of the text, Mr Kavanagh. The Book is powerful in you. Be careful where there is no text. He will be more powerful.'

Kavanagh looked at the second knot. It was similar to the other one, bearing a family resemblance, but also unique. A different part of forever, visible. He closed his palm around it, trying to feel where Nancy had been, wanting to pick up a vestige of her body heat.

'Go and find your daughter, Mr Kavanagh. And do what you have to do.'

'Which is?'

'I have no idea. You will have to write that for yourself.'

Kavanagh inserted the second knot, its edges a perfect match with The Book, feeding several of the stray ends into each other.

The veins on The Book were getting brighter and brighter as though heating up. When they looked almost white-hot, they turned to the purest gold and the whole Book thrummed with energy so powerful every other force in the room abated. The golden light of the cover lit Kavanagh's face and the room was silent.

Kavanagh picked up The Book and opened it.

He began to read.

It coursed through him at a level deeper even than blood.

Every story, poem, play, picture and piece of music originated there. Every work of art or study in science. Stories, tales, yarns, legends, myths and folklore. Every person that ever lived, every journal, diary, record and memoir. An infinite chronicle of parable, fantasy, fact and fiction. The atmosphere and mood, every theme, motif or contrivance was there. Whatever the plot, plan, design, scheme, structure or subtext, it was laid bare before Kavanagh.

It began, and ended, and began again, with The Book.

The pages turned themselves, The Book helping Kavanagh to the right story. The one that would lead to Lucy.

Kavanagh found the page that had been looking for him.

Chapter 64

Through the lines and between the words, The Book gave itself away to Kavanagh. At first, it felt as though he were falling and all its contents were whirling past him like a hurricane. Then he realized he was perfectly still, not going through The Book. The Book was going through him. Pages billowed around him and he was no longer in the fabricated room with Cameron and Nancy. Kavanagh was no longer anywhere except in The Book which, of course, was everywhere and where he had been all the time. Leaves of paper fluttered about him like confetti and the book he held in his hands, the physical manifestation of The Book, fell open to a page and it all stopped.

Kavanagh stood in a clean yellow desert, the sand fine like the grains in an hour-glass. The blue of the sky was too dark, like ink from a bottle, and too wide to take in with a single glance. It was bright but there was no sun, no atmosphere or heat. The air was still and all around was silent apart from the lone sound of a trumpet in Kavanagh's head, an imagined soundtrack.

On the crest of a hillock was a squat building, like a castle. Alone in the desert it looked stately, like an Egyptian tomb. Its granite walls were as hard as the sand around it. There was in this place nothing organic, no wood or fabric. Nothing upon which to write. Apart from The Book.

The solidity of the building in the middle of all the sand was comforting. It was something to head towards, a fixed point that gave him a sense of direction. Kavanagh picked up The Book and walked towards the building. He stepped nearer to it but stopped almost immediately. He felt great threat held within the walls, a trap for him. The Book sent a negative wave through him, warning him. He looked at the volume in his hands. It was the second time it had moved beyond neutrality to help him. The pleasant refrain in his head turned sour and morbid.

On the horizon was a tiny black mark, a spot before his eyes, a full stop on the page. As the dot moved towards Kavanagh, it was liquid in the blur of an unfelt heat.

Nathan.

Where was everyone? Cameron and Lucy. What had happened to Nancy as he watched her dissipate into lines? All he knew was they weren't with him at that moment. They were banished from his mind, as though they had never existed except in The Book. The hands of his watch were poised over the numbers, as though holding their breath. He was nowhere and there was no time.

Nathan's approach was confident and unhurried, trailing forever behind him and approaching an ever shorter future. The boy he had seen briefly in the swimming pool was there, but so was much more. He was like a rock worn to smoothness by time, a sense of the complexity that surrounded him present all over his body like footprints. Kavanagh believed what Cameron had said as he watched Nathan Lucas approach in his solitary procession. He looked like someone who had weathered all time, seen and done all things. All of it was revealed to Kavanagh in the simplicity of a glance, The Book in his grasp seeming to quiver with a mixture of fear and excitement. This man has lived forever; but he can't live forever. The paradox of Nathan Lucas's backwards existence hurt Kavanagh's head as much as the most panicky thoughts about infinity did.

As Nathan passed the building he gave it barely a look as though he knew Kavanagh was already too well-read to be fooled by such an obvious trap. Kavanagh tried to get the story back, to go where he had been, back through the text and to . . . what?

Nathan Lucas, man and boy within the same skin, walked directly up to Kavanagh, who clutched The Book to his chest like a shield. Without speaking, Nathan held up the third knot and Kavanagh felt The Book pull away from him, the force magnetic. Nathan took the top of The Book with one hand and bent it down so he could insert the final knot into the cover. The Book became a frenzy of static, so alive Kavanagh was afraid he would drop it. Nathan Lucas backed away, leaving Kavanagh with The Book.

'Now you have what you want,' Nathan said. 'What do you intend to do with it?'

'Where's Lucy?' he asked.

'Not here. You won't find anything here.'

'Where are we?' Kavanagh asked Nathan. They were face to face. His voice was flat, no echoing acoustics to swallow it up.

'Where you wanted to be,' Nathan said.

'Where's that?'

'Outside of the text. Beyond The Book and beyond reading and writing. You have what you want and you are where you want to be. What are you going to do next?'

'We can't be outside The Book,' Kavanagh said, looking down at the tome, the three knots gushing gold.

'This is Notext, believe me,' Nathan said.

'I told Alex Cameron you were just a boy. Was he telling the truth about you?'

'There is "just a boy" called Nathan Lucas, yes. I imagine he is extremely confused, troubled by small glimpses of eternity. I am he. He is I. I can sense, nascently, what it is like to be him, as he can me.'

'He knows what he's doing? What he did. What you did. To my wife.'

'He did it, in the physical sense, but I know far more about it, am more responsible. He knew what he was doing at the time, but time moves differently for us. Now, he has nothing more than a memory of it as he fades into nothing, losing time.'

'You don't have much time,' Kavanagh said, almost gloating.

'I've had so much time,' said Nathan, accenting the last word. 'Now, you are correct. Time is running out for me and for him. On occasions such as these, which are rare, when I am outside of the text, I am able to view the unfolding, or folding, story of my life from a vantage point. Once inside, I am as innocent or as guilty as you. You forget things as you get younger. There are things I have crafted into the text that even I am not aware of. I imagine Nancy Lloyd would have felt the same about things she had written, the way they could be read by others and interpreted so differently.'

'How is this going to help you?'

'You had the chance to be of such great service. The knotting together of those two companies had much riding on it. The Cameron Trust was a serious attempt to involve myself in the real world, to manifest some of the power of all those stories. Clough Cameron and the children I eventually composed for him should have been part of that. I served so many of his purposes, feeding his desire for wealth, power, children and understanding. He could not bear the pressure of the latter. When he came to know of the true purpose of the Trust and the work I intended it to do, he balked. It was a suspicion of mine that he would do so and it did not trouble me because he was already old and my plans stretched beyond his future. When he began to turn the children against me, children I considered as much mine as his, I had to do something.'

'So you killed them all.'

'Rubbed them out, apart from Alexander, the wiliest of them. The Cameron family were meant to care for me when I became a child, someone to look after me when I grew young.' He paused and smiled, as though allowing himself the humour. 'Alexandra and Alexander would have been my parents – old, but still parents. Like their father, they were not up to the task. Now, there are others serving that purpose, people readying themselves to look after me when I am unable to do it myself. People like Andrew Mathias. And people like you.'

'No,' said Kavanagh. 'I'm no part of it.'

'The merger. No Pendulum or Trellis by the year 2002. Of course, you would have been out of it by then, not concerned with what came after. One of the great, trivial concerns of the world at the moment is the millennium. It is talked about in the most facile of ways, the stuff of a billion bad stories. It will pass, not completely without event, but it will pass. What comes after, what is written, is much more important. By the year 2009, a new religion that begins as nothing more than a cult, rather like Christianity did, will eclipse the globe. The only organizations with more power than the organized religions are corporations. They can give freedom, prosperity, a structure – a process. For a while, that seems like not much more than old-fashioned corporatism, but it moves beyond that and is, for a short time, religion. For many, it is the moment where rationalism and spiritualism are no longer distinguishable from each other. How hypnotic the pattern of the knotwork. It is easy to worship such an effortless combination of eternity and simplicity. All this in a single movement with a child as its figurehead. Those who follow the knot. Gordius. You were the one setting all of that in motion.'

'I don't believe you.'

'I don't need you to. The knotwork can become powerful enough to strangle The Book, take control of the text away from it. It's the paradox of any book, Mr Kavanagh, the way sense will run away from it, the more people come into contact with it. There are as many definitions as there are people, each one of them in the knotwork, ebbing and flowing, touching upon each other. Imagine the potency of pushing all that energy in a common direction. Gordius. It would be like writing a whole new story, one that subverts the original ending, my original ending.'

'But none of that will happen now, not without the merger.'

'There are other ways. I've had so much time. All time. I've allowed the stories to pour from me like my life-blood. Do you know how fast and how slow the world travels for me, watching my seed grow, take form? It goes from simple to complex, the opposite direction to me. I was given a head start on the world, able to be clever while it was simple, old while it was young, but it caught up with me. I've given everything I have. I don't want it to end. I don't want to die, anymore than anyone else does. Surely you can understand that?'

'Tell me where my daughter is,' Kavanagh said.

'Not here. There is nothing here.'

'We're here.'

'You must believe me, Mr Kavanagh. There is no text here, nothing you can grip on to or control.'

'If there was no text, we wouldn't be here talking now. We'd just be obliterated. Even then, if it was The Book which rubbed us out, we'd still be there. That would be our whole point in the story, to not be there.'

'To be erased, you mean?' Nathan asked.

'You're not writing this and neither is The Book. I am,' Kavanagh said.

'How can you be sure? You speak lightly and yet you have hardly held The Book for a moment. The Book reads it and The Book writes it. You can only be read or written.'

'I'm writing this,' Kavanagh warned. 'I can take you out of the story if I want to.'

'How?' Nathan asked. 'If you go through and lift my name out of it, you'll have all these spaces between the words. It would be like taking the key brick from a Chinese puzzle. All the other words would tumble down. Even those bits of the text where my name never appeared in the first place have traces of me, moments where I'm influencing things. They'd have to go as well. Then you would have no story and with no story, you couldn't possibly get your daughter or Nancy Lloyd back.'

'Nancy's gone,' Kavanagh said.

'You know you are not sure about that and neither am I. She's strong, able to write.'

'I could cross your name out rather than erasing it,' Kavanagh said.

'More word games. Draw some bars over my name like a prison and I'll still be able to see through the bars. My name will be legible under the marks. I'm part of this story and The Book is part of us. That's what I'm trying to explain to you, this is about the whole story, not one person in it. It's exactly what you just said – even obliterating us makes us a part of it. It's a paradox,' Nathan said, a weariness in his voice.

'If I write this the way I want, you'll just be a footnote,' Kavanagh said.

Nathan smiled and sighed. 'You're contaminated with me,' he said, holding his hands open. 'If this story of yours is going to be so perfect, the text sealed like a strong-room, why would you have to make excuses for me in a footnote? I'd be like a tiny speck of cancer that would eventually metastasize through the whole story. You don't have the power, the capacity, to erase me.'

Kavanagh knew Nathan was right. Wherever he tried to move Nathan, he would still be there, seeping into the text of his story like damp. Making him absent didn't get rid of him as if he had never been there. In fact, it made him more powerful as though he were the backbone of the story, the key thing on the knot.

'I could change the knot,' he said, as much to himself as to Nathan. 'I could change the knot,' he repeated.

For the first time, Kavanagh saw and felt Nathan falter.

'No,' Nathan said, his mouth already sounding dry. 'No, you can't do that. You'd have to wipe us all out or change us beyond our own recognition. Everything. You can't just think about there being a different knot and then use The Book to write it because it will still be tainted with the old text. Look around you now. Do you want to spend forever in Notext?'

'I won't have to,' Kavanagh said.

'It's your only choice. If you go back to the old knot with The Book, Lucy will die. You cannot save her. The other choice is to stay here forever to stop it happening on the knot.'

'You're lying. This isn't Notext. I'm writing it and you're just trying to taint it through my mind.'

'There is a third alternative. Give me The Book and I'll

write you back. I'm making this offer once only,' Nathan said, holding out his hands.

Kavanagh knew what he had to do.

'I'm going to go outside the text and change the knot,' he said.

Nathan stamped his foot into the gold powder with frustration. 'Why are you so stubborn? There is no outside of it. Haven't you understood that by now? There is Notext but there is nothing outside the text.'

'I don't believe you and I'm bored playing these word games with you. There's more important things than words and language. Things like action,' Kavanagh said.

'The text is infinite like space because The Book is in it and because space is part of The Book. You can travel for all time and never reach the end of it. It goes on forever,' Nathan said.

'But you can see it,' Kavanagh said, tacking it on to the end of Nathan's sentence. He stared at the pulsing knots of The Book.

'If you go outside the text, you lose The Book,' Nathan said gravely. 'You give up the chance to read and write. You're like me, Kavanagh, a very special person. Why change the knot? Share The Book with me.'

'I don't want The Book and I don't want to read and write. Look at you, trapped in this language game. All of your arguments fall down around your ears because they're full of contradictions. I don't want to live under sentence of The Book, but I don't want you to have it.'

Already, Kavanagh could feel the lines of text behind him, long slats of energy opening up in the air, waiting to catch him and carry him to Lucy. The way back into and ultimately out of the text. The lines crackled only inches from his ears.

For all the talk, all the language games and the clever words, it was actions that finally spoke loudest. On Nathan's face was a look of stricken panic that The Book was about to go fully beyond his grasp. Nathan's panic escalated rapidly to hysteria and he lurched at Kavanagh, making a pitiful grab for The Book. It's that simple and petty, thought Kavanagh.

Kavanagh's centre of gravity altered and he let his body topple back towards the strings of text. He felt Nathan's hands on his own, squeezing them. Kavanagh tugged his arms and Nathan's hands came free. He was about to let his weight take him back when Nathan grabbed The Book. There they hung, The Book like a pivot between them as Kavanagh held it by the top and Nathan the sides. It was as though their strength matched perfectly and neither could go anywhere without relinquishing The Book. Kavanagh closed his eyes and tried to imagine himself as the heaviest thing possible. His arm muscles were in a painful spasm as he gripped The Book with all the strength he had. The text sucked at him and he heard Nathan's nails screech like claws down a blackboard as his hands trailed over the cover of The Book.

The hold was gone and Kavanagh fell back gracefully into the lines, their taut strands holding him aloft like wind under wings. As the text gave way and opened itself to allow him in, he fell and the only thing he felt was The Book securely in his hands, Nathan left in the place of no text.

Chapter 65

Lucy stood in the kitchen of her house, Camille Cameron, the Lady, somewhere behind her, and stared into the eyes of Nathan Lucas.

It was, and it wasn't, Nathan. He looked fuller in the face, his skin more worn. Older. Nothing registered as surprise for Lucy. Rather, it was like something coming back to her that she had forgotten, a trivial fact like the name of a film or a friend from infant school. Nathan, the boy calling himself Nathan, had killed her mother. Somehow, her mother had known him and trusted him. What was she doing with a boy his age?

He stood before her, naked and sprayed with her mother's blood. There was nowhere left to run, nowhere she wanted to run. This was where it would end and the certainty, the credibility, of it was chilling. The resignation did not even belong to her, as though her free will was being smothered by a determination far more powerful. Lucy felt bewildered, knowing that the only way to be free was to surrender.

Is this how her mother had felt? Unable to resist? Cut down by the stroke of an unseen pen?

Something very special and very nice . . .

So you trust me then?

Am I hurting you now?

It goes on forever . . .

But you can see it . . .

'I love you, Lucy.'

Real words. Nathan's words, almost shouted, as though he were imprisoned in what now stood before her.

There was a man smothering him, so old he should have been dust, but balanced by the boy. Neither one, young or old, held the balance and Nathan stood there before her, pulled in two directions, man and boy. Lucy wondered where such insight was coming from, sure it did not originate in her own mind.

'I love you,' he said again.

Everything they had done in the short time she had known him crackled in her head, images binding themselves together and releasing feelings she struggled to control. Meeting him for the first time. The first shopping trip. Missing him while she was away in America. Making love with him. She fought the urge to run and embrace him, to tell him everything was going to be all right.

'You love me. You told me you did, at the airport,' he said.

'What are you doing here? Who are you?' she asked.

'I don't know. Anymore than you do. I come to this place all the time, in dreams, Lucy. It scares me.'

Tears ebbed from the corners of his eyes and Lucy wanted to let her own tears go, but knew she had to retain some sort of hold on herself and the situation. She sniffed and swallowed.

'My mum. It was you,' she said.

'No.' He shook his head. 'I can't help it. I don't know what I'm doing. I've been having dreams about this place for as long as I can remember. Ever since you first brought me here, Lucy. It's not my fault,' he pleaded.

'That's not true. It can't be. You know exactly what you're doing.'

He sniffled and wiped at his nose with his wrist. 'It all runs away from me. Men, when they grow up, can forget most of the things they did as a boy. I'm a boy who can't remember what he did as a man. I can't get out of here without you, Lucy.'

The blood was still fresh on him, splattering his bare torso, the very soul of her mother marking him as it left her body with the last of her energy.

'I can't help the things I've done, Lucy. I don't know what's happening to me. None of this here is true. You know that. I know you do. I can feel it. I know you love me and that you understand how hard it is to be me.'

Nathan held his hand out to her. Lucy looked at his open palm, the thin grainy skin that covered his bones. The hand looked old, as though it might have belonged to someone else. She wanted him to say something more, to add more words to the moment and make it all better.

He was not going to speak again, did not need to.

It was written.

He took a step towards Lucy and she felt no fear or resistance, just inevitability, perfectly defined.

They kissed and, after a moment, Lucy realized she was naked too. She closed her eyes and felt everything slip away from her, as the Lady said it would, as though her thoughts were all transferring into his head, sucked out with her breath. Or, that all the thoughts in her head, the things that made her who she was, had been put in there by someone else, as though she were a character in a story. He drew on her, extracting air from her, and it became harder to think for herself.

Lucy felt the cold steel of the screwdriver against her inner thigh, warm spats of her mother's blood trickling onto her leg. The blade eased upwards, ready to split her open.

All the clarity in her brain, the certainty and the inescapability of the situation, translated itself into a perfect silence, a stillness into which a single thought was allowed to speak, one that might just save her.

This isn't real.

The shaft of the screwdriver grazed over her pubic hair, insinuating itself along the folds of skin it concealed.

This isn't real, she thought again.

The tip of the blade touched her navel.

That was not the thought.

I'm not real.

That was the thought and she clung to it even though she knew the only way out was to let go of the thought, to surrender in the way the Lady had told her to.

I am not real
I am not
I am
I
Lucy opened her eyes, Nathan still kissing the life out of her, and saw her father standing there.

I'm not real repeated in her head one more time, as though it were the last thought she would ever have.

Lucy let go of her perspective, allowing herself to be written by another.

Kavanagh lifted The Book above his head and used all his strength to bring it down across the back of Nathan's skull. Contact was heavy and the boy fell away suddenly, as though concussed. Lucy stumbled back and began panting, trying to get her breath back, sucking all the available air in from around her.

Kavanagh longed to go up and find Helen, to save her, but he knew that part of the story was already written and nothing he could do would change it. Lucy was his only concern.

He dropped The Book, picked up the discarded screwdriver and stood over Nathan Lucas.

'Dad,' he heard Lucy say.

Kavanagh ignored her and took a long look into the eyes of what had killed his wife, and Nancy Lloyd.

He pushed the screwdriver into the boy's abdomen, through the protrusion of his navel. It sank in easily and Kavanagh rotated it until the sharpened edge pointed upwards.

'No!' Lucy screamed.

Kavanagh used both hands to wrench the handle upwards, tearing open the taut skin of the boy's belly, splitting it like the skin of a fruit. Kavanagh hollered to give himself the strength needed, as if he were throwing a shot. The blade came to the base of Nathan's ribcage with a tearing sound and Kavanagh moved position, standing on Nathan's throat and struggling to pull the shaft all the way to his neck.

Nathan thrashed about on the floor of the kitchen and Kavanagh could not take his eyes from the open cavity where his torso had once been. He would not have known what to expect in any case, but the inside of the boy's body was a tangle of fuming veins and arteries, connecting to no organs and going nowhere except endlessly around on themselves. All the stories of the world could have been in that mess of nerves, slimy and sinuous. This was the corpus, Kavanagh realized.

The wiry fibres spilled from Nathan as though growing, and Kavanagh sensed danger immediately, not wanting to get caught in the web he knew they would spin. The tendrils undulated seductively, as though they would caress and comfort before closing tightly shut around him. The straggling end of a red lode touched the toe of Kavanagh's shoe and he felt the jolt.

'Lucy, open The Book,' he said.

'Dad . . .'

'Do it. Now!' he shouted.

She did not need to.

The Book turned the page.

Chapter 66

Kavanagh hit the black sand with a bump.

'What are we doing here?' were the first words he heard, in Lucy's voice.

Kavanagh looked around with the same eyes but his perspective was altered. What he saw made him feel giddy, everything out of proportion, things on top of each other, in places they should not have been.

They were on a beach. It was dark, but not so much so they could not see. It did not feel like proper night, more like a blue filter had been placed over everything, day for night. At the point where the beach became the sea, the buildings of downtown Los Angeles were clustered, no pavement in front of them, just water. Pushed together, the buildings looked like a clump of mushrooms growing out of the sand. Stretching off behind the glass and concrete of downtown was the rest of the city, silent and empty.

There were no lights on in all of Los Angeles. The whole town was without light or people, as though the story had no characters, or electricity had not been invented. The only motion was the sea, but even that seemed false, generated by an unseen wave-machine. Or created by a fiction of my mind, Kavanagh thought. Taken individually, everything was a close approximation to Los Angeles, but it was the way Kavanagh remembered it rather than how he knew it actually was. The geography was a mutated dream, deformed by the effort it took for his mind to create it.

This is all in my head, he thought. I'm writing this scene like a story.

'What are we doing here?'

It was Lucy. The real Lucy, trapped in Kavanagh's imaginary story.

'There's no lights on,' she said.

He turned and looked at her and she glowed with authenticity. She saw what he wrote.

The sand under their feet was black and fine, more like salt than the usual beige slurry. The wind picked up around them and waves battered the creaking joists of a pier, the structure reminding Kavanagh of one at Venice Beach and also one at a seaside town he had visited as a child. All of the sounds and sights were not quite real enough, as though they could be switched off at any moment leaving Kavanagh and Lucy in empty silence. Kavanagh's head hurt from the effort of maintaining the fabrication around them.

Nathan was nowhere to be seen, yet Kavanagh felt him, his eyes gazing at them as though they were a page in a book.

'You're writing this. You know that, don't you?' Lucy said to him.

Kavanagh was afraid to speak in case he broke his concentration, so he nodded his head. It seemed as though he could not have speech and writing at the same time, only one or the other. He clenched his hands and felt something.

He had forgotten he was holding The Book. It hummed with all the energy and silence of the universe. It was not as simple as every story being contained between its covers, he realised. The Book *was* every story, not the other way round. He could not open a page and find a story in which his wife and Nancy were magically saved. The text wasn't there on the page, fixed in time for all eternity. It was a process, continual and unfolding. If he wanted to get them back, he'd have to write it that way.

'Where's Nancy?' Lucy asked.

Kavanagh held his breath for a moment and then tried a word.

'She's . . .'

The scene blurred like burning film trapped in a projector. The pier bent like rubber, as though it were melting, the buildings folded like paper. He sensed Lucy's panic and fought to get his mind back to its previous state.

He thought The Book might help him but it remained neutral. The pier resolidified and the scene righted itself. It was going to be hard to concentrate on the scene and the words, like talking to someone while secretly eavesdropping on another conversation.

As Kavanagh wrote, a thought came to him.

Where was Garth Richards?

'Right here,' came his voice and Kavanagh felt a fist in his back, just under his shoulder-blades. It knocked him forward and the wind came out of him in a sick gasp. As he hit the sand, he held on to The Book. In his mind, he tried to imagine putting in a bookmark or dog-earring the page.

'Give me the fucking Book,' Garth said.

Kavanagh struggled to his feet and held The Book out in front of him, walking towards Garth as though it would ward him off.

Garth laughed. 'What do you think I am, a fucking vampire? Keep walking like that and I'll take it from you with open arms.'

Kavanagh stopped a foot or two from Garth, seeing in a flash, in more detail than even the video had shown, all the things Garth had done in the name of The Book. Was this all The Book was worth? Maybe he should just give it away now. He didn't want to spend his life like this.

No. The Book is only ever as good as the person it reads. And as good as the person it writes. Or the person who writes it.

'I made a promise to myself about you, Garth,' he said, tucking The Book into the back of his trousers, forcing it in tight.

Garth looked on in silence.

'I said I would fucking kill you,' Kavanagh said, rushing forwards and gripping Garth's shoulders, taking both of them down.

'Dad!' Lucy shouted.

They wrestled in the sand like children. Garth smelled bad to Kavanagh, like rotting fish.

Garth kneed Kavanagh and he fell onto his back. Before

he could move, Garth had him by the hair and was using his grip to drag him towards the sea. Garth was using all his energy, his face trembling and sweat rolling off it as he pulled on Kavanagh. Hair parted company with follicles and tears filled Kavanagh's eyes as his skull burned.

Kavanagh scrambled his legs round, seized Garth's wrists and found enough body-weight to pull Garth back down, and once more they were grappling with each other in the black sand, Lucy shouting anxiously in the background. Garth manoeuvred himself on top. Kavanagh managed to make his knee connect with Garth's back, using the motion to roll Garth off him. They got to their feet at almost the same time, both stooping from the exertion, breathing erratically.

He rushed at Garth Richards, grabbed the front of his shirt and brought his forehead down onto Garth's nose as hard as he possibly could. The front of Kavanagh's head burned with pain but it was soothed by the scream of agony Garth let out as he fell backwards, leaving a trail of bright crimson blood in the air as it gushed from his nose.

Angry and with no time to waste, Kavanagh sat on Garth's chest. He took a deep breath, held Garth's bloody head in his hands and placed his thumbs on each eye. With just a small amount of pressure applied, his eyeballs felt like the whites of freshly shelled hard-boiled eggs. Kavanagh increased the pressure, straightening his arms and using the weight of his whole body.

There was a squelch and a cry and then Kavanagh fell forward a few inches as his thumbs sank knuckle-deep into the sockets of Garth Richards's eyes. It was warm inside, like sinking his fingers into fresh bread. Garth was convulsing but his strength had diminished. They were the movements of someone using up the last of life, expending their final energy before it radiated away into heat. Garth was grateful for it, Kavanagh could tell. But Garth Richards's eyes were not the only ones of importance.

Nathan.

The bony sockets of Garth's eyes tightened around

Kavanagh's thumbs. He tried but could not retract them. The sockets started to suck on his thumbs like a baby, the drawing sensation stinging the bitten corner of a thumbnail. Then the craters were chomping on his thumbs, the fleshy edges of bone like gums. The whole of Garth's head pulsed like a single muscle as it sucked on him. The drawing feeling throbbed on, making Kavanagh feel sick. He worked himself to a standing position and, bent double, placed a foot on Garth's windpipe. Using it as an anchor and straining with his back muscles, Kavanagh tried to bring himself to a standing position. Garth's bloody head lifted an inch or two off the ground, but Kavanagh's thumbs would not come out of the suppurating sockets.

Garth made a noise, from somewhere far inside him, and forced himself to a standing position, dragging Kavanagh helplessly along at the same time. Kavanagh tried wriggling and sliding his fingers, but he could not get them out of Garth's head. He pulled harder and felt a give in his knuckles, as if the thumbs were about to dislocate. Garth's twisted mouth shaped itself into a smile and the pressure on Kavanagh's thumbs intensified, making him conscious of the bones within them.

Lucy was hitting Garth on the side of the head, staying behind him and landing punches on his back, none of which had any effect.

'Be careful,' Kavanagh warned.

Garth kicked out backwards and caught Lucy on the leg and she fell, calling out in pain.

Kavanagh looked down at Garth's hands and saw the screwdriver in one of them, ready to lunge into him. Garth pulled his arm back in readiness and Kavanagh tried to dance away, but there was no escape from Garth's reach. The blade thrust forwards and Kavanagh heard Lucy shriek.

The gunshot rang out across the fabricated beach and took away the side of Garth's head, all the force in his arm suddenly dissipated as though the energy had run out of the crater in the side of his head. Warm, thick blood and white mush spattered Kavanagh, who had flinched but still managed to get a small piece of spongy matter in his eye. Three more shots, and what little remained of Garth's skull relinquished its grip as the weight of his body made him slip him from Kavanagh's thumbs, the pop audible as the tips pulled free.

A fat man was standing five yards from Kavanagh, holding a gun out in front of him with both hands, the barrel giving off a line of smoke like a chimney.

Garth lay on the sable beach and an ooze of pearl-white ran from his empty eye sockets, lapping away at the blood. The same heavy fluid seeped from his broken nose like snot and from his mouth like dribble. The secretion flowed freely from the side of his head which had taken the blast of the bullets, covering the remains of his face like larvae, and Kavanagh's thumbs were covered with the viscous glue. Gingerly, he raised them to his nose and sniffed. It was semen.

Kavanagh gagged and knelt to rub his thumbs in the sand. The black grains held to them like pepper and Kavanagh dried them off on the back of his trousers. When he had finished, he looked to the man.

'Mr Kavanagh,' he said, lowering the gun. 'My name's Wadlow Grace. I'm a friend of Nancy Lloyd. Did she find you?'

'Yes,' Kavanagh said.

'Where is she?' Lucy asked.

'Mr Kavanagh?' Wadlow asked.

'She was there. Then she wasn't,' Kavanagh said.

'Did she let go of the knot?' Wadlow asked.

'Yes,' Kavanagh said.

'It's time to finish it, Mr Kavanagh,' Wadlow said.

'How?' he asked.

'Where's Nancy? What happened to her, Dad?' Lucy asked, her voice already breaking up. 'Dad?'

'She didn't make it, Luce,' Kavanagh said.

'We don't have much time, Mr Kavanagh.'

'I spoke to Alexander Cameron,' Lucy said.

'So did I,' Kavanagh said, looking at Wadlow Grace.

'He's gone again, Mr Kavanagh.'

'Where?'

'He can do nothing now. It's down to you. You have to finish it.'

'I don't know how,' Kavanagh said.

'Obliterate this fabrication. Tear it down so we can go free.'

Kavanagh's head was a single sensation of pain and he could taste blood in his mouth. There was no way his mind could hold all the things in there at once. He couldn't and he didn't want to. He could feel Nathan's presence in the story, under the surface of the words. He didn't know what to do. He wanted to give up.

The first flake of snow fluttered down and touched the back of Kavanagh's neck, turning to water and trickling down his back, cold as ice. Several more flakes drifted through the air, carried on the low breeze. Gradually, the air thickened with the snow, until a minor blizzard swarmed about them, wiping out the beach in a clean white blanket, as fresh as a new page. On the surface of the sea, ice bobbed and the view became Arctic. The false and overcrowded buildings became a distant city of ice and the temperature started to fall. Kavanagh began to shiver.

Wadlow picked the screwdriver from Garth's whitened body and handed it to Kavanagh. 'Finish it,' he said.

Instinctively, Kavanagh bent down and began to draw on the ground with it, scraping the snow away and revealing the sand as if it were black ink. He marked out a long swirling line and increased the complexity of it as his hand began to move faster. The pattern of the knot welcomed Kavanagh like an old friend and he felt it take some of the strain from his head, bearing part of the burden of the story on his behalf. It was taking shape.

'It goes on forever,' Wadlow said.

'But you can see it.'

The voice belonged to Nathan Lucas.

Kavanagh looked up and Nathan was standing there,

behind Lucy and with his arms around her. They were both naked and Nathan touched his daughter intimately. Lucy's expression of ecstasy was hard for Kavanagh to look at, but he made himself, certain that to do so was to gain control, authorship of the scene.

'Finish it, Mr Kavanagh,' Wadlow said.

Nathan's hand was exploring between his daughter's legs and her eyes were closed, mouth slightly open.

'I can't,' Kavanagh said, his breath misty in the cold.

'If you don't, he'll take your daughter.'

Lucy moaned and Kavanagh watched what he was doing to her.

'Think about the text, Mr Kavanagh,' Wadlow said. 'All of the stored energy in the key words. Stress concentrated on a single point, a focus. What happens when you reach the margin, the edge of the story? Think about where we are. California. Why has he engineered it so we're in this place?'

The words began to make sense to Kavanagh.

'Look for a faultline in the text. Rip it apart, Mr Kavanagh,' Wadlow said.

The sound of the sea abated for a moment and Kavanagh looked across at the pier. It had made a creaking noise, like a tree about to be felled. He was uncertain whether or not he had really seen it move. The sound it made was like a rusty hinge on a door. Kavanagh watched the whole of the pier tear itself away from the promenade and land in the sea.

It displaced water in its wake. The noise was excruciating, as stray pieces of timber and shards of glass flew off in every direction. The weight of the structure sent shudders through the ground. None of it happened in graceful slow motion but in sickeningly heavy and loud real time.

Nathan stopped and looked up, like an animal disturbed. Kavanagh concentrated.

The ground under their feet moved. From side to side. The world was no longer fixed beneath them. The foundations of the fabrication had been moved.

'Be very careful,' Nathan said. 'Make sure you understand what you are doing.'

There was another tremor, strong enough this time to make them all take a step sideways. The waves of the sea fulminated, gaining strength and seeming to brace themselves for what was coming. The dark sky pressed ominously, not a star in it, and the wind carried noise on itself, unfocused and unsettling. The movement of the ground became a continual jarring, one that shook Kavanagh and made his bottom jaw chatter against his top teeth.

A wave like the roll of the ocean spread out beneath the ground and Kavanagh saw the horizon literally ripple towards the buildings in the distance. There was a tearing sound as structures came apart, rented away by a force more powerful than the stored energy that held them together.

The second wave was stronger, fine cracks appearing along the ground. The foundations beneath the huge solid structures were giving way, destroying everything that sat atop them. As the buildings fell, the sound they made was like an explosion, filling the air with diamond clouds of glass, the landslide of concrete leaving mountains of rubble in their wake, a new landscape. Real explosions followed, balls of flame lifting into the air like fireworks.

The third wave split the ground open in a long crack that looked like forked lightning, the blackness of the gap between the two harsh edges seeming bottomless. They were thrown forwards and Lucy fell free of Nathan, scrambling towards Kavanagh. The earth seemed to be mincing itself up, using the movement of its plates to grind away at itself. Kavanagh could hardly see because the force of the shaking made it impossible to focus on any one thing.

Near the edge of the shore, the remains of the high-rise buildings were lifted as the ground rose and tipped them into the sea. They slid off the end and just disappeared beneath a wave that was higher than they themselves had ever reached.

Beneath the feet of Nathan Lucas, the ground parted like

a mouth, ready to swallow him like a word. Kavanagh watched as the man who had formed oceans with his tears and shifted ground with the blink of an eye slipped through the fissure in the text and disappeared, lost in the subtext once again.

All of the basic elements had blended themselves into a single common substance which swept around the three of them like a typhoon. They were engulfed by the essence of the fabrication, every word that had been made solid now sweeping around them. There was no land, no sea, no air, no fire, just a root element. The most core definition of matter swamped them, remaking them as surely as it destroyed itself.

They were pushed together, their three bodies heaved to the eye of the storm. Kavanagh came into contact with the solid bodies of his daughter and Wadlow, the impact revealing the power of the hurricane. Spiralling inwardly, the walls of the tornado, the remains of the fabrication, drew closer to them and Kavanagh was sure they would be crushed. They clung on to each other, the noise so powerful Kavanagh was afraid to attempt speech. The funnel of material touched them and Kavanagh felt his body squashed and his eardrums swelled, ready to burst. His face became rubbery and he was afraid he would lose consciousness as the spinning wave of words reached a climax.

The wave passed through them and was then inside the three of them. Kavanagh felt everything in condensed form, heavy matter that coursed through him. It passed on and became no more than a column of pure content, spinning away into nothing. Kavanagh followed its path and saw it disappear into The Book, which was on the floor, between their feet.

Silence.

The land had closed up and formed a new horizon. There was a different landscape, no longer a fabricated Los Angeles or any part of the world Kavanagh knew. Lucy and Wadlow Grace stood beside him, his daughter clothed once more. The three of them hugged tightly, as though checking each were solid.

Kavanagh looked down at The Book and felt a sick throb that was everywhere in his body at the same time.

One of the knots was gone.

He remembered Nathan's hands screeching down the front of The Book as Kavanagh was about to tumble through the light and out of Notext.

Kavanagh had not been responsible for writing all of it.

He held The Book out, showing its cover to Wadlow Grace.

'Nancy may be lost on the third knot,' Wadlow said.

'Will he be able to get her?' Lucy asked.

'The Book doesn't write it that way,' Wadlow said.

If the lost knot did not come back to The Book, The Book would seek it out. Whichever way it wrote, it would lead to Nathan and, possibly, Nancy Lloyd. Nathan was right – Kavanagh had not succeeded in going beyond the text. Feebly, he tried to find a way to them through his mind, but he could not. He knew he could not. If he could have done that, he could have made it all begin and end, and begin again, there and then on the beach. Instead, it would happen the way The Book wrote it and the way The Book read it.

The silent, reading eyes of Nathan laughed at him.

Kavanagh walked across the beach and stood at the margin of the land and the sea, looking into the dark ice and beyond to the horizon and the night sky. Land, sky and water. The only three places someone could be, and yet he knew Nathan Lucas and Nancy Lloyd were not there.

Where were they?

Like a whisper in his ear from someone close to him, Kavanagh heard a crisp noise, the unmistakable sound of a page being turned in a book. A wave lapped in noisily, rolling over the tops of his shoes. Kavanagh looked down at his feet, the water draining away and leaving suds mixed with black sand and snow.

Nathan would be back for The Book. When it happened,

somewhere in the unending operation of the knotwork, Kavanagh would be ready for him.

In the background, sounds of the real world filtered in as a new day broke. Emergency sirens were everywhere, near and far, at different tones and pitches. Kavanagh wondered how the things he had made happen in the fabrication had affected the real world.

Kavanagh held The Book to his chest and felt himself meld with it. Warmth flooded through his body as though all his blood were being transfused. When he looked down, The Book was no longer in his hands. In his palm, the two knots were threaded to a chain, already lonely.

'I'm going to find you,' he said, words addressed to Nathan Lucas, Alexander Cameron and Nancy Lloyd. He put the chain around his neck.

Reader and writer, read and written, Mike Kavanagh turned and walked across the beach to rejoin his daughter and Wadlow Grace, ready to make his way back to the real world and begin the wait.

Post-Text

Getting to Zero

On the day one millennium would die giving birth to the next, Wadlow Grace dug his boot heels in and took the final strenuous steps to his vantage point. On the apex of the hill at one side of the valley, Wadlow looked down into the basin and saw for real what he had only seen on the news. He trained his binoculars on the mass below.

More than two hundred thousand people moved around in the ravine without any central focus. There was no stage, no leader, no one on a podium telling them what to do. Motor-homes, trailers and tents scattered themselves, small pockets of subsistence clustering around the elements of fire and water. The sheer volume of the assembly and its apparent lack of intent meant the authorities could do little but the same as everyone else – watch and wait. Wadlow observed people at random. An eclectic mix, taking in whole families, groups of friends, couples, loners. Down there in the bowl of dry dust, the harsh heat of the sun was the leveller, and the fatigue showed. Many who had turned up instinctively, unready and ill-equipped, now looked for help from those better prepared.

The media huddled together off to one side, identifiable by dishes on the tops of their vans. Looking closely, Wadlow saw a reporter holding a microphone and using the bodies as a backdrop while she spoke. A helicopter swept over the heads of the crowd and some waved happily while others shook angry fists. The reporter would be saying the same thing in her report that Wadlow had been hearing for the last week and a half. People from all over the world were coming to sit in the sand to wait for it all to begin and end, and begin again. This kind of spontaneous conglomeration had become their trademark. Different people with the same belief – that they alone saw the connections between things, even while the rest of the world dismissed them as paranoid.

In 1997, an earthquake in Los Angeles measuring 8.7 on the Richter scale killed more than sixteen thousand people. The amount of energy released was irrelevant when the severity of the quake was taken into account. At its epicentre, the offices of the Trellis Corporation were simply pounded from existence, as were several tranches of downtown Los Angeles, turned to dust when the Earth chewed on itself like a mouth trying to form words. The concentration of force on the Trellis building was unusual and unpredictable, as though the fault lines and plates of the area had shifted below the surface without the knowledge of the geophysicists.

On the same night, a fire in London reduced the headquarters of Pendulum to ashes. Next to the massive scale of the unfolding tragedy in Los Angeles, the story was lost. The secretive nature of the ill-fated merger between Pendulum and Trellis meant that few people made a connection between the two incidents.

Except for those who believed they saw connections.

From his rucksack, Wadlow removed the notebooks belonging to Randall and Nancy Lloyd. Neither of them made any sense to him but he could not bear to go more than an hour or two without looking at them, as though his existence depended upon them. One day, somewhere in the trail of ink, he would find the truth about his beginning and his end.

The congregation stretching out in the basin, moving like water through a gulch, comprised roughly a fifth of the people across the globe who believed the earthquake in '97 was the first sign of a shift in the text of their lives. A chapter was closing. Under the mark of the knot, they strove to find links, to bring order into the chaos of the stories.

Two years after the quake, a literary theorist and a seismologist had collaborated to write a book which tried to make sense of the shift through a hybrid of plate tectonics, mysticism, alchemy and semantics. Painstaking textual analysis established hidden meanings in certain patterns of words recurring in texts. Seismological study and the mystical linking-together of apparently unrelated events revealed similar enigmatic structures.

The central tenet of the work was to postulate the existence of a Book containing every story in the world. This Book also held a secret, never revealed to a living soul that had survived to tell it to another. The book had been on the bestseller lists since its publication, finding harmony with the nascent feelings specifically of those who followed the knot and more generally of anyone feeling the sense of last things.

On this day, the final of the millennium, those who followed the knot believed the ground would open once again and a young man would issue forth, a youth who held the secret of The Book. Some people in the throng were relatives of those who had died in '97, believing they too would come through the earth, resurrected. Some said the boy would be like a gift from God.

Mike Kavanagh, that night on the fabricated beach in Los Angeles, had hoped to stop Nathan Lucas by losing him through a fissure and burying him deep in the substructure of the text. In reality, the earthquake had lit the fuse. That was the way The Book wrote it.

In the months immediately following the events on the fabricated beach, Wadlow had spent time with Kavanagh and Lucy, teaching them what he knew. In Kavanagh, he felt The Book shift many times and the knots around the man's neck jangle together, making their own unique music. Kavanagh was learning to read and write for the first time, and Wadlow could guide him only so far. The Book was a stern teacher, embedded in Kavanagh and feeding him with itself like a drip. The Book would show him when to make a strategic intervention in the story, a time at which Kavanagh would have no choice but to write Nathan Lucas back into the text.

Now, Wadlow spoke to Kavanagh only from time to

time. Their paths had diverged as surely as they would converge once more when the knot made its final closure around them. Kavanagh was not there with Wadlow because he knew this would not be Nathan's time. Lucy Kavanagh's headaches were still as painful and as frequent as they had been since the quake and it gnawed at both Wadlow and Kavanagh, the true manner of how Nancy Lloyd had carried the knot still concealed from Lucy.

The more Wadlow learned about the knotwork, the smaller and more lost he felt in its tendrils. It had been foolish, illiterate, he realized, to imagine that the incidents in Los Angeles and London comprised the whole knot. Other events had already been layered methodically into the past and future by The Book.

Despite Kavanagh's objections that they should leave her as one of the multitude presumed dead, Wadlow had registered Nancy Lloyd as a missing person, wanting to keep a space in the world warm for her in case they could get to her. Wadlow found himself impatient, wishing Kavanagh could simply pick up The Book and shake it, dislodging Nancy from between whichever pages acted as her prison. He knew it could not be written that way.

Wadlow watched three hot-air balloons rising, propelled by blasts of flame, their warm primary colours perfectly set against the infinite blue of the sky. A roar went up from the gathering, calling in a single voice, and Wadlow quickly looked down, his throat jumping. A space had cleared in the centre of the crowd. He pointed his glasses at the gap, a shake in his hands. He breathed out. A large knot, the size of a running track, had been drawn into the ground, people already starting to walk round it, tracing the arcs and going on forever.

Sitting down on a rock, Wadlow opened his own notebook and took some notes as he waited to see if there would be a tremor in the text on this day of endings and beginnings.

With all the potency, the beauty, the ugliness, the

indifference and the amorality of a god, The Book wrote on.

It had begun and ended in The Book.

It would begin again.

Acknowledgements

The following people are thanked for helping with some aspect of God's Gift:

Andrew Wille for everything. Geoff and Stewart because blood *is* thicker. The two hale Marys – my favourite penance. Elizabeth Pattison for her periodic advice. Julian Spencer for bearing with me. Saul Schneider for lightening all those lunches in hell. Jay Adair for weaving the web. Mark Cousins for teaching me to read. Dan Beach for talking in dialogue. Tim Hughes for promising me the use of his shoes. Felice Picano for saving my death. Helen Pisano for minding my language. Mic Cheetham without whom I'd still be a delivery boy. John Jarrold for getting the pages turning. Paul and Suzie Marsh and Juliet Matthews at the Marsh Agency. Andy McKillop, Jo Tapsell and everyone at Random House.

Visit the John Evans Web Site www.john-evans.com